FURY
of
DESIRE

FURY
of
DESIRE

COREENE CALLAHAN

Text copyright © 2013 Coreene Callahan

Published by Montlake Romance, Seattle
www.apub.com

ISBN-13: 9781477809624
ISBN-10: 1477809627
Library of Congress Control Number: 2013907478

For my readers—those of you who have waited so patiently for Wick's story. It's here, at long last.

Chapter One

The lair was quiet . . . for a fucking change.

Combat boots planted shoulder-width apart, loaded down with an armful of architectural plans, Wick paused beneath the timber-beamed archway separating kitchen from dining room. Senses sharp, he listened, hunting for the smallest sound. No laughter. No rumble of male voices or the zing of good-natured insults. He glanced left along the short corridor that skirted the foundation of a stone fireplace and led into the family room beyond. The large plasma screen was dark. No click of billiard balls either. Barely any sound at all, only the soft crackle of flames in the double-faced hearth, along with the smell of wood smoke.

Nothing and nobody.

Excellent. It was official.

Silence had descended, bringing with it the soothing rush of knowing he had nothing but alone time ahead of him. For the next few hours, anyway: that lovely stretch of quiet as late morning lengthened into early afternoon.

After that, all hell would break loose. But until his brothers-in-arms rolled out of bed and got up for the day, he had Black Diamond—the home he shared with the other dragon-warriors—all to himself. Thank God. He needed the peace and quiet. Maybe even a little R & R to survive the radical changes to the Nightfury pack over the last couple of months. The lair used to be a sane place, a sanctuary after a night spent fighting the Razorback assholes he called enemies.

Too bad all good things came to an end.

Case in point? The female invasion.

Jesus fucking Christ, it was insanity squared. Who knew three human women could cause so much upheaval? Or screw with a male's head so easily? Not him. Then again, what the hell did he know? Wick avoided females whenever possible. He never knew what to say or how to act around them. And after watching the carnival ride called CRAZY his fellow warriors had been on for the last few months, he knew his strategy was straight-up brilliant.

Avoiding females—especially high-energy ones—was the better bet. A necessary measure, self-preservation on a wide scale . . . whatever, 'cause yeah. No way would he end up like his brothers: twisted in knots and downgraded to pathetic while their females rode shotgun.

The soles of his boots thudding on wooden floorboards, Wick crossed to the table dominating the center of the room. High polish made the mahogany gleam beneath the crystal-laden chandelier above its long length. It was a nice piece, eighteenth-century French, pilfered from a swanky palace in Paris. How it had ended up half a world away, a mere twenty minutes from downtown Seattle, was no mystery.

Daimler. The Numbai—and the Nightfuries' go-to guy—had good taste and exercised it on a regular basis.

Which was perfect. A real seal-the-deal kind of thing.

Without Daimler's help, Wick would never have acquired his art collection, never mind gotten his hands on the Gauguin landscape hanging over the mantelpiece. The ever-present heaviness inside him lightened as he studied the painting. Colors swirled. Precise lines intersected. Bold brush strokes and balance reigned, completing the whole—artistry steeped in history, soothing in its entirety.

Storytelling at its best, told by the hand of a master.

Dumping the thick rolls on the tabletop, Wick dragged his gaze away. Later. He'd have time to lock his bedroom door and indulge in his passion, but . . . *later.* Right now required action, not losing himself in a dreamscape.

With a flick, he flipped the elastic band off the first roll and spread the blueprint across the expanse of polished wood. He frowned. Wrong one. He needed the building layout first, not electrical and plumbing schematics. Grabbing the next plan, he repeated the process, opening each roll until the table disappeared beneath heavy paper and . . .

Hell. Wouldn't you know? The last roll contained the information he wanted, the updated version of the architect's floor plan. Not that he needed all the information to break into the human facility—Swedish Medical was a hospital like any other—but thoroughness equaled preparedness, and no matter what the rest of the warriors thought, Wick always arrived prepared.

He didn't blame the Nightfuries for labeling him a loose cannon, though. Wick knew his *fuck you* attitude gave that impression. He should probably do something about that . . . take steps to clean up his reputation and reassure his brothers-in-arms he didn't have a death wish. The problem? Giving a shit had never been his MO. Down and dirty—quick and clean—were more his style. The other warriors would either follow. Or not.

Totally up to them.

His eyes narrowed on the drawing in front of him, Wick trailed his fingertip along a hospital corridor inked in blue lines. With a "huh," he flipped the wide paper back a page. The building's rooftop came into focus. Tricked out with a helipad for incoming medical choppers, the roof was the best bet. Landing in the open space would not only be expedient, but more comfortable too. The more room he had to fly in, land, and fold his wings in dragon form, the better. Tight spaces weren't his favorite thing. Confinement—the mere thought—made his skin crawl and—

Wick suppressed a shiver and locked down the memory, stuffing it into the black hole in the back of his mind. Remembering was never a good idea. The past was the *past*. No sense dredging it up or reliving things best left alone.

Refocusing on the human map, Wick charted the course, memorizing the layout, deciding on the most efficient path through the hospital's labyrinth-like corridors. His target was the ICU. Or rather, the injured female who, at present, lay unconscious inside the critical care unit.

Jamison Jordan Solares.

The right side of Wick's mouth tipped up. *Jamison.* Strange name for a female, but for some reason he liked it.

"Jamison," he murmured, lingering a little, testing the phonetics.

Hmm . . . her name tasted good, tripping off his tongue just right, swirling in the silence, adding spice to his self-imposed solitude. Wick shook his head, his enjoyment morphing into self-mockery. Her name didn't matter. Neither did she, at least not to him. His mission was simple: bust her out of the ICU, keep her safe on the journey to Black Diamond, and hand her off to Mac. All to repay the newest member of the Nightfury pack.

Most males would've said screw it. Forgotten the favor done and the debt owed.

Not him.

Mac had saved Venom's life, a male Wick valued above all others. Without him . . .

Wick's throat tightened. Shit. He didn't want to think about *what ifs*. Venom was his best friend, the only male who accepted him for who and what he was, his savior in more ways than one. And like it or not, a gift of such magnitude couldn't go unanswered. Honor demanded equal treatment, so. . . no question. He would repay the debt he owed by giving the newest member of his pack a gift in return: provide what Mac's chosen female wanted—needed above all else—her younger sister safe, sound, and in the family fold once more.

The trick now would be getting the critically injured Jamison out of the human facility without the assholes guarding her any the wiser. A challenge. Finally. At last. Something complicated that needed a solid plan and brass balls to pull off. Wick hummed, anticipation rising as he angled his wrist and glanced at his MTM military watch.

Seven hours until sundown.

His mouth curved. Fuck him, but he could hardly wait for nightfall. Breaking her out while circumventing a bunch of clueless humans was going to be so much fun.

❋ ❋ ❋

Standing just inside Black Diamond's dining room, Venom watched his best friend sleep. Ass planted in an armchair, Wick sat slumped over the table, crinkled paper beneath bent elbows, cheek pressed to forearms, dark hair gleaming in the low light. Stacked in uneven piles, tattered by dog-eared corners, rolls of architectural plans littered the tabletop. Organized chaos. Made sense. Everywhere Wick went things got messy. And by the looks of it , the male had been at it for hours, buried under paperwork, researching God only knew what.

Why Wick was here, though—laid out in the dining room instead of in his usual spot locked behind his bedroom door—was a mystery.

With a frown, Venom surveyed the untidy arrangement again, zeroing in on the pencil poised between his friend's lax fingertips. He shook his head. Wicked strange. He couldn't remember the last time he'd seen Wick with his eyes closed.

Or so relaxed.

Not surprising, really. Wick possessed an ultrathick guard. Was the kind of male who mistrusted most and rarely showed weakness. Oh, it had been known to happen. Bringing Forge and Mac onside and into their pack was a prime example of Wick's willingness to lay himself on the line. But when moments like that happened, his eyes were always wide open, a wary light in them, body, fists, and a load of lethal at the ready.

Not that Venom blamed him for being so cautious.

All of the Nightfuries were to a certain extent. War did that to a male. Made him suspicious of outsiders and ever watchful, always vigilant, in search of ambush and the enemy. Which was the way it had to be . . .

At least, outside the lair.

But inside Black Diamond? Their home served as a sanctuary, a place of comfort and acceptance, of safety and fun, where the Nightfury warriors could let loose and be themselves. The fact Wick didn't feel that way—wasn't comfortable anywhere—didn't sit well with Venom. No male should live in isolation. Especially a valued member of a Dragonkind pack.

Too bad old habits die hard. Mistrust was a bitch, caging Wick inside a prison of his own making.

No steel bars or barbwire. No guards either. But the male was trapped all the same, brutal experience and past pain locking him up tight.

His gaze still riveted on his best friend, Venom swallowed the bitter taste of disappointment. It was so much bullshit. No matter what he did—or how hard he tried— he couldn't help. Or offer ease. Not if Wick continued to keep his distance.

Always around—with him, but not really.

The condition was a running theme with them. One that worried Venom. It was getting worse. The emotional chasm between them grew by the day. He sensed the distance, the lengthening stretch of a male in full retreat. Wick would raise a brow and brush him off. Tell him he imagined things, that the lair was a busier place with the addition of three females and he needed quiet, that was all. But Venom didn't think so.

Something had changed in recent days.

His friend was pushing him away, setting up psychological roadblocks and emotional blockades. The kind he'd worked for years to drag Wick out from behind. A setback? To be sure. One that sucked? Absolutely. Particularly since it left Venom feeling alone. Isolated and out on a limb without the usual safety net for protection. A place he hadn't been since he'd torn the collar from around Wick's throat, pulled him out of the cage and away from that shithole all those years ago.

The history shouldn't matter, but somehow it did. Wick shutting him out—his refusal to talk about what bothered him—felt like betrayal. Like a boot to the balls. Like exile without the possibility of—

Venom clenched his teeth. Hell, after all they'd survived, he deserved better from Wick. Which was . . . what? Inclusion. Information. Trust from a male who possessed every ounce of his. So, yeah. Here he went again. Hopping on a merry-go-round with heartbreak the main spin. A never-ending ride that revolved at the speed of light, stopping on "screwed up" every once in a while, spinning them both in dangerous directions.

With a sigh, he rolled his shoulders, and putting his combat boots to work, walked toward the end of the table. Time for a showdown. To dig in and turf the obstinate SOB he called best friend. Or kick his ass into reasonableness.

Either scenario worked for Venom.

No one, after all, fought as dirty as Wick. Great on every level. The smackdown held the promise of a double whammy: he'd get the fight he craved while making his point. And Wick? The knuckle-grind would relax his friend enough to facilitate a chat, the words Wick always struggled to find.

Without making a sound, Venom skirted the row of upholstered chairs running along one side of the table. Lined up like soldiers, the square-backed Louis XVIs faced off with the wide expanse of mahogany and the chandelier above it. Dimmed down, light refracted through the antique crystal, sending color arcing across the high ceiling. Ignoring the rainbows, he slipped behind his friend's chair. As he moved past, he reached out and, with a quick strike, flicked the edge of his buddy's ear.

Wick came awake with a snarl and jacked upright. He landed with a thump on the balls of his feet, big hands curled into twin fists, guard up, golden gaze aglow. His back to the double French doors, Venom retreated a step and got ready for—

On a quick pivot, Wick lashed out. Venom blocked the first punch but missed the second. He grunted as Wick connected, ramming through his guard to reach his face. Knuckles slammed against his cheekbone. His head snapped to the side, brutal sound shredding the silence. The chandelier swayed and pain spiraled, sweeping round to hammer the back of his skull. With a growl, Venom slid left and unleashed an uppercut beneath his friend's chin.

Crack!

Bull's-eye. Center-of-the-ring accurate.

Wick's chin came up as his head whiplashed. He stumbled backward, sliding on the soles of his shitkickers. Regaining his balance, Venom reset his stance, expecting another go-around. Except . . .

It never came.

Silence and stillness arrived instead as Wick shook off the last remnants of sleep and paused to take stock. Venom blinked, surprise ambushing him. Weird. Abnormal in more ways than one. And so not his best friend's usual MO. Wick never hesitated to lash out, but retreat? Man, that wasn't even in the male's playbook. But as one second faded into the next, and Venom waited for the sneak attack, his friend did just that. Backed off. Dropped his hands. Unfurled his fists to settle into a more relaxed stance.

Straightening the twisted fabric of his muscle shirt, Wick scowled at him. "What the fuck, Ven?"

"Ring-a-ling-ling," he murmured, not knowing what to make of Wick and the sudden behavioral switch-up. Something to be alarmed about? Or rejoice in? Venom didn't know. One thing for sure, though, the change in demeanor bode watching. "Evening wake-up call."

"Shit. Sun's going down."

"Umm-hmm. We got about an hour."

Wick glanced at the double French doors. Blacked out by magic, the glass writhed, rippling like water, blocking out deadly UV rays. Same old, same old. The windows possessed a mind of their own. Good thing too. No Dragonkind male could withstand daylight—would go blind if he were foolish enough to try—so the magical shift was a necessary one, causing the spell that surrounded Black Diamond to react. The upside? Dark windows during the day—protection in its purest form—which allowed him and his comrades to move around without fear of getting fried by the sun. Soon, though, each pane would lighten, then clear completely, allowing moonlight to flood the aboveground lair.

Flexing his bruised knuckles, Wick turned back toward the table.

Venom followed, curiosity getting the better of him. As he stopped beside his buddy, his gaze wandered over a map of downtown Seattle, hunting for the reason behind Wick's interest. The title atop one of the blueprints caught his eye. Well, well, well. Wasn't that interesting? Wick . . . looking at hospital architectural plans. An inkling—a small whisper of an idea—sparked in his mind's eye. Venom's mouth curved as his focus narrowed on the notes scrawled across a yellow legal pad.

Looked like a grocery list. One that leaned away from eats and tilted toward lethal.

Glancing sideways at Wick, he raised a brow. "You gonna tell me what we're into here?"

"A prison break."

"Tania's sister?"

Wick nodded, nonverbal as always.

Venom frowned. "What the hell, man?"

"I owe Mac." Expression set, eyes serious, Wick met his gaze. "He saved your life. Protected you when I couldn't. I need to repay him for that."

"It's my debt, not yours, so—"

"Bullshit. You're my friend . . . *mine*." Wick rolled his shoulders as though uncomfortable in his own skin and glanced away. His attention settled back on the mountain of paper. "I owe, so I'll pay."

The low murmur tore Venom wide open, messing with his head. It wasn't the words so much, but the force behind them: the ownership in Wick's tone, the concern and pain, the unmistakable acknowledgement of friendship. Of mutual need and the unbreakable bond of brotherhood. And in that moment, he got it . . . understood the reason Wick pushed him away, refusing to allow him close.

Self-protection. Emotional ruin. Wick feared losing him.

And no wonder. The night he'd been injured hadn't been pretty. The Razorbacks had nearly killed him, slicing him open from stem to sternum. Wick's quick thinking saved his life. Myst—the Nightfury commander's female— had done the rest, sewing him up when Wick got him back to the lair. But it had been close, a real toss-up into touch'n go for a while and—

Jeez. No doubt about it. He'd scared his best friend, sending the ever-steady Wick into a tailspin. It was a good theory. Made a lot of sense even as it surprised the hell out of him, 'cause . . . yeah. Emotion from Wick? The realization his friend felt that deeply? Total mind-twist territory.

"Hey, Wick?"

"What?"

"You know I love you, right?"

"Fuck off." Leaning to one side, Wick bumped shoulders with him.

Venom swayed on his feet but grinned at the contact. The gentle collision was as good as any love tap. Sure, Wick might not be able to express his feelings with words, but the male could show them. Which at the end of the day was all that mattered.

"So . . ." Venom trailed off, changing course, bringing the conversation back to its origin. "We're going after the sister."

"Yeah."

"We gonna clue Mac and Forge in?"

"Sloan too." Snagging the pencil off the legal pad, Wick leaned forward and planted his hands, palms flat, against the tabletop. "We'll need backup. She's injured."

"So flying her home in dragon form is out."

Wick shook his head. "Mac and Forge'll secure us a vehicle for transport."

"Why not take an ambulance?"

"Too obvious . . . the humans will notice its theft too fast. Call the cops on us." Wick's eyes narrowed on the city map once more. "Too risky. No . . . we move her in an SUV.

A cube van maybe, depending on if we need the hospital bed or not."

"And Sloan?"

"Hospital computers." Wick tapped the pencil against the surface of the notepad. Soft sound echoed, laying out a soundtrack of tap-a-rap-tap. Tap-a-rap-tap. "We may need info on the fly."

"Her medical records too. Hard copies of X-rays, tests, and shit. Myst'll want to see them."

"Exactly."

The word—and the enthusiasm behind it—tickled Venom's funny bone. His lips twitched. Unprecedented. The excitement, sure, but also the fact Wick was talking to him. For a frigging change. "You're enjoying this."

"Come on, Ven," Wick said, the "duh" in his tone unmistakable. A second later, he pushed away from the table, devilry in his eyes. "How often do we get to bust somebody out of jail?"

Venom snorted. How often, indeed.

Grinning like an idiot, he allowed his own excitement free rein. And why not? With Wick jazzed, the night promised to be a good one. Hell, forget *good*. Goddamn fantastic was more like it, except . . .

For one itty-bitty problem.

"So," he said, tone cautious, starting the conversation off slow. Wick wouldn't like what he said next, but hell, it couldn't be helped. No way could they go after the female without setting a few ground rules first. Which meant getting a face full of flack from his best friend. "We'll need to make a pit stop before hitting the hospital."

Wick's brows collided. "What for?"

"I need to feed." Venom took a deep breath, preparing for the fallout. "And so do you."

A growl slithered through the room, killing the quiet. Tension followed, jacking Wick so tight the muscles roping his arms flickered in protest. Avoiding his gaze, Wick looked away, shook his head, then retreated a step.

"Wick . . ."

"I'm fine."

"Don't lie to me." A quick grab and Venom fisted his hand in the front of Wick's shirt. His friend leaned away, searching for an out. Goddamn. Here they went again. Forcing Wick to feed always started and ended the same way. Wick disliked being touched, and although Venom understood the panic that drove him, he couldn't allow the evasion. The male must feed on female energy, connect to the Meridian or die. No getting around that fact. Or the curse of their kind. So he held firm, preventing Wick's retreat. "I can feel the energy drain in you. You haven't fed in so long, you're slipping into energy-greed."

"Ven—"

"You can't retrieve the female if you're hungry. Tania is high-energy, which means her younger sister probably is too." Knuckles pressed to his best friend's chest, Venom jostled him, hoping to shake some sense into the male, then uncurled his hand and let go. "She's hurt, Wick. You get anywhere near her in this condition . . . touch her while you're hungry? You might lose control, tap into the Meridian without thought, and kill her. Helluva way to repay Mac, don't yah think?"

"Fuck."

A poignant reply with a nasty aftertaste. And the understatement of the century.

But no matter how much Wick fought, he would do right by his best friend. Life or death. Commitment or abandonment. Two choices, only one viable option. Provide what Wick needed to keep breathing or die trying.

Chapter Two

Every time she drifted off, Jamison Jordan Solares woke up in a different location. Musical chairs for the injured and sleep deprived. Not exactly reassuring. Unfamiliar places and strange people had never been her favorite thing. Here, though, surrounded by pale walls, the hum of low-pitched voices and the sharp smell of antiseptic, *foreign* took on a whole new meaning. She didn't recognize anything or anyone and yet knew exactly where she'd landed.

Inside Swedish Medical.

Or more precisely . . . a hospital bed now moving at a steady clip down another ordinary hallway. Such a smooth ride. Too bad she didn't want to be a passenger.

Fluorescent lights gleamed overhead. Each light-filled flash rushed her along, acting like strips on a runway in the long stretch of corridor. Then again, what did she know? She couldn't see straight. Not with one eye half-swollen shut and agony thumping on her skull. Add that to all the stitches, bruises, and . . . God. She didn't have a chance in hell of controlling the pain.

Or saving herself from what came next.

J. J. tried anyway, turning her face away, seeking refuge in her pillow, desperate to block out the glare and get her bearings. A no-go. Pain tightened its grip, making her bones ache and muscles cramp. She shifted on the mattress, but . . . tough luck. Movement didn't help. It hurt instead, and as nausea came calling, brutality twisted the screw. An awful taste flooded her mouth. Swallowing in compulsive desperation, she worked moisture into her dry mouth, past her sore throat, and fisted her hands in the sheet. The tape holding the IV in place pulled, jarring the needle pumping fluids into her vein.

Another round of stomach-churning anguish rolled in. Fighting a bad case of the shakes, J. J. bit down on a moan and prayed for oblivion. Numbness. The mind melt of unconsciousness. It didn't come. Neither did relief. To be expected, she guessed. Agony was the only reasonable outcome after surviving the beat down Daisy had delivered. A badge of honor in many ways. Other inmates hadn't been so lucky. Or lived to tell the tale.

She only wished the *honor* didn't involve bruises, split skin, and the throb of a broken ankle encased in a plaster cast. Those injuries, though, were nothing compared to the stab wounds . . . as in multiple. One sliced across her right forearm. A second slashed over her collarbone on the way to meeting the curve of her shoulder. While the third? That gash was the real kicker. A true testament to Daisy's skill with a blade.

A shiver worked its way down her spine.

God, it had been close. Way too close. Had she hesitated at all—been a millisecond slower—she would be dead. Stabbed through the heart. Laid out in an autopsy room. Not alive to feel the burn of the knife wound running along her right side. As violent as the woman who'd inflicted it, the gash dipped beneath her breast before cutting inward over her rib cage. A terrible injury, every last inch courtesy of a homemade prison shank wielded by a homicidal manic. Now sutures held her together, train-tracking over her skin, a testament to the surgeon's skill and her will to live.

J. J. let her eyes drift closed. Lucky. She'd been so damned lucky.

Strange to think of it that way. Especially after being attacked. But despite the stitches, all the bruises and broken bones, she couldn't help but be thankful. She'd survived. Beaten the odds and made it out alive. So forget crying. Screw the circumstances along with the pain. The fact she felt anything at all was a blessing.

A straight-up miracle when she considered who wanted her dead.

Officer Griggs. Prison guard extraordinaire. Nothing but a thug with a badge at the Washington State Corrections Center she called home.

Ignoring the pulse of pain, she shook her head. Oh, the irony. Four and a half years on the inside. A total of fifty-four months without so much as a paper cut, and now, here she lay . . . bashed up and hurting. Another casualty in one of Griggs's nasty power plays.

One called obsession.

Had his infatuation been with her, J. J. could've found a way around him. Outsmarted him at his own game. Screwed with his head. Manipulated without mercy to save her own skin. Too bad it wasn't that simple. It never was with her sister in the mix. Tania meant the world to her. Was the only person she called family and cared about, so . . . no question. The second Griggs fixated on Tania—harassing her when she visited her at prison, trying to use J. J. as leverage to force Tania to sleep with him—he'd gone from just another prison guard to inmate enemy number one.

All that, though, had been about to change. Griggs had known it. So had she and Tania.

It started and ended with one thing . . . the arrival of a letter. One issued by Washington State Corrections and stamped with parole board letterhead. Call it karma. Call it luck. Call it a reward for good behavior and time served. But whatever the universe labeled it, hope was the principal message. J. J.'s throat tightened. God, freedom. A second chance at a real life. The opportunity to make amends, to help others and give back somehow. Maybe even ensure other girls didn't make the same mistakes she had.

All she'd needed was a month.

A measly thirty-one days and she would've been safe. But oh no, that had been too much to ask. A pie-in-the-sky dream with Griggs breathing down her neck. The weasel liked to snoop, and the instant he found the letter in her file? Game over. He'd come after her with both barrels, sending Daisy and her crew to corner her in the library. His objective had been simple: hurt her, hurt Tania. An excellent strategy . . . with nasty consequences. Ones that left her with the obvious—life-threatening injuries and a truckload of pain. But worse, at least for her? No one else knew about his part in her attack. And she couldn't prove it.

Daisy wouldn't talk. A lifer doing time for triple homicide, she'd kept a lid on things. Refusing to cooperate, after all, was an inmate's specialty. The less the warden and guards knew, the better. Which meant the truth about Griggs would never get out. Not while he played favorites: promising inmates perks on the inside, threatening those who didn't toe the line, manipulating the system without mercy. And what did that make J. J.? Screwed six ways to Sunday, that's what.

No proof. No credibility. No way out.

Twenty-four hours ago, she might've had a shot. But oh my, how the tides turned and fortune shifted. J. J's throat tightened, making her chest ache. It wasn't fair. She'd been so close. So very close. Now the chances of her walking out the prison gates a free woman were slim to none. The warden didn't tolerate fighting. Was no doubt in investigation mode already, putting J. J.'s appointment with the board on hold as she decided who to blame for the incident. And whether charges would be levied.

All without J. J. there to defend herself.

Sorrow circled deep, making her eyes sting. Even knowing the warden wasn't an idiot didn't help. Logic—and the reality that drove the corrections system—dictated the path and required a certain amount of pragmatism. Hope wasn't something she could afford. And luck? She huffed. Right. Fortune was as fickle as fate. J. J. never knew which way either would throw her—into something good or straight into the middle of a whole lot of bad.

The latter seemed more plausible. Especially after what she'd done.

Murderers didn't go free. Society believed in the principle, and so did she. Second chances belonged to other people, not her. Never her. And as regret circled and guilt piled on, J. J. recognized the futility. Damned if she did. Damned if she didn't. Her abusive ex-boyfriend had put her in that position, forcing her to choose between her life and his. A no-brainer all things considered. Self-preservation didn't negotiate and always won out in the end. Truth stacked upon truth. From the moment he threatened to kill her if she didn't stay, the choice became simple and the path clear . . .

Pull the trigger. Take him out of the equation or end up in a body bag.

Unfair? Certainly. A necessary evil? Absolutely. Her fault? Without a doubt.

She'd dug her own grave. Made one bad decision after another. Trusted him too quickly and gotten involved with a violent man willing to use his fists to keep her in line. Her mistake. A heavy cross to bear. Absolution would forever remain out of reach. God would never forgive her. J. J. didn't blame him. She'd never forgive herself, so—

A sharp pop sounded above her.

Startled, J. J. flinched. Sore muscles protested, jabbing her with invisible needles as she glanced up. She sucked in a breath. Different guy. Not the same soft-spoken orderly who pushed her out of the recovery room a while ago. And in his place? A tall stranger with broad shoulders and big hands planted on the head of her bed.

Rimmed by black liner, blue eyes met hers. "Hey, you're awake."

She blinked. Her injured eye squawked, tearing up as pain jabbed her temple. Squinting, she forced her vision into focus and . . . holy moly. A spiderweb tattoo with an ugly red spider at its center was inked on the side of his neck. Her gaze bounced back up, landing on the metal stud piercing his nostril. The black steel glinted beneath the overhead light, winking at its twin just above it, the one calling the guy's eyebrow home.

A chorus of "what the hell" made the rounds inside her head.

"I know, I know," he said, sounding bored. Long bangs with burgundy highlights hung over his forehead, playing keep-away from the buzz cut gracing the sides of his head. "I don't look like an orderly, but trust me . . . no worries, I'll getcha there. Faster than fast too."

Trust *him?* A Goth guy with crazy spider ink? J. J. opened her mouth to . . . well, quite frankly, she wasn't sure. Object to the *no worries* comment maybe? Asking his name was another option. Too bad neither went well. Her brain was in neutral, parked somewhere between confused and quick-witted. Not fun by any stretch, but neither was it priority one. At least, not right now. Why? Goth Guy was picking up speed. Snapping his wad of chewing gum, he wheeled her, bed and all, around a sharp corner. Which . . . oh Jesus, help her . . . prompted a question. What the heck did he mean by "faster than fast too"?

Alarm bells clanged inside her head, making her temples buzz. Her vision wavered, fading in then out. "W-where . . . ?"

He raised a brow. "Where we going?"

Seemed like an important question to ask. An absolutely vital one considering he looked like a vampire. Or an axe murderer. Then again, maybe she should indulge in a combo, a two for one kind of deal, 'cause . . . holy crap. *Vampire axe murderer* fit like a foot in a shoe when it came to him.

He opened his mouth, no doubt to deliver the all-important answer.

"No m-more tests," she said, beating him to the punch. She couldn't go another round with a doctor. No more poking, prodding, or needles. Nothing that included a scope of any kind either. "No more—"

"Nah, you're good. The CAT scan was the last one." Bright-eyed and bushy-tailed, he leaned over the headboard and grinned, looking funny upside down. "Doctor says you're lucky. Gotta pretty hard noggin on you, that's for sure. You only got a mild concussion."

Only. Such an idiotic word. "Super."

Her sarcastic reply made him laugh. A second later, he snapped the wad of bubble gum, blowing a pink bubble. "We're headed two floors up. They got your room ready."

The bed's wheels thumped over an uneven patch of floor. Unfazed by the speed bump, Goth Guy pushed her toward a set of double doors. Collision inevitable, J. J. braced for impact. The foot of her bed thunked, steel and metal rattled, making the mattress vibrate beneath her and . . .

That was all it took. Sensation clawed over frayed nerve endings. J. J. bit down on a moan. Oh God, that hurt. She was beyond raw and into debilitating. And as pain sang her a toxic lullaby, pressure spiraled around her rib cage, stealing her air, compressing her lungs, making her want to throw up. Such a bad idea. Puking wouldn't do her any favors, never mind make her any friends.

Baring down, J. J. clenched her teeth and double-fisted the sheets. The IV zigged then zagged, pinching her skin, tearing at the tape. Blood welled on the back of her hand, and the tube connecting her to the medical cocktail pinged against the bed rail.

Stomach acid churned, sloshing up her windpipe.

With a silent curse, J. J. swallowed the burn and, uncurling her fists, pressed her palms flat against the sheet to ground herself. Little by little, the world stopped spinning, allowing her to take a much-needed breath. The black spots peppering her vision faded and—

Goth Guy snapped his gum again.

Battling her gag reflex, J. J. thanked God when he slowed, bringing her to a rolling stop in front of a bank of elevators. With a soft ping, a set of double doors slid open. Wheels hissed as he swung her bed around and put them in reverse, backing into the elevator. He hit the button for the fifth floor with the side of his fist. With a quiet bump, the doors closed. The floor dipped, then rebounded, slingshotting them into an upward glide. Her stomach gurgled, not liking the shift. J. J. whispered a heartfelt prayer, offering God her services in the prison chapel if she survived the transfer from one room to the next without getting sick.

A likely outcome? Wishful thinking? J. J. couldn't tell. The jury was still out on Goth Guy. And not looking at him in a positive light, 'cause . . .

Man, he was noisy: snapping his gum, humming a tune, making her head ache as he used her headboard like a set of bongo drums. Hands flying, he started another round, beating out a rhythm guaranteed to make anyone—injured or not—scream.

The elevator doors slid sideways, opening in invitation. Goth Guy took the hint and sped into the hallway, the end of her bed leading the way and . . . oh shit. Race-car fast. The guy was speed-of-light ridiculous. Quicker than a runaway grocery cart.

"S-stop," she rasped, a death grip on the sheets.

Oblivious, he roared toward a T-shaped intersection in the corridor. J. J. gagged as he swung wide, taking the corner too fast. She bobbled in bed, wobbling beneath blankets and sheets. As pain ricocheted, colliding with the base of her skull, a counter came into view, file folders and paperwork stacked high. J. J. focused on the lopsided pile. She needed to keep it together, any distraction would do, just as long as—

"Hey!" Sharp with displeasure, the strange voice bit a second before a woman's head popped up from behind the high countertop. Dark eyes narrowed, she glared at Goth Guy. He put the brakes on, skidding to a sliding stop in front of the nurses' station. "We're in a hospital, not on a race track. Slow down!"

"Apologies," he said, grinning, not looking sorry at all. Another snap of gum. The sound ricocheted, banging around inside J. J.'s head as she glanced up at the guy. The pink blob disappeared back inside his mouth. "But I was told to get her here . . . lickety-split quick."

"Lord save and keep me, I swear . . ." With a huff, the nurse pushed out of her chair and stepped around the high countertop. Heavyset with a round face and dark skin, she drilled Goth Guy with another look. Running shoes squeaking, she approached the side of J. J.'s bed. "You do realize there's a difference between efficient and ridiculous, don't you?"

"Just trying to help," he murmured, the gleam in his eyes a little, well . . . J. J. didn't know exactly. Unsettling? Untrustworthy? Aggressive with a touch of amusement? Maybe. Then again, maybe not. She could be imagining things. Might be a tad off her game, fuzzy in the mental realm considering the IV pumping painkillers into her body. "So . . . where you want her?"

Suspicion took a turn across the nurse's face. Her eyes narrowed on him. "I don't recognize you. What's your name?"

"New guy." Big hands flying, he tapped against the headboard as though playing a big drum finale. Rhythmic sound carried, rising in the quiet to drift down the deserted corridor. "All right, I'm outta here. Take good care of her, nurse."

"Hang on just a minute, mister. I need your—"

"Nah, you don't."

The nurse frowned at him.

He winked at her. A moment later, his gaze flicked down to meet J. J.'s. His mouth curved, he tipped his chin at her, then let go of the end of her bed. "Catch yah later, sunshine."

As he turned away, J. J. blinked, the nickname catching her by surprise.

"Impertinent bugger." Looking fifty shades of pissed off, the nurse watched the guy lope back toward the elevators. As he disappeared around a corner, she shook her head. "Double-damned idiot. Don't know where they find them these days, but that one needs an attitude adjustment."

"Driving lessons too."

The nurse's lips twitched. "Shook you up a bit, did he?"

"Feeling like a James Bond martini over here."

"Ha! Shaken, not stirred. Good one, hon."

Thank you would've been the thing to say. But as J. J. opened her mouth, her throat closed, and the words wouldn't come. The burn of nausea, though, was right on time, exploding with inferno-like pressure up her windpipe. As her gag reflex kicked in, muscles bore down, twisting her abdomen into knots. Turning her face into the pillow, J. J. moaned.

"Hell in a handbasket." Leaping toward the nurses' station, the nurse grabbed something off the counter. Back in a flash, she cupped J. J.'s nape and lifted her head. As J. J. dry heaved over the kidney-shaped container, stitches pulled, making her skin scream. She whimpered. The nurse murmured, her tone soothing, her instructions no-nonsense.

"Breathe through it now. In through your nose, out your mouth. That's it, kiddo. You got it."

Sweat broke out on her forehead. The chills set in, making her teeth chatter. Clinging to the sound of the nurse's voice, J. J. listened to her heart pound. The throb multiplied, beating triple-time as she dry heaved again, cresting another excruciating wave. But as she tripped down the other side, dipping into agony's valley, something miraculous happened. Numbness set in, helping her muscles unlock. She drew a lungful of air, thankful she could breathe at all.

"All right now. There we go." Still holding the impromptu puke bucket, the nurse cupped her wrist. Pressing her fingers to J. J.'s pulse point, she glanced at the wide-faced clock hanging on the wall beyond the high counter. "Much better. Your pulse is evening out. Keep up with the breathing. I'll get you sorted out."

Curled on her side now, J. J. nodded, liking the plan. Especially if *sorted out* meant another round of painkillers.

"Good." Releasing her, she set J. J.'s hand down on the mattress. "So there are a few things you should know. I'm Nurse Ashford. I'll be looking after you for a while. How are you doing? Better?"

J. J. dipped her chin, the movement slight. Not much in the way of a response, but it was the best she could do. All she could manage as her muscles twitched in protest, nausea still circling as fatigue set in.

"Demerol will do that to a body," Nurse Ashford said, tone soft and full of sympathy. Adjusting the blanket, she smoothed the bunched fabric and met J. J.'s gaze. Her hand reached out. J. J. tensed, unaccustomed to being touched, expecting the worst. But the worst never came. Instead, Ashford smiled and gave her knee a gentle pat. "Don't you worry, Jamison. You'll be feeling better in no time. Peace and quiet. Lots of rest is what you need. The doctor will be down to check on you soon, but for now, let's get you settled, shall we?"

Kind words wrapped in concern.

The tears J. J.'d been holding back rushed to the surface. As her vision blurred and her chest went tight, she swallowed, fighting the onslaught. Crying wouldn't solve anything. Experience was a great teacher, but . . . wow. She hadn't expected that. Not the patience. Nor the kindness. Convicted felons, as a rule, didn't get much from anyone. Didn't deserve any either. But as Ashford kept up the chit-chat and got them rolling, the squeak of wheels echoing down the corridor, gratefulness made a home inside J. J.'s heart. A *gift*. Whether the nurse knew it or not, she'd given her an incredible gift. One that handed J. J. her dignity. Made her feel normal. Valued. Like a real person instead of a degenerate for a change.

"Nurse Ashford?"

"What is it, kiddo?"

"Thank you." Tilting her head, she glanced at the nurse.

"Don't give it another thought. I got a brother on the inside and things are never what they seem." Expression serious, the nurse's brown eyes met and held hers over the rim of the headboard. "Are they, Jamison?"

"No, ma'am," she said, her voice whisper thin.

The pace gentle—very un-Goth Guy–like—Ashford pushed her past one of the hospital rooms. Slid to one side, the clear glass door stood open, allowing J. J. an unobstructed view of the inside. Her mind took a snapshot, cataloging details, relaying information. Pale walls, the soft beep of medical machines, a wooden U-shaped wall unit

surrounding the bed and . . . nope. Not hers. Someone occupied room number 532 already, the large lump in the center of the bed a dead giveaway. Glancing farther down the
corridor, she spotted another doorway. As they approached,
a man stepped into the hall. Boot soles creaking, he pivoted
in her direction. The hallway light winked off the badge
pinned to his chest.

Fear hit J. J. chest level, stalling the breath in her lungs.
Oh no . . . no, no, no. It couldn't be. It just *couldn't*. She refused to believe the universe was that perverse. But as his
all-too-familiar gaze met hers and she shook her head, the
truth broadsided her. She was a dead woman, the how and
when nothing but a formality.

She knew it deep down, where reason lived and intuition reigned.

Officer Griggs. The man responsible for hurting her—
for organizing the attack and sending Daisy to corner her in
the prison library. Breath stalled in her throat, J. J. stared at
him, mind whirling, suspicion gathering, panic rising . . . the
reason he stood inside the hospital becoming all too clear.

He'd come to finish the job.

She could see it in the hard glint of his gaze. His plan
was simple. Correct his mistake. Silence her before she talked, putting him and his actions under the warden's microscope. Guys like Griggs didn't enjoy that kind of scrutiny.
He thrived in shadow, deep in the dark areas most didn't
want to acknowledge, never mind visit. And as he pulled his
shiny prison issue handcuffs out of his utility belt and strode
toward her, J. J. started to pray.

For divine intervention. Some kind of miracle. A clever
idea—something, anything at all—that would stall fate,
stave off the inevitable, and save her life. Griggs was just that

cunning, a real snake in the grass. One way or another, he'd find a way to shut her up. Accidents happened. Inmates got roughed up all the time for various reasons: mouthing off to the guards, smuggling contraband . . .

While attempting to escape.

All of which might prompt the use of deadly force.

A scenario Griggs could manipulate to his advantage. He would make it look good too. Set the scene. Ensure it ended messy and he came out clean. All in an attempt to cover his own ass. And with Griggs neck-deep in trouble and sinking fast? A cover-up became priority one, so . . . yeah. No way would he hesitate to put her six feet under.

Chapter Three

Filled with more stars than Wick wanted to count, the sky glittered above him, folding over urban edges with majestic sparkle. A rare sight. One he appreciated as cloud cover cleared, leaving nothing but the dark velvety vista in its wake. Wings spread wide, he slowed the velocity of his flight. Cold air slithered over his scales, rattling the weave of his interlocking dragon skin.

His fiery side should've grimaced, complaining about fall's slide into winter. His dragon, though, didn't make a sound. No protest. No wishing for warmer weather or a trip down south. Not even a shiver of discomfort. The silence was an anomaly, signaling his freakish nature. Most fire dragons hated frost and snow, spending more time indoors than out when mountain air turned chilly and north winds blew south, dragging subzero temperatures over the Canadian border.

Not him. A lifetime of deprivation had set the pace.

Now, he simply followed the curve, flying out to meet the enemy no matter the weather. Rikar, a frost dragon and the Nightfuries' first in command, loved him for it. Freezing rain. Snowstorms. Whiteout conditions. It didn't matter.

Wick never missed an opportunity to play hunt-and-kill with the Razorbacks. Which meant while the other warriors hunkered down to wait out a bad squall, he served as Rikar's wingman. Good all the way around. The arrangement gave them both what they needed—a ball-busting fight—while adhering to the rules. Bastian didn't fuck around or tolerate insubordination. No one flew out of the lair without backup.

And if a male was foolish enough to try? B would hand the warrior his ass on a stick.

Not advisable . . . or even close to fun. The rules existed for a reason, one that kept the Nightfury pack healthy and its members breathing. And as much as Wick enjoyed chaos, he liked his brothers-in-arms too much to risk them in the pursuit of foolishness. Smart was always welcome. Dumb-ass stupid, however?

Not so much.

Which meant he couldn't bust a move or go AWOL. Not with Venom and the rest of the boys flying in his wake. Wick ground his fangs together. Fuck him, but he wanted to make a break for it. Fly to his favorite spot deep inside Mount Rainier and curl up next to a river of lava flow while his comrades found suitable females and fed. He snorted in disgust. Droplets of magma swirled from his nostrils, ghosting over his horns as he shook his head. All hail his upbringing. Brutality at the hands of his captor had left him phobic, not wanting to be touched, never mind touch in return.

A bad taste washed into his mouth. Wick swallowed, combating his unease. God. He was a pansy, a lily-livered chicken, for his aversion. Most males relished time with the opposite sex. Enjoyed the slap and tickle. Craved the contact and mutual pleasure. Not him. He dreaded it, feeling

inadequate, unprepared, unable to give the bliss-fueled ecstasy a female demanded while males of his kind fed. Shit.
He didn't even know what that meant. Had never experienced true pleasure, never mind provided any for another
living soul.

Too bad compulsion and hunger didn't care.

He was a slave to his nature and the energy his kind
needed to survive. The Goddess of All Things had seen to
that, cursing his race long ago. Some said she'd cast the
spell to exact revenge. Others thought her methods a judi-
cial righting of wrongs. Wick didn't give a shit either way. All
he cared about was the outcome, and Dragonkind's utter
dependence on human females—to not only procreate but
also connect to the Meridian, the electrostatic current that
fed his kind. Ringing the planet, the energy source nur-
tured plant and animal alike. The process was an automatic
one for all living things, with the exception of Dragonkind.
Thanks to the goddess—and her colossal snit—the direct
link between the Meridian and his kind lay shattered. Now,
a male needed a female to survive. Which entailed connecting to the Meridian's energy stream through her. Getting
up close and personal, so close skin touched skin and . . .

Wick stifled a shiver. Brutal punishment with sharp
teeth and a big-ass bite. Unfair? Without question. Too
bad *fair* had nothing to do with it. Silfer the dragon god
had screwed up, pissing off the wrong deity with his cheat-
ing ways. Now all of Dragonkind suffered for his stupidity.
Which sucked, but hey . . .

It was what it *was*. Flip the dossier closed. File it under
Fucked Up and get on with it.

Good strategy. The best, really . . . logical, straightforward, precise. Too bad none of that helped him. He couldn't

Coreene Callahan

quell the dread. Or turn off his brain as he lined up his approach, gliding over building tops and the avenue below. Cloaked by an invisibility spell, he scanned the city streets. Seattle was busy tonight. Humans were everywhere, huddled into their coats, collars turned up, hands jammed in pockets, the fast click of high heels echoing as they hustled along sidewalks. Music drifted, thumping bass rolling out of nightclubs, enticing males and females out of taxicabs, toward neon signs and closed doors.

Another Friday night. Same outcome.

Humans liked to party. The faint smell of alcohol and perfume told him the scene was in full swing. Good for Venom. Not so great for him. It meant there would be lots to choose from, and more action than he could handle.

The thought cranked Wick one notch tighter. He didn't want to do it. Then again, he never did. The brush of strange hands against his body—the unpleasant rush of sensation—made him cringe and curl inward, away from the prickling pain of overload. Away from bone-bending pressure and the mind-warping hunger that shoved him to the edge of endurance, messing with his control.

Fight or flight.

An instinctive response, nature's own and one Wick couldn't avoid. Not that he didn't try . . . all the time. But Venom was right. He couldn't go after Jamison and repay his debt while hungry. He wanted to rescue the female, not endanger her. So, no getting around it. No negotiating with it either. He needed to grow a pair and allow closeness with a stranger. Someone who didn't give a damn about him. A human who only wanted one thing . . . the promise of pleasure and its rapid delivery.

With a grimace, Wick circled into a holding pattern, wheeling like a bird of prey over a low-lying rooftop. *Pleasure.* The word gave him the chills. His dragon shied, not appreciating the psychological deep freeze or the implications behind it. Shit, he wasn't any good at this, and no matter his eighty-seven years and all past feedings, it never got any easier. He always felt inadequate . . . completely out of his league. Unable to provide what a female demanded as he took what he needed.

All right, so Venom helped. Was ever constant, smoothing out the rough patches, supporting him through the process, providing what he couldn't for himself. Sad, but true. He couldn't feed without Venom present. Panic always picked Wick up, then shut him down, forcing him into freak-out mode the instant a female got too close. Disgust sank deep, cutting through to sear his soul. Damaged. He was beyond redeemable. Shamed by the inability to provide for himself.

Tucking his wings, Wick dropped like a rock between two tall buildings. Glass shuddered and rattled in steel frames, reflecting his black amber-tipped scales and the fierce glow of his gaze. As the golden light refracted, skipping across asphalt, Wick touched down on the brownstone's rooftop. The razor-sharp tips of his talons screeched across metal, setting him on edge.

Not a great start. Especially since he was already wound way too tight.

Dark-green scales flashed overhead, glinting in the moonlight. A moment later, Venom touched down without a sound beside him. Rolling his massive shoulders, his friend wing flapped, sending rock dust swirling into mini-tornados. Muscles rippled along the male's flank, showcasing his strength as he folded his wings, drawing the black webbing against his sides.

Ruby-red eyes shimmering, Venom nodded. *"The Gridiron. Good choice."*

Good had nothing to do with it. The nightclub, and the humans it catered to, drew his friend like a loadstone. Venom liked a rough crowd and lithe, Gothed-out females, so . . . no shit, Sherlock. It was a no-brainer. Considering the favor Venom did him, Wick always went with his friend's favorite.

"Shove over." The low growl, spiked with a hint of the Highlands, came through mind-speak, vibrating between Wick's temples. A second later, the purple-scaled Scot uncloaked, coming in on a fast glide. Smoke swirling in his wake, Forge bared his fangs. *"Or better yet, get gone. Not a lot of real estate down there. We cannae land if you wankers donnae move."*

"Do we have to?" Mac grumbled, rotating into a slow flip behind the Scot as he lined up his approach. *"I hate the Gridiron. It's too fucking loud."*

Venom rolled his eyes but shifted, moving from dragon to human form. Wick followed suit, and stomping his feet into his shitkickers, headed for the rooftop door. The staircase made its home behind steel, and a whole bar full of "just-kill-me-now" lay beyond that. But hey, no time like the present. The quicker he got the job done, the sooner he could go on his way. Be all the way across town, kicking ass inside Swedish Medical.

Not here, looking FUBARed in the face.

"Shut your yap, Mac." Dark-brown scales glimmering, Sloan tucked his horned head, somersaulting in midair to land on the roof edge. Snow-white talons played a game of

clickety-click against the building side as the triple scorpion-like stingers tipping the male's tail glinted in the city glow. *"Not all of us have a personal plaything feeding us at home."*

"My mate's not a plaything," Mac said, the snarl in his tone undeniable. He flexed a huge blue-gray talon, razor-sharp claws promising aggression. *"You say anything like that about Tania again, I'll rip your face off."*

Wick snorted, boots crunching on stone dust as he crossed the roof. He liked Mac's style. Easy to do. The male might be new to Dragonkind—and the magical abilities that accompanied the *change*—but he packed a helluva wallop and didn't take shit from anyone. Both big pluses . . . at least in his opinion.

With a chuckle, Forge thumped the newest member of their pack with the side of his spiked tail.

Mac threw the Scot a dirty look.

Sloan bared his teeth, the smile half-amusement, half-challenge. *"Bring it on, Irish."*

"Stop mucking around." Deep voice rolling like thunder, Venom stretched his shoulders. Leather creaked as his biker jacket protested. *"I'm hungry, and we got a female in the mix tonight. The sooner we feed and get out of here, the better."*

The statement sobered the group.

And no wonder. Pulling an injured female out of danger would take some doing. Strange, but the idea enlivened Wick. Not for the discomfort he would cause, but for the good he might do . . . for the peace he would bring Mac and his female. For the debt he would repay. And, yes, for the chance to screw over human authorities and flout their ridiculous laws. He'd read the police report and court transcripts. Jamison had protected herself. And for that she'd been imprisoned, and now mistreated.

Wick's eyes narrowed. The metal handle settled in his hand, frosting his palm. He cranked the door wide, barely registering the cold. Injustice. It came in so many forms. He was a prime example. His imprisonment—all the agony he'd suffered over the years—didn't matter anymore. It was ancient history. But Jamison still had a chance, and he would see that she got it. But first, he needed to . . . to . . .

His throat went tight. Wick cringed. He forced himself to move forward anyway and descended the stairs. The rank smell of stale alcohol rose, assaulting his senses as his warrior brothers filed in behind him. Multiple boots clanked out a rhythm on steel treads, joining the heavy thump of bass and the high-pitched shriek of a singer's voice. Darkness descended and swelled, enclosing him inside a prison all his own. His night vision sparked, showing him the way as excitement turned to dread, congealing in the pit of his stomach. *But first . . .*

God-awful words. Too bad neither changed the facts. Or lifted the curse of his kind.

A furrow between his brows, Wick paused at the bottom of the staircase. Decision time. Turn right toward the emergency exit, say "fuck it," and pull a fast flash'n fly. Or go left into the alcohol-fueled oblivion of human frenzy. Shitkickers planted, hands curled into fists, he glanced through the open door into the club. Strobe lights backlit those closest to the entrance, holding male and female bodies in silhouette. Some congregated along the back bar, waiting for their drinks. Others stood intertwining, more interested in sex than the surroundings.

Wick's heart squeezed, then rebounded, slamming the inside of his chest. Now or never. No easy choice. Especially considering escape lay a few feet away. A couple quick strides, one swift kick, and he'd be outside . . . in the alley beyond. Deep in the chill, breathing in crisp night air instead of female perfume, the smell of male sweat, and cigarette smoke.

Temptation lit him up. He leaned toward the exit.

A big hand landed on his shoulder.

Clenching his teeth, he glanced left. An uncompromising set of ruby-red eyes met his. Wick shook his head.

Venom tightened his grip. "Let's go."

Mouth gone dry, Wick couldn't answer. He nodded instead and, putting one foot in front of the next, led the way into the last place he wanted to go.

Chapter Four

As the back of the bed's headboard bumped against the wall of her hospital room, J. J. tried not to panic. Fear stuck it to her anyway, punching through to pierce her breastbone. The sharp barbs grabbed hold of her heart, sank deep, and stretched her thin, making it hard to concentrate, never mind control her reaction.

But she needed to. Right now. Before Griggs saw her expression and picked up her distress. The second that happened, she was cooked.

Flambéed with an extra order of screwed on the side.

A consummate manipulator, the slimy good-for-nothing guard would use it against her. Up the ante until nothing but dread remained. Anticipation, after all, was worse than reality. He knew it. So did she. Too bad she couldn't stop the unease. Or stop her palms from sweating.

Curling her hand in the sheets, she wiped the moisture away as he approached the end of her bed. Handcuffs in hand, he swung the metal shackles around the tip of his finger. The move was pure intimidation, 100 percent wild, wild West, the kind of thing gunslingers did with their six-shooters. Twirl. Flip. Point and shoot. The weasel had it down cold.

Not that Ashford noticed.

The nurse was too busy getting her settled. Humming a god-awful tune, Ashford gave the bed one last jiggle, making sure it sat perpendicular to the wall behind J. J., then bent to lock the wheels. Lovely, wasn't it . . . that kind of obliviousness? J. J. wished she possessed a touch of it. Maybe then her heart would stop thumping. Maybe then she could forget the threat, bury her head in the sand, and pretend she was safe for a change.

Maybe then the music would come back.

Her throat so tight she found it hard to breathe, J. J. reached for her fallback. She needed a three-four beat. An up-tempo song. Any melody—a single note—would do, just as long as it blocked out the chaos rebounding between her temples once and for all.

Her gaze riveted to Griggs—and his imminent landing beside her bed—she found the beat on the third try. Rounding the bases like a baseball player at full throttle, the melody came home, sliding in to save her. Acoustic and raw, the guitar thrummed to life. The drums arrived next, snapping imaginary fingers inside her head. B-flat weighed in on the first stroke of piano keys and . . .

Thank God. The piece was fully formed. Only the lyrics stayed away, letting the refrain lead the way to sanity. J. J. clung to the rhythm, let the music take her, and relaxed into the flow of composition like a sunbather in the noonday sun. Warm on her face. Hot in her soul. Beauty tempered by control and partnered with perfection. And as the symphonic sound melded, her body unlocked, allowing her to release the breath she'd been holding.

As air rushed from her lungs, Ashford grumbled. "Stupid . . . stubborn . . . lever."

A double snick sounded a second before the nurse's head popped up over the edge of the mattress. As she straightened, she smiled at J. J.

"Did you get it?" J. J. asked, stalling for time, trying her damnedest to ignore Griggs.

Ashford brushed her hands together. "Got it. You're all set . . . won't be rolling away on me anytime soon."

A smug look on his face, the weasel snorted. "Wheels locked or not, I could've told you that."

The nurse gave him a pointed look, and J. J. tensed. Here it came. Any second now, he'd—

The cuffs rapped against the bed rail. Metal clanged, erupting in the quiet, bouncing off pale walls and a bank of bare windows. A violent twist of his hand, and the loop closed, locking the steel ring against the rail. The familiar zzzz of shackles set J. J.'s teeth on edge. The shivers came next, rattling through her bones. The second he reached for her arm, she cringed and, clinging to the thread of acoustic guitar, breathed out. Panicking wouldn't help. But staying calm, holding firm, standing strong in the face of fear? Those things never failed. Would allow her to think, make a plan, but most of all, beat the weasel at his own game.

Too bad she'd never been much of a player. At least, when it came to poker.

The piano, however? Heck, she could play that puppy all day long. And as she rooted herself in the ascending refrain of a three-four beat, the steel grip on her wrist didn't seem so bad. Neither did the weight. Or the cold against her skin. Griggs could go to hell . . . along with his nasty disposition and obvious agenda.

The asshole had one. Guaranteed. Otherwise he wouldn't have pulled guard duty at the hospital. The question now? How far would he go to keep her quiet? No doubt all the way. She knew it from the look in his eyes. Smug. Victorious. Bastard to the absolute core. And as he squeezed the cuff a notch tighter around her wrist, J. J. gave ground and flinched, shifting sideways on the mattress. The plaster cast dragged at her calf, weighing her leg down and . . .

God. She hated that he stood so close. Despised the warm rush of his breath and sound of his prison issue boots. And in that moment, J. J. almost made a deal with the devil. She wanted him gone. She needed to get away. Couldn't stand the cloying scent of his cheap cologne, or the—

"For the love of Pete, Officer." Tone rift with disapproval, the nurse gestured to the handcuffs. "Is that really necessary?"

"Don't let her baby blues fool you." Expression impassive, he hooked his thumbs into the prison issue utility belt. As far as moves went, it was a good one. With his hands locked on the thick leather, he looked the part—poised, authoritative, and intimidating—with an added bonus. The pose drew attention to the gun holstered at his hip. "She's a stone-cold killer."

J. J. clenched her teeth to keep from retorting. Nothing good would come from mouthing off. Besides, it wasn't as if she could call him a liar. She'd done what she'd done. Taken aim and pulled the trigger. And as recall dredged up the past, her regret sank deep. It always did when she remembered that awful day. The memory was a permanent implant. Unshakable. Undeniable. The ghost she carried with her everywhere she went, so . . .

No. Little sense existed in fighting Griggs. Arguing—stating her case and all the extenuating circumstances—wouldn't change the facts. J. J. didn't want them to either. She'd understood the consequences. Had gone in with full knowledge, and regardless of the nagging guilt, couldn't deny she'd killed a man to save her life, but mostly to protect her sister. J. J.'s ex-boyfriend hadn't been bluffing. He'd meant every word. Would've made good on his threat. Forced her to watch as he put a gun to Tania's head and pulled the trigger before turning the revolver in her direction. Two dead for the price of one, except . . .

She hadn't let it happen. Had countered before he'd gotten his act together.

All of which landed her here . . . injured and alone in Swedish Medical with Griggs and an angry nurse facing off across her hospital bed. Yet as Ashford dug in, glaring at the weasel, J. J. couldn't help but be grateful. No one other than Tania ever championed her. It felt good to find a friend, even one as fleeting as a temporary caregiver. The gesture rated as sweet. Brave as well, considering the mean streak Griggs carried around like a club.

"It's all right, Nurse Ashford," she murmured, hoping to diffuse the situation. Angering Griggs wasn't a good idea. Keeping his pride intact amounted to the safer solution. "The cuffs don't bother me."

A lie. Boldly said and beautifully delivered. But honestly, she didn't want the nurse getting into trouble. Not on her account.

Eyeballing her, Ashford pursed her lips. She paused, indecision written all over her face, then—

"Prison protocol, ma'am," he said, brushing off the unspoken protest.

"I didn't catch your name, Officer . . . ?"

"Griggs, ma'am."

"Well, Officer Griggs, find the key and *un-protocol* her."
A determined look on her face, Ashford stared at him from
the opposite side of the bed. J. J.'s gaze ping-ponged, jumping from Griggs to her would-be savior and back again. Oh
boy. Not good. The nurse was itching for a fight, one that
would get them both bruised in the end. "I need to check
and redress her injuries. I can't do that with the handcuffs
in place."

Blond brows collided over his narrowed eyes.

"You can lock her back up after I'm done, but for now . . ."
The nurse pointed her finger at him in warning.

J. J. swallowed a huff of laughter. God love the woman,
she epitomized tough. Toss in stubborn. Add single-minded
to the mix and . . . yup. It was a whole new ball game. One
that left the weasel out in left field, trying to catch a line
drive without a proper mitt on his hand. She could feel the
sting coming. Could practically see him backpedaling in
the metaphorical sense, and as the nurse shook her finger
at him one more time and turned toward the table next to
the bed, J. J. said a silent "thank you." The weasel might be
a first-rate bully, but Ashford topped him, bringing kick-ass
to life in a contest of wills.

Excellent for J. J. Not so great for Griggs.

The delay gave her what she needed . . . time. An extra
ten, maybe fifteen, minutes to come up with a game plan.
Griggs might be an asshole, but he wasn't stupid. He'd figure out a way to get what he wanted and exploit her sister.
So, first things first. She must protect Tania by warning her.
Tell her to stay away until the shift change and Griggs went
home for the night.

"You hang in there, J. J." Reaching out, Ashford patted the back of her free hand before turning to grab a plastic cup off the bedside table. "I'll get some water for your sore throat and be right back. After that, I'll get you sorted out, okay?"

One eye on Griggs, J. J. nodded. "Thanks."

"No sweat, kiddo." Ample hips swaying, Ashford strode toward the bathroom door. Her hand jostled the cup. The straw rattled, pirouetting around the plastic rim as she glanced over her shoulder. Her gaze locked on Griggs, she arched a manicured brow. "Officer? I don't hear any keys rattling. The cuffs, if you please."

Ashford crossed the threshold into the bathroom. A tap got cranked, and the rush of water drifted through the quiet.

"Pain-in-the-ass woman." Murder in his eyes, Griggs flicked at a button on his belt. The case that held his cuffs flipped open. "Stupid nigger needs to be put in her place."

The slur drew J. J. tight. Her fingers flexed in the sheet. The racist Podunk. She wanted to hit him for insulting Ashford. Just once. Okay, maybe twice. It would feel so good to crank her fist back and let it fly. A knuckle sandwich would smarten him up. Well, at least that was her running theory. Too bad she never got to test it. Punching a guard ranked as stupid, perhaps even suicidal. And yet, the dream lived on, circling inside her head, bringing a certain amount of satisfaction as she imagined him out cold on the floor.

Minus his two front teeth.

"What are you staring at, *Injin?*" His lip curled as he sneered at her.

J. J. reined in a sigh, hiding her reaction. Nothing new about that . . . or the magnitude of his bigotry. He'd taught her well over the last five years. Reacting with outrage didn't work. It simply stoked his fire, feeding him the power to hurt her. A card-carrying member of Haters R Us, Griggs never missed a chance to disparage her heritage. Or insult the Cherokee blood in her veins. It made her less human in his opinion. Disgusting? Absolutely. Rage worthy? No question. Sad in this day and age when skin color shouldn't matter? Without a doubt. But that didn't stop Griggs from spouting his racist views whenever he thought no one else could hear.

The fact she was half white—with blue eyes and light skin—didn't matter to him. A half-breed equaled dirty, less than . . . unworthy of his notice. Too bad the same couldn't be said for Tania. Griggs dismissal of her sister would've solved a lot of problems, 'cause . . . yeah. Had she and her sister shared the same father, Griggs would never have given Tania a second look.

Never mind become obsessed with her.

"Fucking redskin." His low tone set off a buzzing inside her head as Griggs planted his hands on the bed-rail. The bar shifted under his weight, jarring the handcuffs. As the steel shackle tugged at J. J.'s wrist, the panic she'd been try-ing to hold at bay punched through. She shuffled sideways, inchworming beneath the cotton sheet, desperate to main-tain separation. It didn't work. He invaded her space, bring-ing the stench of cologne with him. The muscles along her abdomen clenched in protest. Pain skittered up her side, tightening its grip on her rib cage, pulling at the stitches. "You think you're home free or something? Just because that coon nurse has taken a liking to you?"

J. J. drew in a choppy breath. The guy was beyond sick. A real candidate for the nearest mental institution. "I want my phone call."

"Jesus." With a huff, he pushed away from his perch. As he straightened, rehooking his thumbs in his belt, he shook his head. "You just don't get it do you, *Injin?*"

Fear circled, taking an ugly turn. "I have a right to call my lawyer."

"Bullshit. You have what I give you, nothing more. So listen up, *Injin* . . . and listen good." A nasty gleam in his eyes, his mouth curved, the smile half-smug, half-snarl. Pressure snaked around her torso. As it tightened around her, she breathed in shallow bursts, struggling to keep her expression neutral. The second she let go, gave in, and showed fear was the instant he won. And foolish or not, J. J. refused to hand him a clean victory. "You try anything. Make a call. Warn your sister. Talk shit about me to the warden or anybody else, and you won't make it out of here alive. It's that simple. So go ahead, *Injin.* Cry foul. Test me, but only if you wanna die. Otherwise, keep your fucking yap shut."

"You won't get away with it," she said, faking confidence she didn't feel.

"I already have. And your sister? She's—"

"Smarter than you."

"It's not about being smart. It's about *her* keeping *me* happy. And guess what? The happier I am, the longer you live." One corner of his mouth tipped up. "What do you think Tania's gonna do when she sees you here like this, Solares? Hmm, you want to know what I think?" He paused, satisfaction lighting his eyes as he let her stew a moment. "I think she'll do whatever I say. Spread her legs . . . invite me in . . . blow me whenever I want just to keep you safe."

"You touch one hair on her head, and so help me God, I'll—"

"What?" He flicked at the cuffs chaining her to the bed. "Come on, *Injin* . . . tell me."

"You sick bastard."

He laughed. "About time you caught on."

Door hinges creaked across the room. Dragging her gaze away from the asshole tormenting her, J. J. glanced toward the bathroom. Ashford stood between the jambs, fitting a lid to the top of the plastic mug.

"Got those cuffs off yet, Officer?"

Griggs hesitated.

J. J. swallowed, waiting for the explosion. It never came. He smiled instead, and with a quick twist, inserted the key into the lock. The handcuffs fell away, clanging against metal. Half-relieved, half-sick with dread, she curled her bandaged arm into her chest, moving in slow increments, afraid Griggs would retaliate and reach for her again.

"Excellent. Thank you, Officer Griggs," the nurse said, shooing him out of the room with her free hand. "Now, off you go. There's a coffee machine just down the hall. I'll give you a shout when I've finished with my patient."

Griggs's gaze cut back in her direction. J. J. felt the sting. Not that it mattered. His threats meant nothing in the grand scheme of things. She was accustomed to abuse. Would handle the weasel—and all forms of retribution—to keep her sister safe. Now all she needed to do was figure out how.

The second he cleared the threshold, Ashford stepped alongside her. Setting the mug on the table, she pivoted toward the bank of cabinets running along the wall to her right. Quick hands flipped cupboard doors open, then closed them again. As plastic-wrapped packages, gauze, and tape landed inside a sturdy plastic bin, J. J. shifted on the mattress, trying to get comfortable. Why she bothered, she didn't know. It wasn't as though she had a chance in hell of avoiding the pain. Or outrunning the odds. Comfort wasn't in the cards. Griggs had dealt her a crappy hand, elevating the game to a contact sport.

The best she could do now was ensure no one else got hurt.

Ashford glanced toward the open door. And Griggs. Boots planted and shoulders set, he stood in the hallway with his back to them. He looked one way, then the other, studying the corridor as though he expected a military invasion. J. J. shook her head. Terrific. Just what she didn't need . . . a Neanderthal-in-waiting.

Vigilance piled on top of vigilance.

Moving into her line of sight, Ashford set the mishmash of supplies down on the end of the bed. "Is he always like that?"

"Pretty much."

"Calls you *Injin* a lot, does he?"

"Big racist . . . little brain."

The nurse snorted. "I'll keep that in mind."

"Please do," she whispered, worry tightening her chest. "Please don't cross him. You get in his way, he'll hurt you."

"Don't you worry about me." Sidestepping, Ashford grabbed the edge of the floor-to-ceiling curtain. She pulled. A zing split the silence as tiny wheels whipped around a metal track. Griggs looked over his shoulder. J. J. looked away, avoiding eye contact. A coward's way out? Maybe, but she couldn't take anymore. Not right now. Probably not for a while either. With another tug, the drape zipped full circle, cocooning the area around her bed. "I've dealt with his kind all my life."

"Nobody's like him."

"Nonsense. A bully is a bully. Doesn't matter what kind of uniform he wears. But enough about that." Done checking her IV, Ashford palmed a pair of surgical scissors. "We don't have a lot of time."

J. J. blinked. *Time?* "For what?"

"You know your lawyer's number by heart?"

A crease between her brows, J. J. opened her mouth, then closed it again. No sense trying to figure it out. She sucked at guessing games. "I don't—"

Seeing her confusion, the nurse smiled. "'Cause if you did? You might need one of these."

Slipping her hand into the back pocket of her scrubs, Ashford pulled out a . . .

Oh, Jesus be merciful. A cell phone. The high-tech kind with a wide, flat screen.

Gratefulness hit her chest level. Her heart paused midbeat, then picked up the pace, hammering so hard it echoed inside her head. Not knowing what to say, J. J. went into crybaby mode, tearing up so fast the nurse's face went blurry.

"Make it quick." Her head tilted to one side, the nurse listened for the sound of approaching footsteps. When none came, she murmured, "Don't call. Text him instead."

"I don't know how." Hands trembling, J. J. gripped the phone, staring at the thing like an alien object. The second she'd been charged and denied bail, she lost her privileges. All her belongings too . . . pay-as-you-go cell phone included. "I've never texted anyone."

"Hold on. Here, just . . ."

Quick as a music note, Ashford pressed a button. A picture of a dog dressed in a pink sweater flashed on the viewer. Another stroke across the screen. One more finger tap, and the image morphed, prompting J. J. Insert phone number there. Write a message below. Simple. Effective. Heaven to a girl who had never used it before.

"Clear enough?"

"Got it." Another round of tears flooded her vision. J. J. wiped them away. "Thank you."

Ashford said "uh-huh" and raised her voice, talking loud enough for Griggs to hear her. As she pretended to talk her through the changing of bandages, explaining her injuries and what needed to happen for her to heal, J. J. got busy: heart thumping, mind whirling, hope rising like a hot air balloon inside her head.

Salvation in each stroke, her finger found the right keys.

> *Tania . . . it's J. J. Am hurt. Need help, but*
> *don't come. Not safe. Griggs here. Call lawyer. Get*
> *protective custody. Be smart. Stay safe.*
> *Luv u, sis . . .*

Stress parked on her like a ten-ton truck, she reread the message. One second slid into the next and . . .

She hit the send button.

The praying started next. Along with all the *what ifs*. What if Griggs found out? What if Ashford got in trouble? What if Tania didn't receive the message? What if the warden . . . oh God. Oh shit. Holy hell on a swizzle stick. She hated *what ifs* and all the rotten possibilities each one dragged in its wake. J. J. closed her eyes, physical pain bowing beneath the bend of psychological torment. Someone just shoot her now. Lord knew that would be easier. A quick death, after all, was always preferable to a slow one.

Fury of Desire

❀ ❀ ❀

Biting down on a snarl, Wick crossed the threshold and stepped into Gridiron. His body rebelled, tensing up hard as the cloying stench of eau de nightclub closed in around him. The unconscious reaction ramped him into the danger zone, making his night vision spark. Trace energy flared, coming at him from all directions. He smothered a grimace. Jesus, he hated this place. Despised the strobe lights and Gothed-out décor. Couldn't stand the spine-bending beat of death metal pumping through hidden speakers. Or the shuffle and press of too many bodies in too small a space.

Not that any of the humans ever came near him.

None of them were that stupid. Good thing too. In his current frame of mind, he might snap a few in half just to take the edge off. Most males would've made a beeline for the bar. Downed a drink to combat the distaste. Maybe even an entire bottle to soothe the aversion and set sail into oblivion. Not him. He never touched the stuff. Never would either.

Alcohol wasn't his friend. And tonight? Neither was time.

Rolling his shoulders to loosen the tension, Wick turned left. Upscale VIP section, here he came. Humans scattered like bowling pins, doing what they did best . . . getting out of his way. The stairs took him up five treads onto a raised section that overlooked the dance floor. He didn't bother to look. He knew what lay in that direction. Nothing but the sea of drug-fueled humans pretending they knew how to dance.

Strobe lights flashed overhead, scoring the black walls with bright color.

53

Wick squinted against the glare and slowed, scoping out the lounge, getting a lay of the land, counting the number of humans struggling to talk over the noise pollution. Wick huffed. Surprise, surprise. A full house again tonight . . . along with more females than he could count. Good pickings for Venom and the other warriors.

Not so hot for him.

Unease ghosted deep, pricking the nape of his neck and . . . shit. There went his hands again. Every time he walked into the place the fuckers went numb. A reaction to the stress? Probably. An early warning sign to get the hell out. Absolutely. Not that he could at the moment. With Venom riding his ass, he needed to see the nightmare though. The faster he finished, the quicker he'd get what he wanted . . . out of the club, back into the street and airborne.

He glanced at the door nearest him. The red glow of the Exit sign perched above it bled into the club, burning twin holes in his retinas. An escape hatch, one that led into the alley behind the club. Temptation grabbed hold, cranking his muscles tight. Thirty seconds. Tops. And he'd be gone.

Too bad cowardice wasn't a condition he ever accepted.

Backing off—staying hungry—wasn't an option. Not tonight with his boys at his back and a mission in front of him.

Decked out in short skirts and midriff tops, females were everywhere: lounging in plush booths, sitting at the bar, standing in groups, skin exposed and bodies swaying, drinks in hand while ice swirled in glass tumblers. Wick stifled a shiver as the raw scent of hard alcohol overpowered him. Recall sharpened, sending him sideways inside his own head. God, that smell. It never failed to drag him into a past he didn't want to remember but couldn't forget.

And as he stood, shitkickers planted and shoulders squared, reality faded into memory.

Into the cruelty of another time and place.

Wick shook his head. Even after all these years, he couldn't get a handle on it. Couldn't wrap his brain around the savagery, never mind the abuse. He'd been so young when it started. Too naive to understand what was happening or what it would eventually do to him. Even after eighty years, the horror stayed with him: the collar and cage, the mental whiplash and raw brutality of his captors forcing 40 proof down his throat night after night.

All in the name of entertainment.

Curling his hands into fists, Wick fought the bitter taste of cerebral burn, desperate to douse the psychological flames. But nothing could stem the growing tide of recall. Or the body slam of his physical reaction to the scent of alcohol. Wick knew it. Habit and experience told him so. He tried anyway, combating the sick feeling, swallowing as bitterness rose, making his pulse throb and his heart ache.

Goddamn son of a bitch.

The bastard had locked him in a cage. A fucking *cage*... complete with a steel collar and chains. Why that pissed him off more than anything else, Wick didn't know. Certainly having the booze forced down his throat at age seven had been worse. He'd been addicted by age ten, a raging alcoholic raring for a fix before each fight. Before his captor dragged him onto a stage, slapped a knife in his hand, and forced him to—

The painful memory bit, making him bleed inside his own mind.

The wail of an electric guitar saved him, cutting through the mental noise.

Wick blinked. A second later, he shoved the past away. He wasn't there anymore, in that underground place, scared, alone, and vulnerable. Venom had gotten him out, and the bastard who'd owned him was dead. No sense reliving any of it. The best he could do now was move forward, hit hard, and get out quick.

Which meant finding a female for his friend . . . ASAP.

Turning his attention toward the bar lining the back wall, Wick's gaze skipped over the crowd. He grimaced. Jesus. What a train wreck. The Gridiron was a straight-up travesty. Nothing but hard surfaces that catered to trying-too-hard patrons. An army of Gothed-out pansies who acted tough but didn't have a clue what that meant. Give them a second of hardship, challenge the idiots at all, and . . . yeah. Each and every one would fold like a dirty shirt.

Shaking his head, Wick frowned at the humans.

"Rein it in, buddy."

Wick glanced left and raised a brow in question.

"The pissed-off expression." Amusement in his gaze, Mac slapped a big hand to his shoulder. Skin smacked against his leather jacket, the sharp sound drifting up between them. "You keep looking at them like that, and the females'll run scared. Not the best way to get lucky. A little welcome goes a long way, you know."

His eyes narrowed, Wick glared at the newest member of the Nightfury pack.

"Just saying." With a grin, Mac gave him another love tap. The firm slap rocked him forward, forcing him to widen his stance or fall over. "I'll be at the bar."

"Stay there," he said, silent warning in his tone. A necessary thing. Despite his inexperience, Mac was a wild card, one with the smarts and strength to go it alone. Not exactly what Wick wanted right now. If Mac went commando—not an impossibility considering the mission involved his mate's sister—he would lose his chance to repay his debt. Which would suck in a major way. He needed the score evened and the monkey off his back. And Jamison? She was the best means to that end. "The female is mine to retrieve, not yours."

"Got it." A serious glint in his blue eyes, Mac nodded, backing up word with deed. Brushing shoulders with him, the male moved past him, pointing his boots toward the bar at the back of the lounge. "Have fun, boys. Holler when you're finished."

"No doubt of that, lad." Stopping next to him, Forge threw him a sidelong glance. Anticipation fogged the air around the Scot as he rubbed his hands together. "Time frame?"

"An hour," Wick said, trying not to cringe. Fifteen minutes suited him better, but God knew that wouldn't work. His brothers-in-arms would balk, go grim reaper on his ass if he cut the timeline any shorter. None of them, after all, shared his affliction. Tall, short, thin, curvy, high-energy or not, it didn't matter. Each warrior loved being with a female. Cherished each minute spent with one. Craved the contact and the blast of life-sustaining, orgasmic energy that always followed. Wick knew because he'd seen the way Venom acted around women. Add that to all the chatter at Black Diamond after a night spent carousing and . . .

Shit, no contest. All enjoyed touching—and being touched in return.

Everyone except him.

The admission cranked Wick tight. Unease prickled through him. Anger came next. Jesus. He was a warrior, for fuck's sake. Strong. Able. Lethal in a firefight and feared by his enemies. No way should getting close to the fairer sex set him back a step. But the truth didn't give a damn about convenience or pride. How he felt—his reaction—was what it *was*. No denying it. And as he fought the chill of dread along with his neurosis, Wick rolled his shoulders. The movement didn't help. He did it again anyway, forcing himself to pack up the bag of horrors he carried around like luggage.

With a zip, he closed the thing up tight and reiterated the plan. "I want to be at the hospital before midnight."

"Bloody hell." Forge scowled at him, protesting the time crunch.

"Later," Sloan said, a growl in his voice. Dark eyes intense, he put himself in gear and followed Forge into the thick of the club. "Meet you on the roof in sixty."

"A whole hour." A half smile on his puss, Venom set up shop alongside him. The DJ rolled another track, synthesizing death metal with an older tune. As the remix got going, thumping through the speakers, his best friend raised a brow. "Generous of you. How come you never give me that much time?"

"Fuck off, Ven," he murmured, using his favorite verbal fallback. "Come back later, if you want."

Venom sighed as though resigned to his pissy attitude.

"I'm not leaving Jamison any longer than necessary."

Surprise lit a spark in his ruby-red gaze. "Jamison, is she? When did that happen?"

Wick smoothed his expression, scrambling to cover up the slip. But it was too late. Venom wasn't an idiot. His friend had picked up on his tone . . . on the way he said her name. Super. Just terrific. He'd made a tactical error and let the cat out of the bag. But even as he tried to stuff it back in, Wick knew he was screwed. Like a dog with a bone, Venom wouldn't let it go. He'd poke at him until he admitted the truth.

Jamison fascinated him.

Somehow . . . someway . . . over the last few hours she'd peaked his interest. More than a little strange, not to mention ridiculous. Curiosity never knocked on his door. He was a simple male who enjoyed a simple life. Fight. Rip apart rogues. Come home at the end of each night. Nothing complicated about it, but as the details of her situation surfaced, taunting him, he couldn't dismiss her. Or the novel prickling sensation he experienced when he thought about her.

Now a myriad of questions circled, demanding answers. He wanted to know every single detail. But more than that? He needed to meet the female behind the prison file. The little things made him wonder, and as curiosity burned, his imagination took flight. Such extreme measures. She'd gone the distance, lured a man to his death . . . done the unthinkable. At least, for a female. Most women wouldn't have had the guts. Running and hiding seemed a more likely MO.

Jamison, though, ran contrary to the rule. And like it or not, Wick wanted to know why.

"So . . ." Flexing his hands, Venom cracked his knuckles. The move smacked of impatience. "We getting to it or what?"

Wick nodded. It was now or never. And since *never* wasn't an option with Venom glued to his six, Wick forced himself to move. Picking up his feet, he strode toward the inevitable. The throb behind his temples picked up the pace, making

Wick's head ache. He shoved the discomfort aside, his gaze searching the VIP section and . . .

Bingo. Mac at three o'clock.

Cloaked by magic, invisible to human eyes, Mac stood in the shadows near the end of the bar, shoulder blades pressed to the wall, eyes moving over the crowd, and a pained look on his face. Wick could relate. He didn't want to be here either, but necessity was a motherfucker and finding a female he could stomach, an absolute must.

Dragging his attention away from his comrade, Wick scanned the back bar. High-backed chairs lined its length, elevating those seated into visual inference. A wide-faced mirror winked beyond them, colorful bottles reflecting in the dim light. Acute dragon senses picking up trace energy, he assessed each human. Nah, no decent candidates there. He needed a female with strong energy, powerful enough to feed both him and Venom at the same time.

He skimmed over a corner booth.

His gaze snapped right back. Hmm, that looked promising. Or rather, *she* did. Perfect. Dark-skinned and pretty. She was right up Venom's alley. His friend preferred African American females and . . . yeah. She fit the bill with her dark eyes and silky shoulder-length hair. The barely there white dress didn't hurt either. The fabric clung to her skin, accentuating her breasts and the healthy glow of vitality.

Wick's mouth curved. Excellent. No way Venom would be able to resist her.

Pausing mid-stride, Wick glanced over his shoulder.

Venom tipped his chin. "Decide yet?"

"Back corner booth."

"Goddamn . . . get a load of her." Venom's words rasped beneath a throb of hard-core bass. Wick heard it just the same, registering the interest in his friend's sudden shift. Jackpot. They had liftoff. Venom glanced his way. Simmering ruby-red eyes met his. "You ever gonna pick a female you're attracted to?"

He shrugged, avoiding the question. The answer to which was . . . no chance in hell. It wasn't that he didn't like females. He got off on a long pair of legs as much as the next male, but a big divide lay between looking and touching. The first he did a lot, studying the opposite sex, appreciating a female for what she was: beautiful and soft, arousing with all that smooth skin on display. Contact, though—anything hands-on—he avoided like a face full of acid.

"You want her or not?"

Venom growled. "No question."

"Then move it." Shoving his sleeve up, Wick tapped the face of his watch. "Fifty-seven minutes and counting."

"Hell," his friend muttered, but didn't waste a second.

Boot treads brushing over stained concrete floor, he followed Venom across the lounge. His attention narrowed on the female. Laughing at something her companion said, she took a sip of her drink. Her gaze met his over the rim of her glass. She paused, stiffening as her hand stalled in midair. Locked onto her aura, he registered the spike in her energy. Her eyes went wide. A moment later, alarm picked up her pulse.

Same story. Different night.

Never sure of him, most women shied at first. A normal reaction. One Wick understood, even as regret rose. It wasn't as if he did it on purpose. Given half a chance, he would have assumed a soothing vibe, not the predatory one he knew he wore, but . . . hell. He didn't know how. A hunter through and through, he sent most males running, never mind members of the fairer sex. Even so, he tried to do his part and forced his lips to curve. Maybe a smile would help smooth the way, make her more receptive, help Venom—

His friend stopped in front of her table.

The female blinked and switched focus. The second her gaze landed on Venom, she blew out a pent-up breath, her fear sliding into interest. Tipping her chin up, she gave Venom the once-over, eyes roaming downward, then turned and did the same to him. Wick tensed. She smiled and settled back, relaxing into the seat cushions, her ample charms on display as she made eye contact.

"Well, hello there."

Wick froze as she continued to hold his gaze. Holy shit. Talk about a switch-up. Strange with an extra helping of fucked up too. Usually Venom got all the attention, but as she bit her bottom lip, Wick got the message. Sexual energy was easy to read. So was feminine arousal, and as her pupils dilated and her lips parted, Wick swallowed. She was 100 percent into him, encouraging him to take the lead. To initiate contact, slide in next to her, and coax her to enter the sexual arena.

Which screwed with his chi. Not to mention his mind.

Jesus help him. What the hell was he supposed to do now?

Coming to the rescue, Venom turned her attention. "Hello, beautiful. Mind if I join you?"

She gestured with her hand, inviting his friend into the booth.

"*Mervais, talmina,*" Venom said in Dragonese, his tone low as he acknowledged her acceptance in the way of their kind.

Wielding a mental whip, Wick ousted the guy next to her. As the human skedaddled, moving as though his life depended on it, Venom settled next to her, taking up a sizable chunk of the real estate inside the booth. Per usual, Wick stood stone-still, setting up shop outside the alcove . . . with the pair, but not really. Awkward much? Absolutely, but he didn't know what else do. Two options presented themselves. The first said stay put. The second required walking around the table edge to bookend her on the other side. Seemed like a good move. For a normal male. Too bad he wasn't *normal.* He couldn't make himself move. Shitkickers rooted to the floor, he was stuck in neutral, brain fried, muscles locked, and panic rising. All because she wanted him . . . was throwing him come-hither looks from beneath her lashes.

Slinging his arm along the back of the banquette, Venom got up close and personal with the female. He whispered something in her ear. She tipped her chin, asking for a kiss. His friend gave it to her, pressing his mouth to the corner of hers, then leaned back to meet her gaze. Fingertips playing in her hair, he brushed the dark strands away from the side of her neck. "What's your name, *talmina?*"

"Iesha."

"Pretty name." She murmured a "thanks" and Venom got to the point. "So, Iesha . . . you up for a bit of fun?"

"What kind?" Nibbling on her bottom lip, she glanced in Wick's direction. Interest and desire sparked, making her aura glow bright orange. "A threesome?"

"All right." The tease in his tone unmistakable, Venom's hand dipped beneath the table. She sucked in a quick breath and shifted in her seat. As she tipped her head back, his friend took advantage, uncrossing her legs, spreading her thighs, nuzzling the side of her throat. "You've convinced me."

Her laugh turned into a gasp. "You taking turns?"

"One at a time."

"Here? Or in the bath—"

"Right here."

Wick nearly balked. *Here?* Right fucking *here?* In full view of the club? Bugger him. Trust Venom to grow impatient and neglect the safe side of decency. Gritting his teeth, Wick unleashed his magic, whipping up a cloaking spell. Shadow enveloped them, hiding their happy little trio from human eyes. Venom murmured something naughty against the female's collarbone. Wick cursed under his breath.

"Okay." Her breath hitched as Venom delved deep between her thighs. Lips parted, breasts rising and falling, her eyelashes flickered. As she shuddered in pleasure, the female plugged Wick with a heated look. He went on high alert, then grimaced when she moaned, "I want your friend first."

Wick stayed silent, knowing what was coming.

"No." Nipping her bare shoulder, Venom shook his head. A quick shift put the female in his lap. Some nifty maneuvering later, she sat astride his friend, the fabric of her dress up around her hips. Widening his stance to shield the couple, Wick looked away. Venom groaned, the sound cresting a bliss-filled wave. "I ride first."

Busy settling on what Venom fed her, she didn't argue. Neither did Wick. Particularly since he wouldn't be *riding*. Not her or any other female. He couldn't bring himself into close enough contact. The handful of times he'd tried had ended in disaster, telling him clearer than words sex wasn't his thing.

But as Venom ramped up, getting hot and heavy, working the female hard, Wick wished for something different. For something that didn't begin and end with him standing in a club watching his friend have sex. Not that it was Venom's fault. The male was simply looking after him, doing what Wick couldn't do for himself . . . ramping a female into an orgasmic frenzy. Elevating her energy levels high enough to feed both of them. Forcing him to tap into the Meridian's electrostatic stream to draw the nourishment all Dragonkind males needed to stay healthy and strong.

The fact Wick couldn't feed himself shamed him. Made sorrow rise and disgust circle.

After all this time, he ought to be strong enough to do it on his own. Instead, the idea gave him a raging case of indigestion. A shiver rolled up his spine. Wick shut it down, holding himself steady as the urge to run nudged him again. A mere matter of moments, a few seconds, that's all it would take, and he'd be—

"Wick."

His head snapped back toward his friend.

"Now," Venom said. "She's ready."

Cursing under his breath, Wick cringed. Logic told him to move. Uncertainty wouldn't let him. Stupidity to the next power. The quicker he started, the sooner it would be over, but . . .

He didn't want to touch her. Would prefer to go hungry if given a choice. He'd done it before. Had gone months without nourishment and never succumbed to energy-greed. But as he met Venom's gaze over the top of her head, Wick knew tonight wouldn't be one of those times. If he turned tail and ran, his friend would come after him. Be right on his heels. Drag him back and force him to feed, so . . .

No. There wouldn't be any free passes tonight. No way out either. Just full-on commitment.

"Do it, Wick . . . right now." Venom raised his head, ruby eyes aglow, and mind-spoke, *"And you don't stop until I tell you to. She's prime . . . able to handle us both. No flaking out this time. You feed until you're full, or I'll kick your ass."*

The bossiness should've pissed Wick off. It barely registered. Threat, no threat, it didn't matter. He was too nervous to do anything other than obey. Being told what to do helped. Clear. Concise. No room for error or misinterpretation. Which, oddly enough, gave him courage to move toward the female instead of away.

With a quick flick, Wick shoved the table aside and stepped in behind the female. His leather jacket brushed her shoulder blades. His chest touched down next. She moaned, welcoming his heat, undulating into another thrust, her hips moving in concert with Venom's. Tainted by alcohol, her breath washed into his face. Wick clenched his teeth, but didn't stop. Now or never. Quick in. Faster out. He could do this. Could ride the wave, stay the course, all while making Venom proud.

The thought twisted the screw tighter.

Courage made him reach out and cup her throat. As his hand settled against her skin, she moaned and tipped her chin up, giving him more room. Terrible. Without mercy. Voracious. The beast inside him rose on a greedy growl, begging for sustenance. Driven by instinct, he obliged, and pressing his hand to her lower back, lowered his head. She keened, pleading for pleasure as his mouth brushed the nape of her neck.

Energy surged.

The Meridian opened, blasting him with white-hot energy.

Unable to deny his need, Wick drank deep, pulling the electrostatic current through her into his core as Venom picked up the pace. An erotic switch flipped, powering into orgasm. As the female screamed in bliss, Wick fought a tidal wave of nausea and swallowed another mouthful. Venom growled, encouraging him to take more. He did, drinking hard, feeding fast, taking one pull after another.

But as he fed and his stomach cramped, he faced the awful truth.

He was irredeemable. A bastard beyond redemption for his shortcomings. An honorable male wouldn't need his best friend present when he fed. A normal male would be able to please a female on his own. A dutiful male wouldn't humiliate himself in such ways. And as the female came again, hammering him with another round, shame came calling. Fate had done him a bad turn and twisted his path. Now he lay beyond help. Fucked up in ways that couldn't be reversed, never mind cured.

Chapter Five

Waiting wasn't Ivar's strong suit. He'd never acquired the skill. Had never needed to either. As leader of the Razorbacks, no one ever made him wait. His word was law. The commands he issued absolute. The only voice that mattered in a pack accustomed to taking orders, regardless of the outcome. But as the elevator's smooth ascent took him out of the underground lair, toward street level and the rundown firehouse he now called home, he marveled at the irony.

Hamersveld was late.

All right, not by much. Still the slight bothered Ivar more than he liked. He inhaled long and exhaled smooth, tightening the screws on his temper. No one was ever late. Not when meeting with him. Then again, Hamersveld wasn't just *anyone*. He was a breed apart, a water dragon with a brutal nature, a keen mind, and the wherewithal to use both. A fantastic combo, one Ivar not only admired, but coveted, wanting the male's intellect—along with his propensity for violence—for himself.

And the Razorback pack.

The problem? Accepting Hamersveld put him in the middle of uncharted territory. The male was a true gamble. Powerful. Pissy. And unpredictable. The descriptions fit Hamersveld to a T. So did "severe aversion to authority." The water dragon wore the badge with pride, and by all accounts? Preferred his own company. With a snort, Ivar shoved his hands into the front pockets of his favorite jeans and leaned back. As his shoulder blades touched the mirrored surface of the wall, he ran through the possibilities.

After a moment, he shook his head. Jesus. Talk about an understatement. The male elevated dangerous to whole new levels. Excellent in some respects. Dicey in others. Good thing Ivar had never been averse to underdog odds. Long shots were his specialty. Sometimes playing both ends against the middle worked to his advantage. And Hamersveld? Ivar was betting all he owned, laying it all on the line in the hopes of bringing the lethal SOB onside and into the fold.

Huge risk. Big payoff . . . if he could swing it.

And if he couldn't? Well, death was always an option.

Ivar grimaced, preferring option A over B. He wanted Hamersveld in his corner, kicking Nightfury ass, not spread like fertilizer across his new backyard. But necessity—bitch that it was—demanded a certain amount of practicality. Neither hesitation nor sentiment belonged in the equation. Either the male committed to the Razorback cause or he died. Simple as that. No middle ground. No in between. No going back, changing his mind or the game plan.

All or nothing. Yippee-ki-yay.

The elevator hummed, leveling to a smooth stop, making his heart dip. As it rebounded, settling into a steady rhythm, he stared at his reflection in the steel panels, waiting for the doors to open. It was now or never. Taking a calming breath, Ivar pushed out of his slouch. He checked the contents of his back pocket one last time.

The pads of his fingertips touched hard plastic.

Good. The syringe was still there, safely tucked away, waiting for him to palm it. Filled with powerful neural toxins, the drug was a lethal cocktail, packing enough punch to down three dragons, never mind one. Overkill? Probably, but Ivar wanted to be sure. Nothing could be left to chance, not with a male as powerful as Hamersveld coming to dinner.

He'd sent Hamersveld directions to 28 Walton Street—his new lair—earlier in the day. Which cranked his shit the wrong way. The second he'd connected through mind-speak and relayed the information, apprehension had taken hold. Even now, it poked at him, making his stomach churn. Ivar swallowed, combating a truckload of uncertainty. Had he made the right decision? Was trusting Hamersveld the smart thing to do?

The questions circled, fraying his nerves, filling him with doubt, making him want a do over. A take back . . . whatever. Too bad backing out now wasn't an option. He lay exposed, and no matter how much that chafed him, he must see it through to the end. Bastian and his merry band of bastards had a water dragon in the fold. A young, inexperienced one, sure, but powerful nonetheless. Which . . . fuck a duck . . . qualified as a huge advantage in the war he fought with the Nightfury pack. Ivar needed a male to counteract Bastian's power play, and like it or not Hamersveld was it.

His only means to the end. Still, revealing the secret location of his lair didn't sit well.

And no wonder. Even though he commanded a large pack, three-quarters of his soldiers didn't have a clue where he lived. Where he laid his head down each day and flew away from every night. It was safer that way. A tactical advantage he needed to thwart Bastian's efforts to find him. Beyond ruthless, the Nightfury assholes weren't above torturing the males under his command to acquire the information, so . . .

Right. No doubt. The less his soldiers knew, the better. Although, to be honest, keeping his location on the down low served another purpose too: insulation from the larger Razorback population meant privacy. All he needed, and a commodity he never took for granted. What little quiet time he managed to get was precious. As leader of the Razorback nation, he had too many demands on his time and not enough hours in the day.

Beyond frustrating, but normal, he guessed. Especially since he was now going it alone.

Lothair—his best friend and former XO—had helped lighten the load, taking on half the responsibly, allowing Ivar to spend time in his laboratory. Something he loved, and an environment in which he thrived. Test tubes and microscopes. Air locks and playing with viral loads. Right up his alley. Scientific experimentation enlivened his mind and fed his soul, challenging his skills, all while furthering his cause.

Which was . . . what? Extinction of the human race. Wipe them out and free the planet from the yoke of their stupidity . . . from their selfishness too. For that alone the humans deserved to die. They were fucking up the planet, killing the ozone layer with greenhouse gases, polluting the oceans and water tables, taking more than their fair share while forcing other species into extinction.

All without giving a shit.

It couldn't go on. Mother Earth was dying, the slow, painful death difficult to watch, so . . . no help for it. Only one thing left to do. Treat the underlying cause like an infestation of cockroaches and exterminate the human race. Poof . . . gone . . . done. Problem solved once and for all.

So far, though, success eluded him.

Now he was months behind, unable to keep his promise to Rodin—leader of the Archguard. Head of one of five dynastic families that rule Dragonkind, the male wanted the humans gone almost as much as Ivar did. A political animal, Rodin was a powerful ally, providing funding for Ivar's pet projects and all the soldiers he needed to fill the Razorback ranks. Perfect in so many ways. He got what he required while Rodin cooled his heels in Prague, three thousand miles away. Geographical distance plus money equaled ultimate control. Ivar's favorite kind of equation.

Now all he needed was his experiments to bear fruit.

Easier said than done. Each failure hammered the truth home, and as the memories surfaced, Ivar came full circle, his thoughts landing back on his best friend. Sorrow tightened his throat. Mind-blowing loss. Pain come to life. Son of a bitch, it still hurt. Such a waste of time. No amount of mourning would bring his friend back. Lothair was dead. Gone. Murdered by the enemy. Never to return. Grief cracked him wide open, beating on him until he bled inside: for revenge, for the opportunity to even the score and return the favor. Fucking Nightfuries. The murdering bastards. Bastian had taken the only male Ivar had ever loved.

Clenching his teeth, Ivar snarled, feeding his fury. A life for a life. Somehow—someway—he would make the Nightfury commander pay. Take something precious from the male and even the score. On his honor, he vowed to see it done.

The elevator doors slid open with a gentle hiss.

A soft ping followed, echoing in the silence, coaxing him over the threshold into what would eventually become the Razorbacks' common room. He stepped through, barely noticing the devastation. The smell, though, struck him like an open palm. Musty and damp, the rot of decaying wood mixed with the scent of newly poured concrete. Rubbing the tip of his nose, he headed for the opposite side of the room. Thick dust beneath his boot treads, he left a trail of footprints in his wake and strode toward the floor-to-ceiling windows. Cracked in places, the glass took up the entire back side of the old fire station. Moonlight shone through the panes, casting shadows on the floor and across the exposed, pitted brick walls.

Ivar's mouth curved. The property was a complete travesty. Even so, the old building pleased him. Despite all appearances, the place was solid, and the structure sound, so . . . no. He didn't give a rat's ass that it sat on the brink of decay. Neglected, after all, didn't mean useless. Besides, the humans' abandonment of the fire station, and the thirteen acres that accompanied it, worked in his favor. No one cared what he did. No one noticed either. Not the city or its inspectors or his neighbors. Everyone kept to themselves, happy someone had bought the eyesore, leaving him to fix it up and to his own devices.

Excellent. Just what he needed . . . time, and lots of it.

For what? To finish construction on the underground lair. His worker bees—the humans he imprisoned for the task—were hard at work, in a frenzy to please him and complete the system of hallways, bedroom suites, and living quarters 150 feet below the surface. His laboratory, and the sophisticated equipment it housed, was already set. Thank fuck. At least the place he considered his sanctuary was up and running. A few more months would see the rest of the high-tech facility finished. Only then would he turn his attention to the building aboveground.

Skirting rotten floorboards that gave way to the large hole in the middle of the room, Ivar stopped in front of the double French doors. His dragon radar pinged as he scanned terrain beyond the firehouse. He sighed. Shit. No Hamersveld yet. The male was now a full hour late. Not cool on the punctuality front. Even worse for the fact that he couldn't raise the warrior through mind-speak, the cosmic equivalent of a cell phone for their kind. Every time he tried dialing in to send out the call, static came back at him, washing in, fading out, pissing him off while simultaneously making him worry.

Ivar frowned, suspicion circling. One that involved the Norwegian bugging out and saying the hell with it. He examined the possibility from all angles, not wanting to believe it, hoping it wasn't true. He needed Hamersveld in the fold, not swimming the Atlantic and headed for home, but . . .

Anything was possible. Especially after going another round with the Nightfuries last night.

The bastards had come on strong, backing up their resident water-rat, protecting Tania Solares, KO'ing his plans to put the high-energy female in a cage. He'd had one picked out, the perfect home for her in cellblock A. With her off-the-charts energy, she would've made a spectacular addition to the five females he'd already imprisoned. An incredible bedmate too. Now he had less than nothing. Just an empty cell where Solares belonged and an absentee sea dragon with etiquette issues.

The annoying prick. He could've called. Pinged him through mind-speak to tell him he'd changed his mind . . . that he'd opted out of the Razorback agenda and back into his antisocial tendencies.

"Asshole water-rat." His growl echoed through the quiet, then banged around inside his head. Damn it all, another setback. One more failure to add to the pile. Disappointment circled deep, bringing anger with it. God, what a mind fuck. He'd had such high hopes for Hamersveld and the special brand of strength the warrior would bring to his pack. "Fucking hell."

Everything lay in tatters now. His strategy. His agenda. The hope of a new XO to see to the needs of his pack. Shaking his head, Ivar curled his hands into fists, feeling his internal temperature spike. Ivar put the kibosh on his temper. Anger wouldn't change a thing. Neither would wallowing in the loss. Only action would right the situation and salvage the dream he held in his heart. He was a fighter, goddamn it. A warrior born and bred, with killer skills and a razor-sharp intellect. If he couldn't figure a way out of the mess, no one could and—

A familiar tingle ghosted down his spine.

Ivar's attention snapped back toward the windows. Tilting his head, he called his magic. Heat rose in a powerful wave, setting his senses alight. He held onto the inferno-like rush, allowing it to gather strength, then let it roll. His sonar pinged. Static swirled between his temples.

Mining the connection, he stared through the window glass into the backyard. With nothing more than a thought, he flung the double French doors open and stepped onto the narrow balcony. Cold air closed around him, bringing the fresh scent of midnight with it. He breathed deep, filling his lungs with the chill as he glanced to his right.

A hiss, warped by thick, damp air, slithered on the breeze.

Sensation thumped the inside of his skull. Pain sizzled between his temples. His brows snapped together. Oh shit. Something was off, wrong in a way he couldn't place but knew held weight. A wagon full of it judging by the load of intense, terrible, and scary headed his way.

The wind picked up, howling in displeasure, ripping at the hem of his T-shirt. And still he waited, exposed beneath the night sky, wanting to know what caused the disruption as thunder rumbled and the moon disappeared behind thick cloud cover. As the horizon went dark, lightning forked, striking above the cityscape. Street lights faded in the flash and . . .

Movement flickered in his periphery.

Ivar drew a lungful of frosty air as a dark-gray blur streaked into view. Jesus fucking Christ. Hamersveld . . . moving like an inbound missile, coming in hot, dragging an electrical storm in his wake. More lightning cracked. Another round of thunder boomed. The male wobbling in midair, the angle of his wings all wrong. Christ, he was flying in way too fast. Was completely out of control. No way could the warrior land that way. Unless, of course, he wanted to snap his own neck.

Surprise took a nasty turn into concern. Disbelief whispered next, cranking holy shit into critical territory.

Oh, so not good. The Norwegian was in serious trouble.

Ivar could smell the singed scales and dragon blood. Both wafted on the updraft Hamersveld left in his wake. Which meant one thing. He'd been injured by the Nightfury, taken down a notch while fighting with Bastian's water-rat beneath the surface of the water. In the stupid lake. Over the very HE female Ivar wanted caged and part of his breeding program.

Well, hell. Looked like he owed Hamersveld an apology for his unkind thoughts.

Another time, perhaps, 'cause . . .

Ivar cringed as Hamersveld wobbled, veering toward the beat-to-shit construction equipment that littered his backyard. A second later, the male fell out of the sky, landing without his usual grace. But worse? He skidded then rolled into a death spin, ripping a deep trench into the ground. Dirt mounded on either side of him. The jagged edge of his bladed tail caught a row of rusty oil tanks. The collision flipped him sideways. Steel banged into steel, the clang catastrophic in the silence. Calamity ringing in his ears, Ivar blinked, watching in disbelief as Hamersveld continued to skid, launching a loader skyward.

The thing crash-landed, scattering timber like toothpicks.

With a muttered curse, Ivar leapt over the railing and off the balcony. The chill of midnight rushed over him. Cold wind blasted his cheeks, blowing his hair back as he dropped three stories. He landed hard, knees rebounding toward his chest. Both hammered his breastbone, pushing the air from his lungs. Ivar ignored the burn and, not wasting a second, hauled ass across the backyard.

Coreene Callahan

Frozen blades of grass crunching beneath his boots, he sprinted between two graders. Avoiding the sharp edges of twisted metal, he kept his gaze glued on Hamersveld. Chest heaving, shark-gray scales clicked with each movement. Laying in a tangled heap—wings bent at odd angles, horned head half buried beneath a mound of topsoil, huge talons twitching—blood seeped from a myriad of shallow cuts crisscrossing his torso. Not an issue under normal circumstances. Dragonkind healed quickly, the magic in their DNA closing wounds so fast they usually took care of themselves within hours. The problem here? It had been twenty-four hours since their showdown with the Nightfury pack and . . .

Jesus. The situation was anything but *normal*.

What was his first clue? Hamersveld's tattoo. Running along both sides of his jagged sawtooth spine, the tribal ink was glowing. Not its usual dark blue either . . . but bright frickin' red.

The sight made Ivar's stomach turn.

He approached anyway, keeping his pace slow and even, not wanting to startle the male. A downed dragon was a dangerous one. But one in pain? Even more so, and . . . yeah. No question. Hamersveld was in terrible pain. With the strange glow, he looked like he was on fire, flame eating him from the inside out. Something that wasn't normal for a water dragon. Well, at least as far as Ivar knew. He and the warrior might have teamed up, but that didn't mean he understood the propensities of a rare breed like Hamersveld.

The tattoo pulsed, beating in the frosty swirl, taking on a life of its own.

Ivar kept his feet moving, slipping between a couple of upended oil tanks. Keeping his tone soft, he murmured, "Hamersveld."

"*Ivar?*" he rasped through mind-speak, Norwegian accent thicker than usual. The low, pain-filled growl streamed through Ivar's head. A second later, the warrior groaned and cracked one eyelid open. A black iris rimmed by light blue landed on him. Shimmering in the gloom, Hamersveld's gaze joined the light show along his back and shoulder, piercing the darkness. Ivar bit down on another curse. Holy God, the male was in rough shape, so weak he couldn't lift his head. "*Need help.*"

"I'm here." He laid a hand on the male's scaled shoulder. Keeping his touch light, he examined a deep gash running along the side of the male's neck. "What the hell happened?"

"Fen . . . injured. Nightfury assholes." He coughed, then groaned through clenched fangs. "Sorry . . . had to leave fight. Needed to . . . feed him."

Not following, Ivar frowned. "Who? Fen?"

Hamersveld nodded. A spasm rolled through him, making tense muscles quiver along his flank. Worry glimmered in the warrior's gaze, and Ivar struggled to understand. Fen was a wren, a unique subset of Dragonkind. Light, fast, and vicious in a fight, the miniature dragons had been hunted to near extinction. Considered a sport, tracking and killing wrens had been big business. The practice had been outlawed by the Archguard over a century ago—and with so few wrens remaining, most of his kind couldn't be bothered to hunt them anymore.

Humans, after all, made better prey.

"Where is the wren now?" Ivar asked.

"Safe . . . inside."

Safe inside? What the fuck did that mean? Ivar didn't know. Didn't have time to find out either. Not with Hamersveld looking like a frickin' train wreck. Later—when the warrior was healed and on his feet again—would be soon enough to solve the mystery.

The male's head lulled in the dirt.

"What do you need?" Ivar jostled him a little, uncertain of the best tack to take. As a water dragon, Hamersveld had different needs than he did. "How can I help?"

"A female . . . must feed to keep Fen nourished. Need saltwater too."

"Will a salt bath work?"

"Perfect."

"I've got both inside the lair . . . all high-energy females. So shift, *zi kamir*," he said, using Dragonese, calling him "my brother" to engender trust and get Hamersveld moving. "Let's get you on your feet and into the lair."

With supreme effort, Hamersveld planted his webbed paw on the ground and pressed up. Muscles rippled. Shark-gray scales undulated beneath the faint glow of street lights. With a magical zap, he transformed, moving from dragon to human form. Blond hair matted with blood, he reached for Ivar. He didn't hesitate, and slipping his arm around the male, hauled him off his knees to his feet. Hamersveld cursed as his bare feet touched down. Ivar offered no apology. He gritted his teeth around an f-bomb instead. Jesus, the SOB was heavy. Almost seven feet tall, the male's bulk rivaled a WWE wrestler's.

Great to have as backup during battle. Terrible to support while navigating the war zone that now constituted his backyard.

Half dragging, half carrying Hamersveld, he manhandled him toward the entrance of 28 Walton Street. Halfway across the yard, sensation prickled up Ivar's spine. He clenched his teeth, recognizing the tingle for what it was . . . or should he say who?

With a sigh, Ivar tightened his hold on the warrior in his arms and opened the connection. *"What is it, Denzeil?"*

"Got some info."

"About Tania Solares?" Ivar stumbled sideways. Hamersveld grunted. Ivar tightened his hold and lifted the male over the uneven patch of ground.

"Not exactly, but—"

"Then I don't want to hear it."

"I'm tracking her cell phone. A text message just came in and—"

"Jesus Christ. What did I just say? I don't give a rat's ass, D," he said, tone pissy, his gaze fixed on the fire station's back door. *"Just deal with it. I've got my fucking hands full."*

"Ten-four, boss. I'll send a fighting unit to investigate."

"Do that," he muttered, slamming the door closed on D's connection.

He didn't have time to screw around. Not now that he had Hamersveld right where he wanted the male. Gratitude, after all, was a powerful weapon. He planned to leverage the shit out of it. Crank it so hard, he earned the warrior's trust. If he did it right, loyalty and commitment to the Razorbacks would follow, and he'd get what he needed: a powerful sea dragon in his corner. All he required to turn the tables on Bastian and move forward with his plans.

Chapter Six

The holy shit factor dialed to fuck you, Wick staggered across the Gridiron toward the back exit. Humans squawked, giving him a wide berth and incredulous looks. He didn't blame them. In control, he scared the hell out of most people. His size. The way he looked. The load of lethal he carried around like a bad attitude. All served to make others wary, and that was under optimal circumstances.

But right now . . . while on overload from the feeding and out of control?

Jesus, he was the Dragonkind equivalent of a wrecking ball, swinging on a thin cable of sanity, muscle and joints coming unhinged, coordination nonexistent as he plotted a trajectory toward the other side of the bar.

Wick wanted it to be different. Wished like hell female energy didn't send him into a tailspin—every . . . single . . . frickin' . . . time. But hoping for something didn't garner results. And wishing never made things so. A shame, really. He could've used a little hope right now. Especially since his vision was messed up, blinking off and on like a schizophrenic lightbulb.

Shit, he was in trouble.

He knew the door was over there . . . somewhere. A blurry collection comprised of posts and lintels, but—

Nausea churned, throwing stomach acid up his throat.

His brain went sideways, spinning into a death skid inside his skull. He lost his balance and stumbled, veering into oncoming traffic. The group of females squealed. Wobbling on three-inch heels, the trio hopped out of his way, threw him dirty looks, struggling to steady the drinks in their hands. Liquid sloshed over the rims of glass tumblers. The horrific stench of alcohol hit him like a body shot. Wick gagged and . . .

Fucking hell.

He needed out. Right now. Out of the heat of the club. Away from the stench. Into the alley and boatloads of fresh air. Otherwise, he'd end up flat on the floor, lying in pub scum while a bunch of humans turned him into a zoo exhibit.

Gritting his teeth, Wick forced one foot in front of the other. His shitkickers thudded against the hard floor. His heart kept time, determined to drill a hole in the center of his chest. The energy he'd swallowed didn't help, humming in his veins, attacking his body until he felt like a spaghetti noodle instead of sinew and bone. The psychedelic laser show upped the ante, eating through the darkness. Pulse-pulse-flash. Pulse-pulse-flash. Colorful bursts of light set the pattern, making his head ache and his body hurt.

Another few feet. Just a couple more strides and he'd be free. Out the Gridiron's back door.

A big hand landed on his shoulder.

Wick's stomach heaved. Swallowing the burn, he twisted, fighting the lockdown.

"Easy." Deep, rooted in magic, the voice slithered through his mind, cutting beneath the rage of hard-core bass. *"It's just me."*

Reeling inside his own head, Wick blinked. Boston accent. Kick-ass presence. A familiar hand fisted in his leather jacket. Relief streamed through him. Gratefulness came next, so much of it that Wick greeted his buddy with the usual. *"Fuck off, Mac."*

"You know you love me, right?" Still gripping his jacket, Mac held him steady, keeping him on his feet. *"Need some fresh air?"*

"Yeah."

"I got your six. Let's go." Mac pointed toward the Exit sign. Hanging above the door, the thing looked like salvation. Everything he needed wrapped up in a welcoming red glow. *"It's that way."*

Wick swallowed a harsh comeback, 'cause . . . yeah. The response on the tip of his tongue—the one that went something like, "No shit, Sherlock"—didn't seem wise. If he lipped off, Mac might eighty-six his ass. Which, under the circumstances, constituted a bad plan. Especially given the fact Mac was straight-up awesome, helping him stay on his feet, manhandling him toward the exit, keeping his yap shut.

Thankfulness times a thousand slid through Wick.

His throat went tight. Thank God for family. His brothers-in-arms might not understand him—might even raze him from time to time—but they cared about him. Were 100 percent solid when it counted.

"Mac . . ."

"Hold on, man. Keep it together until we get outside. You can puke out there."

As if on cue, bile sloshed up the back of his throat. Wick forced it back down. Mac gave him a healthy shove, propelling him through the door and into the cramped foyer. Deep in shadow, the stairwell ascended on his right, heading toward the roof. The round handrail followed the rise, keeping time with each tread. Sweat dripped into Wick's eyes. He wiped it away, and dragging his gaze from the stairs, focused on the exit door. Blood-red paint blisters bubbled on its surface, disrupting the smooth contours.

Five feet away. Now three. Almost there. Just a few more seconds and . . .

Shitkickers doing double time, Wick stumbled sideways. Mac's grip on his jacket tightened. As his buddy hauled him upright, he hammered the steel bar locking the door in place with his knee. The portal swung wide and hit the brick wall behind it. The slam-bang echoed, cracking the quiet, rising to meet the night chill. Wick followed suit, bolting into the alleyway.

Cold air blasted him in the face.

His lungs screamed, demanding more oxygen.

He went palms to knees and, doubled over, answered the call. He inhaled hard, sounding like an asthmatic, wheeze after wheeze clawing his chest. A frosty swirl blew into the alleyway, lifting the hem of his jacket. Wick ignored the bluster, dismissing what made most fire dragons shiver in distaste. Contrary to his lava-loving nature, winter didn't bother him. Not surprising considering his upbringing. Raised in devastation, denial and deprivation had been the norm, not the exception, for him.

Excellent training for a warrior. Disastrous emotional whiplash for an ordinary male.

Forcing his lungs to expand, Wick pushed away from his knees. As he stood upright, his muscles cramped, twisting him into knots. With a silent curse, he stomped his feet, then flexed his hands, working blood back into his extremities. Sensation flooded him, rushing back in, making his fingertips tingle, forcing a full-body shiver.

Fighting the deep freeze, he took another deep breath and tipped his head back. Thick clouds obliterated the sky, smothering the stars, playing keep-away with the moon while the first round of snowflakes swirled.

Lovely. Not a distraction in sight.

Just the mind fuck of weakness without possibility of relief. Party central with the added bonus of embarrassment.

Wick glanced sideways at Mac. Standing behind him, the male stood at the ready, willing to step in and prevent him from face-planting. Again. Jesus, what a mess. Humiliation rose, clinging like a bitch in heat, and Wick wanted to disappear. Fight or flight, an instinctual response to a bad situation. As he fought another tremor, getting good and ghost sounded like a plan, but for one problem.

Mac wouldn't let him run.

The male practically oozed concern. And knowing what he knew about the ex-cop? Wick read all the signs. His buddy would become his shadow the second he put his feet in gear. No way would Mac let him out of his sight now, so . . .

Fuck it. *Flight* just got stroked off the list.

Which left him with one option.

Fight. A good brawl always chilled him out, and hammering Mac . . . attacking the male who bore witness to his breakdown? Well, now, the course of action tickled his fancy, jumping to the top of his list. Brutal with his fists, Mac would give him what he needed—a load of pissed off wrapped up in a pretty package called lethal. Serious pain. A truckload of distraction. Redemption in the form of pride-elevating exertion.

Mac would hit hard and never apologize.

Perfect with a capital P.

Boots planted on wet pavement in the middle of the alley, he glanced toward the still-open door. Hope expanded, filling Wick with possibility.

Mac's gaze narrowed in suspicion. *"Forget it. Not happening."*

"What's the matter?" he asked, trying to start a fight. *"You chicken?"*

"Walk it off, Wick." A warning on his puss, Mac slammed the door behind him. The clang reverberated, blocking out the club noise. As the lock clicked into place, Wick cursed under his breath. Freaking guy. Trust their resident water dragon to be reasonable when he'd never been before. *"I'm not tangling with you."*

Fair enough. No doubt the best move too. Especially since Wick never said quit. Or backed down.

He'd never needed to, preferring his special brand of vicious to taking time-outs. His nature set the parameters. He followed the path, walking the line toward one thing . . . death. He fought until someone died. Period. No room for negotiation. No talking him off the ledge. Just straight-up killing, which, yeah, made Mac one wicked smart SOB.

He growled, throwing his comrade a pissy look.

Mac didn't say a word. He scissored his fingers instead, mimicking a walking motion.

Wick dropped another f-bomb, but got with the program. With a quick shift, he pivoted toward the street. Shoulders rolling, footfalls thumping, rage leading the way, he strode toward the sidewalk at the end of the alley. Satisfied with the stomp fest, Mac crossed his arms and, settling in, leaned back against the Gridiron's side door. Eagle eyes on him, Mac tracked his movement. Wick ignored him, traveling over worn pavement, kicking soda cans out of his way, boot treads cracking half-frozen puddles as he bypassed a row of dumpsters.

Energy shards nicked him, making his skin crawl.

Fighting the rush, Wick upped the pace, treating the alley like his personal racetrack. Up. Down. Round and round, each circuit looping into the next. On the third go-around, something strange happened. His body calmed. His heart rate evened out. The prickle abated, slipping from cold and terrible to heated and smooth. His brows furrowed, Wick slowed, tracking the downgrade in sensation. Taut muscles unfurled, relaxing one rigid thread at a time. The benefits of the feeding took hold, settling into his marrow. Powered up, magic crackled through his veins, making him tingle with renewed warmth.

His dragon half sighed.

Relief swirled and dread faded, releasing Wick one talon at a time. Huh. Would you look at that? The pacing crap actually worked.

"Better?" Mac pushed away from the wall.

Not trusting his voice, Wick nodded.

"The others are almost done."

Translation? The sex feast was about to conclude . . . thank God.

Uncrossing his arms, Mac stretched, working out the kinks. *"You got a line on Venom?"*

Good question. *"Not yet."*

But he really should get on that. Hauling Venom curbside wouldn't be easy. It never was. His best friend loved female company too much to rush sex. He liked to take his time, teasing maximum pleasure out of his bedmates. The females no doubt appreciated it. But him? Not so much. Especially since it left him standing outside half the time, waiting for Venom to finish up and get his fill.

Not that he ever complained about his buddy's appetite. No way. He wasn't that selfish. The male was rock solid, worthy in ways Wick would never be. And as much as it pained him to admit it, Wick knew he would be dead by now without Venom in his corner. The warrior knew his secret, understood his background, and didn't care. In spite of his feeding phobia, Venom accepted him anyway. Made sure he fed and stayed healthy, forcing him to do what he couldn't for himself. No one else would've put up with the bullshit or stuck with him for so long.

So . . . no. Under normal circumstances, he never complained. Or tore his best friend out of a female's arms. Tonight, though, didn't qualify as *normal*. He had a mission to complete, a delicate one named Jamison Jordan Solares.

Shoving his sleeve up, Wick glanced at his watch. Twenty minutes to midnight. Right on schedule. Which meant . . . chop-chop, time to roust the others and yank Venom's chain. The sooner it happened, the sooner he'd be in dragon form and airborne. Swedish Medical sat less than five minutes away. And inside it? A female in need of rescue, his ticket to becoming debt-free.

❁ ❁ ❁

J. J. wanted to sleep but was too afraid to close her eyes. People always got killed when they weren't looking. Horror movies proved it. Life and fate followed the trend, attacking when least expected. So elementary, my dear Watson. Fear was a natural part of the equation. At least in her book.

Alertness equaled living to see another day.

An excellent strategy, considering Griggs stood just outside her door. In the hallway. Less than twenty feet away. Yakking it up with his fellow officer. Fighting a yawn, J. J. stared at the uniformed pair. The glass that stretched wall-to-wall across the front of her room afforded her an excellent view. Good in some respects. Awful in others. The clear partition allowed her to keep watch while she waited for Griggs to make his move: the inevitable approach, the next vile threat, the feel of his hands wrapped around her throat.

Nausea churned in the pit of her stomach.

The pitch and sway tossed a bad taste into her mouth. J. J. swallowed, telling herself not to be stupid. Griggs wouldn't try anything with the nursing staff around. She frowned. Would he? Her gaze glued to him, the question circled. His back to her, shoulder blades planted on the glass wall, he laughed. The dog-eared magazine he held jumped in his hand. Big hands. Unkind hands. Owned by a man without conscience or scruples.

Unease turned into dread, heightening her fear.

She shivered. Unable to control it, the quiver rolled into a series of tremors. The handcuff around her wrist rattled against the bed rail. The soft sound cranked her tighter. Oh God. She was trapped. Completely vulnerable.

Nowhere to run. Nowhere to hide. Nowhere to call for help.

Fingertips gone numb, J. J. curled her free hand in the sheet. Cotton rasped against her palm, grounding her in the ultimate question. What to do . . . what to do? Dear God in heaven, she didn't know. With the text message sent, she was out of options. Left to fend for herself, knowing that sooner or later Griggs would try something. His threats weren't idle, neither was his nastiness, so . . . uh-huh. It was a no-brainer. The oily guard was slick with an extra helping of smart. If he wanted her dead, she'd end up that way.

Ice-cold. Toes pointed up. Laid out on a slab in the hospital morgue.

Wiping her sweaty palms on the blanket, she ran through alternatives. Death by strangulation. Murder by pillow suffocation. Overdose via whatever drug he could find. All were distinct possibilities with Griggs in the mix. Her heart picked up a beat, then another, rushing blood through her veins. The accompanying thump-thump made her chest ache as she glanced at her IV. Curled at the edges, strips of medical tape held the shunt in place, presenting the perfect delivery system . . .

For the perfect murder.

Quick. Easy. Diabolical tied up with a neat bow.

Griggs's methods left no room for doubt. None for error either. He'd make sure of it, leaving the ME to draw one of two conclusions: accidental death or natural causes.

Bad luck for her. Even worse for Tania.

Please, God, let her sister pick up the text message.

Closing her eyes for a moment, J. J. asked for extra reassurance and sent a prayer heavenward. As she bargained with God, pleading for a way out, her heart throbbed so hard an answering ache opened behind her breastbone. A terrible pang trailed in its wake and emotion swelled, spilling through the cracks in her defenses. Tears—the ones she'd fought so hard not to shed—pooled behind her eyelids, and she promised to be a better person, to pray more often, to attend church, if only He would grant her this one favor.

Just one. It wasn't too much to ask . . . was it?

Licking the cut on her bottom lip, J. J. glanced toward the bank of windows. Pushed wide, plain curtains framed the skyline. City lights glittered, jewel-like and beautiful, making Seattle look like a postcard picture taken at midnight. Her focus strayed to the digital clock sitting on her bedside table—11:57 P.M. Not bad. A mere three minutes off and a pretty good guess, considering she hadn't seen the night sky in a while.

In almost five years to be exact.

Lockdown inside the prison always happened before dark. And the narrow window in her cell had never satisfied her love of stargazing. Not that she could indulge in her favorite pastime tonight. Or get distracted by the music rising from that secret place inside her. Soulful and restrained, the melody crooned, tempting her to flesh it out, find the beat, create the lyrics, give it life, and follow her bliss. J. J. shoved temptation aside. Composing a song while admiring the constellations wasn't going to happen.

Not right now. Perhaps never again if Griggs made his move before—

"Ready for another adventure, Jamison Jordan?"

Touched by a light accent, the rich baritone jabbed at her.

J. J.'s attention snapped toward the door. The sudden movement sent her brain sideways inside her skull. Her eyesight warped, washing out into streaks. She blinked to clear the visual interference. No such luck. The painkillers were mucking with her ability to focus. She tried anyway, squint-ing hard. A squeak-squawk echoed, laying down an audio track, joining the rumble of male voices in the hall and the soft call of the PA system. A moment later, a man appeared through the blur. Her vision cleared. A dark-blue gaze met hers. J. J. cursed under her breath.

Ah, crap. Not him again.

But despite the ferocity of her denial, her eyes weren't deceiving her. Goth Guy was back, pushing a wheelchair this time.

"Go away." She scowled at him, warning him with a look. If he came anywhere near her, she'd smack him. Just wind up and let her fist fly. No way she wanted to go round two with his particular brand of crazy . . . and get sick again. Too bad her glare didn't do the trick. Despite the load of nasty she threw in his direction, he kept coming, long legs eating the distance between them. Her eyes narrowed on him. "I mean it. Stay away from me."

"Now, now . . ." His nose stud sparkled in the low light. The one piercing his eyebrow took up the cause, flashing in answer. He grinned at her. She glowered back, more deter-mined than ever to hold the line. The wheelchair wasn't a good sign. It signaled big trouble, the kind that would see her speeding down a hospital corridor with him in the driv-er's seat. Oh, so not advisable. Her stomach couldn't take the fallout. Ignoring her unmistakable "screw off, buddy," he abandoned the wheelchair at the end of her bed. "Is that any way to treat an old friend?"

"Friend?" Her gaze landed on the spider tattoo on the side of his neck. Precise black lines spread in a web over his skin, creating a nest for the red spider, which . . . good God, looked so lifelike it freaked her out a little. "Yeah, right. You almost killed me last time."

Stopping alongside her, he threw her an amused glance. "Exaggerate much?"

"You made me sick. I puked . . . nearly popped my stitches because of you."

"Sure you did," he murmured, his attention on the IV embedded in the back of her hand. His mouth curved. She went on high alert. Whatever his agenda, it couldn't be good. He was too intent. Way beyond focused. Fingering the plastic tube connecting her to the cocktail of drugs, saline solution, and antibiotics, he shook his head. "You look fine to me."

Suspicion took a nasty turn, raising her internal alarm system another notch. Something about him was, well . . . all wrong. Not that she could put her finger on the reason. Logic didn't hold sway. Rooted in intuition, her reaction might not make sense, but it was justified.

Shifting with unease, she fisted her free hand. Just in case. She really didn't want to punch him, but she would . . . if he made her. "What do you want? Does Ashford know you're here?"

He ignored the question and, leaning in, examined her IV. Frowning, he studied the jut-out used to inject drugs into the tube. Instinct screamed a warning. He withdrew a syringe from his breast pocket and popped the top off. Air stalled in J. J.'s throat. She shook her head, her voice on temporary lockdown. Oh God. She couldn't scream, and as her heartbeat ramped into apocalyptic territory, J. J. watched him raise his hand.

He inserted the needle into the mouth of the tube.

"Oh my God . . . stop. Stop it!" Horror punched through, mixing with terror. Slow on the uptake, she reached for his arm. "What are you doing?"

He depressed the plunger, pushing God only knew what into her IV, then glanced at her sideways. A strange shimmer gathered in his gaze. "Giving you more juice."

"Don't!" She fought the handcuffs. Steel banged against metal. The clang reverberated, sounding hellish in the quiet. "You'll—"

"I'm not gonna kill you."

Sure. Right. Like she trusted him to tell the truth? A murderer, after all, never warned his intended victim. Oh God. *Scream.* She needed to scream for help . . . right now. Before psycho Goth Guy put her six feet under.

A knowing glint entered his eyes. "Don't bother. Save your energy. No one can hear you."

Bullshit. The guards stood fifteen feet away. They'd hear her—so would Ashford if she yelled loud enough—and come running. Opening her mouth, J. J. filled her lungs. Her rib cage expanded. Agony drove a spike into her side.

Ignoring the pain, she let loose. "Help! Somebody . . . help me!"

Nothing happened. No sudden flap of movement. No shift or glance in her direction. Nothing but business as usual as Griggs laughed at something the other guard said.

A chill snaked across the back of her hand. Oh no . . . the drug was on the move, headed straight into her vein. Frantic now, she moved her left arm toward her right. Her hand might be cuffed, but that didn't mean she was powerless. She must pull the shunt out. Get rid of the IV before—

"Stubborn female." With a quickness that defied description, Goth Guy reached out. He shackled her free hand, preventing her from ripping the needle out. "Relax. You need the extra hit. It's not safe for you here, so I need to move you. The Demerol will keep you comfortable for the duration."

Fighting his grip, she screamed again. He held firm, watching her panic with an impassive expression. Tears pricked the corners of her eyes, making his face waver into a blur.

"I'm sorry," he murmured, his tone soothing. "It's the only way. Had you not sent that text message . . ." A muscle jumped along his jaw as he trailed off. A second later he sighed and shook his head. "But clever girl that you are, you found a way. Now, I have no choice. Change of plan, sunshine."

"Let me go," she rasped, tugging against his hold. A weak attempt, but it was the best she could manage. Goth Guy knew what he was doing. He'd played it just right, shooting her full of enough Demerol to sap her strength. Now she felt the effects, and as tense muscles relaxed, her mind derailed, plunging her into helplessness. "You bastard."

"For sure," he said, his voice coming through the fog. "Go with it anyway, female. Let the drug take effect. You'll thank me later."

Mind gone heavy, body gone light, she started to float inside her own skull. Fighting the pull, she whispered, "Who are you?"

"Azrad."

"Weird name."

"Not for my kind."

The cool rush of relaxation took hold. Her eyelids dipped. Open. Closed. Up. Down. J. J. forced herself to stick with it. Concentrating hard, she forced her eyes back open. "Your *kind*?"

"Nothing to worry about now. You'll learn of Dragonkind soon enough."

Buoyant on soft clouds, J. J. clung to the sound of his voice, using it to ground her in reality. The handcuffs clicked. Steel slid from around her wrist. She blinked, seeing her hand without feeling it. Huh, that was weird. He'd opened the cuff without a key. Had simply brushed his thumb against the lock and . . .

She frowned at the open cuff. "How did you do that?"

"Magic," he whispered.

And J. J. agreed, 'cause . . . wow. The drugs were *magic*, helping her float, holding her high, taking the rest of the pain away. "Oh my . . . this is good stuff."

He snorted. The red spider inked on his neck winked at her. J. J. smiled back. Azrad shook his head, and with a flick, released the bed rail. Folding it down and away, he slid his arms around her and lifted, turning toward the nearby wheelchair. He put her down with care, using gentle hands to adjust her uncooperative limbs. As she settled with a sigh, he straightened one of the footrests, locked it in place, and set her injured foot in the cradle. The plaster cast bumped down. He transferred the IV bag, hanging it on a pole welded to the side of the chair.

J. J. didn't care. She couldn't feel a darned thing, including the tip of her nose. Everything had gone numb.

Grabbing the blanket off the foot of her bed, he knelt in front of her.

Squinting hard, she stared at his face. "Hey, Azrad?"

"Uh-huh?"

"Where we going?"

"To a party." Finished tucking the blanket around her legs, he stood and stepped around the wheelchair. Hands gripping the handles, he pushed her toward the exit. "A mixer, of sorts."

Oh, a party. How lovely. Wonderful. Simply terrific . . . J. J. frowned . . . Wasn't it? She hadn't been invited to a get-together in years. Well, unless the prison yard counted, so . . . yeah. A mixer sounded fun.

She tipped her head back. The back of her skull thumped against Azrad. Tongue gone numb, she tried to make it work, even though talking seemed really difficult all of a sudden. "Do I get a glasssh of wine?"

He chuckled. "No more mind-altering substances for you tonight."

"Killjoy."

He rolled his eyes.

"Hey, Azsh-rad?" she whispered, his name more slur than actual word.

"Yeah?"

"You're my friend." She blinked, the movement a slow up and down. "Right?"

He hesitated. Blue eyes roamed her face. "For the moment, sunshine."

Good news. Although, upon reflection not very inspiring. What the heck did "for the moment" mean?

J. J. hummed. *For the moment . . . for the moment . . .*

The phrase circled, tapping on her frontal lobe. She shook her head. Something about that was all wrong. A bad sign or something, but for the life of her, she couldn't figure out what. Then again, was it really such a big deal? Did it require an all-points bulletin? J. J. frowned. She couldn't tell. Her brain was gone, buoyant in a sea of stupidity as the drug tightened its grip, numbing her mind, taking the pain, making her decide to worry about the conundrum Azrad presented tomorrow.

With a sigh, she slumped in the wheelchair.

It felt better to float and forget . . . if only for a little while. To ignore the warning signs and sink beneath the wave. But as Azrad wheeled her into the corridor—past guards who didn't react and nurses who never looked up—instinct whispered, and J. J. wondered about her *for the moment* friend. Maybe allowing him to steal her away wasn't the best idea after all.

Chapter Seven

With a quick flip, Wick went wings vertical, slicing between two stone-clad high-rises, throwing up dust in a frostbitten swirl. Right on his tail, the other Nightfuries rattled windowpanes. Eyes on the prize, Wick rocketed past another apartment complex. Rotating up and over, green scales glinting in the gloom, Venom settled above his spine. Nothing but a brown blur, snow-white talons and scorpion-like tail at the ready, Sloan flew in below him. Settling in the flank position, Mac and Forge rolled in on his wingtips, becoming wingmen as Wick picked up the pace.

Speed supersonic. Night vision pinpoint sharp. Focus set on a single building rising from the network of city streets below. Check . . . check . . . and triple-check.

Swedish Medical. Dead ahead.

Focus absolute, Wick pulled Jamison's prison jacket to the forefront of his mind. A quick shuffle brought her mug shot front and center. Long dark hair. Pretty oval-shaped face. Full lips on an unsmiling mouth. Arresting sky-blue eyes. He pinned each detail to his mental bulletin board. No sense fucking around. He needed to find her fast. Get in. Get her out. A quick trip home, an even speedier hand-off to her sister and . . .

Jackpot. One female rescued. Mission accomplished. His debt paid in full.

Flying in on a fast glide, Wick lined up his approach. Spread over one corner of the roof, a white cross sat in the center of the dark helipad. He scanned the area again. Nothing but empty space. No helicopter taking up the valuable real estate, and no humans on guard duty.

Perfect. So far, so good.

Above the LZ now, he tucked his wings. Gravity took hold, yanking him out of the sky. He thumped down dead center, hitting the white *X* that marked the spot. The steel support structure groaned. His claws clicked, scraping the hard surface of the LZ a second before he shifted into human form. Magic shimmered, warping the air as he conjured his clothes.

As his shitkickers settled on his feet, he went over the plan. *"Forge and Mac, you're on transpo."*

"SUV?" Blue-gray scales glinting, Mac circled overhead.

Right on his buddy's six, Forge asked, *"Or a cargo van?"*

"Take your pick. Just steal something big enough to transport her comfortably." Already moving across the helipad, Wick mind-spoke to their resident computer genius. *"Sloan—"*

"Hack the system. Steal, then wipe all record of her medical file." The markings on his scales more rattlesnake than dragon, Sloan landed on the roof. The lights planted around the LZ washed his white paws with blue tint. *"I'm on it."*

"Venom . . ."

"On your ass." Folding his wings, his best friend touched down. Dark-green claws bit, gouging the surface of the tiled asphalt as Venom slid to a stop behind him. *"Lead on."*

With a nod, Wick grabbed the handrail and, throwing his legs over, leapt to the concrete lane below used to transport patients on gurneys. His eyes on the door at the end of the ramp, he strode down a slight incline. With nothing but a thought, he flipped the lock, swung the door wide, and crossed the threshold into the large foyer beyond. A bank of elevators waited along the far wall. Wick punched the button with his mind. Magic tingled, zipping along his spine as machinery went to work, propelling the cage up from a lower floor.

Venom joined him in front of the double doors. His gaze narrowed on the numbers above the Otis. The red digits blinked, telling them to get ready.

Wick glanced over his shoulder. *"Room number?"*

"Fifth floor." Dark eyes intent, Sloan met his gaze as he stopped behind him. *"Room 573."*

Purpose roared through Wick, lighting the fuse on his anticipation. Almost there. Five minutes tops, and he'd see Jamison in person. Look into those sky-blue eyes while he made sure she was all right. Ensured her safety. Moved her out of harm's way and into whatever vehicle Forge and Mac (a.k.a. the wonder twins) procured for their getaway. Eyes narrowed, he recalled the mental map he'd made of Swedish Medical. He went over the plan again, charting the fastest route to her room, and nodded in satisfaction.

Good odds. Solid game plan. Success lay just a few floors down and inches away.

The elevator opened with a soft ping.

Thirty seconds and a smooth ride later, Wick stepped out into the fifth-floor hallway. A whole lot of nothing special greeted him. To be expected. Hospitals were designed using strict building codes, where form followed function.

Boring and utilitarian? Both fit the bill. So did all the closed doors. Like soldiers walking a military line, the steel frames interspaced an ocean of pale walls. At an intersection, Wick made the first turn. The narrow corridor dumped him into a much wider one. Excellent. It wouldn't be long now. Another right, two more lefts, and he'd find what he was looking for . . .

The fifth-floor hub.

A processing area, the large circular-shaped space sat at the center of each floor. Its purpose? Traffic control. The hub kept people moving from points A to B in a sprawling complex that felt more like a small city than a single building. The population inside the facility confirmed it. Even at midnight, the halls were busy, nurses scurrying to and fro, doctors making their rounds, patients being shuttled in wheelchairs and gurneys to their next destination.

And speak of the devil. A horde of humans at one o'clock.

Wick paused on the lip of the T-shaped intersection. Rubber wheels on a rolling hospital bed squeaked. Oblivious to the sound, a team of medical professionals surrounded the gurney, voices raised, terms like *intubate* and *chest compressions* fogging the air around them. As the group rushed toward him, a gap between human shoulders opened, and he got a look at the patient. A young girl. Maybe five years old. Wick assessed the situation in under a second flat. The human's biological grid, compete with vital signs, went up on his mental light board.

Wick clenched his teeth. A defect . . . the youngster's heart was failing.

His gaze on her small face, he hesitated a moment and—

Ah, fuck it. He was here anyway. Aiding the child wouldn't cost him a thing. While doing nothing would cost the girl her life. Given those facts, it seemed a shame not to interfere.

With a murmur, he gathered his magic. Heat blazed, swirling like magma-infused whirlpools in the center of his palms. He waited until the girl-child came even with him, then let it roll, enveloping the kid in a healing swirl. She gasped as her heart kicked over. A full breath came next, tiny chest rising and falling beneath a doctor's hands. The medical team paused, hovering above her. One shouted "I got a pulse!" and they were off, galloping down the hallway at breakneck speed.

Venom slapped the back of his shoulder. "Such a do-gooder."

Sloan snorted.

Wick brushed off the comment and stayed silent. What could he say? That he had a soft spot for kids? That seeing one suffer bothered him? That childhood should be full of ice cream, lollipops, and cartwheels? His chest went tight. Shit. Like that would go over well. None of his brothers would understand. Not that it mattered. He did what he wanted. Always had . . . no need to explain further.

Shrugging Venom's big mitt off his shoulder, Wick got back with the program. A speaker crackled overhead, paging Dr. Somebody-or-other to cardiology. His mouth curved. Good. The humans were on the ball. Not that the girl-child needed the attention anymore. His magic had done its job, sewing up the hole in her left ventricle.

Footfalls silent on the industrial-grade floor, he made the last turn and . . .

Strode straight into hell.

He grimaced, registering all the activity. Nurses in scrubs. Doctors in white coats. Visitors and patients sitting in chairs waiting their turn.

"*Goddamn,*" Venom muttered behind him.

No kidding. The place was a logistical nightmare. *"Far corridor on the other side of the hub."*

"The one next to the nurses' station?"

Wick nodded and, scanning the space, moved toward his target. The sooner he entered the hallway, the quicker he'd find Jamison's room.

"Later, boys." Leather bag slung over his shoulder, Sloan peeled off, heading in the opposite direction. Skirting a man on crutches and a child playing hopscotch on different-colored floor tiles, he crossed the threshold. Disappearing inside the belly of the beast, he mind-spoke, *"I'll holler when I'm done at the com-center."*

Venom answered in the affirmative.

Wick didn't say a word. No need. Sloan required no encouragement. The male would do what he did best: crack the database and take what he wanted without leaving a trace. No worries on that front. *"Meet us street level afterward."*

"Uh-huh," Sloan said, mind already on his mission.

Stepping around a row of chairs and the human occupants, Wick moved toward his destination. As he bypassed the high counter of the nurses' station, a prickle ghosted over the nape of his neck. His pace slowed to a stop. Combat boots planted, dragon half rising, Wick sank deep inside his senses, hunting for the signal. Another round of snap, crackle 'n pop. The muscles bracketing his spine tightened, putting him on high alert.

Shit. Trouble. Not the good kind either.

With a growl, Wick glanced over his shoulder.

"I feel it. We've got company." Red eyes shimmering, Venom scanned the hub, searching for an enemy. When he came up empty, he glanced Wick's way. *"Rogue?"*

Wick shook his head. *"Maybe. Can't tell. There's too much electrical interference here."*

His friend cursed.

Wick seconded the motion and put himself in gear. No sense standing around with his thumb up his ass. Hanging back—waiting for something to happen—wasn't his style. The role of game changer suited him better. Natural born killer worked too, and as Wick closed the distance, the predator inside him rose, answering the call of duty. Moving with intent, he crossed into the mouth of the corridor. Static hissed inside his head. He mined the signal, adjusting the dial on his sonar, pinpointing the precise location.

Close. So very close. The unknown male was on the move, but—

Jesus fucking Christ. He spotted the bastard.

Pushing a wheelchair and dressed like an orderly, the male paused, slowing to a stop in the middle of the hallway. Wick stopped walking and widened his stance, blocking the end of the corridor as he sized up the stranger. Tall. Strong, but on the lean side. A Dragonkind male who carried himself with the confidence of a warrior. But odder still, the male sported a spider tattoo on the side of his neck and burgundy streaks in his hair.

Dark-blue eyes met his.

Wick snarled.

The warrior's mouth curved. The stud piercing his eyebrow winked as he dipped his chin and stared at him beneath the curve of his brows. The look was pure challenge, a primal "fuck you" that spoke volumes.

"Heads-up, sunshine." His gaze fixed on Wick, the asshole bent his head, bringing attention to the person seated in the wheelchair. "The party's getting started."

Shifting in her seat, his passenger blinked.

Wick's focus flipped to her and—

"Fucking hell," he growled, recognition instantaneous. "Jamison."

The fucker smirked. "Pretty, isn't she, Nightfury?"

Right, on both counts. Though how the male knew he was a member of the Nightfury pack was a puzzle. One best left for another time as Wick turned his attention to the first declaration. Which was . . . Jesus . . . a total understatement. The female was more than just *pretty*. She was beautiful. Incredible. So powerful her connection to the Meridian pulsed in the air around her.

Unexpected in every regard, considering her injuries.

Some of the bruises he could see. Others he couldn't. But even battered by circumstance, her energy glowed, lighting her up from the inside out.

As his reaction to her went cataclysmic, Wick sucked in a quick breath. High-energy, his ass. She was a Meridian-infused inferno, burning bright, the deep oranges and reds of her aura flickering like firelight. Urgency thrummed through him, making him want to get closer. Reach out. Maybe even . . . he swallowed a mouthful of saliva . . . touch her to see if she zapped him with energy shards. The resulting jolt would no doubt be one for the record books and—

Wick's brows collided.

Holy fuck. What the hell was his problem? Reach out and touch her? God be merciful, he'd lost his mind. Nothing else explained the sudden urge. Or the undeniable tug he felt when he looked at her. Something about her tempted him to a dangerous degree, shaking his foundation, waking his dragon half, cutting through to shred his well-used rule book. The one that housed the no-touch, no-talk, make-very-little-eye-contact edict by which he lived.

Unable to help himself, he looked her over anyway. Not that he wanted to—really he didn't—but he needed the intel. Assessing her injuries would determine the best way forward and . . .

So what?

He enjoyed the way she looked. Big deal. But as sleepy blue eyes met his and his dragon growled, liking what it saw, Wick abandoned his excuses. He wanted her. For the first time in his life, he *wanted* a female. The admission damned him. His dragon didn't care, fixating on her as though she were manna sent from the sky. She blinked, a slow up and down. Wick frowned. Something about her response was all wrong. She was too sluggish. The realization reset his internal barometer in a hurry. Dilated pupils. Lax muscles. Blank expression. His gaze cut to the IV plugged into her arm. Comprehension struck like a sledgehammer.

Drugged.

The male holding her prisoner had cranked up the volume. Now Jamison sat in murky mental shadows. Compliant in the face of danger. Relaxed when she should be fighting. A sitting duck, vulnerable in every sense of the word.

"Venom . . ."

Primed for a fight, Venom growled in answer. *"How dead do you want him?"*

"Alive enough to talk."

A good strategy considering the male's interference. Something about the warrior didn't sit right. The scent he wore—his magical vibe—was all wrong . . . decidedly un-roguelike. So, yeah. No doubt about it. Figuring out what the asshole wanted—the why behind the hostage taking—needed doing before he took the bastard down for touching Jamison.

"Half-dead it is," Venom said, tone full of anticipation. *"You deal with her."*

He intended to.

With his dragon half riveted on her, no other option existed. Primal need had taken hold. Now compulsion ruled, rousing instinct, shoving intellect and reason out of the way. No time to think or ask why. The *how* was more important. He needed to span the distance between them to become her shield. ASAP. Before the clock ticked down and time ran out. Before the tatted bastard used her as leverage. Before the fighting started, and the female he'd sworn to protect got caught in the crossfire.

❀ ❀ ❀

J. J. couldn't believe her eyes. Both were playing tricks on her, making her see things that couldn't be there. Impossible things. Beautiful things. Things like oh, say . . . a sexy as sin dark-haired stranger. Squinting hard, she leaned forward in the wheelchair. Her get-a-little-closer idea didn't help clarify matters. Her vision was shot, wavering in and out of focus, shading everything in an ethereal light . . . making him glow around the edges.

Otherworldly. He must be an alien or something. Nothing else explained the glow. Or the fact his eyes shimmered in the dim light. The golden glimmer drew her deep, held her aloft in the mind-fog and . . .

Huh. Weird, but she recognized him somehow, from somewhere, for some reason.

Which didn't make a lick of sense.

The idea that she knew him was, well . . . far-fetched. Inaccurate. Way off base. Especially since J. J. knew she'd never met him. A girl didn't forget a guy who looked like that. One encounter would sear him into a woman's brain. And that kind of imprint? It never faded or got lost in mental debris. It endured for all time. Logic told her so, gathering evidence, refuting fact, and yet . . . she couldn't shake the feeling. He felt too familiar, safe in the same way a bunker would while a tornado raged, ripping apart the landscape overhead.

Raising her hand, J. J. rubbed her eye. Bad idea. The movement turned her head. Her mind sloshed, sliding sideways inside her skull. As clear thinking went by the wayside, she frowned at Mr. Gorgeous. Where, oh where, had she seen him before? Was he another *for the moment* friend or something better? Both excellent questions. Neither of which she could answer. A shame, really, 'cause . . . yup. The answers seemed important, but as J. J. leaned toward the blunter side of dull, she struggled to care.

Another bad decision no doubt.

The thought tickled her funny bone. Weird, she knew, but . . . God. For some reason that was funny.

Unable to stop herself, she huffed, the sound half-laugh, half-snort. The wheelchair creaked beneath her. Rubber tires rolled forward, and J. J. forced herself to refocus. Hmm, lucky her. He was still there. Boots planted at the opposite end of the corridor, Mr. Gorgeous looked good enough to eat. She ran her gaze over him again and sighed. Wow . . . just, well, wow. Power personified, he exuded a lethal amount of confidence. Big. Strong. And badass. Too handsome for words, never mind reality.

Ah, and there it was . . . bingo, a conclusion that fit.

He wasn't real. Her drug-addled mind was in overdrive. The result? She'd conjured the golden-eyed god out of thin air.

"Shoo," she whispered, hoping the sound of her voice would make the apparition disappear. She craved clarity. Wanted a shot at regaining some semblance of control. Which meant the dark stranger—vision extraordinaire—needed to go . . . and go quickly. No way could she think straight with him standing there, looking beautiful, cluttering up her visual field. "Time for you to go."

Mr. Gorgeous frowned at her.

Azrad shifted behind her. "What did you say?"

"Oh, shut up, Azrad. This is all your fault. Dumb drugs are making me see things. Now I'm imagining *him.*"

"Hate to tell you this, sunshine, but—"

"I'm real." The low growl hung in the air, sounding soft, landing hard.

She blinked. "You are?"

"He is, female." A big blond man moved in behind Mr. Gorgeous. "And so am I."

Azrad cursed under his breath.

"Oh," she said, trying to make sense of the news flash.

A useless endeavor. She couldn't . . . wasn't able to . . .

Good lord, he was real? Beyond a shadow of doubt *real?* J. J. frowned. How was that even possible?

Confusion circled, whacking her with a stick full of "holy crap." He shifted—widening his stance, blocking the corridor, cranking his hands into twin fists—and J. J. stared at him, forcing herself to reevaluate. Okay, no need to panic.

So he wasn't a figment of her imagination. So he looked like death come calling. So the guy next to him didn't look any less lethal. So . . .

Oh, baby Jesus in a bread basket. Someone help her. He was on the move.

Shoulders rolling, long legs eating the distance, he strode up the corridor toward her. Leather creaked and time faded, warping awareness until all she saw was him. Her heart paused mid-thump, then rebounded, throbbing in time with his footfalls. Boom-boom-pause. Boom-boom-throb. Each beat spiraled out, filling her head until static buzzed between her temples. Soft, intense, beyond strange, an electric current flowed on supercharged wings. Her skin prickled, making the fine hairs at her nape stand on end. One instant merged with the next as his heart beat a drum inside her own veins.

Only then did she understand. He was more than real. He was a force of nature: confident in his approach, commanding in the moment, all his focus on her.

A man from another world. The angel of death. He was . . . he was . . .

Oh crap. That's why she recognized him. Anyone would. Death took all forms, after all. And his? The glamour and beauty—his otherworldly quality—made perfect sense. Her time was up. He'd come to punch her ticket. Now she would be made to pay for her mistakes. Be taken to the one place J. J. knew she deserved to go. She'd known the price for pulling the trigger. For becoming judge and jury. For taking another's life.

Eternal restitution in hell.

Murderers, after all, didn't deserve second chances, but . . . God. She wasn't ready to go. Not right now. Too much had been left unsaid. So much undone. All of her wrongs yet to be righted.

Tears welled, burning her throat.

"No." Shaking her head, she met the dark angel's gaze, a desperate plea in her own. Maybe if she begged, Mr. Gorgeous-Death-Angel would show her mercy, come back some other night . . . take her another time. After she'd made amends, gotten to say all the sorrys she owed, starting with the biggest one of all. Her sister. Tania deserved an apology. The words, sure, but also the remorse and closure behind them. She needed one last hug. One more shared meal. A night spent talking, the privilege of contact and a proper good-bye. "I'm not ready to go. Not yet. I'll go quietly, I promise, just . . . please come back later."

Bafflement winged across the dark angel's face.

"Just a little more time. That's all I need. Please, I—"

"Easy." A large hand landed on her shoulder. With a gentle tug, Azrad drew her back, resetting her in the wheelchair. "Apologies, Nightfury. Too much Demerol. She's a little loopy."

"Back away from her," the dark angel said, his voice soft yet somehow deadly. "And I'll let you live."

"You're a bad liar. Tell you what though . . ." Azrad paused, a thoughtful look on his face. "I'll relinquish her without a fight . . . for a price."

"Name it," the blond guy said.

J. J. frowned, her gaze ping-ponging between the two. Huh. Two death angels for the price of one. And the blond one? He was beautiful too, although not in the same way. His dark-haired companion appealed to her more. Sexy vibe. Gorgeous face. Incredible body. A thirteen and a half out of ten on her yum-o-meter, which . . .

Was just plain wrong. In major ways.

Dear God, what was the matter with her? No way should she be admiring him. The guy planned to kill her, for pity's sake. Take her straight to hell, and what was she doing? Scoping him out. Singing his praises. Imagining what notes he might make her hit in bed.

"A meet and greet." Rubber tires humming against hospital floor, Azrad walked her backward. As he retreated, the death angels advanced. "Bastian's presence is required."

"Not going to happen," the dark angel said, an underlying snarl in his voice.

"Two choices, Nightfury." With a quick shift, Azrad slipped his hand over her shoulder. J. J. flinched, shock spinning a sticky web as he palmed the front of her throat. Pressing his thumb against her jugular, he brought her chin up and tilted her head back. "You agree or I snap her neck."

Immobilized, J. J. jerked in her seat to break his hold. Too little, too late. She got nowhere. Azrad was too strong. Her injuries made her weak. And with her reflexes obliterated by drugs, her chances of breaking free landed somewhere south of zero. She swallowed against the hand gripping her throat. A sitting duck. Out of her league. Bait for Mr. Gorgeous. All of which Azrad had intended from the beginning.

Golden eyes aglow, Mr. Gorgeous growled.

The blond bared his teeth on a curse.

J. J. gasped, the sound panicked as helplessness swamped her. She tried anyway. Fighting the lockdown, she grabbed Azrad's forearm. Her nails bit deep to gouge his skin. With a "fuck," Azrad tightened his grip, and she wheezed, struggling to draw air into her lungs. A tremor rolled through her. Fear followed, diving deep to unearth self-preservation.

But it was too late. She knew it. So did Azrad. The jerk had played her to perfection.

And fool that she was, she'd let her guard down. Had ignored instinct—every lesson she'd learned in prison, surrounded by violent offenders—allowing Azrad to slip under her radar. Now she would pay the ultimate price.

Azrad wasn't playing. She felt it in the strength of his grip. Recognized it in the flex and release of his muscled arm. Heard the warning in the intensity of his tone.

J. J.'s breath hitched on a sob. Life or death. He now held hers in the palm of his hand.

"Azrad?"

"Stay very still, sunshine," he said, just loud enough for her to hear.

"You're hurting me," she rasped, pulling at his wrist. "Please let go."

He grumbled something. J. J. wanted to believe it was "sorry," but she wasn't that naïve. He had her by the throat, so . . . no. Only a fool would believe he felt remorse for holding her prisoner.

Mr. Gorgeous took another step toward her.

"Half a second, that's all it'll take." Azrad tensed. J. J. winced as his big hand pressed against her windpipe. "Not enough time for you to reach her, Nightfury. So you decide . . . a dead female or a friendly chat with your commander. What's it gonna be?"

He didn't answer, just kept coming, moving closer in small increments.

The blond guy's gaze narrowed. "You're no rogue. What pack do you call home?"

"Your answer, warrior," Azrad said, a lethal edge in his tone.

"Where and when?"

"Starbucks . . . 1st Avenue and Pike. Tomorrow at midnight."

The blond nodded. "Done."

"Excellent," Azrad murmured. "She's a lovely female. I would have hated to hurt her."

"Let her go." Chilled by violence, the dark angel's voice slithered through the quiet. Goosebumps erupted, spreading like frost across J. J.'s skin.

"With pleasure." With a quick hand, Azrad released the death grip. As she sucked in a quick breath, he grasped the back of her wheelchair. "Hold on tight, Jamison Jordan. He'll catch you . . . I promise."

The lilt of his tone warned her. Intuition spiked. Comprehension followed, laying out Goth Guy's plan like tracks on a runway. "Don't! Azrad . . . don't!"

Too late.

With a hard shove, he sent her rolling. Rubber wheels hummed as she rocketed down the middle of the hallway. Horror shoved shock out of the way. J. J. yelled. Both angels cursed. The IV bag bounced off the metal pole stand, and the speed increased. Careening out of control, J. J. curled her hands around the steel armrests. As her knuckles turned white, each breath came hard, ramping into hyperventilation. Oh God. Oh no. Jesus help her. She was headed for a fall, a serious bone-cracking tumble.

The slam-bang of combat boots echoed down the corridor.

Perception warped and time stretched, spinning everything into slow motion. Fierce golden eyes met hers. She watched him run, arms and legs pumping, a prayer locked in her throat. But even as she sent her entreaty heavenward, hope making her heart throb, pain loomed like a promise at the end of a short trip. And J. J. knew, without a shadow of doubt, Mr. Gorgeous would never catch her in time.

Chapter Eight

Venom sprinted down the corridor, chasing the idiot with the spider tattoo. Wick barely noticed. He was too busy hauling ass, all his focus on the female. Bad odds. Even less time. He ran like a motherfucker anyway, the slam-bang of his boots matching the chaotic rhythm of his heart. Lungs burning, legs and arms pumping, he bared his teeth and pushed hard. He needed to reach her, to stop the furious roll of the wheelchair before . . .

Jesus. He was so fucked. Still too far away. Twenty feet from his target and not closing fast enough. And as each second whirled past, victory slid in the wrong direction. God help him. Any moment now, the chair would destabilize, come apart and send her reeling into a fall. One that would reopen her wounds. Make her bleed. Inflict so much pain she would scream in agony.

None of which Wick could prevent from happening.

The tatted bastard was just that smart.

Azrad cast one hell of an encryption spell. Now Jamison sat wrapped in magic, surrounded by an invisible force field that propelled the wheelchair at breakneck speed. Reaching out with his mind, Wick tore at the enchantment. Powerful and complex, the energy shield whiplashed, holding firm, denying his will to control it. Her bio-energy flared. His concern for her spiked as he registered the extent of her fear. She was in full panic mode, so amped up he felt each painful throb of her heart, saw the flare of her aura and the dread inside her mind.

Her heartbeat drove his, making each breath saw against the back of his throat. Wick pushed past physical limits and hammered the shield again. The structure flexed. Spotting a weakness, his dragon half growled, and Wick sank deep, connecting to the source of his power. Magic exploded through his veins, taking up all the space inside his head. He held it close a moment, then wound up and let it go, hurling the decryption spell like a hardball pitch in a soft-ball game.

Rubber tires whined, picking up speed.

The pitch and sway rocked Jamison in the seat. Her knuckles turned white against the dark padding of the arm-rest. As the steel frame shuddered with catalytic rage, the chair veered, hurtling toward a pair of double doors. Oh shit. Not good. The chair wasn't holding up beneath the strain and—

Metal groaned, threatening to buckle at the joints.

Wide-eyed, Jamison met his gaze. Wick bared his teeth. Already taut muscles tightened over his bones, and fury gave his magic more strength. The cosmic web around the wheelchair shuddered. He hammered it again. The bas-tard's hold trembled, then crumbled, dissipating like vapor in dry air.

Triumph roared through him.

Wick didn't pause to admire his handiwork. Without breaking stride, he reached out with his mind and grabbed the chair. He issued a mental command. The velocity down-graded, slowing little by little. Almost there. A few more seconds, and he'd—

In a panic, she grasped one of the wheels.

"No, Jamison . . . don't!"

His shout went unanswered as the wheelchair flipped, launching her out of the seat. She went up and over, dark hair flying as her head whiplashed. The sight made Wick snarl. Reality made him curse as he watched the IV tube stretch taut. The needle ripped from her arm. The scent of blood filled the air. Wick's heart stalled, pausing mid-thump to hang inside his chest.

Fucking hell. Another wound. More pain. Just what he'd hoped to avoid.

But even as her life's essence splattered across her hospital gown, he didn't hesitate. Or stop running. He reacted instead. With a well-timed thought, he crushed the wheelchair mid-flip. Steel crumpled beneath the force. He hurled the compacted metal like a bowling ball, protecting the female from debris, aiming for the empty nurses' station at the end of the hall. As steel slammed against the half wall, Jamison stopped going up and started to come down. Wick threw himself across the floor. Shitkickers leading the skid, he slid like a baseball player, arms extended, eyes locked on her, body prone to break her fall.

A major-league move. Wicked results.

Jamison landed with a solid bump against him. She whimpered in pain. His stomach clenched, but stayed true. Thank Jesus. He didn't have time to freak out. Or puke. The whole aversion to being touched thing needed to stay where it belonged. On the back burner. Buried six feet under. In the passenger seat, not behind the wheel . . . whatever. Wick didn't care how it happened, just as a long as he kept his shit together.

For his sake, sure. But honestly, right now it was all about her.

She needed him. And strange as it seemed, he wanted to provide whatever he could in the face of her agony.

Jamison trembled against him. Wick cursed and, still in a full-body skid, locked his arms around her, wrapping her up tight to protect her from further injury. Jeans skating across the hospital floor, boot heels digging in, his T-shirt and jacket rode up, exposing his lower back. Wonderful. Just what he didn't need. Rug burn via a heavy-duty industrial floor.

Ignoring the pain, he hung onto his prize. The slip and slide slowed to a stop, leaving him sitting in the middle of the corridor. Breathing hard, shock wreaking havoc, he didn't move. One second slipped into the next as he took stock. Bright lights overhead. Him on the floor. Her in his lap. He blinked. Holy shit, he'd done it. No hesitation. No balking. Just full-on commitment the moment she needed him. Now, she lay in his arms, a warm bundle curled against him, her head tucked beneath his chin.

Pride picked him up, then circled deep. Panic tried to edge it out, closing his throat.

Wick shoved it aside, along with his phobia. He didn't have time for bullshit. She wasn't out of the woods yet. And neither was he. He needed to get her the hell out of Swedish Medical. Down five floors to meet Forge and Mac. All while keeping her comfortable, so—

Voices sounded, coming around a blind corner. His gaze narrowed, Wick's head snapped in that direction. Multiple footfalls, one heavier than the others. At least one male in the group.

"Shit," he growled, knowing what it meant.

Humans. A bunch of them headed his way.

So much for his brilliant crush-the-wheelchair strategy. The crash-bang against the deserted nurses' station had resulted in a ripple effect. Attention from a species known for their curiosity . . . and their ability to call the cops faster than an F-18 going Mach 1. So yeah. No time like the present. He needed to get the hell out of Dodge.

In a big fucking hurry.

Gathering his magic, Wick rolled to his feet. Jamison moaned. He adjusted his hold, gentling his touch, and conjured a cloaking spell. Leading the pack, a security guard entered the corridor with two nurses hot on his heels. Power snapped. Invisibility rippled, hiding Wick and Jamison behind a wall of no-can-see.

As they disappeared into thin air, the guard stopped short. "Good God, did you see that?"

"See what?" one of the nurses asked.

Cradling Jamison close, Wick took a big step backward. His shoulder blades collided with the corridor wall. Excellent plan. The best on every front, 'cause . . . yeah. Getting out of the way—giving the human trio plenty of room to walk past—seemed like a good idea.

"I thought I saw . . ." The human shook his head. His gaze swept the length of the hall, narrowing on the spot where Wick had disappeared. The guard opened his mouth, then closed it again. "It's nothing, I just thought—"

"Holy cow." Nurse number two stepped around the guard. A perplexed look on her face, she hustled toward the balled-up wheelchair. "Would you look at this?"

"What?" Boots squeaking, the guard strode past Wick to rendezvous with the nurse.

"Someone wrecked a wheelchair . . . like in a trash compactor or something."

"Jesus." The guard unclipped the walkie-talkie from his utility belt. "I gotta call this in."

Wick snorted. Good luck with that. All hospital authorities would get was a load of crumpled steel and no explanation. Which meant they'd stay clueless. Perfect. Just the way he liked humans, well . . . at least, most of the time. Jamison, however? He needed to clue her in fast, not to mention get her help. She was bleeding from the cut on her arm, shivering against him . . .

Hurting. In shock. In need of serious care.

Or something.

Wick couldn't be sure. Injured females weren't his specialty. Glancing down at her, he grimaced. God, she was pale, her lips nearly bloodless, eyelashes nothing but dark smudges against her cheeks, and . . .

Ah hell, who was he kidding? He wasn't equipped for this. Didn't know what to do or how to help her. Females, as a rule, belonged anywhere but near him. Venom always dealt with the touchy-feely stuff. It worked better that way, considering his propensity for violence and the phobia he carried around like baggage. But as he scanned her face, Wick refused to cop out. Not tonight. Her care fell to him, at least in the interim. Time to dig in, grow a pair, and get it done.

Inhaling long and smooth, Wick cradled her closer and put himself in gear. Striding past the gaggle of humans still extolling over the wheelchair, he paused at an intersection. Empty in both directions, two options existed: turn right or go left. Recall flared, providing the layout of Swedish Medical. Wick turned right. As he walked toward the stair-well exit, he scanned the hallway for a place to check her wounds. An empty room. A chair pushed up against a wall. Hell, a broom closet would do, just as long as he found a place to put her down and—

Bingo. An empty gurney.

Parked against the wall, the hospital bed was just what the doctor ordered. Solid. Soft. Comfortable. Exactly what Jamison required and he needed for a minute or two.

Wielding his power, Wick enclosed the bed in the cloak-ing spell. Privacy ensured, he sat her down on the cotton sheet. Eyes still closed, her brows puckered. The plaster cast on her foot bumped the inside of his leg, making her list sideways. Instinct made him reach for her. The sleeves of her hospital gown brushed the back of his hand as he grasped her biceps. Upon contact, her bio-energy flared, zapping him with—

Jesus Christ. Holy God. Not even close to good, never mind advisable.

Wick sucked in a quick breath as a channel opened in-side him. Oh fuck, the Meridian. The electrostatic current was . . . it was . . . reversing course, tying him to the female he touched, making it impossible for him to let go. Locked against her, he felt her connect, then link in, becoming one with the energy stream that fed his kind. Except . . .

He wasn't the one doing the feeding.

She was—blocking his ability to fight, drawing heat from his core, rendering him powerless in the face of her need. Wick gritted his teeth. He never should have touched her. Should've known better than to make contact with her bare skin. Jamison was high energy, and his dragon half way too responsive. Despite his aversion—and objections—the beast wanted to feed her. Now the fucker was providing something Wick never had before . . . healing energy. In a gushing torrent, forcing him into serious sensory overload.

His stomach pitched. He flexed his fingers, willing intellect to override instinct. He must let her go . . . right now . . . take his hands from her skin before—

His dragon snarled. Well, so much for that. The idea was a total no-go. The territorial beast inside him refused to back down, robbing him of recourse. No way out. No backtracking either. He was headed into dangerous territory, the kind Wick knew he might not come back from as the energy stream intensified.

The strain put him in lockdown.

He fought the imprisonment along with the rumble of body tremors. All to no avail. Jamison possessed the power, and until she pushed him away, he was stuck. Trapped. Tied to her in irrevocable ways and unable to stop the awful rush of energy moving from him into her. And judging by the look on her face? Not something that was likely to happen anytime soon. Relaxed against him, she took everything he gave, clinging to her connection and the Meridian's power.

With a hum, she nestled in, pressed her cheek to his heart.

"Fucking hell," he rasped, still fighting her hold on him. "Jamison . . . let go. You've got to—"

"No." Eyes closed, voice slurred, she shook her head. The slight movement caressed his chest, cranking him a notch tighter. "Feels too good. You . . . stay . . . with me."

Frozen in place, Wick prayed for mercy. She didn't give him any. Pressing closer, she sighed and wiggled to the edge of the mattress. A second later, she grew bolder, wrapping both of her legs around one of his thighs. The heat of her body snug against his, she murmured in contentment. He cursed and tried one more time to back away. With a grumble, she slid her arms around his waist and hugged him close.

Hugged him, for Christ's sake. *Him*. A male who hated to be touched, and yet . . .

Wick frowned. He didn't feel threatened. Or the need to throw up either. Which didn't jive. Not by a long shot.

He always panicked when near a female. But not with Jamison. Strange, but for some reason, she didn't push him into flee-like-a-motherfucker mode. Wick snorted. All right, so that wasn't quite true. He didn't like it—wasn't sure he wanted to keep touching her—but at least the closeness wasn't freaking him out. And like it or not, that begged a question.

How far could he push it?

An interesting concept. One that made him want to explore a little.

Swallowing past his sudden case of dry mouth, Wick forced his muscles to unlock. As his tension ebbed, the current increased. A prickle rushed over the tops of his shoulders, then slid upward on a mesmerizing glide to stroke the base of his skull. His senses tunneled, attuning him to the female in his arms. He focused on the top of her head. Legs and arms around him, she surrounded him, blurring his vision with flaming energy. His dragon rose to meet her, giving what she demanded, feeding her from the flow. Wick's lids grew heavy. He blinked—once, twice, a third time—struggling to combat the sudden haze of mind-fog.

Oh baby. That felt unbelievable. Nourishing. Gentle. Hot as hell.

And he wanted more. Just a little bit more, but . . .

Hmm, yum. So good. She was so damned good.

Wick swayed on his feet and, forcing his eyes open, stared at the pale wall over her head. Huh. Not home. Not in a club. He frowned, swimming through the river of heat to find the truth. He should be doing something . . . shouldn't he? The question helped his brain kick over. Yeah. Right. No question. He needed to be somewhere doing *something* for someone.

Giving his head a shake, he uncurled his hands from her upper arms. The current downgraded, moving from ball-busting intense to soft and smooth. She grumbled in protest. The urge to reconnect and strengthen the flow poked at him. He ignored the need and inhaled long and deep. The scent of blood reached him. Concern shoved the load of feel-good aside.

Jesus help him. She was hurt.

The realization propelled him into action. Looking for the wound, Wick's gaze skimmed over her. He found the cut in under a second flat. The IV needle had torn her arm open, leaving a gash just above her wrist. Grabbing the blanket edge, he applied pressure to the injury and conjured some medical supplies, only to realize she wasn't bleeding anymore. The plasma had clotted and—

Wow. Would you look at that? The cut was closing too, healing much faster than he would've expected for a human.

Dumping the roll of tape and sterile gauze on the bed beside her, he examined the wound more closely.

She flinched. "Ouch."

"Sorry, baby," he murmured, keeping his tone soft. Holding her steady, he ripped the package of gauze open.

With a quick twist, he wrapped the thick bandage over her wound, then reached for the roll of tape. "Almost done."

"Baby?" Dark lashes flickered. A slow up and down before she opened her eyes. Under the influence of the Meridian, magic went to work on the drugs in her system. As he watched, the empty-eyed expression she wore started to dissipate, helping mental acuity along. "No one ever calls me that."

"No?" Surprising, really. The endearment suited her.

She shook her head. "Get called *Injin* a lot though."

"Who calls you that?"

"Asshole Griggs."

"Sounds like *asshole Griggs* needs his head ripped off."

"Been saying that for years," she said, her words slurring a little.

A half smile on her face, she gazed up at him. Wick's heart flip-flopped, doing a somersault behind his breastbone. Jesus, she was pretty. Even with her split lip, busted leg, and all the bruises, she was the most beautiful female he'd ever seen. Which made him think he'd lost his mind. The fact he wanted to call her "baby" confirmed it. He was officially upside down and backward, waist deep in a stink hole and sinking fast. But even as he told himself to get a grip, the urge to return her smile snaked through him. He retreated instead, playing it safe, putting distance between them as he smoothed tape over the bandage.

She made a face, protesting the pressure of his hands. "That hurts. I hurt . . . all over."

"I know," he said, feeling the need to apologize again.

Christ help him, without meaning to, he kept adding to her pain. Wick swallowed past the knot in his throat. Perfect, wasn't it? She needed gentle. He gave her rough.

The truth slapped him in the face. He wasn't equipped to care for her, never mind provide comfort. Duh . . . made total sense. Kindness had never been part of his makeup. He didn't have a big heart or a gentle nature. Violence and cruelty, however? Wick knew both well. But as she held his gaze, something crazy happened. He saw the trust in her eyes—the kind of acceptance he'd never experienced—and wanted to be different. The idea sparked another, providing guidance, laying the groundwork for know-how and . . .

All of a sudden, he knew how to handle her.

Her eyes slid closed again.

"Jamison, look at me." A crinkle puckered her brows, but she gave him what he asked for and opened her eyes. Nodding his approval, he murmured to her, adopting Venom's method. By all accounts, females liked soothing tones. His friend employed the technique all the time, using the sound of his voice to bring comfort and pleasure. Not something Wick ever indulged in, but . . . hell, why not? No harm in trying, so he got with the program and talked to her. "I'm going to pick you up . . . carry you out, all right? It's going to hurt, but I need to—"

"You know my name."

"Yeah."

Tears welled in her eyes. "I guess that means it's official."

"What?"

"I'm sorry." One tear escaped and rolled down her cheek. The urge to brush the moisture away gripped him. He hesitated a moment, then lifted his hand and gave in to the compulsion. And why not? With her clinging to him, his no-touching rule was already history. No sense freaking out about it. "I know it's your job, but I'm not ready. I don't want to die."

His lips twitched. Amazing, but even overloaded by the Meridian, she was astute. Him and killing, after all, went hand and hand. "I'm not here to kill you."

"You're not?"

He shook his head.

"But you and the other angel were—"

Wick snorted. *Angel.* Now that was a stretch. "I'm here to help. Tania sent me."

She blinked again. Another slow up and down. "Wow, that was fast. I only just sent the text message."

The whispered words wound him tight. "You called Tania?"

"Nurse's cell phone."

"Shit."

"Is that bad?" Injury and exhaustion made her lean on him. Wick shifted toward her instead of away, catching her forward slump. The electrostatic prickle connecting them intensified, making him wince. "Sorry, but I couldn't wait. Asshole Griggs is here, remember? He's mean, and I need a lawyer."

"It's all right," he said, reacting to her fear even as he fought what she made him feel. Intense, raw, beyond normal, she made him *feel* far too much. Dangerous things. Wholly unfamiliar things. Things that could never be taken back. And as she turned him inside out, snuggling in, putting them skin-to-skin again, Wick wanted to be anywhere but here, holding her, caring for her . . . frickin' feeding her. "We gotta move, *vanzäla.*"

"*Vanzäla* . . . that's pretty," she said, holding in a yawn. "What does it mean?"

Wick cursed under his breath. Nice going, hot shot. The last thing he needed was to give her a pet name in Dragonese. "Nothing."

"Tania and I have a rule."

"Really."

"Yup." Fading fast, she stopped fighting it and yawned. "No lying allowed."

Sucky rule. Particularly since lying would be easier. More expedient too, but . . . whatever. If she wanted honesty, he'd give it to her. What could it possibly hurt? Not much. Half baked by the drugs, deep in the energy stream, she wouldn't remember anything he said anyway.

Shrugging out of his jacket, he settled the leather around her shoulders. "*Vanzäla* means 'songbird' in my native tongue."

"Oh, that's nice," she whispered, her eyes half-closed. "I like you. You're nice."

Nice? Wick stifled a snort. Sure, he was. "And you're completely shitfaced."

"Drugs will do that to a girl."

"No doubt."

With a tug, he pulled the coat lapels closed, cocooning her in the lingering warmth left by his body. It was cold outside. He didn't want her getting a chill when he stepped into the alleyway, a few strides away from the extraction point. And speaking of which? Time to find that door. Wick glanced down the corridor. A quick shift, and he gathered her up. Less than a second later, he was on the move, the exit into the stairwell in his sights.

Her face half-buried in his coat collar, she took a deep breath. "Hey, you know what else?"

"What?"

"You smell nice too."

Wick flinched. Good Christ. What the hell was he sup-posed to say to that? He didn't have a clue. Polite conversa-tion wasn't his strong suit. He only talked when necessity required it. In fact, the whole convo with Jamison qualified as bizarre. But as he stared down at the top of her head, he thought maybe . . . shouldn't he . . . well, say something? Respect her effort—along with the compliment—by an-swering her in some way?

Silence expanded around the idea. Inspiration struck, prompting him. "Thanks."

"Don't mention it."

No worries. He wouldn't be *mentioning* it anytime soon. The entire topic was out of his league. A different one, how-ever, circled, demanding clarification. "Hey, *vanzäla?*"

"Yeah?"

"You know the text message you sent?"

"Sure."

"Did you sign your name?"

"I dunno." She took another deep breath and hummed on the exhale, the sound one of pleasure. Wick gritted his teeth, determined to keep his shit together. Turning into a pansy over the fact a female enjoyed his scent wasn't on his list of things to do tonight. "Maybe."

Terrific. Trouble lived behind that *maybe.*

Wick upped his pace. The Razorbacks weren't idiots. Masters of technology, the rogues monitored human chan-nels and databases the same way Sloan did. So if Jamison had used her name while contacting her sister, the enemy would investigate. Which put him on an even tighter sched-ule. He needed to get out of the area fast. Before the en-emy picked up the Nightfury energy signal. Under normal circumstances, the frequency a large pack of males emitted while in the same area worked in their favor, making it easy to draw multiple Razorbacks into the kill zone.

Not tonight. Wick wanted to fly below enemy radar for a while. At least long enough to ensure Jamison's safety.

With a mental flick, he swung the door into the stairwell wide. Careful not to jar her, he kept each stride smooth. She grumbled, not liking the jog as he descended the first flight of steps. With a murmured apology, Wick adjusted his hold and slowed the pace. The sound of his voice soothed her, and she settled as he rounded the second landing.

Two floors down, three to go.

She yawned again. "What's your name?"

"Wick."

"Huh," she murmured. "Another weird one . . . like Goth Guy's."

Par for the course. The tatted bastard was Dragonkind. Stood to reason the male would be named according to the traditions of his kind. Not that Wick would tell her that. Oh no. The whole dragon/secret race powder keg would be blown up at Black Diamond. And not by him. He refused to be the messenger. It wasn't his place to inform her she'd just stepped inside another world . . . one where dragons ruled and humans remained clueless. Tania and Mac could handle that nightmare. So the sooner she stopped asking questions, the easier it would be for him.

"Jamison?"

"Yup."

"Go to sleep."

Unimpressed by the direct order, she huffed. "You're very warm . . . like a fire."

"Uh-huh," he said, agreeing just to agree. Refuting the facts was a waste of time. As a fire dragon, his core temperature always ran north of hot.

"It's nice . . . the heat." Tipping her head back, she opened her eyes, and he got nailed with sky-blue peepers.

Beyond distracted, he cleared his throat. "Good to know."

"And you know what else?"

"Jesus help me," he muttered. "What else?"

"It's J. J. No one ever calls me Jamison." Slipping her arm out of his jacket, she held up her hand. The slight weight of her in his arms, Wick stared at it, wondering what the hell she was doing. "Nice to meet you."

Oh for Christ's sake. She wanted to shake his hand? Right now?

Amusement whispered through him. Frickin' female. She was one of a kind. Ridiculous in the way only the fairer sex could manage, but . . . shit. He couldn't deny there was something special about her, adorable even.

Ignoring her hand, he took the next flight of stairs. "I like Jamison better."

"Not your call. It's my name."

"Nickname," he corrected. "I'll call you what I want. Now, go to sleep."

"Bully," she said, her amused tone contradicting the word choice.

Wick bit down on a laugh. Had he said adorable earlier? Times that by a thousand and call him screwed.

Giving into the inevitable—desperate for some peace and quiet—Wick opened the cosmic channel wider, increasing the Meridian's flow to feed her more energy. He hoped the excess would knock her out. Send her into a tailspin.

Push her deep into a healing state . . . or whatever. He didn't care how it happened just as long as she fell into a deep sleep. He needed a break before the husky sound of her voice sent him over the edge.

"Close your eyes, baby."

Overwhelmed by the energy, she obeyed and succumbed to the warm rush. As she slipped into slumber, Wick breathed out in relief.

Holding her was hard enough. But talking with her—being impressed and amused by her? Pure torture, both good and bad. On the one hand, he preferred his own company. Was more comfortable in silence, in the shadows, than he was in another's presence. To be expected, he guessed, considering the first twenty years of his life had been spent alone in the dark, his sole contact the brutal fist of a harsh master and the violent conditions of slavery. The only time he'd touched another was when he fought under glaring spotlights and the watchful eye of Dragonkind males who paid to watch young boys fight to the death.

A fight club complete with membership dues. As vile a concept as it was vicious.

Even now, all these years later, he couldn't shake the violence of his past. Or forgive himself for all the lives he'd taken. Innocent lives in the bud of youth. Did it matter he had been nothing but a boy himself? Made to pick up a knife at the age of seven and forced into combat? To become an instrument of death for other males' amusement? Wick swallowed past the tight knot in his throat. Do or die, the story of his life. Not a very good one either. Had he been stronger, he would've done the right thing and perished: defied his master, refused to fight, and died in the squalor so that another boy might triumph and live.

But he hadn't. He'd done the unforgiveable instead and . . . Survived.

So many dead to preserve one life. *His* life. Now he lived with the guilt. Day in. Day out. Night after night. Which meant one thing.

He didn't deserve enjoyment of any kind. And certainly not the ease Jamison made him feel. She was off limits. Nothing more than a means to an end. He needed to remember that. Otherwise he would overstep his bounds, do the unthinkable, and seek her out to discover what she was like after the healing was done.

Dangerous. In so many ways. Too many to count.

Navigating the last flight, Wick focused on the reinforced steel door at the bottom.

"Wick," Mac said through mind-speak, his Boston accent more pronounced. The tonal shift put Wick on high alert. The male always became more intense, accent included, when trouble approached. *"ETA?"*

"Now. I'm at the alley door."

"Move it. We're picking up a shitload of static. Company's coming."

"How many?"

"Not sure." A car door slammed, coming through mind-speak along with Forge's voice. *"My guess? A full fighting unit."*

"Fuck." Disengaging the security system, Wick shoved the door open. Reinforced steel swung wide, opening into the night. Frigid air rushed in, ruffling his hair as he stepped into the alleyway. Jamison shivered. Wick reacted, pulling the edges of the coat tighter together to keep her warm. The tug-and-draw should've been enough. It wasn't. He wanted to do more. To make sure she stayed comfortable at all costs. Without thought, he unleashed magic and upped

the temperature, surrounding her in a heated bubble, insulating her against the cold. Boot treads crunching over broken glass, he headed for the mouth of the alley, searching for his brother-in-arms street side. *"Venom, where—"*

"Headed to the roof with Sloan."

"The male?"

"Gone." Venom made a sound of disgust. *"He's a slippery little bastard, I'll give him that. But don't worry, I'll crack his skull tomorrow night."*

At the meet and greet Azrad wanted. Venom didn't say it. He didn't need to. After years of living together, Wick knew his friend better than he did himself. *"Get airborne, Ven. We're gonna need cover."*

"On it. What vehicle you got?"

The purr of an engine rumbled from the south end of the alleyway. Headlights lit the building's facade, arching across dull brick. An SUV rolled into view, pulling up curbside.

Mac chimed in. *"Red Suburban . . . blinged-out front grille, fancy running lights."*

"Jesus fucking Christ," Wick growled, spotting the poor excuse for a truck. Nothing like picking something with too much flash. The thing screamed "look at me!" *"Red? You stole a—"*

"Sorry, man." Putting the pimpmobile in park, Mac popped the driver's door open and stepped out onto the sidewalk. He glanced at the stripe of chrome running along the Suburban's side, then back at Wick. He shrugged. *"It was this or an orange Prius."*

Hopping out of the passenger side, Forge met his gaze over the SUV's roof. *"We picked the lesser of two evils."*

Lucky him. The wonder twins were at it again, backing each other's play.

Wick didn't bother to razz the pair for it. The mentor/apprentice thing was serious shit. A bond not unlike the one he shared with Venom: unbreakable, intense, the kind of friendship that lasted a lifetime and made males sacrifice for one another. That Mac and Forge fell into that category so quickly after meeting was a good thing. No sense getting bent out of shape about it. Or their dumb-ass choices.

Especially with a squadron of Razorbacks flying in hot.

Now that he was outside, Wick could smell the acrid burn in the air. Add that to the static buzzing between his temples and . . . yeah. There were multiple rogues in the area. Minutes away probably.

Footfalls hammering the quiet, Wick ran toward the only way out. Moments before he reached the tricked-out SUV, Mac swung the rear door wide. Wick pivoted mid-stride, spinning into a 180-degree turn. Ass-planting himself on the edge of the backseat, he slipped inside with Jamison in his lap and inchwormed until his boots cleared the cushion edge.

The truck doors slammed.

Forge met his gaze over the top of the passenger seat. Purple eyes drifted over the female asleep in his arms, then snapped back to Wick. The Scot raised a brow, the look on his comrade's face all about "are you, okay?" Wick stayed silent. What could he say? No, not even close to okay? Yes, totally fine? Neither answer seemed adequate. Or anywhere near truthful, so instead of answering, he told Mac to punch it, hoping the ex-cop drove like a speed demon. Otherwise, the enemy would close ranks around them, and Jamison would end up with a bull's-eye on her back.

Chapter Nine

Home on his mind, Nian took the treads two at a time. The rhythm of his footfalls echoed up the stairwell, bouncing off concrete and steel. The scent of stale beer and sex lingered in the narrow space, telling the tale, revealing the stairwell's secrets, highlighting the truth of club goers' amorous pursuits in dark corners. Not a problem most nights. He didn't give a damn about what went down in his clubs. Right now, though, he thanked God for the quiet and the coming dawn. All the patrons had left, stumbling into the night, leaving the Emblem Club, and the nightclub that sat one floor above it, empty.

A blessing, if ever there was one.

After the strain of the last week, he needed a break. Could feel exhaustion settle into his bones, then reach deep to touch his heart. An unusual occurrence for him. The hustle and bustle never bothered him before. He liked to keep busy. Thrived on all the activity. Enjoyed the income his many businesses provided too. Tonight, however, proved to be the exception, not the rule. He was tapped out . . . tired of the constant barrage of questions from employees and the heavy load of responsibility. He needed peace. He needed quiet. He needed the Metallics to call him the hell back.

Hellfire and brimstone. What in God's name were the pair doing? Well, besides ducking his calls and avoiding his presence. No matter how many messages he left, nothing came back. It was frustrating. Annoying. Beyond disrespectful. Something he never tolerated from anyone. His pride—and position as a member of the Archguard—disliked disdain. From anyone. But true to form, the Nightfury warriors didn't give a damn about him.

Or what he planned.

Now he had less than diddly-squat. Nothing but all's quiet on the eastern front. A never-ending string of stalling on Gage and Haider's part. Nian gritted his teeth and, grasping the handrail, ascended another flight of stairs. What the devil was Haider's game? The warrior seemed sincere enough, promising him a face-to-face with Bastian. But despite everything, it hadn't happened. At least, not yet. Which was why he always put together a contingency plan, one for every occasion. He'd done the same for the Nightfury situation over a month ago . . . long before he approached Bastian's warriors.

A brilliant strategy, but for one thing.

The male in charge of plan B wasn't returning his calls either.

Two weeks had passed and . . . nothing. Not a peep from the warrior he'd freed from indentured servitude for the sole purpose of infiltrating the Seattle scene. He needed viable intel to tempt Bastian into an alliance with him. A two-pronged attack. Step one involved him. As a member of the high council and Archguard elite—head of one of the dynastic families that ruled Dragonkind—he sat at the very top of Dragonkind hierarchy, able to collect insider information Bastian wouldn't be privy to on his own. Details of which he would share with the Nightfury commander to win his trust.

And step two? Plant a spy inside the Nightfury camp.

A risky proposition? No question. But success required calculated risk, and Nian needed an edge. One that would allow him to keep an eye on Bastian and the Razorback situation. The best way to accomplish that was from inside the Nightfury pack. The plan held tremendous promise but wasn't without problems. Bastian didn't run an adoption agency. The male was too guarded to accept a new pack member without vetting him first. So the chance of planting an ally loyal to Nian next to the Nightfury commander was slim to none. But if his warrior proved useful to Bastian—figured out a way to exist on the fringes of his pack—it would be enough. Enough to feed him information. Enough to help him keep his thumb on the pulse of Bastian's mood. Enough to give him the advantage while he furthered his own agenda in Europe.

But only if the bastard he'd sent to Seattle did his job.

Impatience beat on Nian as he reached the last landing. With a snarl, he upped his pace. His gaze on the Exit sign, he hammered the security bar. The door swung wide, flying back to slam into the building facade. The violent bang pinged off brick and mortar, raging across the cityscape to touch the heart of Old Town. Sidestepping, he avoided the backlash of reinforced steel and strode across the roof.

Five stories up. Not a lot of height to get airborne. Nian didn't care. He needed to fly. To shift into dragon form, feel the rush of frigid air and experience Prague in the predawn hours.

Arms and legs pumping, Nian sprinted toward the edge. Street lights flashed in his periphery. His magic flared, swirling in the center of his palm, warming the air around him as he transformed and leapt skyward. The burnished gold of his interlocking dragon skin glimmered in the gloom. With a growl, he unfolded his wings and rotated into an ascending spiral. Pushed south by the north wind, frost rushed over him, stripping away the city filth. The tri-headed spikes running along his spine rattled, shivering down to touch the tip of his barbed tail. Baring his fangs, he hummed, reveling in winter's sweet smells as urban lights fell away beneath him.

Oh, so good. Better than *good*, actually. Perfection. Bliss. Excellence wrapped up in open skies and the brutal stretch of taut muscle.

Fast flying took him out of the city, over thick forests and rocky terrain. Nian sighed. Almost there. Another few minutes, and he'd be where he yearned to be . . . home. Safe within the confines of his mountain lair. Away from the demands of his many businesses and all the Archguard tripe.

Fine golden mist rising from his nostrils, Nian shook his head. Something needed to change, and quickly. He couldn't stand much more of Rodin's foolishness. The leader of the Archguard was out of control: arrogant, over-confident, infected with idiotic notions driven by twisted ideology. So blind. So stubborn. So very foolish. The depravity—the female slave auctions . . . the fight clubs with ten-year-old boys playing gladiator—turned Nian's stomach, driving him to the point of rage.

Not good. Or the least bit productive.

Showing his cards too soon wouldn't get him what he wanted. Neither would anger or grief. Only deliberate action and a clever plan would achieve his end. He wanted so much better for his race. But change would never occur with Rodin at the helm. Fact, not fiction. He'd watched and waited since ascending to his position, searching for a light at the end of the tunnel. It hadn't come. Now—after three months of enduring the Archguard's corruption—Nian knew it never would.

Disgust settled deep. Frustration followed, tightening his chest.

He banished both and, eyes on the treetops, dove toward the forest below. Seconds before he collided with the canopy, Nian dodged, slicing between two enormous tree trunks. Increasing his velocity, he swooped beneath the outstretched arms of ancient beeches, navigating tight turns in the towering Eastwood. Snowflakes drifted like glitter only to fall away as he rushed the cliff face. Rising like a pale wraith in the dark, the mountain wall rose, calling him home, calming his mind, helping him decide the way forward.

Time to face the facts. The entire Archguard must be executed. Right alongside Rodin.

Necessity and honor—the health of his race—dictated the path. He must do what needed to be done. No doubt. No room for hesitation. No leaving it to someone else either. Just sure knowledge coupled with the wherewithal to deal the final death blows. Nian shook his horned head. Christ. What a waste. All the violence. All the death. All the destruction to come. If only he could convince the Archguard to listen. If only the council would abandon the old ways and send Dragonkind down a new road . . . a safer one, a better one for future generations, one without the threat of war.

War. On a global scale.

Nian knew it was coming. He smelled it in the air. Felt it in the wind. Saw it in the tension and mistrust between Dragonkind packs the world over. All eyes turned to Seattle and the feud raging between Nightfury and Razorback. Members of his race were picking sides—supporting one pack over the other—and soon . . . very, *very* soon . . . each commander would decide. Make their allegiances known. Draw the battle lines. Allow the fighting to spread from its epicenter—Washington State—to other areas of the globe.

A state that would put all of Dragonkind in jeopardy.

Stretching his wings to capacity, Nian came up over the last rise. A quick flip. An elegant twist. A whisper of sound. Nothing more, and he hung, suspended in midair, his eyes fixed on the manor house nestled into the curve of the mountainside. Built by a duke centuries earlier, his home perched on a wide-faced ledge, its foothold on the rocky outcropping more certain than a mountain goat's. Neither the mountain nor the howling winds challenged its dominion. The house simply belonged, growing out of jagged stone like a tree from the ground. And as Nian set down on the balcony overlooking the valley below, he blew out a long-drawn breath.

His razor-sharp claws clicked as his paws touched down on worn stone. Without thought, he shifted, moving from dragon to human form, and conjured his clothes. As the baggy workout pants and long-sleeved T settled against his skin, a shadow passed behind the bank of French doors along the far side of the balcony. His mouth curved. A deadbolt clicked. The doorknob turned, and his trusted servant stepped out into the winter chill.

Dressed in his usual fair, tuxedo and tails, the Numbai bowed his head. "Welcome home, my lord."

"Lapier."

"What news?"

"None," he said, moving toward the only male he considered family. The Numbai served him well, caring for him as he had every male of his line for generations. Thank God. Nian didn't know what he would do without him. Friend. Confidant. Caretaker. Lapier did it all, more than his fair share most nights. "The council is blind to Rodin's ways. They remain loyal to the bastard. I can find no crack to slip through."

"Then it is as we feared."

Worse, actually. But Nian refused to argue the point. "Any word from our other pursuits?"

"Not yet."

"Christ."

His hands curled into twin fists, Nian scowled at the awakening sky. It shouldn't be this hard. He was trying to do the right thing, but as was her habit, fate intervened, turning her tiresome wheel. Getting in his way. Mucking up an excellent strategy. And as he raged at the setbacks, mind churning to see all the angles, to adjust and forge a new way forward, to somehow salvage—

"My lord." Concern in his eyes, the framework of glass and stone archways rising behind him, Lapier paused, and Nian knew what he was thinking. The "look"—the one Lapier reserved for when he misbehaved—said it all. The Numbai didn't agree with his plan . . . or the ambition that drove it. Nian sighed. Lapier clasped his hands together, making the rings he wore wink in the low light. "Perhaps, it's for the best, Nian. A sign to leave well enough alone."

The best? Not a chance.

Leaving Rodin to his own devices wasn't a good idea. The bastard corroded everything he touched. Not that Lapier gave a damn about the big picture. The Numbai's duties extended to him . . . and him alone. He didn't care about the greater health of Dragonkind, just that Nian lived to see a new night.

Biting down on a curse, he padded across the balcony on bare feet. "I'll be in my study."

"Would you like a bourbon?"

"Bring me the bottle."

"As you wish, my lord."

Nian huffed. *As you wish.* Right. As if. *If only* . . . what a load of BS. So only one thing left to do. Get roaring drunk. Find some oblivion and stay there for a while. At least, throughout the day. Maybe blunting his thoughts, forgetting his troubles, would help jump-start a new strategy. Frustration and fixation weren't a good pair. Both made males act in unpredictable ways. Not something a warrior in his position could afford, so . . . why not? Hitting the bottle for a few hours was as good a plan as any.

Exhaling long and slow, Nian reached for his magic. The mental flick swung one of the double doors wide. Cold stone chilling the soles of his bare feet, he strode over the threshold and into the central corridor. Pale walls slid into Arab archways, then reached up to touch the fluted ceiling overhead. Lush with tradition, Turkish rugs streamed the length of the hallway to cover colorful mosaic floor tiles underfoot. Simple yet beautiful. He loved the house, appreciated its isolation, enjoyed the flawless symmetry along with the craftsmanship that spoke of another culture in another time.

Home sweet home. Warm. Inviting. Safe.

Crossing into his study, he gave the windows dominating one side of the room a quick once-over. Enchanted by a spell, the clear glass rippled, darkening by the second, protecting him from the awakening sun. His focus on the magical metamorphosis, Nian reached into the pocket of his pants. The lighter he carried slid into his palm.

Instant relaxation. Perfection in solace.

With a flick, he thumbed the gold top. The lighter snapped open. Nian stared at the wick a moment, then snapped the lid closed. The sharp sound echoed like a question. What should he do? Force the issue? Disappear for a few days and make a secret trip to Seattle to corner Bastian himself? Rolling his shoulders, Nian stared at the fresco on the domed ceiling. Wood nymphs in full frolic. He frowned at the half-naked females. No answers there. He flipped the lighter again. Click-click-snap. Click-click—

Ding-ding . . . ping.

Nian blinked. What the hell was that?

Frowning, he scanned his study. The noise came again. His attention snapped toward his desk. Ding-ding . . . ping. His gaze narrowed on the computer he'd set up a month ago. Not his favorite thing. Technology belonged to humans, not Dragonkind. But he couldn't argue with progress. Or his inability to connect to his contact through mind-speak. The male was too far away for him to link in and use the cosmic connection his kind favored, which made the computer a necessary evil.

One he really needed to learn how to use.

Oriental rug soft beneath his feet, he rounded the corner of his desk and glanced at the monitor. Black from disuse, a small red icon blinked in the center of the screen.

Nian drew in a quick breath. Oh, thank Christ. A message. He had a—

Ding-ding . . . ping.

Focused on the icon, he tossed his lighter on his desk blotter and reached for the mouse. The second he touched it, the screen went active. A box with the words "video conference" flashed in the middle. Hope hit hard, banding around his chest, making his heart thump and throat go tight. He swallowed past the knot and, repositioning the cursor, clicked on the link. A circular whirligig spun center screen a moment, then . . .

Movement flashed as a male looked away from the book he held. Dark-blue eyes narrowed on him. "Where the hell have you been?"

The tone should've pissed him off. Nian's lips curved, instead. He couldn't help it. Was so glad to see the warrior, relief superseded the usual respect he demanded. "Around. It's good to see you, Azrad."

"Wish I could say the same." Raptor flat, Azrad's gaze ate across time and space, threatening to devour him. The metal-stud piercing in his eyebrow winked, drawing attention to the burgundy highlights in his hair. A rough look. All Goth, no sophistication in sight. Not that it mattered. Nian didn't care how the warrior looked. Lethal with loads of cunning, the male wielded know-how like a razor-toothed club . . . without mercy or an ounce of hesitation. The perfect instrument in the game Nian played. "The Nightfuries are a pain in the ass. There's some really strange shit going on over here."

Hope lit Nian up. "But you're in?"

"Set up and on a roll," Azrad said, looking more like a kingpin than a former slave kicking back in the office chair. "Haven't met Bastian yet, but that'll come."

"And the rest of the Nightfuries?"

"Nearly got clipped by two of them tonight."

"But you—"

"Yeah. First contact's been made. Meeting's set for to-morrow at midnight . . . Seattle time. Bastian'll be there."

"You're sure?"

"Positive." The chair squeaked as Azrad cupped the back of his head with both hands. Elbows folded out, he leaned into the backrest. "I put on a good show . . . got their attention in a big way. He won't be able to resist meeting me. Will wanna know what I'm up to . . . and why I'm in his territory."

"Well done."

The warrior snorted. "Was there any doubt?"

Some. Nian didn't voice the opinion, though. Azrad, for all his skill, wasn't the most trustworthy. He was too strong-willed. Far too smart. Forget the fact he'd been little more than a slave less than two months ago, the warrior did as he pleased. Nian had known it the moment he secured Azrad's release. He'd done it in secret. Made a deal with the devil right under the Archguard's nose and offered the one thing the warrior wanted most in the world . . .

Freedom. Payback too, a chance to right the wrongs Rodin had done him.

Nian tipped his chin. "I'll be at my computer, waiting for your call."

"Uh-huh." Staring at him from half a world away, Azrad lowered his arms and reached forward. His finger poised above the keyboard, the warrior winked at him. "Later."

Hell, he hoped so. One never knew with Azrad.

All he could do was cross his fingers and pray Azrad kept his word.

Faith and honor. Two very big words he hoped played in his favor. 'Cause sure as he lived in Prague, Azrad possessed an agenda of his own. The warrior had craved more than just his freedom. He'd *wanted* to travel to Seattle. And now, for the first time, Nian wondered why.

Chapter Ten

Venom took the flight of stairs at a dead run. Three treads at a time. His chest heaved, burning from lack of oxygen. Clenching his teeth, his gaze riveted to the next landing, he pushed the pain away and pumped his arms, turning his legs into pistons.

Up. Up. Up.

He needed to reach the roof. Shift into dragon form and get airborne.

Knees acting like shock absorbers, the slam of his combat boots echoed the urgency, banging out a harsh rhythm. Sound reverberated in the enclosed space, taking up all the room inside his head. Grabbing the steel railing, Venom pulled, propelling himself into another tight turn and up another set of stairs. Muscles along his arm screamed in protest. He ignored the pain. Only one thing mattered . . . reaching his brothers-in-arms before the Razorbacks zeroed in and took out the SUV.

Zip. Bang. Gone.

That's how it would go down. The Razorbacks would blow the vehicle sky-high the second they spotted it. And realized who sat inside. Unless, of course, he did something . . .

Like, oh, say, reach Swedish Medical's frigging rooftop. Become rogue bait and his brothers' shield. Buy enough time for everyone to find cover.

Cover. Right. Wishful thinking much? Probably. The Razorbacks might not be rocket scientists, but once locked on, the pack became efficient. Proof positive lay in the fact the bastards had nearly killed him two weeks ago. Venom wanted to say it had been a lucky shot but knew the truth. The enemy had used superior numbers to effect, cutting him off from the other Nightfuries in order to pick him apart in the swarm.

Pretty good strategy, all things considered. One-on-one, none could beat him. Hell, strike that. Three against one still came out in his favor, 'cause . . . yeah. He was just that strong, a powerhouse in a physical fight. The biggest, strongest, most—

All right, maybe not the most vicious.

Wick topped him in that department, but not by much. So, no question. He needed to get the hell out there. Right now. Before the extraction plan went from dicey to deadly.

Though, how that had happened, he didn't know. Wick's plan had been solid. Well thought out and executed to perfection. His eyes narrowed, Venom rounded the second to last stair landing. Something had tipped the rogues off. Or maybe *someone.* Venom growled. Azrad. Frigging male. Had to be him. Nothing else explained the warrior's presence inside the hospital, never mind his interest in the female.

Well, other than angling for the "meeting" with Bastian.

A setup. The entire scenario smacked of an ambush. A way to draw the Nightfury commander into a trap in order to kill him. Sneaky. Smart. Well executed too. Especially since Azrad didn't smell like a Razorback. But then, Ivar the psycho was just that cunning. Plant the seed, let curiosity fester, and wait for it to play out.

The perfect plan.

"Goddamn it," he said, half-snarl, half exhale. "The bastard."

One that wouldn't last long. Why? Tomorrow night, at the meet and greet, Venom planned to rip Azrad's balls off. Make him squeal like a stuck pig, crank the pain level to apocalyptic before he tore his head off, leaving nothing but a pile of dragon ash.

Red light flashed up ahead, bleeding onto the stair treads in front of him.

With a growl, Venom unleashed magic. Power unfurled, cracking like a whip. Pressure expanded in the narrow space, warping the air. Bolts popped, exploding from their holes like bullets. Metal pinged against metal. Venom ducked, avoiding the barrage, and hammered the emergency exit. Reinforced steel buckled. The door ripped off its hinges, blowing outward into the night sky. As the panel cartwheeled, then slammed into the helipad, Venom cleared the threshold.

Stone dust crunched beneath his boots. Within seconds, he planted his foot on the lip of the building and—

He was up and over, diving toward the pavement below.

Street lights flared below him. His night vision sparked, and winter wind blew his heavy trench coat wide open. Leather streaming behind him, Venom sighted the ground, tucked into a somersault, and . . . oh yeah. The switch-up felt good. Like a gift, hands and feet turning into talons as the tips of his razor-sharp claws clicked together. Dark-green scales accompanied the shift, wrapping him in interlocking dragon skin, snaking around the venomous barbs of his tail. Armored up and buttoned down, Venom unfurled his wings. Frigid air slid over his horned head, then moved on, rattling the spikes along his spine.

Spiraling into a side flip, he banked hard. The trajectory swung him around hospital smoke stacks. As his wing tip grazed a chimney, his eyes glowed. Blood-red gaze staining the air in front of him, he scanned the street below.

Nothing and nobody. No squeal of tires against the asphalt. No cherry-red SUV in sight either.

Relief hit Venom chest level. Wick and the others must be gone. Were hopefully hauling ass, taking the most direct route across the city, heading toward the bridge and I-90.

Intent on covering their retreat, Venom circled around again. Flying east seemed like the best option. If he played his cards right, he could not only cover their retreat, but stay in between his boys and any inbound rogues.

"Ven . . . I'm airborne." A dark-brown blur streaking through the gloom, Sloan flew in. Snow-white talons flashed as his buddy rotated into a flip, taking the wingman position on Venom's right side. *"You feel that?"*

Goddamn, did he ever. No male worth his salt could ignore the static. The buzz hammered his temples, feeding him information. His sonar pinged, marrying instinct with experience. No mistaking the signs. Razorbacks. A shitload of them, rolling in hot.

Venom cursed under his breath. *"No way we'll outfly the bastards."*

"So what? You wanna play bait and switch?"

"Sounds like a plan."

Not a very good one, but . . . hell. Talk about a nasty twist.

Venom ground his fangs together. So much for getting away free and clear. He didn't have much time. A minute—maybe two—before the rogues intercepted him. Wanting to be sure of the time frame, he mined the signal. Magic sparked and sensation spiraled, confirming his suspicions. The rogues had just broken through the three-mile barrier, allowing him to pinpoint their location. And if he could feel them? The bastards could track the magical trace he left in his wake too.

Sloan threw him a sideways glance.

He ignored the warning. Acknowledging it wouldn't change anything. Neither would failing to make a plan.

Wheeling around a tall high-rise, Venom fired up mind-speak. *"Wick . . . give me a grid."*

"Heading east on Jefferson. We'll make a left on 23rd and head for the bridge."

"No good. The rogues are locked in now." Following his trajectory, Sloan sliced between two apartment buildings. A quick flip took him up and over Venom's spine. *"Find a hole and disappear until we clear the sky."*

"Motherfuck."

Ignoring Mac's curse, Sloan inhaled, drawing deep to scent the air. *"I count ten."*

Venom shook his head. *"Fourteen . . . minimum."*

"Jesus H. Christ," Sloan said. *"We need B and Rikar."*

No kidding. But that wouldn't happen. Not in a hurry anyway.

Bastian and the Nightfury first in command were twenty minutes away, taking a night off, getting some well-deserved R & R with their chosen females at Black Diamond. A new occurrence for their pack. Until a month ago, none of them had ever taken a break. But some rules were meant to be broken. Now a new normal reigned. One that included the occasional night off—to rest, recharge, and recuperate.

Not a bad thing, just . . . different.

The bigger adjustment—at least for him—stemmed from another source altogether. The expansion of their pack.

At first, Venom resisted the change, not liking the paradigm shift, fearing the new members would get one of them killed. But after seeing what Forge and Mac could do . . . their special brand of kick-ass and how the warriors complimented one another? He'd changed his mind in a hurry. All right, so he still couldn't resist busting Mac's chops— razzing the resident water dragon was way too fun to ever stop—but neither could Venom deny that the wonder twins fit right in. The pair were viciousness squared. And honestly? Lethal with a heaping side order of brutal always got Venom jazzed.

Still, no matter how talented, the warriors couldn't replace their commander.

Bastian had skills. Ones Venom needed right now. Without B in the mix—and his ability to read the enemies' strengths and weaknesses from a distance—he was flying blind. Were there fourteen or more Razorbacks on the horizon? Experience told him multiple rogues of varying skill levels. But beyond that? He didn't know. Worrisome. Nowhere near optimal heading into battle. Too bad beggars can't be choosers. In order to protect his pack and J. J., no other choice existed.

Increasing his wing speed, Venom glanced over his shoulder. He cursed. Rogues at six o'clock, flying in fighting formation, white frost curling from their wingtips . . . coming down the pipe, right on their asses.

"Listen up, boys." Watching the circus unfold behind him, Venom assessed the situation. He indulged in a quick head count. Huh. Only eleven rogues on the horizon, three short of two full fighting units. Instinct whispered. Something about the numbers didn't add up. Neither did their strategy. Frowning, Venom laid it out for his brothers. *"The bastards are splitting up. Half are headed our way, but I've also got multiple males landing on the hospital roof."*

"Shite," Forge said, Scottish accent rolling. *"They know about J. J."*

"Looks like it."

Wick growled. *"Stupid text message."*

"She sent a text?" Sloan asked.

"To Tania."

"Motherfuck. Way too resourceful. Just like her sister," Mac said, a growl in his undertone. As he dropped another f-bomb, the SUV's engine snarled, the violent rumble coming through mind-speak as the ex-cop put his foot down. *"Wick . . . put J. J. down and get ready to take the wheel. Forge and I need to get airborne."*

Frigging right. Excellent plan. Mac's strategy hit all the markers. Outnumbered three to one didn't equal great odds in a firefight, but—

Venom blinked. Wait a minute. Back up a step.

What had Mac just said? Something about . . . *put J. J. down.* Venom frowned so hard the space between his eyebrows stung. What the hell did that mean? Was Wick actually touching the female? Holding her in his lap or something? The thought seemed ridiculous. Way off base. His friend avoided physical contact like field mice did snakes. And given the fact J. J. had been sitting in a wheelchair when he saw her last?

No need to inquire further.

Wick always took the path of least resistance. His friend would've wheeled the female out, then handed her over the moment he made contact with the wonder twins. Venom would bet his fangs on it.

"Heads up, lads," Forge said. *"We're making a right onto—"*

Yellow flame exploded across the night sky.

"Shit!" Mac hit the brakes.

Tires squealed, shrieking inside Venom's head as an enemy dragon uncloaked. Wings spread wide, the bastard hung above the cityscape and exhaled. Fire hissed between the rogue's fangs. And Venom knew they were screwed. The male was a Flame Thrower, able to exhale a continuous stream of fire for minutes on end.

The steady inferno roared, rocketing over building tops, flashing off dark windows, polluting the air with the smell of sulfur.

More cursing came from inside the SUV.

Rage twisted through Venom. No way. Not on his watch. The rogue might be a tricky bastard—flying around the perimeter to come in the backdoor—but that meant nothing with him in the mix. He was faster, stronger, more deadly, and now . . .

In the prime position.

Speed supersonic, Venom torqued into a full-body twist. His wingtip grazed the surface of a top-floor window. Glass rattled. He set his sights on the rogue, lining his enemy up for the kill shot. Bull's-eye, right on the male's chest. The idiot should know better. An immobile dragon was a dead one. Good for him. Not so great for the Razorback trying to kill his best friend.

The frigging asshole.

Rising like a viper over rooftops, Venom exhaled hard. Luminous green fog shot from between his fangs. Like a pulsing wave, the venomous froth ate at the air, devouring the oxygen in a toxic curl. The rogue squawked. Too late. The glowing toxin engulfed the bastard, settling into his lungs, making him grab his throat.

The stream of flame ceased, turning off like a tap.

Talons deployed, Venom broadsided the male. He dug in, sinking his claws through scales to reach muscle and bone. The rogue screamed. Warm dragon blood flowed over his talons as the Razorback flailed. Showing no mercy, Venom bared his fangs and increased the pressure. Pain, oh the pain. Great fun to deliver to the male in his grasp. Well deserved too. The asshole had tried to scorch his brothers, so . . . yeah. He wanted to take his time, make it last, hear every last scream as the rogue begged for death.

Not that it would happen that way.

With multiple rogues converging on him from behind, he didn't have time to screw around. Adjusting his grip, he pinwheeled, spinning the rogue full circle. An instant before Venom let go, he grabbed the bastard by the throat. A quick slash. A sharp upward thrust, and . . .

Eureka! One dead rogue. Nothing but an explosion of dragon ash.

The gray cinder flew, colliding with a building facade. The puff swirled like smoke, coating the glass as another Razorback attacked from behind. An instant before enemy claws touched him, Venom tucked his wings. With a grunt, he rotated into a somersault and scanned the street below. Blistered from the flames, tar bubbled up through the asphalt and—

Thank God. Cherry-red SUV dead ahead.

Ass end smoking from the almost charbroil, the Suburban roared toward the other end of the street, heading toward an intersection. Both the driver and passenger side windows opened. Mac and Forge slid out. Shitkickers planted on the running boards, the pair made like a couple of natural born surfers.

Relief grabbed Venom by the balls as Forge left his perch. As the Scot leapt skyward, he shifted, purple scales flashing, his growl loaded with nasty undertones.

On the move behind his buddy, Mac's feet landed on the truck's rooftop. Aquamarine eyes aglow, his gaze narrowed on a spot over Venom's shoulder. *"Ven . . . hard right."*

Muscle torqueing, Venom banked wide, and Mac unleashed. Water hissed through the air with violent intent. Forming mid-throw, a triple-headed javelin whistled toward him. Venom ducked. The rogue behind him squawked, then wing flapped, pulling up short, but—

Crack!

The water spear struck, piercing scales to reach the enemy's heart.

The rogue gurgled, choking on his own blood. Another round of ash swirled in a wind-filled updraft.

Forge hoorahed, and claws leading the way engaged three rogues at once. *"Top marks, lad. Keep that shite coming."*

"Will do," Mac murmured, his eyes on the sky.

Venom grinned, showing fangs as he swiped at an enemy dragon on the flyby. Blood splashed up his forearm. Mac hurled another javelin and . . . thud! Match. Set. Game. Another Razorback down for the count. Goddamn. *Top marks* was right. Mac owned a first-class arm. One that would make the Seattle Mariners drool. But just this second? He was glad his buddy played for Team Nightfury, not in the human world. That water spear crap was wicked.

"Mac, move your ass," Wick growled from behind the wheel. Hitting the brakes, he locked the tires. The SUV's ass end swung around. Rubber pulsed against asphalt as the truck went into a controlled skid, snaking onto 23rd Avenue. The second his best friend cleared the corner, he gunned it. Big V8 screaming, huge trees from a municipal park casting shadows across pavement. *"Get airborne, for fuck's sake."*

"Wick . . ."

"What?"

Balanced on the SUV's roof, Mac slid on steel as Wick changed lanes. *"Get ready to pop the hood."*

"Say when."

"Now!"

The cherry-red panel flipped up.

Shifting into dragon form, Mac leapt up and out, clearing the truck as he grabbed hold of the steel shield. Two Razorbacks attacked. Venom snarled and, flying in fast, grabbed the second rogue by the tail. Sharp spikes bit into his palm. He hauled him backward in midair. Idiot number one squawked. Venom ignored the outcry. With a quick twist, he snapped the enemy's neck while Mac shit-canned the other, treating the rogue to a face full of steel. Another smash with the sharp edge of the hood and—

Dragon teeth flew through the air. The splatter hit Venom in the chest, spraying across his scales. *"Ugh."*

"Suck it up, Ven." Flashing a grin, Mac attacked another rogue.

"Easy for you to say."

Course set to intercept, focus riveted on a bright-blue Razorback, Venom rocketed over a high-rise. Stone dust flying in his wake, he reached out and grabbed the tip of the male's wing. Enemy claws raked his chest. Venom clamped down, ignoring the pain along with the Razorback's freak-out routine and . . . crack! Bone snapped, disabling the ass-hole as his wing's webbing tore.

"You don't have . . ." Already looking for his next target, Venom sent the bastard into a free fall and growled, *" . . . teeth stuck in your scales."*

Mac laughed.

Sloan streaked past, chasing a pair of rogues.

"Ven," Wick said. *"Heads up. I'm getting off the road."*

"Headed into the park?"

"Going to lose 'em in the trees."

Good plan.

With Razorbacks in full swarm, and only four of them to hold the line, finding a safe place to hide the female sound-ed about right. Excellent strategy—really, it was—but for one teensy-weensy problem. Wick lived to fight. Hated to be left on the sidelines. Which meant . . . what? His friend would be hard-pressed to stay put while he and the others cleared the sky. The knowledge gave Venom a bad case of indigestion. But then, that tended to happen with a male as unpredictable as Wick in the mix.

❁ ❁ ❁

J. J. woke up like an astronaut shooting into outer space, with gut-wrenching velocity. Surging awareness sliced through her. Sensation cut deep, making sound explode inside her head. Somebody cursed. Something high-pow-ered rumbled. And the wind. God, it was howling, whistling against . . .

She frowned. Where the devil was she exactly?

Good question. With her sense of bearing shot to hell, she couldn't tell. Too bad, really. She could've used a clue, particularly since she kept getting jostled. Each sway rolled her forward, then back. Surge and release. Bump. A lot of noisy rattling. More bone-jagging shudders and—

Her stomach clenched. Ah, crap. Not again.

The nausea, though, didn't care what she wanted. The sick feeling spread, scalding her insides, tightening her throat, making her stomach heave. An awful taste washed over her tongue. J. J. gagged, but refused to give in. Nothing but pain lay in that direction. Raising her hand, she cupped one hand over her mouth. Bad decision. With her arm raised, her side squawked and agony swirled, joining the party, pulling at her ribs, forcing her to remember . . .

Everything.

The attack at the prison. Her injuries, all the stitches, the god-awful drugs, and something else too.

A guy. There had been a man at the hospital. A stranger, an angel with a compelling voice and calming presence.

J. J. frowned. God, that voice. Deep. Sure. Beyond incredible. Something about it called to her, making awareness spike and her interest turn. She wanted to hear it again. Needed the rich timbre to ground her in the here and now. Maybe then her mind would clear. Maybe then coherence would return. Maybe then she would remember.

Concentrating hard, she chased the soft sound of his murmur through her mind, hunting for the truth. Recall played a cruel game of keep-away. She dug deeper, needing to know. Fragmented pieces bubbled to the surface. J. J. shook her head. None of it seemed real and yet she couldn't dismiss him. He'd been so warm. So powerful. So present and potent that the impression he left clung like seaweed in sun-warmed shallows. He'd done something to her. Saved her somehow. Soothed her while he took the pain away. And, hmm, that had been nice. The rush of sensation. The warm curl of comfort. The intense heat of his body along with his scent as he carried her away.

J. J. drew a soft breath. *Carried her away?* Now wait just a minute. Was she imagining that or—

A low curse interrupted her train of thought.

The scraping sound came next, then the bumping thump over something big.

She cracked her eyes open, and . . . wham! Instant recognition. Not to mention full-on alarm. Holy moly. She wasn't in the hospital anymore, but in the front seat of an SUV. The backrest cranked all the way back, she lay curled on her side, snug inside a leather jacket with a blanket covering her legs, facing . . .

An angel. A man she now remembered with total clarity.

Odd, to say the least. With the drugs mucking up her mind, she'd doubted he was real when she saw him in the corridor. Now, with the effects of the Demerol gone, lucidity returned, helping her catalog the details. J. J. licked over the cut splitting her bottom lip. Tall. Strong. Amber-gold eyes set in a too-handsome face. Big, bad, and brawny. He owned them all, sporting each one like a junkyard dog wore spikes, razor-sharp teeth at the ready.

Ignoring the discomfort, J. J. swallowed past her sore throat. "Wick."

"Shit." He glanced sideways at her. "You're awake."

"Not an angel."

His mouth curved. "Not even close."

Good to know. Better to remember. Why? Something about him wasn't quite tame. He was too intense to be considered safe. But even as instinct squawked, warning her of the danger, J. J. couldn't muster an ounce of fear. He wouldn't hurt her. Crazy to believe it? Probably. But for some reason, the observation didn't change a thing.

She wasn't afraid of him.

"Where are we?" Excellent question. One that needed answering—fast—considering her companion and his lead foot. Jeez, he was driving at breakneck speed . . . heading God only knew where. Glancing out the side window, J. J. forced her eyes into focus. Tree trunks raced past, galloping in the opposite direction. The engine roared. Wick cranked the wheel, spinning the truck around a tight corner. Dirt flew, spraying the undercarriage. Moonlight pierced the darkness as branches raked the SUV like gnarled fingernails. "Where are you taking me?"

"Somewhere safe," he said, eyes on the road, big hands on the wheel, expression set. "Go back to sleep."

"Can't." More insistent now, anguish throbbed against her side, working its way down her leg to beat on her broken ankle. "I'm hurting."

"I know. Hold on, *vanzäla*. I'll get you help."

Not soon enough. It wouldn't be soon enough. She needed something right now. A something she knew from experience he could give her. "Can you . . ."

He arched a brow. "What?"

"Hold my hand?"

Throwing her a startled look, he shook his head. "No."

"Please?" She hated to beg—she really did—but touching him would help. Or, at the very least, get her through. Did it matter he was a stranger? Or that he didn't want to touch her (yeah, that came through loud and clear), but . . . no. Forget logic. Only one thing mattered. She needed him, for some bizarre reason. So like it or not, he was going to hold her hand. "It's getting worse, and I think touching you will help."

A muscle twitched along his jaw.

"Please, Wick?"

Agony tightened its grip, snaking around her rib cage. As she gasped, silence stretched, one second lengthening into the next. J. J. drew her knees closer, curling into a fetal position, tucking her face into the collar of his leather jacket as she struggled to waylay the pain. A no-go. Brutal sensation told her all she needed to know. The last of the Demerol had worn off, leaving her unable to do anything but feel. Fighting the onslaught, her teeth started to chatter.

"Fuck."

The growl swirled in the cab a second before his hand left the steering wheel. He held it aloft a moment, poised in midair, then laid his forearm across the SUV's center console. J. J. didn't hesitate. She reached out and, with a whispered "thank you," slid her hand into his much larger one. Skin on skin, his unbelievable heat spread. Warm prickles ghosted up her arm, chasing her chills away. She sighed in relief. Wick flinched and, white-knuckling the wheel, cursed again.

"Sorry," she said, trying to sound convincing.

She didn't pull it off. Lying wasn't her forte. Neither was faking it and—

A warm curl of sensation swirled through her. Something clicked, opening a channel deep inside her. Relief rolled in, breaking like a wave against a beachhead at high tide. The siphoning rush picked her up, blissed her out, relaxing her completely, and . . . oh wow. Thank you, God. *That* was un-believable. An instant reprieve from the pain.

Her eyes grew heavy-lidded. His fingers twitched against hers. "Am I hurting you?"

"No."

"But you don't like it?"

"I didn't say that."

True. Then again, he didn't say much of anything. He liked short answers, one to three words at a time. Not a problem for her. Quiet by nature, she appreciated silence—along with concise answers—more than most people. She'd learned that skill in prison. The more silent she became, the less others noticed her. An excellent skill to embrace when surrounded by violent offenders with impulse-control issues. Dum-Dum Daisy was proof enough of that.

And speaking of which? The whole jailbreak thing wasn't a great idea.

"You should take me back, you know," she said, her mind working better as the pain subsided. Which meant . . . no more room for denial. The dash and dodge through the forest told her all she needed to know. They were on the run. No doubt from cruisers with SPD's logo plastered along the side. And once the cops caught up with them? Forget about parole. It would be bye-bye freedom, hello extended sentence. "Don't get me wrong, I appreciate what you're doing, but I'm up for parole in a month and—"

"Forget it, Jamison." His grip tightened as he glanced over his shoulder. His gaze narrowed on the back window. "I'm not taking you back to that shithole."

Well, would you look at that? More than three words in a row. They were making progress. "But if the police catch us—"

"Fuck the cops."

"Don't swear at me."

He huffed, the sound half-snort, half-laugh.

And she knew what he meant. Her reaction was ridiculous. She was accustomed to prison life, for goodness sake—the land where harsh language abounded. Still, his attitude annoyed her. He'd given her the brush-off, dismissing her problems, asserting his control, making her feel . . . well . . . helpless, for lack of a better word. Yes, he controlled the play, no question. Was behind the wheel, calling the shots, roaring down some stupid dirt road in the middle of nowhere, but this was her life. *Hers.* Her future on the line. Her freedom hung out to dry. Her ass in the sling. So for him to pooh-pooh her concern, flush all she'd worked so hard to achieve down the toilet? Well . . .

The dismissal pissed her off. Pushed all the wrong buttons. Now all she wanted to do was wind up, let loose, and knock some sense into him. Too bad that time had come and gone. With the jailbreak in full swing, she was pretty much screwed. The cops wouldn't understand or believe the escape hadn't been her idea. So instead of the scathing comeback he deserved, she said, "I'm serious."

Amusement sparked in his eyes. "I can see that."

"You know what I said about you being nice before?"

"Yeah."

"I take it back."

"I'm relieved. About time you pulled your head out of your . . ." Dark brows furrowed, Wick trailed off. He tilted his head, almost as if he was listening to something, and J. J. got a bad, *bad* feeling. "Shit."

Bingo. Score one for women's intuition. The intensity of his tone said it all. Trouble. A lot of it headed their way. "What is it?"

"Company." A muscle twitched along his jaw. He tugged his hand away from hers. Each breath sawing in her throat, J. J. clung a moment, then let go. As a whisper of pain returned, he met her gaze. "Whatever happens, *vanzäla,* keep your head down. Don't make a sound. It's about to get rough."

"Oh my God."

The police.

Her heart beating an erratic pace, J. J. glanced out the rear window. Nothing yet. No wail of sirens or revolving splashes of flashing lights, but she knew they were coming. It was only a matter of time before the SPD closed in and . . .

She curled her arms against her chest. God. She was so screwed. About to be caught, cuffed, and sent back to prison. For a very long time.

Dread spiraled deep, causing a nasty chain reaction. One that tightened her throat and made panic rise. Tears surfaced in an irrepressible wave. And as moisture pricked the corners of her eyes, J. J. shook her head. This wasn't happening. It *couldn't* be happening. Less than a day ago, she'd held all the hope in the world. A chance at freedom and a second start in life. And now? All her hard work lay in ruins. Wrecked by a man she didn't know, but who clearly had an agenda of his own.

Chapter Eleven

Shock absorbers working overtime, the SUV sped over another rough patch on the deserted dirt road. Tree trunks and skeletal branches flashed in Wick's periphery, casting shadows over the forest floor. Headlights turned off, his night vision pinpoint sharp, he scanned the narrow lane ahead, looking for the next turn, and almost snorted.

Lane. Right. A total exaggeration. God-awful trail was a better description.

Cursing under his breath, Wick slowed down to wheel around a rocky outcropping. Pine needles played on the windshield, jumping against glass as the front tires dipped and . . .

Bam!

Shit. Another pothole, one of many and—

A gasp sounded to his right.

A quick glance confirmed his suspicions. Jamison was in pain, tears welling in her eyes even as she tried to be brave. To ride it out without complaining or distracting him. Wick clenched his teeth, debating. What should he do . . . reach over? Take her hand again? Or say the hell with it? She was a grown female, for fuck's sake. Well past the point of baby-ing. More than able to care for herself.

Great argument. One that absolutely worked for him.

Too bad his dragon half didn't agree. The bastard kept poking him—with a barbed stick—urging him to do some-thing stupid. Like what? Murmur her name. Bridge the dis-tance over the center console to touch her. Soothe her until she believed he wasn't the enemy, but her only way out.

Totally screwed up reaction? No doubt. He wasn't any-one's knight in shining armor.

He was the other guy. The asshole in black. The one who brought death and destruction everywhere he went. The male no female wanted to be near. So the compulsion to reassure her surpassed idiotic to land in laughable. Yet, he couldn't suppress the urge. And as the beast inside him rose, he did the unthinkable. He reached out and cupped her cheek. Sky-blue eyes glistening with unshed tears, she turned her face into his touch. Her bottom lip quivered, and his heart went tight, balling up inside his chest.

Shit on a stick. He disliked her distress. Hated her fear almost as much as what he was about to do. And what did that entail? Frightening her again by showing her all his cards.

"It's bad, isn't it?" she asked, her voice less than a whis-per. "We're going to get caught."

"No, baby."

"Please don't lie to me."

Brushing his thumb over her cheek, Wick shook his head. He should've guessed she was astute. Any other time he would've admired her for it. He appreciated smart—straightforward too—but not tonight. He preferred she stay oblivious. Or better yet, went back to sleep before she got a look at what hunted them. But inevitable was just that . . . *inevitable*. Meant to be, so to speak, so he'd just have to go with it. Make the best of a bad situation while he hoped she didn't freak out and have a heart attack or something.

Static buzzed between his temples. One eye on the sky through the towering pines, Wick fired up mind-speak. *"Venom."*

"What?"

"You busy?"

"Just a tad." The shriek of claws against scales sounded. A male screamed. Venom grunted and . . . *crack!* The snap of bone echoed inside Wick's head. *"One down . . . two to go. Whatcha need?"*

"Backup." Wick cringed as the word left his mouth. He never asked for help in a firefight. He never needed any. Tonight, though, bypassed normal, heading straight into clusterfuck country. So to hell with his pride. With Jamison curled up beside him in the passenger seat, all bets were off. The more warriors to watch his six so he could protect her, the better. *"I got a trio of rogues on my ass."*

"Shite." Forge snarled and metal rattled, joining a symphony of breaking glass. A wet gurgle sounded as a male choked on his own blood. Wick's mouth curved. Dollars to donuts, the Scot had just used the sharp side of a building to gut a Razorback. *"How much time we got tae get there?"*

Hard to tell. With the forest providing cover, it might take a while for the rogues to find the opening they needed to attack. *"A couple of minutes . . . three tops."*

"J. J.?" Mac asked.

Wick drew a gentle circle on her temple. *"Scared but alive."*

"*Keep her that way.*" Venom growled. Another rogue screamed. "*Stall, Wick. Give me a minute to break free. I'll come after you.*"

Stellar plan. Except for one thing.

The forest was thinning, trees becoming scarcer by the moment. The road dipped, veering into a sloping turn and . . . fuck him. A clearing. Dead ahead.

Biting down on a curse, his gaze swept the terrain. Nowhere to go. Which meant he was headed into open space, one the rogues would use to their advantage . . . if he didn't do something. Right now.

"Jamison." He glanced out the window, gauging the distance. Shit. Three winged shadows off the driver's side. Thirty seconds out and closing fast. "Buckle your seatbelt."

"But—"

"Don't argue." His grip on her chin firmed. "Do it."

Nylon hissed as she pulled on the strap. The buckle clicked home with a snick. Wick nodded and withdrew, letting go of her to put both hands on the wheel. Moonlight shone through a break in the trees, illuminating the trail and—

Jackpot. A small alcove between a boulder and two huge redwoods. The perfect spot to shield Jamison—and hide the SUV—while he went after the assholes chasing him.

Ancient trees on either side of the road tunneled, branches curving overhead. Wick stamped on the gas pedal. The Suburban responded, rocketing toward the lip of the clearing. Small shrubs pressed in, scraping along the running boards. Jamison flinched. Wick murmured, hoping the sound of his voice would calm her. It didn't work. He smelled her fear. Felt each frantic beat of her heart. Heard each breath she took, the rasp and draw, the hitch in the back of her throat, and watched her curl into a ball in the passenger seat.

Fucking hell. The Razorbacks would pay for that. For scaring her. For causing her more pain. For the folly of hunting him while he protected a female.

A snarl locked in his throat, Wick rechecked his sight-line. So far, so good. If he timed it just right, the rogues wouldn't know what hit them.

The trailhead widened into a V, opening into a field. Long grass undulated, moving with the wind.

The lead rogue wheeled overhead.

Wick bared his teeth, half smile, half snarl. Come on. Come on. Almost there. Another few seconds, and he'd have the male right where he wanted him . . . in prime strike position and at the end of his talons.

Bright scales flashed at the end of the roadway. Eyes aglow, the enemy dragon spread his wings, stopping his flight to hang in midair, obliterating the view of the field beyond. Black horns curled over his ears, the rogue snarled. Wick tightened his grip on the steering wheel and counted off the seconds. Three. Two—

"Oh shit!" Jamison's startled cry echoed inside the truck. Her eyes went wide. Panic struck, making her scramble on the seat as she stared at the Razorback through the windshield. "Oh . . . my . . . God . . . Wick!"

The rogue inhaled past razor-sharp fangs.

One!

He hit the brakes and cranked the wheel. All-terrain tires bit, swinging the rear of the truck around. The vehicle rocked side to side. Dirt flew, arching in a circle, loam and pine needles raining against the SUV's rooftop. He heard Jamison gasp in alarm. Ignoring her, he slammed the truck in reverse and gunned the engine. Steel shrieked against stone as he sandwiched the vehicle between the boulder and the redwoods. A stream of acid flew through the air. The dragon's toxic exhale splattered the ground, then splashed over the front bumper. Bark crackled and sizzled, smoldering into smoke. Noxious fumes puffed against the SUV's grille, then rolled toward the windshield.

A millisecond—that's all it took—and Wick exited the truck.

Out. Up. And over. He landed with a thump in front of the SUV. Magic exploded, swirling around him as he shifted into dragon form. Black amber-tipped scales flowed over his body to reach his spiked tail. Dragon talons took up the cause, turning his hands and feet to razor-sharp claws. In full battle mode, he slammed the driver's door closed with his mind, enclosing Jamison inside. Her scream echoed inside his head, filling him with regret. Too bad for her. For him too. He didn't have time to go back and coddle her. Not with the Razorback poised to strike again.

In less than a second, he closed the distance. The enemy dodged, wing flapping to avoid his upward surge. Wick wanted to snort. He snarled instead. The dumb-ass. Like a complete idiot, the male hung in the kill zone, hemmed in by trees, immobile in midair, prime pickings with nowhere to go.

Tucking his wings, Wick spiraled into a sideways flip and lashed out. Halfway through the revolution, his claws caught. Dragon blood splashed up his arm. He grinned and dug in, claws cutting through scales to find muscle and bone. The Razorback flailed, fighting the lockdown and . . . oh, Nelly. The screaming never got old. Neither did inflicting the pain.

The rogue bastard. Asshole male. Threaten a female, would he?

No fucking way.

He wouldn't permit Razorback filth anywhere near Jamison. Or allow her to be hurt. Not anymore. Never again. The male deserved every ounce of agony. And as the stink of his enemy's desperation rose, Wick showed no mercy. Clamping down. Claws ripping at the rogue's throat. Ignoring the backlash of claws against the wall of his chest. The pain was nothing, but killing the rogue? That was everything. And as he took the male apart scale by scale, he reveled in dominance and, for once, honor. Tonight he fought for something greater than himself. To protect. To serve. For a female who needed him to shield her.

A death rattle rose on the night breeze.

Wick growled as the Razorback disintegrated in his grip. Ash flew like snowflakes, covering his talons, whirling over his horned head—as he searched the sky. Oh goody. There they were . . . assholes number two and three flying in fast. Leaping straight up, he unfurled his wings. The rogues attacked in tandem, tag-teaming him. He spun in midair and nailed asshole number two with his barbed tail. The rogue's head whiplashed. Using his momentum, Wick whirled around and grabbed him by the throat. He jerked his arm back. The fucker's larynx ripped from the front of his neck, coming away in Wick's talon. The rogue plummeted out of the sky, ashing out before he hit the ground. Wick pivoted, hoping—

Ah, hell. No such luck.

Asshole number three was bugging out, hauling ass over the forest, no doubt praying Wick decided not to give chase. Under normal circumstances, he would've gone after the pansy-ass. Not tonight, though. Murder and mayhem weren't the top priority. Too bad. He could've used the exercise. But with Jamison curled up in the SUV less than a hundred yards away, killing anything else tonight didn't seem like a good idea. Wick sighed and, folding his wings, set down in the middle of the field. Shit. He'd probably traumatized her. Scared her so badly she would no doubt freak out if he came anywhere near her now.

A green blur flew overhead. *"Wick. . . you clear?"*

Wick bit down on a curse. Not even close. He still had Jamison to deal with. *"Two dead. Last rogue bugged out."*

"The female?"

"Still in the truck."

Ruby eyes aglow, Venom dropped out of the sky. Scales rattling from the free fall, his friend's talons thumped down, flattening the field grass a few feet away. *"I'll get her."*

"The fuck you will."

Venom's brows popped skyward.

Wick ignored the show of surprise. He didn't want to explain. Couldn't begin to either. What the hell could he say? That his wires were crossed—tangled up, on the fritz or something—and he didn't want another male anywhere near Jamison. That if Venom approached her for any reason, he'd be forced to tear his best friend a new body orifice. Wick shook his head. Right. Like that would go over well. The entire Nightfury crew would ask questions. Razz him about his need to protect her. Demand he explain the compulsion. Not something he wanted to get into with the other warriors when he didn't understand it himself.

"Stay here." He eyeballed Venom, warning him with a look. *"Give me a minute with her."*

His best friend grimaced. *"She saw?"*

"Front row seat."

"Goddamn it."

Uh-huh. That about summed it up.

Shifting into human form, Wick conjured his clothes. Worn jeans and a T-shirt settled on his skin, and stomping shitkickers on his feet, he crossed to the dirt road. His chest went tight as the front of the SUV came into view. Her bio-energy thrummed, pulsing in her aura, making the inside of the cab glow with fiery light. The muscles along his spine tightened with each step he took. The closer he got, the more awareness expanded, folding around him, telling all he needed to know.

She was scared shitless. And he was to blame.

Approaching the passenger-side door, he glanced through the window. Ah, hell. Not good. Tucked into a fetal position, Jamison lay curled in a ball. But worse? She trembled so hard his leather jacket shivered around her. Remorse struck him chest level. Wick smothered the reaction. Emotion was a bad idea. And feeling sorry about something he couldn't change? Complete folly. It wouldn't help him, never mind her. He needed to get her moving—and head to Black Diamond.

"Jamison." Reaching out, he popped the truck door open.

Her head snapped toward him. Wide, terror-filled eyes met his. "D-don't! Don't touch me!"

"Easy." Standing in the V—between the open door and the truck frame—he held his hands out to the sides, the move one of reassurance. "It's just me . . . Wick. Remember?"

"W-wick." Huddled inside his jacket, a tear spilled over her bottom lashes. "You . . . I saw y-you. You're not . . . n-not . . ."

"Human?"

Another tear fell. "What are you?"

"Dragonkind. One of the good guys."

Incomprehension in her gaze, she shook her head. Wick didn't blame her for not believing him. He'd never been one of the *good guys*. Didn't look or act the part, so . . . she was right on the money. It was only natural for her to fear him. But that didn't change the facts. Or what he must do. And yet, he wanted to give her a moment to acclimate. A chance to understand. To come to terms with the idea that he intended to touch her again.

"Look, *vanzäla*. I know it's hard to understand, but I want you to trust me a little longer." Meeting her gaze, he stepped forward. Trapped by her injuries, hemmed in by him, she squirmed on the seat, retreating even though she had nowhere to go. He watched her a moment, feeling helpless, not knowing how to help her, then leaned in. Angling his body through the open door, he planted his hand on the center console. As she whimpered, he said, "I won't hurt you."

"Liar," she rasped. "I saw you. I saw you change into a . . . a . . ."

"Dragon?"

Her small hands made an appearance between the lapels of his jacket. Curled into twin balls of fury, she leveled her white-knuckled fists at him. Amusement sparked. Respect for her followed. Jesus. What a spitfire, a female with courage and the chops to hold her own against him. So, time to change tactics.

Wick smoothed his expression. No sense pissing her off. Laugh at her, and he knew she'd pop him with a left jab. "You wanna see your sister?"

She blinked. "You have Tania?"

"Yes." Short, sweet, and to the point . . . always the best strategy.

"If you've hurt her, I'll—"

"No need to threaten," he murmured, his respect for her rising another notch. "She's in good hands . . . mated to a friend of mine."

The news flash made her mouth fall open. Wick took advantage of her momentary confusion and, tucking her fists away, tugged his jacket closed around her. Half a second, and he scooped her up, one arm supporting her back, the other beneath her knees. A quick reverse in course. A nifty shift to the left. A tight turn, and he walked away from the truck with her in his arms. All before she could protest.

She squirmed against him.

Wick secured his hold on her. "Relax, female. It's all good."

"Relax," she said, her sarcastic tone all about "yeah, right." Face half covered by the collar, she coughed into the leather, the sound raspy with pain. "You gotta be kidding me with that crap."

His chin brushing the top of her head, Wick's mouth curved. After a moment, he gave in to impulse and grinned. He couldn't help it. He liked her moxie. Admired her for not crying like a baby too. All right, so a few tears had fallen. No big deal. Most females would be sobbing by now—be in postdragon freak-out mode or some shit. So, yeah. Jamison got full marks for keeping it together. He only hoped she continued on that track as he strode into the clearing toward his best friend.

Still in dragon form, Venom tipped his chin.

Wick nodded. Getting a load of Venom in all his scaly glory, Jamison gasped. He murmured, trying to reassure her, and called on his magic. Power sparked, warping the night air as she whispered "this isn't happening . . . oh my God, this *can't* be happening" against his shoulder. Careful to hold her gently, he shifted into dragon form. As he transferred her into his left talon, she winced, but settled fast, making him proud, slipping past his guard to touch a soft spot deep inside him.

Unprecedented. Not very smart either.

No matter how intriguing he found her, Wick refused to be lured. He wasn't wet behind the ears, a green warrior without the sense God gave him. He didn't want to feel anything for Jamison. Or be plagued by the need other males suffered for a female. He wasn't built for connection. Didn't want to experience closeness or yearn for another. He was a lone male, best suited to solitude, not to keeping a female happy.

Unfurling his wings, Wick nodded and leapt skyward. Exactly. Perfect. Excellent conclusion. A no-brainer, really. He didn't want her. She clearly harbored no liking for him. Now only one job remained . . . reach Black Diamond. The sooner he handed Jamison over to her sister, the better it would be for both of them.

❖ ❖ ❖

Hamersveld snarled as Ivar dragged him away from the female. Black eyes half-open, the tattoo bracketing his spine still glowing, the male fought the pull and reached for her again. With a muttered curse, Ivar tightened his grip and muscled the male to one side of the prison cell. Enough was enough. Tapped out already, she couldn't afford to give another ounce of energy. And the warrior in his arms didn't need anymore. But as she collapsed into an unconscious heap on the floor, he shook his head.

Hell's bells. He'd never seen anything like it. Hamersveld was voracious. So hungry, energy-greed drove him, propelling him toward female after female, KO'ing reason in favor of self-preservation.

Not surprising considering the Norwegian's condition, never mind his crash landing in the backyard. Since then, he'd gone through three HE females, mainlining energy the way an addict injects heroin. All in between salt baths. In. Out. Lift, carry . . . dunk. He'd been doing it all night, hauling the warrior away from one female after another, lifting him in and out of the tub between feedings. But that was over now. The worst had passed. At least, Ivar hoped so, 'cause . . .

God, his arms were about to give out.

Muscles screaming with fatigue, Ivar slung his new friend's arm around his shoulder. One hand gripping Hamersveld's wrist, the other around his waist, he turned toward the front of the cell. Wet skin touched his. He ignored the slip 'n slide and half carried, half dragged the male toward the glass stretched wall-to-wall across the front of the cell. Satisfaction hummed as he admired the seamlessness. Perfection in application, a clear expanse of quadruple-paned glory instead of steel bars . . . more fishbowl than prison.

Modern. Contained. The perfect cage for his exotic collection of human birds.

Pleasure filled him as he glanced at the unconscious female. Curled up on the floor, blond hair in disarray around her head, the number three was branded on the back of her shoulder. A fitting mark, one that reinforced her purpose.

She was livestock, captured for one reason . . . to breed the next generation of Dragonkind, and hopefully—if the serum he'd created proved successful—produce the first female offspring of his kind.

It was a lofty goal. A risky venture too. One he needed to work.

Science drove him. The thrill of discovery its twin as he hunted for the chromosomal sequence to unlock dragon DNA and lift the spell that cursed Dragonkind. No other outcome would be satisfactory. The promise of freedom burned deep inside him, driving him to do better. To find the answers and save his race from inevitable destruction. He'd seen the path long ago. With females of their own, Dragonkind would no longer rely on humans to survive.

And the moment that happened? He'd eliminate the inferior race. Wipe them from the face of the earth once and for all.

The pissants deserved no better. Only a horrible death would do. Why? It was simple, really. No matter how many times Mother Nature warned them, the humans refused to act responsibly. The proof lay in the pudding . . . or rather, the result. Global warming. Catastrophic weather patterns and extreme storms. Species all over the planet driven into extinction. Air pollution, ozone reduction, oil spills, and the poisoning of groundwater. The list went on and on . . . and on.

Each one when added to the next equaled one thing . . .

The rape of Planet Earth.

So, fuck 'em. He was through pulling political strings, hoping the assholes would do the right thing. The time for talking had come and gone. Nothing left to do now but find the perfect superbug. The incurable disease that would infect them one by one when released into the wilds of human society. Mass genocide via supervirus on a global scale. The perfect plan.

Flicking the lock with his mind, Ivar gave the cell exit a mental push. The glass panel slid out and to the side. Hauling Hamersveld with him, he crossed into the central corridor of cellblock A. The door closed behind him with a suctioning hiss. He barely noticed. Bare feet brushing over concrete, his focus was on one thing. The lab. He wanted to get back to his superbugs. With his pack out hunting—and his new friend practically asleep on his feet—he'd get in a few hours before dawn threatened and his soldiers arrived home.

If he hurried. And Hamersveld decided to cooperate.

Hoping beyond hope, he muscled the male through a complex series of doors. Steel dead bolts clicked, releasing only to reengage behind him. Sharp sounds echoed, the clang of doors closing along deserted corridors. As he turned into the main hallway, the male he held up twitched.

"Ivar."

"Yeah?"

"Want more." Chin bobbling, Hamersveld tried to open his eyes. His blond lashes fluttered. Ivar glimpsed the blue rimming his black irises a second before the warrior gave up and let his lids fall again. "Give me another."

"No chance of that, my friend. You're already topped up."

"Are we?"

Laboring under the Norwegian's weight, Ivar frowned. "Are we what?"

"Friends."

"After the last few hours? Hell, we'd better be," he said, only half joking. "Otherwise I'll KO your ass, scrape you into an ash bucket, and toss you into the nearest trash bin."

Hamersveld snorted. "Nah. We're friends now. Definitely. Kind of strange, though."

"Why's that?"

"Never had a friend before."

"You and me both," Ivar said, even though it wasn't true.

Lothair had been his friend—an impulsive one, sure— but a close companion nonetheless. Well, at least until his murder a few months ago. Ivar's chest went tight as he muscled Hamersveld along the corridor. God, he missed the male. Much more than he ever expected. Missed the early morning bullshit sessions. Missed having someone who shared his goals and worked hard to see them realized. Even missed making the crazy-ass SOB sandwiches after coming home from a successful raid. The bigger problem, though? No matter what he tried, he couldn't find a way around the grief. The pain remained, getting in his face, refusing to abate, damning him with each passing day.

Now, he hurt whenever he thought of Lothair.

Ivar shook his head. The result equaled a total mind-fuck. One he didn't need, never mind want.

"You sure I can't have another?"

Ivar's lips twitched. Persistent with a slaphappy helping of "ah, come on," the warrior clearly didn't have an off switch. Three females in as many hours. A record by anyone's standards, but unheard of inside the complex beneath 28 Walton Street. His new lair hadn't seen that much action. Ivar liked it that way. Only males he trusted gained entrance to his new home, and even fewer to cellblock A, where he housed his HE captives.

"How about another salt bath, instead?"

Hamersveld grumbled but shook his head. "Bed. Sleep."

Thank God. It was about time. "Just a bit farther. You can crash in my room until yours is ready."

His new friend nodded, and Ivar upped the pace, turning right toward his bedroom suite and into the main corridor. Still under construction, bare lightbulbs cast shadows across walls marred by splotches of joint compound. Soon, though, his worker bees—the forty-odd humans he'd imprisoned—would complete the project, leaving glossy wood floors and no dust behind. A minute later, Ivar stopped in front of his door. Hamersveld sagged in his arms. With a grunt, he swung the door wide. The lights flicked on, illuminating the space Ivar called his own. A place of solace for him, he loved it here. The sea grass wallpaper and bamboo floor blissed him out, helping him relax in the arms of organic cotton and eco-friendly feather-down every day.

Crossing the threshold, he flipped the duvet back with his mind and settled Hamersveld on pale sheets. Belly down, the male sighed and threw his arms wide. Pillows went flying, rolling over the side of the king-size mattress as the warrior burrowed in. A quick flick of the coverlet and . . .

Fantastic. Mission accomplished.

The newest member of the Razorbacks was covered up, bare ass no longer waving in the breeze. Good thing too. With Hamersveld sleeping it off, he could get back to business. The next superbug waited inside his laboratory, its nastiness caged inside liquid nitrogen. Pressing his chin to his chest, Ivar rubbed the back of his neck. The knots left by tension and fatigue loosened as he turned toward the door. A couple of hours . . . that's all he needed. Maybe if he played with the viral load—tweaked the dosage, upped the incubation-to-infection rate—virus number three would prove more—

A blue light flashed in his periphery.

Ivar glanced toward the flat screen TV mounted on the wall opposite him. The video chat blinked on and then off, a name written in neon at its center.

"Ah, Christ."

Lacing his fingers on top of his head, Ivar blew out a long breath. Just what he didn't need. Rodin skyping in from Prague. He'd called every week for the past month, demanding an update. Denzeil usually fielded the calls, leaving Ivar to avoid the prick along with the fallout. But with his warrior out hunting, answering the phone fell to him.

Ivar sighed. First Hamersveld, now Rodin. The night kept going from bad to worse.

Annoyance mixing with dread, he skirted the end of the bed. His bare feet brushing over bamboo planks, Ivar crossed to the laptop sitting on the marble-topped bar. A quick flick opened the computer. He tapped on the mouse and . . .

Terrific. Rodin in all his glory.

"Ivar," the male growled, dark eyes narrowed on him. "About time you answered my call. Denzeil and his trucker talk annoy me. Where have you been?"

Good to know. Another reason to keep his warrior around. "In the lab working out the viral load sequence."

"Any progress?"

"Some. I'm still unsatisfied with the results. I'll be testing another bug soon."

"Good." Fingering an expensive Mont Blanc, Rodin picked up the pen and turned it in his hand. "And the breeding program?"

"Underway on our end," he said, watching the older male closely. Rodin was after more than just an update. Sure, he asked all the right questions, but something about the way he held himself warned Ivar. The leader of the Archguard might be an ally now, but one never knew about tomorrow. "Yours?"

"We're on the hunt. I've got a dependable crew searching the city for HE females," Rodin said, the pride in his tone telling. *A dependable crew.* Right. The word choice could only mean one thing . . . Zidane, Rodin's firstborn son was involved. "So far, we've come up empty."

"Keep looking," Ivar murmured. "If you find one, you'll find more. HEs gravitate toward one another. They tend to be related or live together."

Rodin grunted and changed the subject. "How's your cash flow?"

"I could use more."

"You always want more."

Ivar shrugged. "Science is an expensive sport."

"A bloody one, I hear."

"It's better that way."

The male huffed. "I knew there was a reason I like you."

"Just working with what God gave me."

A sparkle lit in Rodin's eyes. Ivar narrowed his and unleashed what he did best. Analysis. Ferreting out facts. Putting each into context. Funny, but . . . huh. He swore the gleam in the older male's eyes approached paternal pride. A strange thing considering Rodin was as cold-blooded as they came. Hell, the prick had never looked at Lothair that way, and his late XO had been Rodin's youngest son.

Turning his head to one side, Rodin tapped his pen against the keyboard. "Check your accounts. I just wired you another half mill."

"In exchange for?"

"Information and . . . your honesty."

Weighing the pros and cons, Ivar examined the idea, searching for pitfalls. Truth, after all, was a tricky beast. It owned varying shades of gray. The kind a male could manipulate if he were smart enough to see the shift in color. "What is it you wish to know?"

"I hear there is a member of the Scottish pack in Seattle."

Ivar frowned, not liking the implication in the inquiry. The intel was far too accurate. Forge, the only Scot he knew, had arrived a few months ago. The warrior had briefly danced to the Razorback tune before switching alliances to join the Nightfury pack. The loss still rankled, leaving a bad taste in Ivar's mouth. Clenching his teeth, he bit down on a snarl. The backstabbing Scot had promised one thing, but delivered quite another.

The lying bastard. Forge had screwed with his plans.

Not that it mattered now. The past belonged where it already sat . . . in the *past*. He couldn't change it. The future, however? Hmm, that bad boy was up for grabs, which meant he must be careful. Rodin's interest in Forge—and how he'd come by the information—raised his internal radar. Something was off. Way, way off, 'cause . . . shit. It sounded as though the leader of the Archguard had a spy inside the Razorback ranks.

Not surprising. But by no means good either.

In order to function well, Ivar needed less scrutiny, not more. So, what to do, what to do? Share the information or stonewall Rodin? Misdirection, after all, was his specialty.

Ivar debated a moment, determining the course that would best service him and—

Why not? "His name is Forge. He is a member of the Nightfury pack."

"One of Bastian's warriors now," Rodin said, his pallor turning ashen.

Ivar nodded, wondering at Rodin's reaction. The male didn't scare easily. He knew it firsthand. Had witnessed the older male wield his power while under the Archguard's thumb. But something about the Bastian/Forge connection shook the male from his lofty perch.

Interesting. Maybe even fortuitous.

With Rodin shaken up, now might be the time to cut through all the bullshit, get straight to the point, and reveal Lothair's death.

He'd held onto the information, hiding the truth for fear of Rodin's wrath. Not against him. Ivar could handle whatever the asshole sent his way. What he didn't want was the male in Seattle. He needed to avenge his best friend without any outside interference. And Rodin, with one of his death squads in tow, amounted to a serious disruption.

"One other thing you should know, Rodin."

Dark eyes snapped back to his.

"Lothair is dead . . . murdered by the Nightfuries."

Rodin snarled, baring his teeth as rage flamed in his gaze. Raising his hands, he slammed both fists against the desktop. Wood crackled. The computer jumped, jarring the image. With a roar of fury, the male exploded in a flurry of movement. Mouth hanging wide open, Ivar watched the leader of the Archguard lose control from halfway around the world. A blurry swipe of arms, a brutal thrust of a booted foot, and . . . slam-bang! Lift off. The desk toppled, sending the computer tumbling end over end. Pale walls whirled past in the frenzy. The screen slammed into something. Static came through the breach, replacing the picture as the connection shattered.

Chapter Twelve

Ahead of the pack, Venom came down through the clouds like a serial killer in search of his next victim. Alert. Focused. Watchful. Too bad he didn't have a target. He'd left all hope of one behind in the city . . . along with the rogues. Now nothing but thick forest stretched out for miles, staring up at him as a storm gathered in the sky above him. Rain threatened, the distant rumble of thunder a warning, the thick mist that hung over the land another.

Condensation gathered, wicking off his scales as he glanced over his shoulder. His gaze landed on the warriors flying in his wake. Venom's mouth curved. Man, what a sight. Symmetry in motion, his brothers assembled behind him, a lethal collection of kick-ass flying in perfect formation. The forest thinned in front of them. A rock face rose, jutting out at odd angles into the night sky. Angling his wings, Venom banked into a tight turn. Curls of air swirled from his wing-tips, rushing over the side of the cliff. Shale rattled and let go, tumbling down the rocky outcropping as he flipped into a fast roll and rocketed over the beachhead. Settling into a smooth glide over the river, he followed the snake-like flow, his gaze on the surface of the water below.

Another round of thunder rumbled overhead.

The first raindrop hit, splattering over one of his horns. Sensation swirled at his temples as Wick fired up mind-speak.

"Mac."

"Yeah?"

"Delay the waterworks."

The female cradled in one of his talons, Wick raised the other, curling it over her head, protecting her from rain. Magic gathered between his friend's claws. Venom frowned. Holy jeez. His friend's reaction to her was bizarre. Way beyond the pale. Outside his usual boundaries, using his body heat and a spell to keep her warm.

Good for J. J. Confusing as hell for him. He'd never seen Wick act so . . . so . . . goddamn protective. Of anyone.

Tucking her closer, Wick shielded her from the rising wind. *"I don't want her to get wet."*

Forge grunted. *"Tae chilly for her."*

"Got that covered." More warmth rose to surround J. J., creating a bubble-like barrier around Wick's claws. *"But her cast—"*

"On it." Bladed spine glinting in the storm flash, Mac murmured a command. Magic flared, and water droplets evaporated into thin air. The blackening sky froze, as though pausing mid-breath, cutting off the sound of thunder. *"I'll deal with the waterfall too."*

Good plan. They were almost home.

The river rushed into a 45-degree turn.

Increasing his wing speed, Venom wheeled around the corner. Majestic and full, the waterfall cascaded from three hundred feet up, roaring toward the river below. Mist bellowed, rising in wet clouds, tumbling into spray as each tendril reached for the sky. Upon approach, Mac did his thing, suppressing the drizzle, subduing the fog and . . .

The waterfall split in half, parting like curtains.

"Shite . . . would you look at that?" Purple scales flashing, Forge broke formation, dipping in behind Wick. The others followed suit, abandoning the fighting triangle to form a single line.

"Like it," Sloan said, rotating into a slow flip at the rear of the procession. *"Wicked move."*

Mac laughed.

Wick growled in approval.

Venom grinned, agreeing without hesitation. Their resident water dragon deserved the accolade. The move was *wicked.* He liked the cause and effect. No splashdown. No wet scales or chilly blow back. Just clear sailing as he went wings vertical. The sound of rushing water roared in his ears. His heartbeat picked up as he threaded the needle— slicing through the opening, wet curtain flowing on either side of him—and rocketed into the underground tunnel. Musty air rushed at him. Complete darkness descended. His senses spiked, narrowing until his night vision took over. The red glow of his gaze rolled out in front of him, guiding him, illuminating the darkness, allowing him to see each jagged edge.

Navigating the tight space, Venom banked into the last turn. A soft yellow glow penetrated the gloom, narrowing his flight path. He closed the distance and flew into the cavern. The domed ceiling rose above him. Held aloft by magic, light globes bobbed, bumping into each other seventy-five feet above his head. Quick on the trigger, he tucked his wings and set down fast.

The pads of his talons slid against stone.

Venom dug in and, claws shrieking, shifted into human form mid-skid. With a mental flick, he conjured his clothes and hightailed it to the rear of the landing zone. Standing around wasn't a good idea. Not with the lethal group hot on his heels. His pack would turn him into a bowling pin— eighty-six his ass as each one landed—if he didn't get out of the way. The LZ might be long, wide, deep, so expansive it launched four dragons at a time, but . . .

Hell. He'd chosen to lead the flight home. Which made him lucky number five tonight.

Circling around the Honda in the middle of the LZ, Venom watched his brothers-in-arms rocket into the cave. True to form, Mac and Forge landed in tandem at opposite ends of the platform, leaving lots of room for the final two. As both warriors transformed, stomping their feet into their shitkickers, Wick flew in with Sloan on his tail. The work of seconds, his best friend set down. Poised on his back paws, Wick wing flapped once and shifted into human form. Sinking to his knees on the stone floor, he wrapped his arms around J. J.

Cradled in his lap with her eyes squeezed shut, her bottom lip quivered.

"It's all right," Wick said, his tone soft and sure. "Jamison . . . look at me."

She shook her head.

Venom's heart sank. God, she looked so small. So pale bundled inside the harsh black of the too-large leather jacket. Way too scared to weather the storm and come through unscathed.

Not that he blamed Wick for her near panic.

His best friend was doing all he could—holding her gently, using a reassuring tone, being sympathetic instead of sociopathic . . . acting like a normal male might under similar circumstances. But Venom knew the truth. Wick wasn't *normal*. Honed by brutality and abuse, the male wasn't equipped to interact with a female, never mind give her what she needed. And any minute now? His friend would freak out. Lose his cool. React as he always did when faced with a female.

The realization drew Venom tight. He needed to step in. Step up. Intercede and neutralize Wick in order to save J. J. from additional pain, but . . . hell. Convincing Wick to release her wasn't going to be fun.

Rolling his shoulders, Venom fisted his hands, then uncurled his fingers and repeated the process. Flex. Release. Open. Close. The movement helped him think. Strategy was paramount when it came to Wick. If he moved too fast, his friend would fight. If he didn't move fast enough, J. J. would suffer the consequences. Not something he wanted to contemplate, never mind explain to his commander. Bastian might be reasonable—well, at least most of the time—but fact was *fact*. B didn't tolerate ineptitude, never mind idiocy. His commander appreciated neat and enjoyed tidy.

Especially when it came to protecting females.

So . . . yeah. No time like the present to put his ass in gear. The sooner Wick handed her over, the better it would be for—

"*Venom.*" The deep voice thumped the inside of his skull.

As the vicious vibe played ping-pong between his temples, Venom sighed. Great. Just perfect. Exactly what he didn't need. "*Yeah, B?*"

"*What's taking so long?*"

His gaze cut to the couple intertwined a few feet away. "*Got a bit of a situation.*"

"*Well, figure it out,*" Bastian said, impatience in his tone. "*My female's wearing the soles of her shoes thin in here, begging me to open the portal. No way I'm doing that until I know it's kosher out there.*"

Venom stifled a snort. *Kosher?* Right. The word didn't come close to describing the situation. Not with Wick playing keep-away with a female.

"*How's Tania?*" Mac asked.

Bastian snorted. "*On a hair trigger.*"

"*Hold on.*" As Mac jogged across the LZ, the thud-thud of his boots echoed in the vastness, making the light globes sway above their heads. Stone dust drifted from the ceiling, sprinkling Venom's shoulders as Mac engaged the energy shield that protected Black Diamond, hiding their home from outsiders. Static electricity buzzed. The cave wall rippled, opening the magical doorway into the underground lair. "*I'm coming.*"

"*Thank fuck,*" Bastian murmured. "*I don't know what to do with her.*"

Venom could relate. He didn't know what to do with Wick either.

Looking for help, he glanced in Sloan's direction. Shitkickers planted beside the decapitated Honda, his buddy shrugged and turned his hands palm up, the gesture one of "how the hell should I know?" Wonderful. No help from that quarter, but maybe . . .

Glancing over his shoulder, he met Forge's gaze.

The Scot shook his head. "*Donnae look at me, lad. You know him better than anyone.*"

True enough. "*Give me the floor, guys. I'll get him moving.*"

As the guys "uh-huhed" and beat feet toward the exit, Venom strode in the opposite direction. A couple of feet from his target, he crouched in front of his best friend. "Wick, let me—"

"Tell me what to do, Ven."

Venom blinked, not understanding.

"I don't know how to soothe her." Nestling his cheek against the top of J. J.'s head, Wick met his gaze. Venom flinched, getting nailed by the concern in his friend's eyes along with, well . . . something else too. Panic maybe? Worry too? Wick's expression bordered on both. Except that didn't make any sense. Nothing made Wick lose his cool. Ever. "You're good at this shit. Tell me what to do."

He wanted to say "give her to me," but knew that wouldn't fly. Wick was too tense, and after getting told not to touch her in the park? He didn't like his chances of surviving a hostile takeover. Wick would fight to keep her, and . . . yeah. All of a sudden—and as strange as it sounded—helping his friend care for her seemed like a better option than taking her away.

A healthier one too.

"Keep talking to her." Balanced on the balls of his feet, Venom rested his elbows on the tops of his thighs. "You're doing fine."

"Should I . . . I mean . . ." Wick trailed off, his hesitation palpable. "Touch her or something?"

Like a sucker punch to the gut, the question stole his air and . . . holy hell. The situation had just gone from semi-weird to full-on sci-fi. "Do you want to?"

"I don't know. Maybe." Frowning, Wick broke eye contact, looking lost—so confused it broke Venom's heart. So damaged. So unsure. So stuck in the past. His friend was the poster boy for abuse. But as he stared at Wick, realization struck. He stood on a precipice, the defining moment that might change Wick's life. Right here. Right now. Surrounded by stone and musty air, possibility held Wick in the palm of its hand. Venom recognized the opportunity. Saw the difference in the male he'd known almost all his life. Wick wanted to help—to give of himself—instead of turn away. "She liked holding my hand in the truck. Said it helped with the pain."

Venom cleared his throat. "Then go for it."

"All right."

Inhaling deep, Wick exhaled smooth and raised his hand. His fingertips stroked over her temple, brushing the thick strands of dark hair away from her face. With a sigh, J. J. stirred, turning into the touch instead of away. Another gentle caress across her skin. Her bio-energy flared, nearly blinding Venom with the fiery pulse in her aura. He turned his face away to shield his eyes. The Meridian hummed, rising in a powerful wave to forge a connection between the two.

Venom's mouth fell open. Goddamn. Talk about insane, bizarre . . . whatever. The descriptor didn't matter. The sudden flare-up, however? Jeez. That mattered. Without knowing it, Wick was feeding her: opening an energy channel, letting her link in, nourishing her with the healing flow drawn from the Meridian.

"*Vanzäla,*" Wick murmured, cupping her cheek, giving Venom another shock as he called her songbird in Dragonese. He shook his head. Wick didn't notice. All his focus on J. J., he caressed her again. "Open your eyes and look at me."

She shivered, trembling in Wick's arms.

"Come on, baby."

Wet lashes fluttered, lifting to reveal brilliant blue irises. "You're back."

Wick stroked along her jaw. "I never left."

"Yes, you did," she whispered. "How did you do it?"

"What . . . shift forms?"

She nodded.

"Dragon DNA," Wick said, giving her the simplest answer.

"Figures, I guess, since you turned into one." Wick traced the fine arch of her eyebrow, then changed tact to caress her cheek. With a hum, J. J. turned her head, seeking more of his friend's touch. "You scared me."

"I know."

"Please don't do that again."

Wick huffed. "I'll try."

"Good," she said, and Venom cringed.

Goddamn it. The exchange made him feel like a first-class heel. Like a voyeur, butting in where he didn't belong. It was beyond awkward, starting to border on embarrassing now. Venom shifted on the balls of his feet. He wanted to turn and walk away. Leave the situation behind and never look back. The strategy was a good one, except for one problem.

He couldn't leave.

Duty called. Honor rode shotgun, refusing to give him a get-out-of-jail-free card. He'd given his word. Bastian expected him to get the pair inside the lair. Which left him playing monkey in the middle, baring witness to an intimate moment between two people so absorbed in each other they'd forgotten he existed.

Venom cleared his throat, hoping to break up the party.

J. J. ignored him. Raising her hand, she touched her fingertip to the corner of Wick's mouth. His friend tensed, but stayed true, allowing her to touch him. She drew a soft circle on his skin. In reaction, Wick's gaze began to glow. "You're not human."

"Half," Wick said. "We're a different species."

"Oh," she said, a frown on her face. The expression pained Venom. It made her look as though she carried the weight of the world on her shoulders. Not something any female should be made to do. "Hey, Wick?"

"Yeah."

"I'm really tired." As though admitting the truth elevated her fatigue, her body gave out. She dropped her hand, tucking it back in her lap. Pressing her face to Wick's shoulder, her eyes drifted closed. "I can't think anymore. I'm just . . . done."

Wick nodded, even though she couldn't see him anymore. "Sleep, *vanzäla*. You'll feel better."

"Promise me something?"

"What?"

"Don't leave me alone with strangers," she whispered, strain in her tone. "Promise you'll be here when I wake up."

"You don't need me." Shifting her in his arms, Wick pushed to his feet. The movement was smooth, measured, designed for her comfort. "Your sister will—"

"Please?"

The whispered plea tipped the balance. Folding like a bad poker hand, Wick gave it up, promising her as exhaustion drew J. J. into slumber. Cradling her close, Wick strode across the LZ. Venom followed, trailing his friend, wondering what the hell had just happened. None of it made sense. Not Wick's reaction to J. J. Not her lack of fear or her acceptance of a male most females avoided at every turn. Not the wretched sense of loss Venom suffered in the aftermath of their exchange either.

His response was screwed up. Completely backward, it smacked of selfishness. He should be happy for his friend, not feel uptight, out of sorts, and . . . yes . . . even a bit jealous of Wick's good fortune.

Knowing it, though, didn't stop envy from grabbing hold. And as Venom walked across the LZ, he couldn't deny the emotion. He'd been displaced . . . shoved aside and replaced. After sixty years together—of relying solely on each other—he was about to lose his best friend. To a female.

Instinct warned him. Logic hammered the truth home.

Energy-fuse was serious stuff, a magical bond, a connection that only occurred when a male's dragon half found its mate. Not exactly something a male could fight. At least not for very long. B, Rikar, and Mac were proof enough of that, which meant sooner or later Wick would succumb too. The realization reached deep, made him ache from the inside out, stirring up ugly emotion.

Everything was about to change.

And Venom knew . . . just *knew* . . . it wouldn't be for the better.

❂ ❂ ❂

A warm bundle, Jamison lay like a gift in his arms. So relaxed. Too trusting. Beyond precious. Wick clenched his teeth, his footfalls echoing as he approached the magical barrier into Black Diamond. At some point in the last few hours, he'd lost his mind. It was the only explanation for his behavior, never mind his promise. Add that to the fact he kept likening her to a *gift* and . . .

Jesus. No doubt about it. He needed his ass kicked. Or his brain rebooted. One or the other, and in the next few minutes. Otherwise, he'd suffer another short circuit and wade even further into the land of holy fuck. A huge first for him.

Like that damned promise.

Wick cringed. He never should've given his word. Being there when she woke up wasn't a good idea. A clean break would be better for all concerned. But oh no, he'd deviated from the plan. Now he was hemmed in, stuck between two schools of thought, which . . . oh goody . . . happened to be polar opposites.

Help or hinder. Keep his promise or head for safer ground.

He couldn't do both. Couldn't stay and go at the same time, and as opposing forces stretched him thin, his head started to pound. He cradled Jamison closer, looking for guidance, fighting the urge to bail on her, wishing he wasn't so screwed up. A normal male would know what to do to make it right for her. He huffed. *Normal.* Right. As if. He didn't know what ordinary entailed. Or how to act the part.

Case in point? Jamison needed gentle. He'd never been kindhearted or soft-handed in his life. She required care and comfort. He didn't have the first clue about how to deliver either. She trusted him to keep his word and be there for her. He couldn't wait to put her down and beat feet in the other direction.

The comparisons made his stomach cramp.

Fucking hell. He deserved to be drawn and quartered. Hung by his entrails. Taken out and shot. Take your pick.

The method of torture didn't matter. Not while he contemplated betraying her trust. Abandonment with the backlash of duplicity. God help him, he hated the mere idea of it. But fact was just that . . . *fact*. If he broke his word, he was nothing but a first-class cheat. A betrayer. A coward for abandoning the credo he'd lived by all his life. Granted, the list of principles was a short one, but at the top sat one unbendable dictate—a promise made was a promise kept.

Wick sighed. Shit. He couldn't do it. Jamison was too important. Honor demanded he finish what he started. His dragon half concurred, refusing to let him retreat or cause her any more pain.

So . . . here he went, veering away from safe and straight into fucked up.

Adjusting his hold on her, Wick unleashed his magic and engaged the energy shield. Static crackled, prickling over his skin as the cave wall reacted. Solid stone rippled, turning milky white. Wick drew in another breath. Time to face the music and the females on the other side of the wall. Tania and Myst were waiting. He registered their presence inside the lair. Frustration poured off both, sending out a vibe that polluted the air as each paced, ready to tear a strip off him for keeping Jamison out on the LZ so long. Normal, he guessed. From what he knew, females liked to worry. Enjoyed coddling people too.

Not a bad thing. He was glad they cared about Jamison. But that didn't mean he wanted either of them in his grill the second he strode over the threshold. So . . . new plan. One that would provide some breathing room. Enough to get him inside the clinic instead of accosted in the corridor.

He fired up mind-speak. *"Mac."*

"You coming through?"

"Yeah."

Raising a mental fist, he thumped on the energy shield, requesting safe passage. Another major first tonight. Usually, he blasted his way through, challenging the magic that safeguarded Black Diamond from outsiders. The provocation was a test of sorts—a way to make sure the shield continued to do its job, one that played out the same way. The pissy thing enjoyed taking a chunk out of him every time he walked into the lair. Wick tucked his female closer, hoping the shield would take a pass tonight.

He didn't need another lesson. Or any of the spell's usual bullshit.

Jamison was already hurting. Was far too fragile to be treated to another round of pain, never mind the magical tantrum the energy shield loved to deliver.

Rolling his shoulders, Wick got ready anyway. One never knew. The shield had a mind of its own. No sense underestimating the thing. *"Make sure the females stay in the clinic."*

"Already done," Mac said, a female voice rising in the background. Wick's lips twitched. Wow, she didn't sound happy and . . . Mac cursed. A scraping noise came through the cosmic connection, echoing inside Wick's head as his comrade grunted. The scuffle continued a moment before all went quiet. *"I got her. You're good to go."*

Murmuring a "thanks," Wick knocked on the portal again. Magic hummed. Energy surged, kicking up dust motes in the musty air. Wick kept walking, his pace smooth and even, his gaze glued to the ripple of light in front of the solid stone. One moment slid into another and—

The shield snarled and stared out through narrowed eyes, locked onto him from within the void. Adrenaline punched through. His heartbeat picked up the pace, hammering the inside of his chest. Looping his magic end over end, he cocooned Jamison, leaving himself vulnerable as he stepped into the breach. A growl rumbled through the quiet, and Wick tensed. Any moment now, he'd see the flash and hear the whistle of—

Full of fury, the blue flame of a magical whip exploded across the abyss.

Right on his heels, Venom cursed behind him.

Upping the pace, Wick ramped into a run. Legs pumping, breath sawing in his chest, he watched the sharp multi-headed lash slice through the air. He turned his back to take the brunt. A second before the magical cat-o'-nine struck, the spell shifted focus, zeroing in on the female in his arms. Oh shit. Not good. The beast didn't permit outsiders and . . .

Jamison twitched against him.

Wick bared his teeth. No way. Not going to happen. If the shield so much as touched her, he'd make it pay. Just KO the motherfucker. Rip it apart without conscience or mercy . . . Black Diamond and his brothers-in-arms' reactions be damned. But as he held the line, threatening without words, the spell paused. Magic cracked like thunder. Wick felt the shift in intention a second before the beast reversed course. The whip swung wide, missing him by inches, and whirled away. The fiery tendrils vanished with a loud pop as it shoved him out the other side.

Light flared. The scent of pine floor cleaner reached him. His feet thumped down. Fighting to keep his balance, Wick cursed as his combat boots slid on polished concrete.

"Holy shit." Shifting mid-stride, Rikar scrambled out of his way.

Breathing hard, Wick skidded to a stop in the middle of the corridor. Shock riding shotgun, he stood rooted to the floor. *Holy shit,* indeed. Crazy too, considering the energy shield had left him untouched. He glanced down at Jamison. Relief rolled through him. Fast asleep in his arms, she was none the worse for wear. He tapped into her bio-energy anyway, wanting to make sure. Heartbeat steady. Energy levels good. Each breath soft and even.

Thank God.

"Christ, I hate it when you do that." The grumble came from his right.

Glancing away from the top of her head, he met Rikar's gaze.

A sour look on his puss, his XO glared at him. "Stop provoking it, and the bastard might let you through without trying to kill you every once in a while."

"That work for you?"

"Never mind." Amusement sparked in Rikar's pale eyes. His mouth curved in response. He couldn't help it. Despite the fact his XO enjoyed razzing him, he liked the tough-minded SOB. He was lethal in a fight and loyal to a fault, the kind of warrior a male wanted watching his six. "Nasty fucking thing. Always will be."

With an "uh-huh," Wick put his boots to good use and headed for the clinic.

"How is she?"

"Alive."

Rikar huffed. "Always a bonus."

No kidding. A big one too, considering the alternative. The idea of her dead, laid out on a cold slab somewhere, made his skin crawl. He didn't want to imagine the possibility, never mind entertain it.

A few hours ago, it hadn't mattered.

Rescuing her started out as a lark. A challenge in the form of a jailbreak. Now, though—after meeting her, holding her . . . talking to her—it mattered a whole hell of a lot. More than he wanted to admit. Which cranked his screw the wrong way. His fixation on her couldn't be healthy. It was too raw. Too intense. Smacked too much of obsession to be anything other than bad. And yet, even knowing the danger, Wick couldn't shake the fascination. Like a moth to a flame, he yearned to move toward the inferno—feel the heat, touch the flame, experience the burn—instead of doing the smart thing and back away.

The very definition of insanity.

Bypassing Rikar in the corridor, Wick strode up the slight incline. Roughhewn walls led the way, moving him past scarred stone toward his salvation. The clinic lay just ahead. Soon, he'd be able to put her down. To relinquish his responsibility, set Jamison in capable hands, and reclaim his sanity. He needed to leave her behind. Balance. Peace. A lot of quiet. Severing their connection—all the energy flowing between them—would provide all three. Retreating into the silence of his room—isolating himself from the others—would help too. But even as he acknowledged the wisdom of the plan, Wick battled the urge to hold on tight and . . .

Never let her go.

God, he was messed up. Beyond confused. And as Rikar kept pace alongside him, Wick considered asking the male for advice. The warrior knew a lot about females. He was mated to one, for Christ's sake, and well . . . Angela seemed happy enough. So yeah. Rikar would no doubt make an excellent mentor. His XO wouldn't bullshit him, but as Wick opened his mouth to ask, his throat closed, and he clammed up. He didn't know how to broach the subject, never mind word it right. Shit, he was an emotional illiterate—stunted, unsure of himself, incapable of reaching out for help—so instead of asking, he shut it down, abandoning difficult in favor of easy.

"Myst ready for us?"

"Triage is set up," Rikar said, his boots thudding in concert with Wick's. Running a critical eye over Jamison, he raised a brow. "Not sure the female's gonna need it, though. She looks pretty good, all things—"

The energy shield snapped behind them.

"Goddamn it!"

Wick grinned. Things were about to get interesting. About time too. Venom had been right behind him upon entry. He should've come through the portal long before now.

Venom snarled as the beast spit him out. Velocity set to breakneck, he flew into the corridor, head and shoulders leading the way. Twisting in midair, arms and legs pinwheeling, he struggled to get his feet under him.

"Christ." With a wince, Rikar grimaced. "Did I say nasty earlier?"

"You did," Wick said, watching his friend's free-for-all scramble.

Cursing a blue streak, Venom landed with a thud. Forward momentum made him slide. Wick winced as he collided with the stone wall. Rolling belly-up on the floor, Venom groaned, "Son of a bitch."

"Whatcha think, Wick?"

"Eight out of ten. He didn't stick the landing."

"Nice," Venom said, sarcasm out in full force. Looking ready to kill something, he pushed to his feet. As he dusted himself off, he grumbled, "How can I hate that thing, yet love it at the same time?"

Rikar laughed.

Wick fought an eye roll, but as he continued walking, the contrast wasn't lost on him. Love and hate. Polar opposites that created one helluva combination. One he now owned when it came to Jamison. Not that he hated her. Far from it. The way she made him feel—confused, uptight . . . out of control—wasn't her fault. She'd done nothing wrong. The defect belonged to him. He was the damaged one, not her.

And yet, he continued to feed her . . . even though he knew he shouldn't. It would only bring him more grief in the end. Too bad his dragon didn't care. Despite his will to control it, instinct won out over common sense, and he submitted, allowing her to take from him. Without ever putting up a fight. She needed him too much, and as strange as it seemed, he couldn't deny her, increasing the flow of healing energy the moment she asked for more.

Awful. Complicated. Undesirable.

All three applied, turning him inside out.

Throat gone tight, Wick shook his head. He was in big trouble, the kind that came with a label . . . energy-fuse. The realization cracked him wide open, making him feel sick. But even as his stomach clenched, he rejected the truth. Impossible. The conclusion couldn't be right. He was a soulless bastard, well past the point of saving. Intimacy wasn't his thing. He didn't want it to be either. Every ounce of kindness—along with the instinct that drove a Dragonkind male to mate—had been beaten out of him years ago.

And honestly? He liked it that way.

Detachment allowed him to do his job. Had shaped him into the kind of warrior his brothers valued, needed, and expected him to be—a natural born killer without conscience or mercy. He didn't want what the other Nightfuries shared with their chosen females. Juggling a relationship and his responsibilities as a warrior didn't belong in his lexicon. The first would distract him from the second, ensuring he failed at both.

It all came down to one thing . . .

Choice.

He'd made one years ago when he joined the Nightfury pack. His brothers—his vow to protect each—came before all else. Bewitching females included. So enough foolishness. His attraction to Jamison must die a swift, unholy death. No good would come from straying from a path already taken.

Air hissed as the glass door to the medical clinic slid open.

In a state of complete panic, Tania shot over the threshold. Time slowed as she pivoted toward him, spinning into an endless stretch. Horror darkened her brown eyes. Wick wiped his expression clean, preparing for the worst. Mac's female didn't like him. She'd made it clear that he frightened her . . . even though he hadn't done a thing to make her fear him. He was who he was: quiet, reserved, so baffled by social situations he never knew what to say, never mind how to make someone like him. Wick understood the truth of it . . . accepted it too. Most females reacted to him the same way, but as tears pooled in Tania's eyes, Wick suddenly wished he wasn't so inept.

A few well-placed words would no doubt reassure her, but—

"Oh my God . . . oh God. Mac!" Her terror-filled rasp wrung Wick out, twisting his insides into knots as Tania froze in the middle of the corridor. Her gaze glued to him, both feet rooted to the floor, she shook her head. "She's dead, isn't she? You . . . you . . . oh God, you—"

Wick growled, cutting her off mid-accusation. How typical. Tania thought he'd killed her fucking sister. Her reaction pissed him off, even though it shouldn't have. The conclusion wasn't a bad one considering his reputation and temperament. Toss in his propensity for violence, and . . .

Ah, hell. Her assumption made a certain amount of sense.

"She's isn't dead, female."

Tania blinked. "But—"

"Motherfuck." Mac growled, stepping out of the clinic behind his female. "Tania, I told you to stay put."

"I can't . . . I couldn't," she whispered. "Why isn't she moving? Why does he have her? You promised . . . you said she was okay."

"She is, honey. Your sister's been injured. She's exhausted . . . sleeping hard, that's all." Throwing him an apologetic look, Mac cupped her shoulders and tugged Tania into his arms. As her back met his chest, he wrapped her tight against him. "Wick saved J. J.'s life tonight. He's taken good care of her. You owe him an—"

"Thank you," she said, cutting off her mate mid-scold. Eyes still huge in her small face, she met his gaze, and Wick blinked. Wow, would you look at that? Tania had never looked at him before, never mind spoken to him. Both were huge firsts, and she didn't stop there. "I'm sorry, Wick. Please forgive me, I didn't mean to . . . it's just I've been so worried and . . ." Tears escaped, rolling down her cheeks. "Thank you. Thank you for bringing her home."

"You're welcome," he murmured, reciprocating for once, giving Tania her due. It was only fair. Courage, after all, deserved acknowledgement. "She's all right, Tania. A little banged up, but it's nothing time won't heal."

A lie. Boldly told and beautifully delivered.

No one knew better than him that time didn't heal all wounds. Jamison would heal from the physical trauma, no question. The healing energy he shared with her would see to that, but five years spent in prison damaged a person. Readjusting to being on the outside—to the real world and her newfound freedom—would take more than just time. Pile on surviving a vicious knife attack and witnessing a dragon battle on top of that and . . . yeah.

D-day. Detonation inevitable. Psychological scarring times ten.

Movement flashed in his periphery.

Glancing through the open door, he spotted Myst inside the clinic. Snapping her rubber gloves in place, B's female tilted her head, inviting him inside. "I'm ready. Bring her in."

With a nod, Wick crossed the threshold. Shitkickers rasping across the industrial-grade hospital floor, he eyed the examination table. Warrior-sized, the surface stretched beneath the bright overhead lights. Stainless steel cabinets rose beyond the setup, hugging the back wall, framing the female who now stood alongside the stretch of cabinetry. The scent of antiseptic soap added to the medical ambiance, making his nose twitch and his heart hammer.

Different night. Same story.

Except that wasn't quite true.

The medical supplies laid out in tidy rows on the rollaway cart weren't for him. Or one of his brothers. Not right now. Tonight, each plastic-wrapped package—all those metal tools along with the stethoscope and blood pressure cuff—belonged to Jamison. The thought bored a hole through his breastbone, piercing his heart. All of a sudden, Wick couldn't breathe. Jesus. He didn't want to put her down . . . or leave her here all by herself.

Totally ridiculous, considering who stood in the room.

Myst would take good care of her. Treat her with kid gloves and gentle hands, ensure Jamison received all she needed to heal. But as Wick stopped beside the table—seeing all the bandages and other packages up close—something snapped deep inside him. He felt the splintering shock wave. Heard the roar of denial along with the blood rush in his ears. The throb hammered his temples. Wick shook his head, fighting the buzzing surge of awareness, and waged an internal war. Logic told him to put her down. The territorial bastard inside him overrode the system, unleashing a torrent of possessiveness.

Shit. He couldn't do it. Couldn't relinquish—

"Wick."

The sharpness of Myst's tone brought his chin up. She nailed him with serious violet eyes. "I need you to put her down. "

Holding onto Jamison like a greedy two-year-old, he shook his head.

"Trust me . . . I know what I'm doing."

"I know," he rasped, not doubting her skill for a moment. The female possessed a shitload of know-how. She sewed up the Nightfury warriors on a regular basis. Hell, Venom owed his life to Myst and her talent with a needle.

But relinquishing Jamison wasn't about that. It was about something more. Duty, maybe. Honor, certainly. A strange sense of entitlement too, 'cause . . . God. After caring for her the last couple of hours, abandoning her to another's care seemed, well . . . wrong. "I'm just . . ."

"I get it. I really do, but I need to examine her. Make sure the hospital did their job, and she wasn't reinjured on the way here." Reaching out, she patted the top of the examination table. The sheet rustled, crinkling under the gentle pressure, ratcheting his tension up another notch. His dragon urged him to hold on. Myst wanted him to let go, and as Tania stopped at the head of the table, backing up her friend, denial rose on a violent wave. "One of us will come get you if she needs you. Deal?"

Wick hesitated. A big hand landed on his shoulder, giving him a gentle squeeze. Thank God. Venom. Trust his best friend to arrive in the nick of time. The male always helped him pull his head out of his ass.

Exhaling hard, he unlocked his muscles. The cage he made with his embrace opened, and just like that, it was done. His arms were empty. Jamison lay on the table: his leather jacket half covering her face, the blanket twisted around her hips, plaster cast sticking out to expose her bare toes. The sight tipped the balance. Pressure banded around his rib cage, making it hard to breathe. So fragile . . . too many bruises . . . beyond vulnerable without him to protect her.

Venom pumped his shoulder again.

He shrugged, throwing off the hold, and cleared his throat. "I'll come back later."

"Good. She'll need you," Myst said, somehow managing to reassure and praise him at the same time. How the hell she did that, Wick didn't know, but he said a silent "thank you" anyway. Her no-nonsense tone eased his worry, smoothed down the ragged edges of concern. "We'll put her in recovery room one."

Wick nodded and, flexing his fist, cut the cord with a vicious mental swipe. As much as he yearned to stay, watching wasn't an option. He'd go ape-shit crazy as her wounds were revealed. He didn't need to see it to believe it . . . or understand the brutality of what had been done to her. So instead, he dragged his gaze away and pivoted toward the exit. A distraction. He needed one. Right now. Before he did something stupid, like turn into a first-class pansy and refuse to leave her side.

Chapter Thirteen

From his position at the back of the room, Wick watched the other Nightfury warriors file into the com-center. Heavy footfalls bounced off pale walls, making the room's generous portions shrink and his head pound. The sting slid around to hammer the base of his skull. Rolling his shoulders, he resisted the urge to rub his temples. Fuck the pain. The frustration and confusion too. All he wanted was out. Out of a space filled with males who took up too much room. Away from the hustle 'n bustle and all the chitchat. Into the silence of his room and the comfort it brought him.

Too bad that wouldn't happen anytime soon.

His gaze narrowed on the male responsible for screwing up his plans. Or rather messing with his escape route.

Boots planted beside the desk across the lab, Bastian stood alongside their resident computer genius. Seated in his uglier-than-shit chair, Sloan nodded at B, his eyes on the wall-mounted screens, fingers flying over the keyboard, making his supercomputer sing in the predawn hours. Watching the byplay, Wick flexed his fists, trying to alleviate the tension. It didn't work. He was too far gone. On edge. On the brink of exploding into aggression-laced agitation.

In need of space and a shitload of alone time to power down. But as his comrades fanned out, taking up most of the available real estate, stealing all the air in the room, the harder he worked to keep his cool.

It was nothing but an act. A game of cover-up he'd played for years.

Not even Venom understood the depths of his emotion. He was good at keeping it contained and out of the spotlight. He understood the coping mechanism. Crossing his arms over his chest, Wick growled. He should too. He'd read every book the field of psychology had to offer—Jung, Freud, fucking Alfred Adler. He knew them all, every single one of their theories. It was all so much bullshit. None had helped him get past his problem. Or cured his phobia.

The thought twisted his stomach into knots.

Wick swallowed the burn and tossed his commander another nasty look. "All right, already. Get the fucking show on the road."

The low grumble brought Bastian's head around. Piercing green eyes met his. Wick tensed. His commander left Sloan's side, coming toward him from the other side of the room. Ah, hell. Here it came . . . the inevitable question and answer routine the second B reached him.

Stopping beside him, B propped his shoulder against the wall and raised a brow. "You okay?"

"Never better."

"Don't bullshit a bullshitter."

Wick snorted, the sound full of amusement. He couldn't help it. He liked B. Respected the male too. A step up for Wick. Sentiment wasn't his thing, after all. But after years spent fighting side by side with the warrior, proximity had turned to friendship . . . and loyalty to love. Now, he trusted

Bastian with his life. The male was solid: stout of heart, whip-cord smart, with a wicked amount of lethal on top. Always a good combination. But that didn't mean he wanted to share what had gone down in Seattle a few hours ago.

The upheaval was still too fresh. Way too raw to get into with B.

So only one thing left to do . . . deflect his commander's concern.

Crossing his arms, Wick bent one knee and planted his boot against the wall. "You gonna get this party started or what?"

"Nice try, my brother, but . . ." As B trailed off, Wick tensed. Jesus, he was in for it now. His commander refused to let it go, which put him in the hot seat. Lovely. Just what he wanted to avoid—an in-depth examination with Bastian in the driver's seat. "You wanna explain what happened out there, or would you prefer I take a guess?"

"Fuck off, B." The fail-safe response acted like a shield, deflecting inquiry, shutting down conversation with the added bonus of forcing others to keep their distance. Per usual, Bastian wasn't fooled, and as a muscle twitched along his jaw, Wick relented. "I'm not ready to talk about it yet."

"Fair enough." Bastian nodded and backed down. At least, in the metaphorical sense. The male was still close enough to nail him with a no-nonsense look. "But when you are, come to me. I'll talk you through it."

A prickle of discomfort rippled through him. He didn't want to *talk* about it. Not now. Not ever. Wick dipped his chin anyway, agreeing without words . . . if only to get B off his back.

"Energy-fuse is serious shit, Wick. You can't fight it," he said, his voice low to prevent the others from overhearing.

"My advice? Don't try. Embrace it. Thank God you found her. Give your female what she needs, and you'll end up with more than you can imagine."

Your female. Holy fuck. Bastian thought Jamison belonged to him.

Denial clogged his throat. Wick shoved the emotion down deep, combating the sting. It couldn't be true. He didn't deserve good fortune or a female of his own. Could barely take care of himself, never mind someone else. B was wrong—was talking out his ass if he thought Wick capable of forming a lasting bond with a female. Fairy tales existed in human nursery rhymes, not in his world.

Uncomfortable with the topic, Wick broke eye contact and changed tack. "Venom tell you about what happened at Swedish Medical?"

"Not yet. Fill me in."

With a nod, Wick laid it out, describing his encounter with Azrad in detail.

Bastian frowned. "He targeted the female to force a sit-down with me?"

"Yeah."

"And he wants to meet at a coffee shop?"

"Pine and 1st Avenue. Midnight tomorrow," Wick growled, replaying the encounter, seeing the wheelchair whirling down the corridor. The fear on Jamison's face came next, coalescing into vivid imagery, making his heart pound, pissing him off. His nostrils flared. The bastard. Azrad might not smell like a rogue, but he sure as hell acted like one . . . disregarding a female's safety to achieve his own end. For that alone Wick would tear him apart the next time he saw the male. "He hurt her, B. Had her by the throat."

"And what?" Green eyes knowing, his commander eye-balled him. "Now you want him dead?"

"It's my right."

"No argument. But I'm curious now, so . . ." Rubbing his hand over the back of his neck, Bastian sighed. "We talk to him first. I want to know the *why* before you take him out. Agreed?"

"Deal," Wick murmured, relief grabbing him by the balls.

Rogue or not, Bastian had sanctioned the hit. So . . . yeah. He'd get his shot at the tatted bastard. Would get all the time he needed to go to work on the male. Make it painful. Rip Azrad apart scale by scale, without any interference from the Nightfury commander. Nothing better than that, especially if—

"Hey, B?" Swiveling in his chair, Sloan glanced in their direction. "We're all set."

"On-screen." Thumping Wick on the shoulder, Bastian pushed away from the wall and grabbed one end of the cedar conference table. Wood legs bumping across the polished concrete floor, he dragged it into the middle of the room. The tug 'n tow put his brothers in gear. As they stepped to, snagging the leather chairs, resetting the seating arrangement, the screen in front of Sloan flickered. "Everybody take a seat."

Multiple chair legs scraped across the floor.

Grabbing a seat back, Wick sat in his usual spot along one side of the table. As Venom set up shop next to him, an image flared on the monitor, putting Gage and Haider up front and center. Wick's mouth curved. Shit, it was good to see the pair. Especially Gage. He missed both males' presence in the lair, sure, but the warrior with the intense bronze gaze—and an attitude full of fuck you—was his favorite of the two. Vicious to the point of self-destruction, Gage never backed down or said quit.

His kind of male.

Haider, on the other hand, was harder to figure out. A silver dragon, the male epitomized the stereotype of his sub-set—and not just because he looked the part with his mercury eyes and black, gray, and silver-streaked hair. Talented in the art of deductive reasoning, his IQ landed in the upper echelon of intelligent. Toss in his ability to keep secrets, a lethal amount of charm, and the fact Haider wielded both like a weapon, and . . . yeah. He was the perfect diplomat, a male equal to any task and able to ferret out information no one wanted him to know.

A useful skill. One Haider used to effect.

Good thing too, considering the pair were ass-planted in Prague, playing nice at the Archguard festival. All an act, of course. Bastian didn't care about keeping the members of the high council happy. The trip—under the guise of honoring the traditions of their kind—was more of a fact-finding mission. One Wick could get behind without hesitation. He liked the subterfuge. It suited his nature, if not his temperament, and as he settled in, he hoped the Metallics had hit pay dirt.

Accurate intel, after all, equaled opportunity. Opportunity opened up possibility. And possibility? Well now, that created a myriad of options. One that might achieve what the entire Nightfury pack wanted done. Namely, a clear break from the Archguard and Rodin's toxic hold on their kind.

Taking his seat at the head of the table, Bastian greeted the Metallics.

"Fuck me." Leaning forward in his chair, Gage brought his face closer to the camera. Bronze gaze roaming around the crowded table, he zeroed in on Angela. "Since when do we invite females to our meetings?"

"Since now." The last to join the party, Rikar's mate pulled up a chair. Ex-SPD with an incredible nose for investigation, Angela threw a file folder onto the tabletop. As the paper slapped down, she glared at Gage. The look sent a clear message—smarten up or get your ass kicked . . . by a girl. "Cut the crap, Gage, and get with the program."

An amused gleam in his eyes, Haider snorted.

Shifting focus, Gage grinned at Rikar. "I like her."

"Me too." Returning the male's smile, Rikar reached out and cupped her hand. "She's a keeper."

Angela rolled her eyes. "Screw off . . . both of you."

With a laugh, B tipped his chin in her direction. "Ange, you start. Whatcha got?"

"It's a little thin, but I think I've got a lead." Untangling her fingers from Rikar's, she opened the red folder. Inside sat three sheets of foolscap laminated in plastic. Shredded by the Razorbacks and left inside one of their abandoned lairs, the info had led Angela down a rabbit hole, one they all hoped would end at Ivar the Asshole. "These are just a couple of the shredded documents I've put back together, but they're the most promising."

Forge snagged one of the pages. "Why is that, lass?"

"It's a list of inventory for a club of some kind."

"A nightclub?" Venom asked.

"Maybe," she said. "Too soon to tell. There's no name on the documents to point us to any one establishment, but there's a definite money trail. A history and pattern to follow. Sloan's set me up with a computer." Glancing Sloan's way, she smiled at their resident computer genius. "He's teaching me how to hack the system too. With a little luck, I might be able to find the distributor. If I can match their accounts payable to the quantities of alcohol the club ordered, along with the corresponding dates, I may be able to pinpoint the place. It'll take—"

"Fucking forever," Mac said, interrupting his best friend and former SPD partner. She scowled at him. He backed off. "But it's worth a shot."

"Myst and Tania are helping me sort through the other boxes." Tapping her fingertip against the tabletop, she shuffled in her seat . . . as though she couldn't wait to get started. "It'll go faster than you think with the three of us working at it."

"Jamison will want to help too."

The second Wick opened his mouth, he regretted it. Particularly since all eyes snapped in his direction. Surprise winged across each warrior's face. Wick hid a grimace, berating himself for abandoning his usual silence, but . . . God. He couldn't stop thinking about her. Couldn't forget that she lay just down the hall—one right turn and seventy-three paces away—never mind squash the urge to go check on her. And frankly? Including her in the mix seemed, well . . . halfway natural.

Wick frowned. The impulse signaled a huge problem. One that put his holy-shit meter on high alert.

"I mean . . . probably," he murmured, backpedaling. "The female is Tania's sister, after all."

A multitude of grunts greeted his explanation.

Wick breathed out in relief. The last thing he needed was for any of his brothers to catch on. Bastian knowing about his obsession with Jamison was one thing. But the whole pack? Jesus. What a clusterfuck that would turn out to be.

"Haider," Rikar said, getting back on track. "Anything from your end?"

"Nian's becoming a serious player." Forearms planted on the desktop, Haider shifted in his office chair. "He's spending a lot of time in Rodin's inner circle. He's been to at least three private parties in the last week as far as I can tell. Rumor has it he purchased an expensive female at one of them."

"Shit."

"No kidding, Sloan. But I'm not convinced that's a bad thing."

"Why?" Bastian growled. "If the fucker's dealing in the sex trade, I'll give Gage the green light right now."

Gage perked up. "Fantastic. I've been dying to rip the prick apart since we got here."

"I hear yah, but here's the thing . . ." Holding up a piece of paper, Haider flapped it in front of the screen. "The next day, Nian purchased a first class plane ticket out of the country, so . . ."

Forge cursed. "He wasnae the one tae use it?"

Haider shook his head.

"Hell," Gage grumbled, snatching the invoice out of his buddy's hand. "Where did you get that?"

"Doesn't matter."

"I agree," B said, sounding unhappy. "Set up the meeting with Nian. I want to talk to the bastard face-to-face. And one other thing . . ." Trailing off, he glanced Wick's way. "Anything else you want to know before we break it up?"

Catching his commander's drift, his mouth curved. Bastian was the best . . . no question about it. "Either of you ever heard the name Azrad?"

"No," both males said in unison.

"Can you stir the pot?" he asked. "See what floats to the surface?"

Haider nodded. "Got any more than that for me to go on?"

"Longer-style mohawk . . . black hair, burgundy highlights, dark-blue eyes," Venom said, throwing Wick a sidelong glance. "A metal head. He wears eyebrow and nose studs."

"Tattoo on the left side of his neck," Wick murmured, picking up the description where Venom left off. "Black web. Red spider at its center."

Gage's brows popped skyward "Freaky, but distinct. If there's any info to be had, we'll unearth it for you."

"You've got twenty-four hours," Bastian said. "Do what you need to, then pack it up. The instant the festival's closing ceremony concludes I want you to get your asses home. We need you here."

"How about that, Gage." With a flash of teeth, Haider nudged his buddy with his elbow. "I think he misses us."

Rikar snorted. "Yeah, about as much as an extra hole in the head."

Bronze eyes gleaming, Gage's mouth curved. "That can always be arranged."

"Not unless you want to deal with me," Angela said, a load of pissed off in her tone.

"Such a feisty female, Rikar," Gage murmured. "Bet she keeps you in line."

Venom laughed along with the others.

His XO growled something obscene.

Grinning like a devil, Gage rapped his knuckles against the desktop. "B, I'll set up the meet with Nian and let you know when. We find out anything else, I'll e-mail Sloan. Otherwise, we'll see you on the flip side."

One hand poised above the keyboard, Haider tapped a button, and . . .

Lights out.

The second the computer screen went blank, Wick pushed away from the table and stood. No time like the present to make a break for it. He'd lasted long enough. Now he needed a little peace, a lot of silence, and the space that heralded both.

Passing behind his chair, he thumped Venom on the shoulder.

Ruby-red eyes met his. "Halo or World of Warcraft?"

Wick shook his head, turning the male down. Odd, really. Most mornings, he jumped at the chance to hang out with Venom and his high-tech system. Video games allowed them both to wind down after a long night of fighting. But after the showdown in Seattle—and his bizarre reaction to Jamison—he'd had enough games for one night.

"Later."

As Venom "uh-huhed," he headed for the door. Almost home free. One turn and a short walk up the corridor, he'd be in front of the elevator doors. Nothing but a quick ascent from the aboveground lair. And his room. But as he left the rumble of male voices behind and stepped into the hallway, the strangest urge struck. He wanted to turn right instead of left . . . toward the clinic instead of away.

Such a bad idea.

Jamison was in good hands. Would no doubt be asleep for a while. She didn't need him at her bedside. Despite his promise, experience told him she hadn't meant what she said. She no more wanted to see him when she woke up than he wanted a boot to the balls. Her request to be close to him stemmed from desperation . . . from fear and uncertainty. He'd been her lifeline in a moment of crisis. Nothing more, no less. The second she became clearheaded again, she'd react to him the way other females did . . .

With terror-filled revulsion.

He knew it. Had lived through it time and again. Even so, the thought of her looking at him that way made his chest ache and his heart hurt. And as the pain expanded to engulf his rib cage, Wick fought the growing tide to keep his feet moving. It didn't work. With his dragon fixated, compulsion drove the spike deep, stalling his forward progress. With a curse, Wick paused in the middle of the corridor. Bowing his head, he fisted his hands, and pivoting 180 degrees, glared at the sliding glass doors.

Son of a bitch. He couldn't do it.

Couldn't walk away without checking on her. One more time.

Calling himself a fool, Wick put himself in gear. Maybe all he needed was a sneak peak. Maybe a quick glimpse through the glass would do it. Or a moment parked at the end of her bed—watching her sleep . . . seeing her safe, sound, and at peace—would alleviate the worry. But as Wick neared the entrance into the clinic, nerves got the better of him. Unease followed, pricking the nape of his neck before slithering down his spine. Nothing about the situation rang true. His need to be near her wasn't right. Not exactly smart either. Instinct and self-preservation existed for a reason. He needed to exercise both, exorcise the demons that drove him in her direction, and stop thinking about her altogether.

Safer for him. A helluva lot better for her.

Too bad it was easier said than done.

❀ ❀ ❀

Close to the edge of the mattress, J. J. lay flat on her back in a huge bed. Man, the thing could fit five of her across. Maybe more . . . easily. Ridiculous. Especially since her prison cot had only been twenty-eight inches wide. Narrow sure, but familiar too. Her home behind the safety of a locked door. The one place in the world she'd found solace after a long day spent avoiding trouble in general population.

Sad, wasn't it? Instead of comfort, all the extra space made her uneasy.

Breathing in, she filled her lungs, counted to five, then exhaled and glanced at the clock across the room. Mounted above white cabinets, its wide face, the endless ticktock of the second hand, taunted her . . . kind of like Chinese water torture would a prisoner of war. She swallowed past the knot lodged in her throat. POW. Ha. Surprise, surprise . . . the title fit, working in a way that surpassed alarm to skid smack-dab into surreal. Not that she was in chains or locked in a dingy hut in a godforsaken jungle somewhere. Her room was beautiful: pale-walled, high-tech, and, above all, spotless.

Normally, she would've approved. Clean, after all, meant tidy. Everything put away in its proper place. Always a good thing in her estimation, but not today.

Tidiness didn't work for her. Not after what she'd seen last night.

Blowing out another shaky breath, J. J. returned to staring at the ceiling. Not that there was much to see. Nothing to count either. No pockmarks in the plaster. No brush swipes or straight edges left by the push-pull of a paint roller. Just smooth sailing, a sea of white interspaced by dimmed-down halogens overhead.

Which sucked. In a big way.

She needed a distraction. One that would keep her from obsessing over the fact Wick lay next to her. J. J. huffed. All right, so n*ext to her* leaned toward exaggeration, but not by much. Seated on a stool beside the bed, he slouched against the mattress, taking the real estate along her right side. Dark head pillowed on his forearm, he'd tucked his face against her hip, nestled in, and gone to sleep. Not that she blamed him for being tired. After breaking her out of Swedish Medical, he deserved the rest, but . . .

Was it really necessary for him to . . . to . . .

Oh boy. She was in so much trouble. The kind that sent her into a tailspin. Now she didn't know what to do. Or the best way to react. Not with his arm pressed against a, well . . . rather sensitive place.

Sometime while she'd slept, he'd tunneled under the covers. Now the back of her knee rested on his muscled bicep while his forearm traveled across country, allowing his hand . . . holy moly . . . to curl over her bare hip. Big. Strong. Calloused. Fingers spread wide on her skin, he claimed the spot under her hospital gown, making her aware of every nerve ending she owned. Throw in the fact his position left a certain part of her anatomy vulnerable and unease turned the corner. Panic upped the pace, dumping her into apocalyptic territory with two very different choices.

Stay still and enjoy—the zip in her veins and buzzing effect of his touch—while she waited for him to wake on his own. Or freak out and punch him in the face.

Fisting her hands in the sheet, J. J. debated the pros and cons. It was a toss-up. After five years on the inside, she'd lost her bearings. Most of her autonomy too. And her ability to trust? Long gone. Prison did that to a person. Everyone— good, bad, or indifferent—became suspect, another enemy in the struggle to stay alive in a place where hardened criminals called the shots. But as she lay in the dim light, under the welling warmth of Wick's palm, she didn't want to fight. She wanted to stay still, enjoy the echoing quiet along with the man, if only for a little while.

Which . . . ding-ding-ding, give the girl a prize . . . didn't make any sense.

Her reaction to him bordered on stupidity. She should've hammered him by now. Wound up and let fly the moment she woke up with him all over her. Under normal circumstances, she would've made him pay for getting too close. But for some reason, the situation didn't qualify as *normal*. Forget the dragon stuff. Her hesitation started and ended with Wick—the man, not the monster. Odd in more ways than one. Particularly since she never allowed men anywhere near her.

At least, not anymore.

She'd learned her lesson the hard way. Mistrust might not look nice on paper, but it kept a girl safe. Not to mention alive.

But with Wick, her defenses were shot. Down for the count and disengaged from the motherboard. Something about him rang true. Despite the man-to-dragon switch-up, she recognized safe when she saw it. Most women would've jumped for joy at the news flash. Gotten off on his trustworthiness and gone shopping for his and her towels or some crap. Not her. J. J. didn't *like* the imaginary juxtaposition.

The attraction she felt for him scared her too much.

Careful not to jostle him, she shifted on the mattress. Next she drew a fortifying breath, screwed up her courage, and glanced his way. Oh God. Unfair. He looked unbelievable lying there, like a fallen angel with his thick lashes and messed-up dark hair. Chewing on the inside of her lower lip, she ran her gaze over him again. Boy, he was big. Intriguing as well, all male with wide-set shoulders, hard-muscled arms, and a gorgeous face. Lingering on his mouth, she listened to him breathe, watched his back rise and fall—

"Good lord," she whispered. "What should I do?"

She racked her brain and waited, hoping *He* might take pity and toss her a bone. An idea. An inkling. A certified escape plan. Anything at all to help her out of the mess. But as the clock's hands walked around its face, tick-tick-tocking in the quiet, her mind went blank, refusing to cooperate. Annoying much? No question. Beyond frustrating too, particularly when temptation called, infecting her with curiosity, making her stare at the top of his head and wonder things like . . .

Would his hair be as soft as it looked? Would the day-old stubble along his jaw be as prickly as she thought? Would the heat he radiated warm her chilly fingertips within moments . . . or would it take longer?

Stupid questions. All of them. She knew it the moment each one drifted through her mind. Her reaction to him—the awful pull of attraction—bordered on ridiculous.

Illogical and insane worked too, considering what she knew about him.

An image of him rose in her mind's eye.

Horned head framing golden eyes. Black amber-tipped scales flashing in the moonlight. Razor-sharp claws crowning huge talons that had ripped other dragons apart.

Dragons. Oh dear God. The sky had been full of them last night and—

J. J. swallowed as panic sent her sideways. Practicality stopped the psychological slide. Freaking out wouldn't help. It never did. She'd seen what she'd *seen.* No going back or denying it. And yet as she stared at him, replaying the events, she fought to reconcile what she'd witnessed with the man asleep next to her. With the very human hands holding her and the realization that his touch brought her comfort. J. J. wanted to deny it, but facts were tricky things. Uncompromising, each one got in her face, making her admit the truth. She wasn't hurting anymore. The pain was gone, leaving nothing but a nagging ache along her rib cage where she'd been sliced wide open.

Oh, and a slight throb in her ankle too.

Wiggling her toes, she lifted her leg beneath the sheet. Propped on a pillow, the plaster cast rustled against cotton, but . . . huh. Some discomfort, but nothing like before, which prompted a realization. He'd done something to her. It didn't take a genius to figure out what. Human beings didn't heal that fast, so . . .

She owed her fast recovery to Wick.

Frowning, J. J. dug deep, examining her conclusion, turning it over in her mind, looking for holes in the theory. Nothing but certainty surfaced. Proof positive lay in the strange current buzzing though her. She could feel the ebb and flow of sensation swirl. Closing her eyes, J. J. pinpointed the epicenter. The heated rush radiated from the center of his palm, sizzled across her skin, spread out, sank deep, enfolding her body to embrace her from the inside out.

Between one heartbeat and the next, J. J. made her decision. Waking him up had just become priority number one. She had questions. He possessed the answers. A conversation was in order. One problem, though. She didn't know how he'd react. Experience told her men didn't like to be shaken awake. So poking at Wick while he slept? Probably not the best idea. He might wake up swinging, and considering the size of the hand gripping her hipbone, avoiding a knuckle sandwich a la Wick seemed like an excellent strategy.

Apprehension cocked like a gun about to go off, J. J. cleared her throat, hoping the sound would wake him. Nothing. No reaction. Not even an eyelash flutter.

"Wick?" She kept her tone soft, nonthreatening. "Time to wake up."

Again, he didn't move.

Out of options, J. J. reached out. Her hand touched his shoulder. She nudged. He frowned. J. J. added a jostle to the equation. He grumbled something. She blinked. Surprise folded into annoyance. Frigging guy. She wasn't completely certain, but it sounded as though he'd just told her to fuck off.

Irritation strangled self-preservation. She jabbed him with her fingertip. "Hey!"

His hand flexed, tightening on her hip a second before he snarled. J. J. squeaked in alarm as his head came off his forearm. Intense golden eyes met hers, then narrowed. The breath stalled in her throat. Memory grabbed hold, dragging her back five years to a time and place she didn't want to go. Oh shit. Jesus help her. She should never have lost her patience. Now he would make her pay. Eat her alive. Hurt her for pissing him off. The lash of experience struck and left welts behind, forcing her to remember what she wanted to forget. She recognized the expression Wick wore . . . understood history often repeated itself and that hers had come to claim her. And even though being hit was nothing new, J. J. screamed inside, howling at the unfairness.

Not again. Never again. She'd made herself a promise. Had shot and killed a man to keep it and herself safe. But here, in a strange room, under the dim light, the past came back to haunt her. And as fear stripped away reason, she froze under the threat of brutality, not knowing which way to turn or where to go.

"I'm sorry," she whispered, hating the plea and the weakness that drove it. She was broken. Beyond fragile. So pathetic the rasp of her voice made her cringe. But even after five years, habit—years of training meted out by an ex with a sadistic side—forced J. J. into an awful pattern of surrender. A quick roll. A fast jerk, and she curled into a ball. With efficiency born of desperation, she brought her arms up to protect her face. "Please don't h-hit me. Please don't. I'm sorry . . . s-sorry."

As the ugliness spilled out of her, Wick flinched. "Holy fuck."

His curse banged around inside her skull. Her heartbeat took up the cause, ricocheting inside her chest, throbbing hard as J. J. waited. For the violent rush of air. For the first punch to land. For the pain that always followed. Except . . .

She blinked. Nothing happened. The worse didn't arrive.

And as quiet expanded in the wake of her outburst, J. J. stopped reacting and started thinking. Drawing a lungful of air, she listened hard. No sound. No movement. Nothing at all. Just the warm, heavy weight of his hand on the outside of her thigh. His absolute stillness reassured her. His silence gave her courage.

Lifting her elbow, she peeked through the space between her forearms. A furrow between his brows, he stared at her, confusion and more in his eyes. A slight tremor in her hands, she lowered her guard halfway to test him. When he stayed perfectly still, J. J. released a choppy breath. Thank God. He wasn't going to retaliate. Had no intention of hitting her at all.

Tears gathered as the realization settled deep.

Her gaze locked on him, she exhaled and allowed her muscles to unlock. As the tension eased, she called herself a fool. *Dumb-ass,* though, worked even better. She'd shocked the hell out of him. She could tell by the look on his face. The mixture of concern and wariness made her chest go tight. Jeepers, she'd done it again. Gone deep six without proof and overreacted, allowing her past to infect the present. Which made Wick a casualty in her sad little war, didn't it?

Not fun for him. Embarrassing as hell for her.

Unable to stop the shame, her cheeks warmed to a full blush. Forcing herself to meet his gaze, she uncurled her limbs and, with a push, sat upright. Drawing away, his hand slid from beneath the sheet, leaving a cold spot on her thigh. Rubbing her lips together, she searched for the right words. "I just insulted you, didn't I?"

He shrugged, downplaying her explosive reaction.

"Sorry." She shook her head. "I should've known better. Especially after last night."

"Why? You don't know me."

"I saw you, remember?" Another image of him streamed into her head. Of him at the hospital, gentle hands on her arm, strong arms around her as he carried her down the stairs, the deep timbre of his voice in her ear. "You protected me and saved my life while doing it. There's no reason you would hurt me now. I just . . ."

Her voice cracked, cutting off her words.

He raised a brow and waited for her to continue. The gesture struck her as odd. Not in a bad way, simply different. Most men would've rushed her along. Looked at their watch, maybe even tapped on its face and said, "chop-chop, honey." Not Wick. He sat unmoving, patient, silent, giving her the gift of his time, allowing her to regroup. And as J. J. stared at him, letting the quiet drift, she debated.

The pros. The cons. How much to admit . . . what to hold back.

Honesty was a rare commodity, one she liked more than most, but the truth didn't always set a person free. She knew it, but as she held his gaze, something strange happened. J. J. decided to be brave. She was tired of running. Tired of hiding. Tired of the games too. As the silence stretched and he remained patient in the face of her uncertainty, she lost her usual caution. Screw it. He seemed solid, trustworthy even, so . . . the heck with it. Time to test him and see where she landed.

Nervousness clogged her throat. J. J. cleared it away. "I react before I think sometimes. My track record with men isn't great, but that's no excuse. So, if I hurt your feelings, I'm—"

"Who hit you?" he asked, his gaze so intense it scared her a little.

"My ex."

"The male you shot?"

"Murdered, you mean?"

"Bullshit." Shifting his weight on the stool, he pushed away from the side of the bed. Wheels squeaked as the distance between them grew. Two feet widened into three before he stopped the backward glide. "I read your file."

J. J.'s mouth fell open. "You read my—"

"Every last word." As surprise spun her full circle, he growled, "Worthy males don't hurt females, Jamison. The asshole deserved to die."

Well, that was one way of looking at it. Another would be that she'd shot him in cold blood. The DA certainly thought so. Her regret, and the guilt that went with it, tended to agree. Gathering her hair in one hand, J. J. pulled the heavy mass over her shoulder. As the blunt ends brushed over her breast, she shook her head. She'd done it all wrong. If she'd been smart, she would've listened to her sister and done the right thing: gone to the hospital, reported the abuse, and pressed charges. But hindsight was twenty-twenty, and she couldn't go back. The past was *past*. It was over and done. Now she must live with the consequences along with the pain.

"No one *deserves* to die, Wick."

"Not true," he said, conviction in his tone. "I kill males who deserve it all the time."

J. J. blinked. *All the time?* Oh boy, that didn't sound good.

"Like, ah . . ." J. J. swallowed, wondering whether or not to ask. She didn't want to piss him off, but safety required a

Fury of Desire

certain amount of due diligence. Despite her reservations, she needed to know. "The dragons in the clearing?"

Watching her with predatory interest, he nodded and rolled his shoulders. Muscle reacted, rippling under his T-shirt, tightening over his biceps, sending shockwaves through her. Wow, he was strong. Way out of her league. Far too dangerous, and yet, intriguing too. A puzzle in need of solving. One she found difficult to resist.

Which posed a huge problem.

She didn't need any more trouble. Didn't want to feel the fascination either, but denying the pull wouldn't make it go away. Wick owned her attention . . . and something else too. Her interest. Not good. Or even close to smart. He was a Dragonkind guy. She was a damaged girl. Nothing good would come from setting herself up for a fall. Now if only she could stop the questions whirling inside her head.

And her love of a good mystery.

Easier said than done.

Wick presented a fascinating conundrum. Quiet. Reserved. Yet willing to sit with her. She saw the dichotomy. Recognized its ilk and labeled it within seconds. Wick carried the mark of the *exiled*. Was branded by pain and the past . . . just like her.

"So you killed them because . . ." Flipping her hands palm up, she paused, playing fill in the blanks.

"We're at war."

"Why?"

"Long story and—"

"I've got time."

"I'm more interested in you." Boots flat on the floor, he planted his elbows on his knees and leaned toward her.

A stranglehold on the sheets, she shuffled on the mattress. Silly, she knew, but no matter how much he interested her, she didn't want him to come any closer. Not yet. Maybe not ever. A death grip on her urge to turn tail and run, J. J. bit the inside of her cheek. Her reaction bordered on irrational, but knowing it didn't stop the pit of her stomach from churning. Or her relief when he straightened and pushed back another foot, making the stool squawk, giving her space, making her wonder . . .

Could he feel her apprehension? J. J. frowned, rolling the assumption over in her mind. Logic said no. Instinct countered, throwing a big, fat yes into the ring.

His expression unreadable, he ran his gaze over her. "How are you feeling?"

"About what . . . the scary dragon stuff? Or in general?"

His lips twitched. "In general."

"Okay, I guess. A lot better than before, but then . . ." Dropping her gaze to the bandage on her forearm, she picked at the tape and peeled the gauze away. J. J. sucked in a soft breath. Holy moly, that was weird. Blood on the bandage, but no cut in sight. No scar either. A little freaked out but mostly grateful, she rubbed the smooth skin, then held her arm out for Wick's inspection. "You already knew that, didn't you?"

"Hoping and knowing are two different things, *vanzäla*."

Vanzäla? An endearment of some kind?

J. J. smiled, enjoying the possibility. No one had ever given her a pet name before. The idea struck a chord, making her insides warm with appreciation. Why? She had no godly idea. It was a stupid, knee-jerk response to the deep timbre of his voice, but . . . ah, hell. He sounded so good, like coffee ice cream smothered in dark chocolate sauce.

Her absolute favorite. And foolish or not, she couldn't deny she liked the sound of him.

"How did you do it?"

"The healing?" When she nodded, he said, "I'm half dragon, remember?"

Right. Of course. Dumb question, considering she'd spent the last hour watching him sleep, trying to come to terms with that fact. "So it's magic or something?"

"Or something."

"Well, aren't you a wealth of information," she said, reacting to his deflection. Or his unwillingness to share. Whatever the case, he preferred short answers. Four words or less seemed to be the norm for Wick. "All right, I'll leave that one alone . . . for now . . . but—"

He snorted.

"But," she said, a warning in her tone. Not that he cared. He was too busy laughing at her. Okay, not out loud or any-thing—he was too smart for that—but she could see the amusement in his eyes. Which honestly? Rubbed her the wrong way. "You can at least answer the next one."

"What's that?"

Sliding her legs over the side of the bed, she sat sideways on the mattress, allowing her cast to dangle alongside her bare foot. She twirled her hand in the air, the gesture en-compassing the room. "Where did you bring me?"

"Black Diamond. My home." Tilting his head to one side, he glanced toward the door. "Your sister's now too."

Hope hammered her, punching through to her heart. "Tania's here?"

With a nod, he pushed to his feet. Footfalls thumping, he rounded the end of the bed, his trajectory a straight shot to the door. "She was with you until dawn."

Her breath hitched. "What?"

"You were out of it, but—"

"Where is she?" she asked, anticipation making her twitch. Unable to stay still, she hopped off the bed. Balanced on her good leg, she hobbled alongside the metal frame, following Wick's retreat. "Can you take me to her?"

"No need, *vanzäla*." Already across the room, he cranked down on the handle and shoved the door wide. A second later, he crossed the threshold into the corridor beyond. His deep voice drifted over his shoulder, sliding between the door and its frame. "She's already here."

She frowned, not understanding. What did he mean? She couldn't see a—

The door started to swing shut.

A silhouette appeared in the hallway.

A death grip on the footboard, she sucked in a quick breath. Long hair pulled into a ponytail, Tania raced into the room. Feet doing double time, her sister yelled her name. Tears pooled in J. J.'s eyes. She couldn't help it. Could hardly believe it was real, never mind happening.

Freedom. A reunion with her sister. Both of them safe at long last.

Three things J. J. knew never to take for granted.

And as she met Tania in the middle of the room and hugged her tight, J. J. knew who to thank. Wick. He'd made it possible. Had not only saved her life, but given her back the only thing she regretted losing . . . her family. For that, she owed him a debt of gratitude. One she would never be able to repay. But she would try, give him every ounce of appreciation he deserved . . . just as soon as she managed to let go of her sister.

Chapter Fourteen

Wings spread in flight, Nian descended through thick cloud cover. As cold wind gusts blew the last wisp away, rushing over his scales, he tightened the cloaking spell. Magic spiraled around his torso, making him disappear into thin air. With a low growl, he bared his fangs on a smile.

Perfect. Per usual. The humans wouldn't suspect a thing.

Exactly the outcome he wanted.

He didn't have time to fool around. Or to play memory scrub with inferior human minds. Not tonight. Not with the meeting less than two hours away. Sensation curled in the pit of his stomach. Nerves? Anticipation? Probably a bit of both considering the high stakes . . . and even more dangerous circumstances. Playing both ends against the middle took patience, and steering Dragonkind in a new direction—one rooted in honor, instead of depravity—incredible skill.

Good thing he possessed both. Now all he needed was an ace in the hole.

Only one male fit the bill. Bastian.

The Nightfury commander was a formidable leader. The kind Nian required in his corner. An unequaled strategist, Bastian saw the whole board, moving each piece with skill and unbending commitment. A warrior's warrior. A male's male. Which explained his caution . . . along with his failures. He'd tried the polite way first, approaching Haider and Gage in the hopes of gaining their trust and cooperation. Too smart by half, the Metallics played the game with a precision that he admired. But he couldn't continue to be diplomatic. Or wait any longer. Actions spoke louder than words, so tonight he planned to roust the chess master and convince the Nightfury commander to knock Rodin off the board for good.

Not a bad plan, all things considered.

As long as he survived to see it put into motion.

Nian banked east toward the city center. Awash in the glitter of moonlight, the Vltava River snaked through Prague, leading him over red-tiled rooftops and cobblestone streets. Nestled at the heart of Old Town, the Emblem Club held down one corner of Main Street, a fixture along an avenue noted for them. Of the many establishments he owned, the Emblem was his favorite. Old school. Distinguished. A gentlemen's cigar club steeped in tradition.

The perfect venue for his conference call with Bastian.

Night vision sharp, he circled overhead. Seeing nothing but deserted, fog-soaked streets, he folded his wings. Gravity took hold. With a hum, he dropped like stone between rooftops, paws thumping down on cracked pavement. The spikes along his spine rattled, clicking together a moment before he shifted to human form and conjured his clothes, opting for casual instead of his usual fare. A suit and tie wouldn't impress the Nightfury commander. From what he knew, the male preferred rough around the edges, so . . . why the hell not? Might as well do the unexpected, dress like a warrior instead of a pampered aristocrat.

The gold lighter, though, Nian couldn't forgo.

He never left home without it. And as he turned to-ward the Emblem's back entrance, disengaged the alarm and swung the door wide, habit took hold. Or maybe it was compulsion. Nian didn't know. Didn't want to examine the need too closely either. Instead, he slipped his hand into his pocket, pulled the lighter into the open air, and thumped the top.

Click-click-snap. Click-click-snap. Click-click-snap.

The sound centered him. The repetitive motion soothed him. And the cool metal against his palm? Well now, that brought clarity, sharpening his focus as he strode out of the damp alley and into the open foyer. Glancing to his left, his gaze skimmed the staircase leading to the upper floor and another of his nightclubs. Nothing and nobody. Excellent. All the patrons had gone home. His employees had done their jobs, locking up before doing the same. Another men-tal twist opened the security door, and the Emblem Club beckoned. Sharp and pungent, the scent of cigar smoke mixed with a hint of alcohol, the combo welcoming him into his home away from home.

Nian smiled as he crossed into the club. Dark but for a single light behind the long wooden bar, his night vision sparked. He scanned the space like a businessman, ensur-ing everything was in its proper place. Details jumped out at him: chairs upended on tabletops, the wide-planked floors shined to a polish, the green-and-gold damask curtains tied back while the tasseled edges—

A tingle slid over the nape of his neck. The muscles bracketing his spine tightened as Nian swallowed a curse and glanced toward the rear of the club. Clad in shadow, a male stared out from the midst of darkness.

"About time you got here, Nian." The voice slithered out from a corner booth, cracking through the quiet, a slight slur in the intonation. Ice clinked against glass. "Where the hell have you been all night?"

Nian bit down on another curse. Accustomed to ambushes, he smoothed his expression. No sense giving away the game before it began. But as he met his nemesis's gaze, he nearly slipped off the I'm-in-control wagon. Hellfire and brimstone. Rodin. The tiresome bastard had the worst timing.

"With my accountant." Not a lie, exactly. A half-truth at best. Moving farther into the club, Nian skirted a couple of tables.

Dark eyes glittering, Rodin raised his half-empty glass in salute. "Responsible of you."

"I run a tight ship," he said, running a critical eye over the leader of the Archguard.

Rodin didn't look good. Tie askew. Brown hair disheveled. Face drawn and blurry-eyed, the male slumped in the back corner of the booth. Nian frowned and shifted focus to the bottles of booze sitting on the table. Glenlivet single malt whiskey . . . one empty, the other magnum halfway there. Drunk and disorderly. Rodin epitomized the first and was about to land face first in the second.

Caution yanked his chain. Something was wrong . . . very, *very* wrong.

Grabbing a chair from the tabletop, Nian dropped its legs to the floor. Wood scraped against wood. A soft thump echoed as he flipped the chair backward and, folding his arms over the backrest, sat directly across from one of the most powerful males of his kind. "What's wrong?"

"What makes you think there's anything wrong?"

Aw, come on. Were they really going to play this game? He didn't have time for the sideshow. Only an hour remained until showtime, for Silfer's sake. Gritting his teeth, Nian resisted the urge to glance at his Rolex. He raised a brow instead, asking without words. Patience, after all, was the better part of valor. And right now, silence seemed like the best policy. He couldn't afford to turn the older male away. He needed Rodin's trust. Had worked hard to make inroads these last few months, and the fact Rodin now sat inside his club instead of halfway across the city in his pleasure pavilion was a good sign.

Breaking eye contact, Rodin frowned into his drink. "Lothair is dead."

"How?"

"Murdered by the Nightfury pack."

"Ah, hell, Rodin . . . I'm sorry," he said, even though he didn't mean it. Lothair. The male didn't deserve to be mourned. Rodin's second son represented everything Nian wanted to change about Dragonkind. And as far as he was concerned? Bastian had done the world a favor by taking the bastard out. Not that he would ever admit it. "But Lothair knew what he was signing up for when he joined Ivar's camp. Any male involved in that war is—"

"Bullshit!" With a snarl, Rodin slammed his fist against the tabletop. The whiskey bottle jumped, skittering across the wooden surface. Teeth bared and dark eyes aglow, he leaned forward in his seat, violent intent throbbing at his temple. "He was my son. Mine! Immune from death. Do you know how this reflects upon me? I am the leader of the Archguard . . . the most powerful Dragonkind male in a sea of them. No one touches what belongs to me."

And there it was—the real reason behind the rage. Rodin didn't care that his son was dead. His concern centered on his own reputation.

"And your plan is . . . ?"

"To kill them all."

The announcement sent Nian back a step. The conviction he saw in Rodin's eyes gave him pause. The bastard might be drunk, but he wasn't stupid. He'd thought it through. Had a plan in mind. Which meant the ball was already rolling . . . in nasty directions.

"How?" he asked, needing more info. Intel, after all, amounted to power. The right information fed to the right male at the right time could make all the difference. To him, at least. He didn't give a rat's ass about Rodin. "The Nightfuries are a warrior pack . . . one of the strongest and most lethal. Bastian is well loved. Many follow him . . . are begging him to serve as High Chancellor over the Archguard as his sire did before him. You try and assassinate him, and packs will choose sides. Dragonkind will splinter. You will start a war, Rodin."

"Not if I reinstate *Xzinile.*"

Nian blinked. Oh Christ. Not good. *Xzinile* was an ancient state of law, a legal way to label someone a traitor. Once invoked and voted upon by the high council, the male—or pack of males—became outcasts, fair game for legalized assassination. Sanctioned execution by the Archguard put a bounty on the warrior, making him an attractive target for any Dragonkind male in need of money, prestige . . . or simply a way into the Archguard's good graces.

Dangerous. Foolhardy. Brilliant in a sick kind of way.

It also endangered Nian's agenda. He needed Bastian to support his hostile takeover of the high council. But if the Nightfury pack came under threat of *Xzinile?* He'd be screwed. Stuck waiting for another opportunity to strike at the upper echelon and take the power for himself.

"Who is responsible for Lothair's murder?"

"A Scottish warrior," Rodin said. "Goes by the name Forge."

Uh-huh. Not even close to accurate.

The bastard lied. Nian recognized the slither in his tone. Rodin didn't have a clue who'd killed his son. Which begged a question, didn't it? Why pin the murder on an individual member of Bastian's pack? His eyes narrowed. The entire thing stunk. Not surprising. Nothing Rodin ever handled came out smelling like roses. The leader of the Archguard targeted Forge for a reason. A very specific one. One Nian would bet his fangs had more to do with Rodin covering his own ass than the truth.

Shifting in his seat, Nian stared at the wallpaper above Rodin's head. As he pretended to consider all the angles, he shook his head. "It'll be a hard sell."

"Not if you're behind me." One corner of his mouth twisted up, the bastard smirked, making Nian want to take his head off . . . just for the fun of it. "The other members of the high council will follow our lead."

"You want my word I'll vote with you."

"I want your loyalty and support."

Two things Rodin would never possess, but what else could he do? If he said no, he jeopardized his position. If he said yes, he condemned an innocent pack to death.

"I'll think about it," he said, refusing to lie down like a fifty-dollar whore. Strength respected strength. It was time he showed Rodin some. "When's the vote?"

"Night after tomorrow, just before the festival's closing ceremony . . . if I call it."

Nian nodded. "Call it."

"Can I count on you?"

"I'll be there."

"Good." Downing the rest of the whiskey, Rodin slid out of the booth and pushed to his feet. Heavy-handed, the bastard slapped him on the shoulder, then turned toward the door. "In the meantime, see that Gage and Haider are rounded up, will you?"

Alarm bells went off inside his head. "To what end?"

"They will be held until Bastian complies and delivers the Scottish whelp to me for execution."

Held, his ass. Nian stifled a snort. Imprisoned was more like it. "He won't do it."

"Exactly." Halfway across the club, Rodin glanced over his shoulder. A terrible gleam in his eyes, he murmured, "This is a power play, Nian. When Bastian refuses to hand over Forge, all of the Nightfuries . . . every last fucking one . . . will fall under the rule of *Xzinile* and—"

"The Metallics become fair game."

"Duel beheadings at the festival's closing ceremony sound good to you?"

"Could be fun."

"I think so too," he said, dark voice drifting.

The handle clicked. The door opened then closed behind Rodin.

Christ help him, he felt sick. A stomach full of rotgut would be more pleasant. But as Nian pushed to his feet, automatically returning the chair to the upside-down perch alongside its fellows, he refused to acknowledge the chop and churn. He tilted his wrist and glanced at his watch, checking the time instead. So much to do, so little time. Just under an hour to reevaluate his plan, formulate a new one and . . . Nian swallowed . . . decide how much to tell Bastian. All while he tried to figure out a way to smuggle Gage and Haider the hell out of Prague without compromising his position.

Or getting caught.

Chapter Fifteen

Silence seeped from the ground, licking through chilly air to electrify the neighborhood. A good sign. The fewer humans around the better.

Wick didn't want to be interrupted. Not while hunting Azrad.

All right. Maybe *hunting* wasn't the right word. Rendezvous might be more accurate considering Bastian wanted to talk to the bastard first. But as Wick scanned building tops, searching for hidden threats behind steel and concrete, his commander's agenda didn't concern him. Not at the moment, anyway. His need for retribution trumped the party line. Payback sounded better. A lot more fun too, so . . .

No. The tatted warrior who liked to hurt females wouldn't get a free pass. Not this time. Not with him involved.

Night vision pinpoint sharp, he looked across the cityscape. Puget Sound sparkled in the distance, water rolling in to wash up on shore. The corner of his mouth curled, exposing one huge fang. Frigid air ghosted over his teeth. He relished the chill. Jack Frost enlivened him, coating his scales, prepping him for the showdown and . . .

Jackpot. About time too. Coffee shop at twelve o'clock.

Slithering in on a slow glide, Wick swung wide, banking into a holding pattern. He revolved into a continuous series of concentric circles, widening the grid with each pass, reconning the area, searching for hostiles within the target zone while avoiding the airspace above Starbucks. No sense tipping the bastard off. Better to arrive undetected. And if he flew directly overhead? He risked alerting the enemy to his presence.

Not advisable. Particularly while planning a sneak attack.

Eyes narrowed on the city below, his sonar pinged. Alive with magic, the cosmic net spread, molding over rooftops to flow unrestricted into the street. Or rather . . . the avenue. First and Pike, a veritable hub of activity during the day. Completely deserted at night. Nothing but tidy street corners, stone-clad buildings, and wide, pedestrian-friendly sidewalks. Charming with its old style, three-globed lampposts and inlaid-brick intersection, both throwbacks to a simpler time and place.

The golden age of wholesome.

Wick snorted. *Wholesome.* Jesus. Where the hell had that comparison come from?

It took him less than a second to figure it out.

Jamison. Despite her past, she embodied innocence with her big blue eyes, smooth as silk skin, and innate beauty. Wick shook his head, told himself to stay on task, but . . . God. It was hard. She was so damn pretty, her dark hair so long and straight he wondered what it would feel like wrapped around his fist. Or sifting through his fingers, caressing his palm in a sensual sweep. The visual made him swallow. The imagined sensation drew him tight. His muscles flickered in reaction, forcing a shiver down his spine.

Killing the twitch mid-shudder, Wick flexed a talon. The tips of his claws met the center of his palm. Pinpricks of pain nicked interlocking dragon skin, setting him straight. He needed to get a grip. Fast. Obsessing about her wouldn't change the facts. He wasn't built for connection, never mind the intimacy that went with it. And yet, he couldn't deny his curiosity. For the first time—ever—he allowed himself the possibility. Wanted to follow the trail of bread crumbs to its conclusion, maybe get closer to her and see what happened.

Damned strange. More than a little bent too, considering his phobia. And the fact he never touched anyone or fed . . . unless forced by desperate need and Venom's pain-in-the-ass prodding. Wasn't inclined to modify his behavior either, except . . .

Shit. He'd done a lot of touching in the past twenty-four hours, hadn't he? Caring for her. Holding her. Waking up with his hand pressed to the softness of her skin.

With a frown, Wick swung around a chimney stack. Smoke swirled in his wake, dancing with the frosty air. He watched tendrils curl, then drift, disappearing against the dark sky and—

"*Wick,*" Bastian growled. Sensation swirled against his temples, turning his attention back to the mission. Thank fuck. He needed his head in the game, not on Jamison. Thinking about her distracted him, splitting his focus in two directions. Never a good thing when headed into a potential firefight. "*How close are you?*"

"*Thirty seconds out.*"

On point, five minutes ahead of the pack, he played lead male tonight. Although, maybe *bait* described his role better. Venom had balked, not liking the plan. He'd insisted. No way he wanted his commander on-site—or anywhere near Azrad—until he assessed the situation. An ambush? Could be. Probably was too. Wick huffed. Hell, the meet and greet inside the human-owned coffee house had bait and switch written all over it.

Which made him the best male for the job.

The most maneuverable in flight, stealth was his specialty. Good at covering his tracks—able to camouflage the unique energy signal he left in his wake—most males never saw him coming. Unless, of course, he wanted them to, which . . . truth be told . . . happened nine times out of ten. He couldn't abide a quick kill. Liked the claw-grinding, muscle-stretching challenge of a good fight and engaging one-on-one. Or in his case, three-to-one odds. Being outnumbered equaled fun on a grand scale. A way to test his skill each night while out on patrol.

Not that it ever amounted to much.

The rogues were woefully inept. Unskilled. Lily-livered. Inexperienced. A damning combination that amounted to even less satisfaction.

More's the pity.

"Heads up." Flipping into a slow spiral, he went head-to-head with an apartment building. The angle gave him a clear shot down Pike Street, and in turn? The Corner Market building situated across the street from Starbucks. All clear. Nothing to be alarmed about . . . at least not yet. Banking right at the last moment, he circled behind a skyscraper. *"Making a final sweep."*

"Watch your six." With a curse, Venom growled long and low. *"No screwing around. You see anything hinky, bug out first, holler second."*

Hinky? Wick frowned. What kind of word was that? Not a very good one considering he wanted hellish, not hinky. Nasty sounded good too. And fatal? Even better . . . as long as it referred to the enemy. Hell, he hoped he got that lucky. With his dragon half itching for a fight, he craved scale-splitting calamity. Wanted to sink his claws deep. Watch rogue blood flow between his talons and splatter, warm and wet, up his forearms.

Only death would do.

The natural born killer he kept caged agreed, humming in anticipation. Oh-so-much promise. The next few hours held loads of bright and shiny hope: the kiss of possibility, the probability of foreplay, the skills required in an assassin's game. As he made one more pass, the spikes along his spine rattling, Wick could taste the potential. He felt it in his bones too. Smelled its stench on the night air, allowing it to invigorate him as he picked his spot.

The perfect insertion point.

One that would put him close to the target, yet allow for some wiggle room.

Tucking his wings in fast, Wick set down hard. His talons thumped against the ground. Windowpanes rattled in their frames, and momentum took up the cause. Slick with recent rain, the blacktop sent him into a sideways skid. Gritting his teeth, Wick bore down to control the slide. Friction burned the pads of his paws. The tips of his claws bit, ripping narrow grooves in the asphalt. Chunks of rock flew. Sound rippled like a wave, ricocheting off glass and steel, undulating down the avenue to reach the waterfront.

With a silent curse, he slid to a stop in the middle of the street.

Alert, ever watchful, tail flicking back and forth, he crouched like a cat poised to strike, ready to kill, magic feeding him information. Like gaping wounds in a pale face, the windows stared back at him. No reflection. No surprise. Cloaked in magic, invisibility didn't allow for detection. Sound either, and as Wick searched the perimeter, looking first left, then right, quiet stroked over building facades to tumble down the empty street.

Nothing and nobody. Two thumbs up so far.

"Just landed on Pike." Lifting his forepaw, Wick shook tiny bits of gravel from between his toes. A repeat performance on the other side freed his other foot of debris, and switching gears, Wick transformed, shifting into human form. Without thought, he conjured his clothes. Leather settled against his skin. Protected by his fighting gear, he veered into the shadowed enclave of a building. *"I'm going to walk the block. No one moves without my say-so."*

As the other Nightfuries "uh-huhed," Venom grumbled.

Wick ignored his best friend. The overprotective SOB would have to wait. He was a grown male, for fuck's sake. Well able to take care of himself. So screw Venom and his opinions. Clearing the scene came before his brother's skewed sense of responsibility.

Footfalls silent, he walked toward the corner of 1st and Pike. Planted not long ago, young trees lined both sides of the street, skinny limbs bobbing under the influence of saltwater breezes. The scent of brine hung in the air, and Wick paused under an eave, his gaze locked on the coffee house. An outdoor terrace hugged one side of the establishment, providing humans with the benefit of sunshine. Empty now but for tables and chairs set at odd angles, the patio abutted a bank of large windows that rose toward the second floor and the ornate architectural frieze above.

Shadows moved behind the thick panes.

"B? I sense three males inside. Sound about right?"

"Same. All in human form."

"Skill set?" Wick asked, tapping Bastian's talent for assessing a male from a distance.

"The first breathes acid, the second . . . Scald." As his commander paused, magic vibrated in the void. And Wick hummed in anticipation, 'cause . . . oh baby. *Scald.* Such an interesting weapon. One not many Dragonkind males possessed. Natural napalm mixed with venom, the exhale was potent—toxic swill that ate through scales and sent deadly neural inhibitors deep into muscle. A real challenge to avoid, which made doing so all the more fun. *"But the third? Shit, I don't know. I can't get a read on him."*

"Azrad . . . guaranteed," Wick murmured. *"The fucker's powerful."*

"Christ," Rikar said, entering the fray. *"All right, guys . . . here's the plan."*

Mac chimed in. *"Break it down."*

"You, Sloan, and Forge set up post outside. Nothing and no one comes in or out."

"Anybody tries, we'll pull the trigger," Forge murmured, his brogue thicker than usual.

A telltale sign. The Scot's accent always became more pronounced at the first hint of battle. Excitement, maybe. Eagerness, certainly. Wick related. He couldn't wait to get started. Or put his fist in Azrad's face.

Rikar growled. *"Good."*

"The rest of you . . . with me. Let's rattle the bastard's cage," Bastian said. *"And Wick?"*

"What?" His attention riveted to the front door, Wick crossed the street.

"Remember our deal. Stay put until we land. We go in together."

Bullshit. Screw the deal along with the direct order.

Wick could see the assholes moving around inside. Fate had given him a single shot. A moment in time to wrong a right. Now he stood just a hop, skip, and jump away from the male who had hurt a female. No way would he allow B or anyone else to get in his way. He needed to unleash, exact retribution, make Azrad pay the price for Jamison's pain.

Not wasting a second, Wick ramped into a run.

Shitkickers hammering concrete, he sprinted beneath the steel overhang fronting the shop. B snarled a warning. Venom seconded the motion, cursing a blue streak as Wick slammed the door open with a mental shove. Reinforced steel whiplashed, rattling the glass pane in its frame. Claws clicked down on asphalt behind him. Wick didn't care. All he needed was thirty seconds. Time enough to snap Azrad like a twig, and as he roared over the threshold—heart thumping, aggression level topped out, ready to unleash hell—he zeroed in on his target.

Spinning on his heels alongside his two companions, Azrad settled into a fighting stance beside the coffee bar, fists raised and eyes flashing. Wick bared his teeth. Oh goody. Kick-ass came in size extra-large, it seemed, 'cause . . . yeah. The male was ready, and oh so willing, to engage. Too perfect. Beyond satisfactory. Azrad deserved every ounce of pain he was about to deliver.

Forget reason. Sideline sensible. Fuck it all.

Jamison belonged to him. She'd become his responsibility the moment he saved her. Now his retaliation would be her revenge.

❀ ❀ ❀

Venom grunted as he got elbowed in the face. The shot to his chin backed him up a step, making his skull bobble-head on his shoulders. Blood washed over his teeth, filling his mouth with an awful metallic flavor. Pain streaked along his jaw, then clawed up the side of his face to hammer his temple. Scrambling to avoid another elbow, he lunged forward, boots sliding on the wooden floor, his gaze centered on Wick and the flurry of fists.

Frigging male. So much for the chitchat with Azrad.

Wick had started a war inside Starbucks. Now a full-on brawl was in progress . . . Nightfury pitted against three strange males in a battle of wills that trumped good sense. Goddamn it. Trust Wick to toss a monkey wrench into the mix and twist the screw the wrong way. Not that he blamed his best friend. Wick was who he *was*—violent, unpredictable, merciless—and after what had gone down at Swedish Medical, Venom understood. He really did, 'cause . . . hell. Had it been him protecting a female? Azrad would be dead already.

Wick cracked the male again.

Azrad cursed and stumbled backward as a cut opened beneath his eye.

"Fucking hell, Ven." Low and lethal, the growled words whiplashed, giving Venom chills as Rikar entered the fray behind him. An enemy male cursed. Ice crackled and frost spread, coating the inside of the coffee house's windows, dropping the temperature until each breath became white puffs of air. "Get a hold of him, for Christ's sake!"

He lost his grip on Wick a second time.

"Goddamn it." Venom gritted his teeth. "Like I'm not trying?"

Easier said than frigging done.

Wick was a force of nature on a good night. On a bad one? He was the devil incarnate. Un-frigging-stoppable.

Venom made another grab for him.

Slippery as a water snake, Wick slid right. Venom's hands caught nothing but air, throwing him off balance. As he compensated, shifting mid-stride, Wick widened the gap, driving the male backward across the shop. The scramble of footfalls echoed against the high ceiling. Frustration riding shotgun, Venom went after the pair as his best friend slammed Azrad against the wall. Picture frames rattled against plaster. One let go, plummeting into a free fall. Wood splintered against wood. Glass shattered, spilling across the floor as Wick hammered his opponent again.

And again. Then one more time.

Venom closed the distance between them. Quick hands bought him a fingerhold on his friend's leather jacket. Determination sealed the deal, intensifying his grip. He yanked. Wick rocked backward, but resisted, regaining his momentum. Thrusting his knee forward, he unleashed more hell, nailing Azrad in the stomach.

The male doubled over.

"Son of a bitch." Locked in a battle of his own, Bastian kicked a male's feet out from under him. The warrior hit the floor with a thud. With a nifty move, B wrenched his arm back and flipped him belly down. Driving his knee into the male's spine, he pressed him to the floor. "Put a leash on him, Venom."

"You think it's so easy . . ." Out of breath, he lodged his forearm against Wick's throat. "You come over here and do it."

Wick raised his combat boot, aiming for Azrad's head.

The warrior swung around and countered, hammering his friend with a right cross. Bone cracked against bone. Wick's head cranked to one side, and Venom took advantage. One arm at his throat, the other around his chest, he wrapped his friend up from behind and hauled him sideways. Up. Off. And over. Fantastic. He had liftoff . . . the kind that arrived with a crapload of imbalance.

Venom cursed as he careened backward. His arms locked around Wick's chest, the male came with him, both of them acting like pinballs, bouncing off tables, sending chairs flying, reeling across the narrow space. Bolted to the floor in the center of the room, a massive hardwood table stood strong and—

Ah, hell. This was going to hurt.

He was right.

Pain bit, scoring his hipbone as he collided with the thing. The table edge sent him up and over. With his friend along for the ride, he hit the floor on the other side with a bone-jarring thump and slid, knocking a quartet of club chairs askew. Refusing to let go, he clamped down on Wick. An unnecessary move. His buddy stayed put—thank God—and glanced over his shoulder. Shimmering golden eyes met his. Calm. Steady. Not an ounce of pissed off in sight. Venom frowned. What the hell was going on? After that display, he'd figured Wick would fight to regain his footing.

Go ape-shit crazy to take another shot at Azrad.

The corner of Wick's mouth curved instead. "I made my point."

"Did you ever," Azrad grumbled from the other side of the room. "Fuck me, I think my front teeth are loose."

"You deserved it." Shoving out of his hold, Wick rolled to his feet.

Not trusting his friend for a second, Venom scrambled to join him next to the table. No sense making the same mistake twice. The free-for-all was his fault. He should've been ready. Should've known Wick would go after Azrad at the first possible opportunity.

"I know." On one knee next to the coffee bar, Azrad swiped at the blood dripping from his chin. He missed a drop and it went splat on the wooden floor. With a curse, he grabbed the edge of his T-shirt and wiped the mess off his face. "You always make statements like that, Nightfury?"

Wick shrugged. "Usually."

"Effective."

"Get the message?"

"Yeah. No fucking with females under your protection." With a grimace, Azrad pushed to his feet. Rotating his shoulder, he stretched out sore muscles, then paused to frown at his bruised knuckles. As he flexed his hand, the male threw Wick an intense look. "How is she?"

"Hurt."

"I had no wish to harm her."

Skirting a downed chair, Wick moved into the center of the room. "Why did you then?"

Amazed by the exchange, Venom's attention volleyed. As he looked from Wick to Azrad, then back again, he shook his head. His friend never talked to anyone, so . . . why was he now? What was the impetus? His eyes narrowed. There had to be one. Wick might be quiet, but he possessed more than his fair share of brains. The male was wicked smart. Add in hyper-observant and . . . yeah.

Wick knew something he didn't.

Dealing with a load of WTF, Venom glanced toward his XO.

Pale eyes sharp, Rikar pinged him through mind-speak. *"You see what he does?"*

"Not yet," he said, following his XO's lead, keeping the conversation on the down low.

"Take a closer look at Azrad," Rikar murmured. *"Look like anyone we know?"*

Venom reversed course. He glanced at Azrad, scanning the male's face, looking past the nicks and cuts, trying to make the connection. It was hard. All the heavy metal—the eyebrow and nose stud—distracted him. The tattoo, black web supporting a freaky-looking red spider on the side of his neck, didn't help either. He stared at Azrad a little harder, stripped away all the bells and whistles—the spiked mohawk, the tat, the hard-core attitude—to reach the truth. The male's coloring and features moved to the forefront, and—

Venom sucked in a quick breath. *"Holy shit."*

"Bingo."

Rendered speechless, Venom opened his mouth, then closed it again.

"I regret the necessity, warrior," Azrad said, his soft tone full of sincerity.

"The name's Wick."

Azrad nodded. "I wouldn't have taken her out of the hospital room, but with a squadron of rogues inbound, my options were—"

"Limited?" Bastian raised a brow.

The comment turned Azrad's attention. His gaze landed on B. Something akin to awe washed over his expression. He swallowed so hard Venom saw his throat bob. "I . . . I'm . . . you're . . ."

"Bastian, commander of the Nightfury pack." Green eyes locked on Azrad, B hauled his captive to his feet. He gave the male a solid shove. The blond growled, but took the hint and crossed the room. Rikar followed his commander's lead, unlocking the full nelson on the warrior with a black patch over one eye. Silence descended. The room reshuffled, all players headed to their respective corners to surround and shield their leaders. "But the greater question . . . the only one I'm more interested in . . . is: who the fuck are you?"

"I have something to show you." Reaching inside his jacket pocket, Azrad pulled out a slim leather-bound book. Worn by age, cracked along the spine, the journal bobbed in his fingertips. "I received this just over a year ago. It belonged to—"

"I know who it belonged to." Aggression rolling off him in waves, B put his boots in gear and crossed the shop. His target? Take a guess. The new boy with the old book. Azrad had just painted a bull's-eye on his forehead. Not advisable or even close to smart. An angry Bastian amounted to the equivalent of a shark-infested marina with blood in the water. "Where did you get it?"

"It was given to me by a Numbai. It belonged to my sire."

"Bullshit," Bastian said, his tone dipping into melodic. Venom smoothed his expression, smothering a grimace, and got ready to move. The proverbial shit was about to hit the imaginary fan. He knew it from B's intonation. Whenever his commander used it, death almost always followed. "My father didn't sire anymore sons before his death. I have no siblings."

"Not true." Dark-blue eyes full of emotion, he stared at Bastian. "You have me."

Magic rippled, electrifying the air as Bastian snarled.

The warning was low and lethal, the kind of growl that sent smart males running. Venom tightened the loop instead, moving to stand at his commander's shoulder, showing support as Rikar and Wick took up post positions behind them. Trapped between a wall of male muscle and the raised countertop behind him, Azrad leveled his chin and stood his ground. Stupid? Brave? Venom couldn't decide. It was far too soon to tell. One thing for sure, though? Despite the uncanny resemblance between Bastian and Azrad, the male needed to tread lightly. Whatever the newcomer said in the next thirty seconds would seal his fate.

"Do you know how long I have waited to meet you?" Azrad asked, desperation in his voice. "From the moment I learned the truth. From the second I read the journals, I . . . Jesus. Months of rotting in that godforsaken place . . . of knowing the truth with little chance of escape. Of living with the hope of meeting a brother I never knew existed." A muscle twitched along his jaw. He flexed his fist, fighting for control. "Bastian . . . I would no sooner lie to you now than cut off my own balls. You are my brother. We are blood kin. I swear it on my life."

Unwilling to believe, Bastian glared at him.

With a growl, Azrad shrugged out of his coat. As the army jacket hit the floor, he grabbed the hem of his T-shirt and pulled it over his head. Bare chested in the dim light, muscle flexed as he bared his teeth and threw the crumpled cotton at Venom's chest. Reflex made him catch it, the scent of blood and male rising from its folds. "Blood doesn't lie. Check the fucking DNA."

As far as bluffs went, it was a good one. Better than good considering the veracity in the statement. Dragon DNA *didn't* lie.

Which meant one of two things.

Either Azrad told the truth. Or he'd played his last card and now stalled for time, the kind that would get him and his boys the hell out of hostile territory. It made sense from a tactical standpoint. DNA needed to be run in a lab, alleles and familial markers matched across four dragon chromosomal strands wrapped in unbreakable magic. Not an easy process. Isolating specific genetic threads took time, no doubt something Azrad knew.

Venom pursed his lips. Smart. Beyond dangerous too. The SOB had graduated at the top of his class. "Pretty good cover story, Azrad."

"No cover. Just the truth."

His brow furrowed, Bastian glanced his way. As Venom met his gaze, his commander held out his hand. Relinquishing the prize, he tossed B the bloody shirt. Fingers shifting through the folds, Bastian brushed his thumb over one of the stains. "It can't be."

"I don't think he's lying," Wick murmured, breaking formation. Footfalls joining the quiet buzz of overhead lights, he brushed shoulders with Venom, then swung wide to pace a circle around the male who claimed the impossible. Golden eyes alight, Wick breathed deep, filtering scent through keen senses, and ran a critical eye over Azrad. "He carries a variation of your scent . . . the same magical signature in his veins. I smelled it the second I made him bleed."

Silence met that pronouncement.

Venom huffed. Well, that explained the switch-up. Wick had backed off, delivering a cordial beat down to make his point instead of an agonizing death. And yet, even given his friend's certainty, Venom remained skeptical. It was a good story, one that nudged at the truth and smacked of sincerity. But then, wasn't that what made a lie believable? Give just enough verifiable detail. Provide a smattering of veracity, an equal amount of honesty and . . .

Poof.

Everyone believed. Everyone got fooled. Everyone ended up dead.

No mistakes could be made. Not with the Razorbacks angling to take out the entire Nightfury pack: his family, the males he loved and valued above all others.

Ivar would stop at nothing to win. And planting a spy inside the Nightfury camp—one who claimed to be Bastian's long-lost brother? Hell, that qualified as a major coup. Would be a real victory for the son of a bitch, so . . . yeah. Brother or not, Venom wanted to know everything. Down to the last digit and decimal point. Only after Azrad was vetted would he decide which way to jump. Into belief and acceptance. Or death and destruction as he split the male in half to protect his pack.

Chapter Sixteen

Tension spread like nuclear fallout, clouding the air inside the coffee shop with suspicion. Wick didn't mind. Uncomfortable and tense worked for him. Caution kept a male alive. And with the proverbial plutonium planted and the timer set, vigilance seemed like a good idea right now.

Then again, when didn't it?

The thud of his boots soft in the quiet, Wick paced another circle around Azrad. The males he commanded shifted with unease. He didn't blame them. No one messed with him—or his brothers-in-arms—unless forced, and these two? The pair looked smarter than most, recognized that a ticking time bomb was about to go off. Wick could practically hear the countdown. The snick of the clock as the second hand ground down to blastoff.

Which meant he needed to do something.

Lickety-split. As in, right fucking now. Otherwise the situation would detonate, leaving his pack with a crater full of speculation and no real answers, so . . . no question. Diffusing the situation sounded like a plan. A good one, except for one thing.

Coreene Callahan

Meditation wasn't his strength. His expertise lay in other areas—namely, killing things—but that didn't change the facts. Nor the urgency. With Bastian set to go off, he figured he had a minute tops before his commander lost his patience and went nuclear. The resulting fallout wouldn't be pretty. Neither would the cleanup. And scraping what was left of Azrad and his boys off the floor? Not on his list of things to do tonight. He had other plans. A strategy that included discovering if he was right about Azrad.

Like, after all, recognized like. An undisputable fact.

Now suspicion gave rise to certainty, grabbing Wick by the balls. Azrad carried all the markers. The truth of it—of who and what he was—went more than skin deep. It was embedded in the male's bones. Was present in the way he moved, smelled, and thought. Wick could practically hear the mental wheels turning inside Azrad's head, so . . .

Not a chance. He wouldn't be leaving B to his own devices until he knew for sure, one way or the other.

Hooking a chair leg on the flyby, Wick kicked it into the center of the room. Metal screeched against wood. The nails-on-chalkboard racket shattered the silence, doing what he intended . . . making the other warriors in the room flinch. The ripple of muscle widened the gap, unlocking the stalemate as everyone glanced his way. Venom frowned at him. Wick met his gaze and tipped his chin, the move all about one thing. Trust. He needed Venom to back him up if things got critical, and Bastian went sideways. As his buddy nodded back, Wick grabbed another chair and shoved it in Azrad's direction.

The male stopped the sliding invitation with his foot.

Not bothering to explain what he wanted, Wick showed him instead. Flipping his own chair backward, he straddled

270

the seat and stacked his forearms on the backrest. He forced
tense muscles to relax, playing it cool to put Azrad at ease.
The body language sent a clear message—it was all about the
chat. No one needed to die here.

Wick stifled a snort. Jesus. His move beat the shit out of
irony. Him . . . receptive to conversation. What a fucking
joke. But hey, dialing down the boom-boom factor required
a certain amount of finesse. And if giving diplomacy a shot
got the job done—relaxed Azrad enough to acquire the
information Wick wanted? Well then, taking patience and
tactfulness to the next level seemed like the best way to go.

"Got a few questions." His gaze riveted on the male
standing a few feet away, Wick pointed to the second chair.
"You in a talking frame of mind?"

The nice guy approach triggered a chain reaction.
Surprise spread like the plague, killing silence in the room.
Murmurs full of "WTF" fogged the air. Wick ignored the incredulous looks his comrades threw his way. He didn't care
what the other Nightfuries thought. Didn't have time for
the usual BS either. Not if what he suspected about Azrad
turned out to be true.

"Depends." Mistrust in his eyes, Azrad grabbed the
chair. Rotating it into a 180-degree turn, he mirrored Wick's
move, adopting the same position.

"On what?" Wick asked, raising a brow.

Azrad frowned. Light winked off his eyebrow stud.
"What you want to know."

Everything. But he'd get to that. "Show me the inside of
your forearm."

Blondie and Eye Patch shifted, covering their leader's
six.

The warning was subtle. The show of muscle was not. Wick's mouth curved. The pair were devoted to Azrad. Good. Solidarity equaled strength. An excellent sign. It said a lot about the male seated across from him. A leader who instilled loyalty and love instead of fear was admirable. Maybe even ally worthy.

His expression closed, Azrad shook his head.

Wick held the line. "I need to see it."

"Fuck," the male growled under his breath. A moment later, he complied. Unlacing his fingers, he turned his wrist out. A muscle jumped along his jaw as he glared at Wick. "Satisfied?"

Not even close. *Satisfied* didn't have anything to do with it.

Wick nodded anyway, his gaze on the scar that marred the inside of Azrad's forearm. Fucking hell. Never mind suspicion, instinct made a better bedmate. His had been right. Then again, having graduated from the same hellhole, calling Azrad out hadn't been all that difficult. Even so, the sight of the brand drove revulsion to the surface, making Wick remember and his stomach churn. He swallowed the burn, unable to look away from the proof of the Archguard's cruelty.

So obscene. So barbaric. So completely unnecessary.

And yet, the depravity of the mark remained.

Shrugging out of his jacket, Wick dropped it behind him. As the leather hit the floor, he rolled up his sleeve. An inch below his elbow joint, the Dragonese symbols—seven digits strong—marred the skin on the inside of his own forearm.

Azrad sucked in a quick breath.

"Wick," Venom murmured, stepping in behind him. "There's no need—"

"It's time, Ven. I'm tired of hiding it."

He'd done a good job, though, hadn't he? None of his brothers-in-arms knew the truth. None had seen the mark either. In dragon form, he hid it, using his magic to camouflage his shame. In human form, he couldn't conceal the scar. Which meant he never took off his shirt or wore short sleeves. But now, after all these years, he wanted to come clean. To have the others understand why he kept to himself and didn't talk much.

He'd been trained from an early age to be that way. No talking. No physical contact. No warmth of any kind. Deprivation like that changed a male. Made him quiet. Kept him apart. Bred mistrust and suspicion.

The ultimate way to build a killing machine.

Flexing his hand, Wick watched his muscles work, undulating beneath the brand, distorting the numbers his captor had burned into his skin . . . remembering what had made it.

Molten dragon venom, the only substance that could mark his kind.

If used before a male went into his *change*—before the magic in his blood activated—the stamp of ownership scarred and never faded. The burden became something to carry, a blatant reminder seared into skin. One to look at and live with every day. One that dragged the past, no matter how distant, into the present.

He should know.

Every time Wick looked at it, his stomach rolled, taking him to the night he'd received his number. As memory spun him around, things he yearned to forget bubbled to the surface. In a blinding flash, he was back in the filth and squalor, reliving the brutality—the flames burning high in the fire pit, the red glow of steel as the bastard lifted the brand from the bubbling vat of dragon venom, the acrid smell of smoke in the air, the hard hands holding him down, the bite of steel against his throat.

Wick clenched his teeth. He should be over it by now. Sixty years was a long time to hold onto the pain, but . . . God. Recall was a bitch with a mind of its own. No matter how many times he tried to blot out the details, the experience stayed with him, haunting him. The helplessness in the face of savagery. The bitter taste of defeat. His rage as they forced him to submit.

Not that it had taken much to subdue him.

His captor had done it right. Waiting until his body chemistry dipped, landing him on the edge of his *change*. He'd been too weak to fight . . . so ill, beyond vulnerable, in need of help from a senior male to get him through his first shift. Most males anticipated the occurrence. Dreamed of the night it would happen and rejoiced when it came. Then again, those males had sires who loved them. He'd had a sadistic bastard who wanted him dead at the first sign of true strength. The second Wick's magic spiked, his captor had realized his peril, recognized the warrior inside the male, and understood Wick would hunt him to the ends of the earth—tear him limb from limb—the instant he woke in dragon form.

So yeah. He understood Azrad. And as he looked at the male seated across from him, Wick saw everything he felt reflected back at him.

"They didn't send you . . ." Clearing his throat, Azrad trailed off. His brow furrowed, he shifted in his seat. A moment later, he broke eye contact and traced the edges of his own scar. "You were never at Tanzenmed. I would have seen you there."

The name made Wick tense. Tanzenmed. A Dragonkind prison so terrible, males begged for death, a merciful kill when faced with the prospect of imprisonment there.

"I never got that far." Thanks to Venom. His best friend had risked everything. Given up a cushy life inside Dragonkind's aristocracy to rescue him. Throat gone tight, he glanced over his shoulder. As always, Venom stood at the ready, willing to back him up at a moment's notice. Just like the night he'd defied the general and intervened to save his life. "Which club did you come up in?"

"Rodin's." A hard gleam in his eyes, Azrad's nostrils flared. "You?"

"The general's."

"My sire's club," Venom said at the same time, his voice overlapping Wick's, revealing what neither of them ever had before. "Rodin's right hand back in the day."

"Jesus H. Christ. A fight club run by Dragonkind elite?" Grabbing a chair, Rikar dragged it over and joined their circle. Concern in his pale eyes, he shook his head. "The practice has been outlawed for hundreds of years."

"Doesn't mean the clubs don't exist. The new law simply pushed them underground." One shitkicker crossed over the other, Bastian leaned back against the table edge. The pose was relaxed. Wick knew better. His commander didn't do nonthreatening. "Thought they only used human fighters, though."

"Probably still do," Wick said, a prickle of unease nipping at his nape. He didn't want to talk about it. Hated the power of recall and what it did to him. "But they bet on boys too."

"I entered the ring for the first time on my seventh birthday."

"Same." A bad taste entered his mouth. Fuck. No more secrets. Nothing to hide behind anymore. Wick flexed his hands, not knowing what to do with the knowledge . . . or how to act now that his brothers-in-arms knew the truth. "They kept me caged by day and fighting by night until—"

"You went into the *change*," Azrad said, completing his sentence.

Wick nodded. "After that, I was too much of a risk. I was slotted for Tanzenmed, but Venom intervened, pulling me out before the general loaded me on the truck."

Resulting in the death of Venom's sire.

Wick swallowed past the knot in his throat. Patricide. Jesus, what an awful burden to bear. One Venom carried every day. A moment in time that had put a price on both their heads and sealed their fate. An act that made them instant fugitives, sending them running with nothing but the clothes on their backs.

"I did what was needed," Venom murmured, shrugging off the sacrifice. He always did, downplaying his bravery. But Wick knew the truth. That night had taken a terrible toll on both of them. The strain in his friend's voice broadcasted that fact loud and clear. "But you were already inside Tanzenmed by then."

Azrad nodded. "Godforsaken place."

No doubt.

Established to train the elite, the prison used live targets—Dragonkind sentenced to death, males drawn from the fight clubs, or anyone the Archguard wanted silenced—in a series of war games designed to teach fledging dragons how to fight. Spread out over vast acreage in rural Russia, the compound kept the live targets enclosed in a limited area via an electronic collar, allowing the hunters to track and kill their prey. Packed with explosives, the collars would detonate, blowing a male's head off if he crossed the boundary to flee the compound.

Death via C-4. Or try to fight your way out.

A depraved practice with an equally revolting endgame. Once imprisoned, no one walked out of Tanzenmed alive.

Which begged a question, didn't it?

His gaze narrowed, he looked Azrad over.

Quick on the uptake, Venom caught his mental string. "The compound is reputed to be impenetrable. Only one way in. No way out, so . . ."

Rikar huffed. "Wanna explain how you managed to escape, Azrad?"

"Wrong question, my brother," Bastian said.

"Exactly." Intuition spiked, and Wick growled. Ah, yes . . . the plot thickened. "*How* isn't important, Rikar. It's the *who* we want to know."

"Fucking hell," Rikar growled.

"Nian," Venom said, the anger in his tone unmistakable. "You're in the bastard's back pocket."

"No." Sitting up straighter, Azrad shook his head. The violent movement backed up his denial, making his irises shimmer like blue diamonds. "I used the Archguard asshole to get out of that hellhole . . . nothing more."

"Nothing is ever that easy." Pushing away from the table edge, Bastian stood. Suspicion made the air crackle with hostility. Patience worthy of a commander stayed his hand. "What did you promise him . . . my head on a platter?"

"Never," Azrad said. "Nian came to me three months ago with a proposition."

"Why you?" B asked.

"I earned a certain reputation in prison."

"Oh really?" Sarcasm out in full force, Rikar flashed his pearly whites, half smile, mostly snarl. "Mind sharing what that was exactly?"

His gaze predatory flat, Azrad cracked his knuckles. "I kill whatever comes near me."

Wick snorted. "Handy."

"It worked for me. So here's how it breaks down." Azrad glanced from him to Bastian, then back again. "You know how the pampered bastards think. Nian is the same. He needed a warrior outside the Archguard's grid, a player they'd never see coming, never mind miss. He offered me a deal . . . freedom and a first-class ticket to Seattle for one thing."

"A face-to-face with me."

"Bingo." Azrad shrugged. "The deal is: I get close enough to facilitate the meeting. After that, I'm to get in your good graces . . . in tight enough to feed him information about Bastian and the Nightfury pack. I never agreed to that part of the bargain, but . . ." Trailing off, the male frowned at his bruised knuckles. "I wanted to meet you, so lying to him about the spying shit seemed like the play to make."

"Not a bad plan," Venom said, sounding impressed.

"It got me here, didn't it?"

Venom rolled his eyes.

Azrad grinned, then smoothed his expression. As amusement slid into seriousness once more, the male met B's gaze. "Look, I know you don't trust me. I don't blame you. If someone showed up claiming to be my blood kin, I'd hurt him first and ask questions second. All I ask is that you run the DNA. Give me that much, at least."

Expression impassive, Bastian eyed the male. "No promises, but . . . give us a few days. The blood work will get run. In the meantime—"

"In the meantime," Azrad said. "I'm into something else you should know about."

Curiosity nudged Wick. "What's the cherry on top?"

"I'm inside the enemy camp." A nasty gleam in his eyes, Azrad smiled, the expression making him look like a kingpin. A dangerous one with his finger on the trigger. "I figured you might need a gesture of goodwill to take me seriously, so I infiltrated the Razorback ranks over two weeks ago."

"Christ," Rikar said, looking like he'd been hit upside the head. With an axe, sharp side up.

Venom blinked. "For real?"

"For real. The bastards think I'm one of them."

"A spy." Wick grinned. He couldn't help it. The plan struck him as ingenious. Smart. Bold. A gutsy move by a gusty male. Right up Wick's alley. "That's how you knew about Jamison."

Dark-blue eyes met his. "Razorback chatter and some research put the female in the mix. You ruffled some feathers when you stole Tania out from underneath Ivar. Logic suggested you'd go after the sister next."

Rikar dropped another f-bomb. "We're that predictable?"

"Only when it comes to females." Heavy metal on his face winking in the low light, Azrad stared at the Nightfury first in command. "Otherwise, you're a fucking mystery. Good thing too. With the Razorbacks hunting you, secrecy is—"

"So little brother wants to join our cause." When Azrad nodded, B approached on silent feet. Skirting the end of the coffee bar, his commander rolled up beside his *maybe* brother. Azrad froze. Wick didn't blame him. As calm as B looked, everyone in the room knew he wasn't playing. Raising his foot, B nudged the side of Azrad's chair. "What's in it for you?"

"Payback."

"Ivar piss you off or something?"

"Too soon to tell. I haven't met him yet." His head tilted back, the male looked up at Bastian, meeting his bright-green eyes. "I'm still working my way up the Razorback food chain. But Ivar's just a stepping stone, one I'll use to catch a bigger fish."

Wick hummed. "You're talking about Rodin."

"I owe him a lifetime of pain." Azrad smiled, the show of teeth animalistic. "Besides, Rodin and his cronies are bank-rolling the Razorbacks."

Looming above them, interest sparked in B's gaze. "Do you have proof of that?"

"Not yet, but—"

An alarm went off, beeping double time.

Azrad glanced at his watch. Midnight on the dot. "Nian's on the hunt for it. You interested in talking to him?"

"You got a go bag with a computer here?"

The male nodded.

Bastian tipped his chin. "Then set it up."

He didn't need to be asked twice. The second B agreed, Azrad pushed out of his seat so fast the chair wobbled. As he turned to his warriors, Eye Patch handed him a black back-pack. Slinging it over his shoulder, he crossed to the large table in the center of the room and went to work: unzipping the bag, pulling out a laptop, fingers flying as he typed in coordinates and set up the video chat.

Wall-mounted above a cluster of club chairs, a large flat screen TV flipped on. Wick strode over for a better look. The video prompt box blinked on center screen, washing the coffee shop's pale walls with bright-blue light. Smart move on Azrad's part. The wide-angle webcam hooked on top of the TV would capture the entire room, allowing Nian to view all of them from the other side of the world.

Azrad tapped a few more keys and—

"About flipping time."

"Good to see you too, Nian."

Seated behind a desk, a dark-haired male stared out at them. Eyes the color of opals swept the inside of Starbucks. "Which one of you is Bastian?"

"Right here." Impassive, Bastian sat down, unloading his weight on a club chair. As he set his shitkickers on the coffee table, he met the youngest member of the Archguard head-on. With more growl in his voice than patience, he said, "What the fuck do you want, Nian?"

"Any number of things," the male said. "But first things first. You need to get your warriors the hell out of Prague. Rodin's hatching a scheme . . . one that includes Gage and Haider's execution. At nightfall, a death squad will be sent out to secure them."

Wick bared his teeth on a snarl.

"Goddamn it," Venom growled.

"Exactly." A row of bookcases behind him, Nian leaned forward in his office chair. Not bothering to hide his concern, he nailed Bastian with shimmering multihued eyes. "I don't know where the Metallics sleep, so I can't reach them. But if you can . . . do it. Tell them to stay out of dragon form. No flying. The city will be crawling with Rodin's thugs come sundown. Tell them to contact me via this web link. I'll smuggle them out of the city."

Lovely in theory. Big problem with its proposed execution.

Wick didn't trust the Archguard whelp any farther than he could throw him. No male in his right mind would. Especially considering Nian's pedigree and history. Any number of possibilities might play out. The bastard could be in league with Rodin. He might be setting the leader of the Archguard up to take the fall for whatever scheme he had in the works. Could be lying through his teeth in order to lead the Metallics into a trap too. Any combination of which would see his brothers-in-arms murdered in cold blood.

All losing propositions.

"*Sloan,*" Wick said to his buddy standing sentry outside.

"*Here.*"

"*Find a computer.*"

Scales clicked as Sloan shifted on a nearby rooftop. "*What do you need?*"

"*Warn the Metallics. Rodin's got a price on their heads.*" One ear on his commander's conversation with Nian, Wick met his XO's gaze. Rikar nodded, and he continued. "*Tell 'em to get out of Prague. Under the radar. Most ricky-tick.*"

"*Roger that.*"

The thump of boots on stairs came through mind-speak.

The sound lit Wick up, making his muscles tighten and tension creep across his shoulders. He wanted to yell "hurry!" at his buddy. Wick stayed silent instead. Sloan would do his level best. But computers weren't as reliable as mind-speak. The message might not get through or be picked up in time. The entire Nightfury pack had just been forced into a holding pattern. Nothing left to do now but pray Gage and Haider made it out in one piece.

☼ ☼ ☼

Chair springs squeaked as Nian shifted in his seat, bringing him closer to the computer screen. Forearms stacked on the desktop, he leaned in, picking up details, assessing the situation as he stared at Bastian. Holy Christ and a baseball bat. He'd expected fierce from the Nightfury commander. What he saw topped it. The male was more than warrior strong. Kick-ass with a healthy dose of dangerous, his vibe screamed "don't mess with me," and with Bastian's green gaze pointed in his direction, Nian believed it. Every rumor. Every story. Every word whispered in dark corners about the male and his tactics.

Lucky for him he sat half a world away. Safe enough. Out of range with an entire ocean between them. At least, Nian hoped so. Bastian no doubt possessed a long reach and many allies on both sides of the Atlantic. Males willing to do his bidding without question or at a moment's notice.

The thought wasn't a pleasant one.

Good thing he wasn't faint of heart. Or without power of his own.

Readjusting his position, Nian looked into the screen, out into an open room framed by large windows. Clustered behind Bastian's chair, the Nightfuries backed their commander. Tall. Strong. Unwavering. Warriors driven to protect, every last one. Nian recognized the breed, but held the line, meeting each male's gaze before returning his attention to Bastian. So far, so good. All systems were a go.

Mission almost accomplished. Leading with the Gage and Haider angle had been a brilliant stroke of genius. The ploy had captured the Nightfury commander's attention like nothing else could. Any fool could see Bastian cared about his comrades. His concern was palpable, fogging the air around him, coming through from over five thousand miles away. He wanted Gage and Haider safe. He wanted them secure. He wanted the pair home in Seattle.

Perfect in every way.

Ironic too. In his quest to bring Bastian down, Rodin—and his asinine scheme—had provided the one thing Nian needed above all else . . . an in with the Nightfury pack. Now he sat nose-to-screen with one of the most powerful males of his kind, minutes away from procuring the support he required to cut the leader of the Archguard off at the knees.

But only if he played his cards right.

Bastian wasn't stupid. Then again, neither was he.

Gaze still narrowed on him, Bastian lifted his boots from the coffee table. Shifting in the leather club chair, he leaned forward, feet planted on the floor, elbows on his knees, fingers laced between the spread of his thighs. The move brought him closer to the camera. Nian swallowed, resisting the urge to lean back . . . get out of range before things went apocalyptic. A stupid reaction. Bastian couldn't touch him. Not right now anyway.

"How did you come by the information, Nian?" Bastian asked, his voice soft. The melodic pitch pricked the nape of Nian's neck, warning him without words. Something about the tone was off. Far too dangerous to ignore. "You in Rodin's back pocket?"

Nian shook his head. "No, but I've worked hard to culti-
vate his trust. I'm there now. He's begun to confide in me.
Any information I have comes directly from the bastard.
You can trust it."

"Then tell me . . ." Same tone. Shivers rolled down
Nian's spine as the Nightfury commander nailed him with
shimmering green eyes. "What's the real reason behind the
roundup? What's Rodin's true intention?"

Christ. Had he said smart earlier? Well, he'd meant brilliant. Bastian was astute in a way that made a male sit up
and take notice. "He knows of Lothair's death. Learned of
it from someone in Seattle."

"Fucking hell." Standing behind his commander's chair,
a blond, pale-eyed warrior scowled at him. "Ivar. The asshole's been chatting with Rodin."

"I assume as much," Nian said, dragging his focus from
the blond warrior back to Bastian. "I can't prove the connection yet, but I think Rodin is funding the Razorbacks.
He's running underground fight clubs and female slave auctions. Making a ton of money from both enterprises and—"

"How do you know?" A knowing light in his eyes, Bastian
tilted his head and stared at him, the glare full of predatory
intent. "You been visiting Rodin's playground?"

Nian opened his mouth to answer.

Bastian cut him off. "Why don't you tell me about the
female?"

"What female?"

"The one you purchased last week at an auction."

Surprise made him twitch. Recall made his throat go
dry. Ah, Christ. Not good. He didn't want anyone digging
up that skeleton. It needed to stay buried, six feet under
where it belonged. Otherwise, the truth of that night would

get him killed. But even as Nian told himself to keep it under wraps, to remain impassive, calm, well able to deny the accusation, memory spun him in dangerous directions.

Grace von Ziger. The beautiful blond with big brown eyes and gorgeous energy. Not that most males noticed. His talent for illusion had unearthed her deception when she woke in his home. An HE female—rarest of the rare— Grace was a *zinmera*, so evolved she could disguise her connection to the Meridian. The chameleon-like ability served her well, allowing her to fool members of his kind into believing she was low energy, prompting them to overlook her.

Too bad that didn't apply to him.

From the moment he'd laid eyes on her, he'd been unable to look away. Or allow another male to own her. Touch her. Possess and treat her like a sexual prize.

Lifting his hand from the leather blotter, he sat back and, reaching beneath the desk edge, fingered the driver's license he'd wedged under the wooden lip. Lapier thought he'd thrown it away, erasing all trace of her, but he'd been unable to do it. He liked the laminated paper within easy reach. Often flipped it open to look at her picture. To imagine her safe in America, starting a new life with the seed money he'd provided. But as his fingertips ghosted over the crisp fold and he held Bastian's gaze, Nian knew he should throw it away . . . burn it along with the file folder in his floor safe, the one that held all her personal information.

Keeping a piece of her, after all, was foolhardy, not to mention dangerous.

As dangerous as the warrior pack seated in Seattle.

"How long have you been spying on me?" he asked, feeling stupid for not realizing it sooner. Hell, Bastian no doubt had someone watching him right now.

"Long enough to know you bought a first-class ticket out of Prague. Question is . . . who was on the plane? Not you, so . . ." Bastian raised a brow. "The flight landed in New York. You want me to do some digging? Check passenger manifests? Track travel plans stateside? I can send a couple of warriors to—"

"Stay away from her," he growled, rage lighting his fuse.

"She mean that much to you?"

Nian stayed silent, a warning in his eyes. He understood Bastian's intent . . . received the message loud and clear. The bastard wanted him to know he wasn't invulnerable, that anyone could be gotten to with the right amount of leverage. And Bastian—clever tactician that he was—knew how to crank the hell out of it. But if the Nightfury warriors went anywhere near Grace, Nian would show no mercy. He'd use every ounce of power he possessed to level the Nightfury pack. Alliance be damned. She deserved a fresh start, and he hadn't saved her life—and risked his own in the doing—to turn around and thrust her back into danger.

"All right," Bastian murmured, watching him closely. "But the offer stands. We don't hurt females, Nian. If she gets into trouble . . . needs help . . . let me know. My pack is closer, able to reach her faster."

Nian should've appreciated the offer. It pissed him off instead. If Grace got into trouble, he'd jump the pond to ensure her safety. No one else would be involved, and the Nightfury commander would be the last to know.

Done with the bullshit, Nian challenged the warrior threatening him. "You done screwing around? Can we get back on point now?"

A slow smile spread across Bastian's face. The amusement didn't quite reach his eyes. "As long as we understand each other."

"No doubt of that," Nian said, anger mixing with respect. Bold bastard. Whatever else his claim to fame, Bastian knew how to operate, and as much as it chafed Nian to admit it, he admired the warrior for it. "I'm almost positive Rodin and Ivar are in league together. All the income from the fight clubs and slave auctions . . . and there is a lot of it . . . isn't hitting his personal accounts. It's being funneled elsewhere."

"You tracking it?" the blond male asked.

Nian nodded. "Trying to, but he's clever. Good at hiding his illegal holdings along with the money trail. But that's not the most immediate problem."

Bastian raised a brow. "How do you figure?"

"Rodin is calling a special meeting of the high counsel. He wants Lothair's death ruled illegal . . . treated as murder. Charges will be levied against a member of your pack."

"Who?"

"Forge."

Bastian cursed. The Nightfury warriors standing behind him backed the sentiment. As f-bombs dropped, clouding the airwaves, Nian dished the rest. "He will demand you deliver Forge to Prague for trial."

"And execution," Bastian said, quick on the uptake. The trial would be nothing more than a ruse. A sham conducted behind closed doors. Oh, Rodin would make it look good. Court favor among Dragonkind by playing make-believe—using sleight of hand and rumor to establish the male's guilt—when in reality, Forge would never see the inside of the Archguard's tribunal courtroom. "Why Forge?"

"I don't know, but . . ." Nian trailed off, then let his suspicions loose. "Rodin is rattled, scrambling to cover up something . . . afraid of Forge for some reason. But he has no proof of his involvement in Lothair's death, of that I am certain."

Bastian snorted. "He'll manufacture what he needs."

"Probably, but here's the kicker." Plucking his lighter from its perch beside the laptop, Nian flicked at the top. The snap echoed, sounding loud in the quiet. "When you fail to produce Forge, the entire Nightfury pack will fall under suspicion. Rodin will then have reason to reinstate the old laws and—"

"Jesus," Bastian growled. "*Xzinile.*"

"Exile." The blond snarled, showing a row of straight white teeth. "And a bull's-eye on our backs for every bounty hunter around."

"It's a power play, Rikar." Twisting in his seat, the Nightfury commander glanced over his shoulder. He met his warrior's gaze and shook his head. "Hell, the bastard's after me."

As Nian nodded, another round of low curses came through the speakers.

Facing forward once more, Bastian pushed to his feet. Both hands curled into fists, he walked closer to the camera and plugged Nian with an intense look. "When's the vote?"

"Night after tomorrow."

"Can you stall it?"

"Maybe." Nian frowned, mind churning over viable options. The best ones lay in the letter of the law. If he put up too many roadblocks, suspicion would fall on him, and Rodin would guess his game. Turning the lighter over in his hand, he brushed his thumb over the crest engraved in the gold. "There are certain criteria Rodin must follow to reinstate *Xzinile*. If I make him jump through all the hoops, it'll take more time."

"Good," Bastian said with a nod. "Keep me in the loop."

Nian leaned forward in his chair. "Can I count on you to keep me in yours?"

A bold inquiry with potentially disastrous consequences. A wise male didn't tweak a powerful dragon's tail. Nian knew it but didn't care . . . couldn't pass up the opportunity to secure Bastian's support. He'd waited months for a face-to-face with the Nightfury commander—to acquire what he needed to move forward with his plans for the Archguard. Now that he'd done his part and given Bastian valuable intel along with his trust? Nian wanted something in return. The warrior's stamp of approval. Something that wouldn't cost Bastian much up front, but held the potential to yield vast returns for years to come.

Green eyes narrowed on him. "Excuse me?"

"I scratch your back . . . you scratch mine." Holding the lethal male's gaze, Nian pushed his agenda. "I want what you want, Bastian . . . Rodin's head on a platter. I can't achieve that without your backing. Do I have it?"

Silence met his question. Terrible and effective, the quiet spread, filling the void, slithering in like a poisonous snake—silent, venomous, deadly. Cranked tight by uncertainty, tension wrung him dry as pressure banded around his chest. Smothering his reaction, Nian breathed around the knot in his throat and stayed true, refusing to back down. The outcome was too important. Everything hinged on the next few moments. On Bastian's decision and—

"You have it," Bastian murmured. "But Nian?"

"Yes?"

"Disappoint me, and you die."

A promise in his eyes, Bastian warned him with a look, then turned and walked away. Unease picked up his heart, making it slam against his breastbone as Nian watched the Nightfury commander stride toward the door across the room. A second later, the computer screen went black, severing the connection, leaving him in the dark and without the reassurance he craved. Nor the triumphant moment he'd expected.

Christ help him. After months of planning, he'd finally gotten what he wanted, so . . . Nian frowned. Why wasn't he celebrating? He should be. Should be relieved, thankful he now had the powerful male's backing, but . . .

He wasn't grateful at all. Not happy either. Instead, he felt wary. Out on the tip of a very thin limb. Uncomfortable in his own skin, 'cause . . . no doubt about it. He had a bad, *bad* feeling. One that suggested he'd just allowed a shark into shallow water, inviting him to swim in his private wading pool.

Chapter Seventeen

Still perched on the examination table after her checkup, J. J. pulled a T-shirt over her head and eyed her fancy new walking cast, although it looked more like a boot than anything else. A royal blue one with ugly Velcro straps and no fashion sense. She refused to complain. Beggars couldn't be choosers, and given the fact she'd just been given a clean bill of health, ungratefulness seemed like a stretch.

A big one, considering she was still breathing.

Alive and well. An excellent state of grace.

Wiggling her toes, J. J. shifted on the tabletop. Paper crinkled beneath her as a faint ache ghosted up her calf. She huffed. Well all right, *clean bill of health* might be a bit of an exaggeration. Her broken ankle still hurt, and her side? Even though Myst had removed the neat row of sutures—declaring her almost healed—it still ached like the devil, nailing her with a sharp jab if she moved too fast. But other than that? She was good to go.

All thanks to Wick. The guy packed one heck of a punch on the healing front. Miraculous? Sure. A welcome turn of events? Absolutely. Especially since she'd come out of surgery just under forty-eight hours ago.

Another round of thankfulness sank deep.

Lucky. She was so damned lucky. Evidence of it lay in the way he'd treated her, but also across the room.

J. J. glanced toward the bank of stainless steel cabinets and the two women who'd served as her lifeline over the last hour. Busy stowing medical tools and extra supplies, the pair stood side by side in front of the countertop. A pretty picture. One J. J. knew well. She'd grown up watching them. Best friends forever. Most girls said that at some point but then let it go, drifting away from each other as life pulled them in different directions. Not these two. Myst and her sister were rock solid. Had been since the third grade, and as J. J. listened to her sister laugh—the sound lightening her heart by the second—she marveled at the irony.

Such different life paths. Prison for her. Career and community for them. Two completely different roads, and yet, here she sat . . .

Sharing the same space inside Black Diamond's medical clinic.

Rotating into a 180-degree turn, she sat sideways. With her legs dangling over the side of the table, her gaze skimmed over the space. High-tech equipment pushed against the back wall. Boxy fluorescents hummed overhead, washing everything with warm light. She stifled a shiver, the pale paint and soft electrical buzz reminding her of days gone by and the community center in the old neighborhood. Everything had been colorless there too. Pale walls. Whey-faced people. Anemic opportunity . . . thin beyond measure.

J. J. swallowed past the lump in her throat. It seemed like a lifetime ago. All the times Myst had knocked on their door, asking if Tania could come out to play. Then later—after the hormones hit and adolescent angst settled in—if her sister could go with her to the Four Corners Community Center after school and on weekends. The memory made J. J. smile. Made her happy for her sister, if not a little sad for herself. She'd always wanted a friend like Myst. Someone willing to put themselves on the line, stand by her side . . . simply be there when everyone else bailed.

The sentiment smacked of jealousy.

But it wasn't that.

Funny enough, J. J. didn't envy their friendship. Never had either. Oh, she'd tried to copy it a few times, hoping to find a best friend of her own. All to no avail. She wasn't like Tania: charming, confident in social situations, able to put people at ease and win their trust. Her sister's innate ability to say the right thing at precisely the right time flummoxed J. J. She'd never acquired the skill. Silence was more her thing. Throw in her powers of observation and love of people watching and . . . yup. She flew under the radar as much as possible. Was a regular operator, a covert player who saw more than most.

An excellent skill to own, as it turned out. The talent had saved her more than once in prison. Knowing which way to jump, after all, equaled staying alive.

"Hey, guys?" Her voice interrupted the stream of conversation across the room.

A plastic packet in her hand, Tania glanced over her shoulder. "You ready to go?"

"All dressed," she said, smoothing her hands over the gray sweatpants. Careful not to tweak her ribs, she slid off her perch and hopped to the floor. The tie at her waist slipped. Grabbing a handful of material, J. J. turned the band under a second time. As the cotton settled at her hipbones, she palmed the cane hanging from the table edge. Plunking it on the floor, she kept most of her weight on her good leg and turned toward the sliding glass door. "Where are we headed now? To the gym to help Ange?"

"In a minute." Pulling the stethoscope from around her neck, Myst set it on the countertop. With a quick pivot, she leaned back against the cabinets and rubbed her hand over the flat curve of her belly. She did that a lot, no doubt thinking about the baby she carried . . . and her mate, the dragon-guy responsible for her condition. Two months pregnant and hardly able to contain her excitement. J. J.'s mouth curved. Impending motherhood. It looked good on Myst. "We need to discuss something first."

J.J. blinked. Uh, oh. That didn't sound good. Particularly since they'd been *talking* for the last couple of hours. Great in a lot of ways. She now knew the lay of the land: all about Black Diamond and the dragon-guys who called it home. Toss in Daimler—the adorable tuxedo-wearing butler who'd shown up with a tray of cupcakes, begging them to take a stroll down Treat Street while they curled up in the recovery room bed—and . . . uh-huh. She was officially on the other side of the wall. Smack-dab in the middle of weird.

Or not. She didn't know yet.

Tania, Myst, and Angela didn't seem like the crazy type, and their reassurance went a long way, helping her climb the mountain of holy crap banging around inside her head. Still . . .

Despite the assurances, it wasn't an easy sell.

All right, the dragon stuff she could handle. Disputing the truth after witnessing Wick's transformation—complete with fangs, claws, and scales—seemed counterproductive. Not to mention ridiculous. She couldn't go back, after all, and *un-see* it, but believe it or not . . . strange as it sounded . . . the man-to-dragon switch-up wasn't the problem. The whole energy thing, however? Yeah, that freaked her out. She couldn't wrap her brain around it.

Commitment. Connection. Energy feedings, a bond formed by a force outside her control. The entire concept was scary as hell.

She didn't do relationships. Not well, at least. Her track record spoke volumes . . . none of it good. But that didn't change the facts. According to Tania, the Meridian—the all-powerful source that enveloped the planet, nourishing all living things and, by extension, Dragonkind—didn't lie. Or make mistakes. Which meant she and Wick were now linked through cosmic connection. J. J. shivered as unease slithered deep.

Energy-fuse. The magical bond between mates.

Destroyer of independence and her peace of mind.

Blowing out a shaky breath, J. J. forced herself to stay calm. Her nerves didn't listen, jangling like a ring of runaway keys as she met Myst's gaze. "Are you sure about this . . . the whole energy thing?"

"He fed you, J. J. Healed all but your most severe injuries in less than twelve hours." Picking up a pair of surgical scissors, Myst turned them over in her hands. After pressing the pad of her thumb to one of the blunted tips, she sighed. "The only way that happens is if a male's dragon half recognizes and—"

"Accepts you as his mate," Tania said, jumping in with a soothing tone.

"What if I don't want to be mated?"

J. J. cringed. She hated the question. For some reason, asking it felt disloyal, as though she betrayed Wick by thinking it, never mind saying it aloud. Which was just plain stupid. In every way that mattered. She barely knew the guy. All right, so he'd been good to her—kind, gentle, patient in the face of her freak-out attack—but that didn't mean she wanted to walk down the aisle. Or commit to a relationship that would no doubt end in disaster.

Again.

The thought stopped her cold. Ah, and there it was. The entire reason for her fear. Past experience. Her reaction didn't have a thing to do with Wick and everything to do with her. J. J. frowned so hard her forehead stung. Did that make her a coward? Or simply cautious? She didn't know, but one thing for sure? He moved her in ways no one else ever had, and like it or not she felt the pull. Even with him out of the lair, the almost imperceptible hum of synergy buzzed in her veins. The tug held sway. Drew her attention. Pushed her north of center, tightening its grip, making her feel so alive her senses crackled in reaction.

And she knew . . . without a shadow of a doubt . . . he was the reason.

"Look," Tania murmured. "I know you're scared. If Wick was fixated on me, I would be terrified too. He's a dangerous guy, totally unpredictable and—"

"What are you talking about?" All right, so she'd been scared of Wick at first. More than a little unsure of him, but that hadn't lasted long. He was too solid to fear. Too straightforward to mistrust, and despite her track record with men, J. J. knew a good thing when she saw it. The realization, however, didn't help matters. Or mean she wanted to jump into a relationship with him. The mere idea sent her spinning. Too many things could go wrong. She'd make another mistake. Take another wrong turn. End up neck-deep in trouble all over again. "I'm not afraid of Wick. This isn't about him. I mean . . . not exactly."

"You aren't?" Tania asked, surprise winging across her face. "It isn't?"

"No. He's been great."

Myst's mouth fell open. "He has?"

"Yes." Completely true. Every last word, and as her gaze ping-ponged between the two women, J. J. admitted the truth. At least to herself. She may not want to hook up right this minute, but maybe . . . just maybe . . . if she spent more time with Wick, she'd get over her aversion. Energy-fuse aside, her attraction to him was powerful. Undeniable. And if she were honest? Not something she wanted to ignore. "Really patient too, talking me through the—"

"He *talks* to you?" Glancing sideways, her sister threw Myst an incredulous look.

J. J. wanted to roll her eyes. She crossed her arms instead, letting the cane dangle from her fingertips. What the hell was wrong with them? Of course, he talked to her. All right, so maybe not in run-on sentences, but hey . . . short responses she could handle.

"Hey, Tania?" Straight teeth working overtime, Myst nibbled her bottom lip. "If he's responding to her, we may have jumped the gun."

"Daimler won't be happy."

Myst shook her head. "No worries. Her new identity won't go to waste. She'll need the proper paperwork if she wants to leave the lair during the day anyway."

Surprise blinded J. J. *New identity?* "What are you—"

"You know, it makes total sense now that I think about it," Tania said, cutting her off as she tilted her head. And oh boy. Not good. J. J. recognized that look, and whenever her sister wore it, trouble always followed. "He stayed with her all day. Practically kicked me out of the room to be with her."

"Really?" Rabid interest sparked in Myst's eyes. "What did he say?"

"Nothing," Tania said, a clear "duh" in her tone. "He looked at me sideways. Mac said it was all right, so I made him promise we'd sleep in the next room—"

"Within earshot." Myst grinned. "Smart move."

"Thank you," Tania said without losing a beat. "Then I got the hell out of there."

J. J. opened her mouth, then closed it again. What could she say? The exchange made her feel like a twelve-year-old. A clueless one with overbearing parents who intended to take over her life. Lock. Stock. And barrel. Which was . . . yup. An all-too-familiar occurrence with her big sister around.

God give her strength.

"Okay then," Myst said. "New plan. We'll keep Daimler in the loop, but ask him to continue preparations on the safe house anyway . . . just in case things go south. Now all we need to figure out is—"

"All right, that's enough." Done listening to plans for what amounted to her inevitable demise, J. J. glared at them both. She might enjoy a good mystery upon occasion, but playing monkey in the middle? Not really her style. "What the heck is going on?"

Straight teeth worrying her bottom lip, Myst glanced away while Tania pretended to examine her cuticles. The stall tactic didn't work. J. J. knew trouble when she spotted it. The pair were hedging, no doubt wondering how much to tell her. Which didn't bode well. Not for her anyway. Tania times Myst equaled smart squared. A scheme was definitely afoot. One that included her—probably Wick too—so . . .

No. Letting sleeping dogs lie wasn't an option.

"Well?" Ignoring the twinge of pain along her side, J. J. shoved away from the table. Expression set in militant lines, she raised a brow. When neither folded under the pressure, J. J. dug in. No way would she walk around Black Diamond blind, deaf, and dumb while Tania plotted the equivalent of a military coup. "Spill or all bets are off."

Sheepish her new middle name, Tania sighed. "I was worried about you."

"Since when?" J. J. asked, sarcasm out in full force. A chronic fixer, her sister worried about everything. Normally, she didn't mind. The constant barrage of concern reassured her, telling her plainer than words that her sister loved her. Today, though, she could've done with a little less fretting and a lot more forthrightness. "Tell me why you're in fixer mode."

"I freaked out when Wick carried you in."

Myst huffed. "She accused him of killing you."

"What?"

"I know," Tania murmured. "Totally uncalled for and I apologized, but that doesn't mean I trust him not to hurt you. He's a straight-up killer, J. J."

"So am I," she said, making her sister cringe. J. J. felt the answering ping soul deep. A terrible ache rose in its wake. She didn't like reminding Tania, but fact was *fact*. She'd killed a man. Was guilty of the same crime her sister now accused Wick of committing. And honestly? The double standard bothered her. Wick didn't deserve the distain. "He would never hurt me."

"You don't know that."

"Yes . . . I do." Saying the words helped solidify her certainty. Wick might be rough around the edges. He might even scare the hell out of Myst and her sister, but labeling him a woman beater was unfair. She'd insulted him once by fearing he might hit her. J. J. refused to do it again. Or let anyone else think badly of him either. "He saved my life, Tania. Got me away from Griggs, out of the hospital, and here in one piece. All while keeping me pain-free. So, I don't care that he scares you. I like him. I'm attracted to him. I want to know more about him . . . even if the thought of commitment makes me want to run. So back off."

Her outburst echoed, bouncing around the clinic like automatic gunfire.

Stunned into silence, the women stared at her. J. J. glared back, anger helping her hold the line. She was a grown woman, for God's sake. Well able to take care of herself. So screw the new ID and her sister's idea of a safe house. She wanted the chance to get to know Wick better. The decision was noteworthy, her first self-affirming one since getting out of prison. A tribute to autonomy and her newfound freedom. And if she made the wrong choice and it turned out badly? Well then, she would have no one to blame but herself.

Chapter Eighteen

Bare feet planted on the bathmat, Ivar raked a hand through his wet hair and yanked a towel off the top rack. The silver shelf rattled. Terry cloth snapped its tail, protesting the rough treatment. Ivar didn't care. He wanted to trash the entire bathroom. Just let loose and put his fist through the wall. The only thing that stopped him was the sight of fancy light fixtures bookending the antique mirror.

He frowned at the fuckers. Ah, hell, he couldn't do it.

Installed less than a week ago, the expensive pair heralded a momentous occasion. Construction on the underground lair was almost complete. Proof positive lay in the finishing touches that now graced his en suite. After months of waiting, the vanity finally sat in its place, the last tiles had been laid, and, yes, he now owned wall sconces. Small details. Big impact. Which meant he needed to reel it in before he took his frustration out on the wrong thing. And set his plans back another step. With his bedroom suite now complete, he didn't want his worker bees back in his space. The human construction workers he imprisoned had enough on their plates without him fucking up the flow.

Reasonable. Logical. Annoying as hell.

He wanted to kill something. Maybe then he'd kick the cabin fever. Two days. Almost forty-eight hours of nothing. No progress in the lab. No contact with his soldiers. No fresh air either. Why? One answer. He'd been stuck inside his bedroom with Hamersveld. The male was still out of it, flaked out in his bed, suffering from God only knew what for a wren Ivar couldn't find.

With a growl, he tossed the towel into the corner and conjured his clothes. Jesus. Could it get any worse? Another entire night wasted. The confinement was getting old. Inactivity drove him insane. Was the kiss of death, a sign of an idle mind and—

A groan sounded from the other side of the closed door.

Ivar sighed. Terrific. Time to go another round with Hamersveld.

Not bothering with shoes, he padded across the heated floor tile and swung the door wide. Light from the bathroom cut a swath across the bamboo floor, spilling onto the bed beyond. His head half-buried beneath a pillow, blond hair matted with sweat, Hamersveld lay belly down, one arm hanging over the side of the mattress. Not much different there. The warrior had been that way since collapsing on the bed, but . . .

Ivar frowned and, sidestepping the chair he'd parked beside the bed, stared at the male's back. The tattoo bracketing both sides of his spine shifted and . . . holy shit. Ivar drew a quick breath in surprise. Nothing normal about that. The tribal marking Hamersveld wore like a badge of honor wasn't red anymore, but morphing, changing, sifting through the color palate to land on polished silver. Mesmerized, he took a step closer, changing his vantage point for a better view. The tattoo went mirror smooth, reflecting the pink of his irises back at him.

A sizzling hiss rolled through the quiet. Mist rose, twisting like steam from Hamersveld's skin.

A pattern formed in the smoky swirl.

Ivar stilled, then reversed course, backing away a step at a time. Distance seemed like a good idea, and caution an absolute must. Especially right now. Something nasty stared out from the mist, yellow-slitted pupils narrowed on him. Self-preservation punched through. Ivar called on his magic and conjured a protection spell. The invisible shield settled in his hand and—

The thing shrieked, coming through the fog fangs first.

With a curse, Ivar dodged as the miniature dragon lunged at him. Shield up, he avoided the quick strike of a duel-clawed forepaw and countered, feeding the wren a face full of magical steel. A brutal *crack!* ricocheted. Fen's horned head snapped to the side. Scales the same shark-gray as his master's clicked as the wren's gaze swung back to him. The move was slow, measured, full of aggression and twice as deadly. Ivar froze, hoping the male got the message. He meant no harm. Didn't know much about wrens either. By all accounts, the subspecies of Dragonkind owned a matched set . . . equal parts vicious and merciless.

Lovely for Hamersveld. Not so hot for him at the moment.

Fen didn't know him from Adam. And it showed.

Tilting his small head, the spikes lying flat against the wren's neck flipped out, making him look as though he wore a barbed collar. The thing looked positively wicked. Deadly too. Attributes Ivar appreciated. At least under normal circumstances. But here . . . locked in combat with a miniature dragon inside his bedroom? Not so much. He couldn't shift into dragon form to protect himself. Deep underground, surrounded by bedrock and concrete, the space was nowhere near sufficient. He'd get squished while Hamersveld and his wren ended up dead. A terrible outcome, considering he'd spent hours playing nursemaid to the Norwegian.

"Hamersveld!" Half-yell, half-growl, the entreaty bounced around the room. "Wake the fuck up!"

Venomous tail rattling, Fen curled his paws over the footboard. Yellow eyes full of lethal intent, he bared his razor-sharp teeth, leaned into the crouch, and—

"Fen . . . stop!" Hamersveld lunged to his feet behind the wren. Big hands encircled the male's throat from behind. The second skin touched scales, Fen submitted. The collar of dragon spikes flattened, folding back against his neck as the wren turned and pressed his horned head beneath his master's chin. Ivar blinked. Jesus. The thing wanted a hug. Hamersveld didn't deny him. Blond hair sticking up at odd angles, the warrior stood on the mattress and ran his hands over Fen, petting him like a dog. "It's all right. You're all right."

"I'm all right too." With a grumble, Ivar dropped his guard. Magic crackled, then dissipated, taking his invisible shield with it. "Thanks for asking."

Black eyes rimmed by pale blue met his over Fen's head. "Sorry about that. He's always a bit jumpy when he transitions out."

Just a bit? Fuck him, if that constituted *a bit,* Ivar needed a new set of parameters. Or a new dictionary. One or the other, 'cause . . . hell. Hamersveld's description lacked a certain something when it came to the entire wren experience. "Protective of you too."

"Believe it," Hamersveld murmured. "I'm his host. If I die, so does he."

Not understanding, Ivar shook his head and ran a critical eye over Fen. Less than half his size in dragon form, the wren looked tiny to him. Then again, allowance must be made considering the male didn't have an ounce of human in him. A pure species, the wrens' chromosomal DNA diverged, making them related to Dragonkind but separate too. Which meant the subspecies operated under the yoke of a different set of magical principles. Interesting. Especially from an empirical point of view. Chromosomal mutations fascinated him, putting his love of all things scientific to work.

And the wren? Shit, the miniature dragon was a gold mine. Mapping the structure of Fen's DNA would keep him busy for months, if not years. And now—with Hamersveld in the fold—he had the perfect opportunity to explore the possibility.

Careful in his approach, Ivar crossed to the foot of the bed. He ran his gaze over Fen's flank and reached out. As his hand touched down on shark-gray scales, the wren hissed. Hamersveld murmured, soothing the male, allowing Ivar the examination. Huh. Very cool. The miniature dragon wasn't much different from the rest of Dragonkind: ridged scales, sharp claws, spikes running the length of his spine to the tip of his tail. He was quite simply a smaller specimen of a bigger version, the only deviation being the two-taloned forepaws instead of the regular five claws.

Extreme curiosity picked Ivar up, driving him toward the need to know. "How does it work?"

"The bond he and I share?"

Ivar nodded.

"What do you know about wrens?"

"Not much beyond the fact they are a magically distinct species." Stepping around the end of the bed, Ivar touched one of the spikes along the wren's spine. A pinprick of blood welled on his fingertip. "And that we nearly hunted them into extinction a few centuries ago."

"A brutal practice that forced wrens underground . . . or rather, into the Ether."

"Jesus," Ivar murmured, surprise spinning him full circle. No one entered the Ether and lived to tell about it. Owned by a deity, the vast space lay between Heaven and Earth. The magical wasteland acted as a cushion, protecting the creators of all things from the earthly realm, but was ruled by one. "The Goddess of All Things allowed this?"

"She offered all wrens sanctuary, inviting them to make a home within the enchanted lands." Dark eyes intense, Hamersveld pushed Fen away to sit on the side of the bed. As the Norwegian's bare feet touched down, the wren curled around his master from behind, half on the bed, half off, and laid his head in his lap. "With a proviso."

Typical fare for the goddess. She was a vindictive bitch. One who never gave without taking something in return. Witness the fact she'd punished all of Dragonkind for the mistake of a philandering idiot—Silfer, the dragon god—tying his race to humankind, cursing them to procreate with the inferior species, taking their ability to feed themselves from the Meridian and sire female offspring. A circumstance Ivar hoped to change with his serum and the breeding program.

"What did she demand in return?" Ivar asked, repositioning the chair beside the bed. Angled toward Hamersveld now, he sat and, lifting his legs, propped his feet on the bed. The journal he'd left perched on the arm slid sideways. Quick reflexes allowed him to snap it up. His gaze glued to his new friend, he rotated the red leather-bound book in his hands. "A lifetime of servitude?"

Hamersveld shook his head. "Her hatred of us does not extend to our relatives."

"What then?"

"She changed their magical makeup."

"Forced evolution." Made sense. A species might evolve over time, helping the subset adjust to changing ecological conditions, but it didn't happen fast. Or all at once. Which gave Ivar a clue. Hell. She'd remade an entire species to protect them from inevitable extinction. "So now a wren must bond to a Dragonkind male to ensure his survival. He doesn't feed in the usual fashion, does he? You nourish him via your energy, the same way human females feed us."

"Very good, Ivar. You're a quick study." Hands moving in continuous sweeps, he stroked his pet's scales. Fen purred in reaction. "The tribal ink I wear acts as an outlet . . . a kind of conduit. Whenever Fen is hungry, he plugs in, becoming one with the tattoo and connects to the Meridian through me."

"And only a male with the right ink can own a wren."

"Exactly."

"How can I get one?"

"You can't. The marking comes with the *change*. Either a male is gifted with the ink or he isn't. No negotiating it." Hamersveld's focus cut to the journal in his hands. "The moment a male transitions, the tattoo sends out a beacon, allowing the colony of wrens to detect him. After that, it's a race to the finish line. All wrens wish to return to Earth. It's a better life. But only the strongest and fastest will reach the Dragonkind male first and—"

"Create the bond necessary for him to remain on Earth."

As Hamersveld nodded, Ivar cursed. "So the Nightfury water-rat?"

"He wears the ink. It is only a matter of time before a wren reaches him."

"How soon will it happen?"

"Depends. The journey out of the Ether is a long one. It took Fen almost a year to reach me."

"We need to kill him before that happens." As in . . . right fucking now. "Bastian has enough weapons at his disposal. With a wren in their camp . . . Jesus. We don't need that kind of trouble."

"The whelp may not live through the bonding period. Only the strongest males survive it. I became very sick when Fen melded his life force with mine." Lost in the memory, Hamersveld shook his head. "But don't worry. One way or the other, my son will be dead soon enough."

Ivar blinked. "Your *son*?"

"Only a water dragon can breed another, Ivar."

"Will killing him be a problem for you?"

"Not even a small one," Hamersveld murmured, a deadly thread in his tone. "I am unique among our kind. I have killed my offspring for centuries to ensure I stay that way. The Nightfury will be no exception."

Well, all right then. Crisis averted. In the nick of time too. He wanted to get back to the lab. After losing days caring for Hamersveld, he'd fallen behind on Project Supervirus. So much to do, so little time. Ivar thumbed the tattered pages of his notebook. He needed to round up a new batch of humans to—

"What's in the journal?" Holding his gaze, Hamersveld raised a brow.

Ivar hesitated, playing a game of should-he shouldn't-he with himself. How much should he share? Every detail? Or only the basics? He debated a moment, intuition urging him to take the plunge while logic advocated caution. Up until this point, only one male had known the ins and outs of his plan. A pang hit him chest level as he thought of Lothair. God, he missed the male, but mourning him didn't change the facts. His best friend was dead, long gone thanks to his enemies. Now he must start over. And Hamersveld—a warrior who was willing to kill his own son? Hell, he might never find a better counterpart in the war he waged against the Nightfuries, and by extension, humankind.

"How much do you know about science?"

"Enough."

Satisfied with the answer, Ivar nodded and laid it out. As he talked, Hamersveld interrupted here and there, asking questions, making astute observations, affirming his choice to bring the warrior into the fold. The Norwegian was wicked smart with an equal dose of lethal. Happiness sank deep, lightening his mood. Fantastic. The male was more than he had hoped, and everything he needed to continue his work.

As Ivar finished the rundown, Hamersveld shoved Fen aside and pushed to his feet. With a stretch, he worked out the kinks and plugged him with a thoughtful look. "Why work out of the lab? Why not release a virus directly into a human population? See how it performs in the wild?"

"I haven't perfected the viral delivery system yet." His brows furrowed, Ivar abandoned his seat and paced to the far end of the room. Skirting the bar and a wall of flat screen

TVs, he pivoted and strode back toward the bed. "I need to be certain it'll take before—"

"What if I can guarantee it'll take?"

"How?"

"You provide the superbug," Hamersveld said. "I'll introduce the virus into the water supply. Any human who drinks it will become infected."

Hitting the pause button on the pacing, Ivar stopped in the center of the room. He opened his mouth, then closed it again. Jesus. That was brilliant.

"But we test it first." Magic whispered on the air as Hamersveld conjured a map of Washington State. Folded into pamphlet size, he tossed it to Ivar. "Pick a small town. Some place rural with a water treatment plant."

"Then we sit back and watch how it spreads." Excitement spiked, hitting Ivar with a shot of adrenaline. "Record and process the data. Make adjustments as needed."

A nasty gleam in his eyes, Hamersveld grinned.

Ivar returned the smile and unfolded the map. Fucking hell, he couldn't wait to get started.

Chapter Nineteen

The frosting smelled like fresh strawberries.

Seated on a stool at the kitchen island, J. J. smiled as she scooped more pink icing out of the bowl. Who would've guessed she'd enjoy baking so much? Not her, that was for sure. A little over an hour ago, she'd scoffed at the idea. Now she couldn't wait to tackle the next cupcake. For some reason, the simple task relaxed her.

It was strangely freeing. No one telling her what to do or how to do it. Just her, a homemade batch of frosting, and a butter knife. Nothing but scads of mini-cakes to decorate any way she saw fit.

J. J.'s smile widened into a grin. All the taste testing didn't hurt either.

She held up her next victim and eyed the white cake top with consideration. What to do . . . what to do? Tried and true? Or should she elevate her game and test her new skill set? With a quick twist of her butter knife, she iced the top, leaving swirls in its wake, then glanced at the toppings beside her. Set out in small bowls, the sheer variety blew her away. Colorful sprinkles. Candies and chocolate curls. Marzipan decorations of all shapes and sizes. She perused the selection crowding the marble countertop, then looked at the already finished cupcakes. Sitting on a plate tree with three tiers, her pretty creations made the rounds, filling up most of the available real estate on Sweet Street. Only a few more left to do, so . . .

She reached for the piping bag full of chocolate icing.

"Ah, getting brave, I see." British accent full of approval, Daimler raised a brow.

J. J. crossed her eyes, making a funny face at him.

He snorted and, tapping a wooden spoon on the edge of a huge pot, turned away from the six-burner stove. Like everything in Black Diamond's kitchen, the range looked expensive. Gourmet on top of gourmet, hard-core gas burners surrounded by steel and stylish designer cabinetry. Not surprising, really. Anyone with eyes could see Daimler was a culinary tour de force. And honestly? The sophisticated white-on-white décor suited him.

An elegant space for an elegant elf.

Bridging the distance between stove and island, he examined her handiwork. "Well done, my lady. I had a feeling you would make a wonderful baker."

The compliment pleased her. The title on the other hand? J. J. fought the urge to cringe. *My lady.* Right. As if she deserved to be called such a thing. "Daimler, for the millionth time, please call me J. J. I'm not comfortable with—"

"These are gorgeous, my lady!" His exclamation rolled over her request. J. J. sighed. She couldn't win the argument. No matter how many times she objected, he ignored her wishes. Something told her that was typical behavior. His claim to fame . . . politely disregard anything he didn't like and go on his merry way with every intention of doing whatever he wanted. Like now, while he twirled the cake stand in a circle on the countertop, eyes sparkling with enthusiasm, gushing compliments . . . making her want to hug him so hard his head popped off. "It's such a treat to have you here."

Uh-huh. And there it was . . . distraction in the form of a compliment.

J. J. knew she shouldn't fall for it. Should stand strong in the face of obvious manipulation, but . . . well, crap. Just crap. She enjoyed the way he treated her—how quickly he had accepted her, despite her shady past. Her chest went tight under the weight of heavy-handed thankfulness. God, it felt good: to be valued, to be welcomed, to be included. A novel experience after five years of receiving the complete opposite.

"Thanks for letting me do it," she murmured, listening to the low hum of female voices in the adjoining room. Beyond the wide timber-beamed archway, a long table occupied the center of the dining room. A magnificent chandelier hung above the mahogany surface, cut crystal reflecting the light, casting an ethereal glow over the three women in its circle. Her gaze landed on Tania, then bounced, sweeping over Myst and Angela. Busy doing Daimler's bidding, the trio circled like sharks in a holding pattern, laying plates, cutlery, and wine glasses in prearranged places. "It's a lot more fun than setting the table."

"Complete selfishness on my part, I assure you." Gazing at her like a proud papa, Daimler watched her pipe fancy chocolate trim around the edge of the cupcake. He grinned, gold front tooth winking at her. "You're a natural, my lady. I'll make a master baker out of you yet."

J. J. huffed. "And I'll end up gaining three hundred pounds."

He laughed, and she fell head over heels for him. He was just too cute with his elfin face and pointy ears peeking through his dark hair. Daimler was a definite keeper.

With a steady hand, she set a marzipan flower in the frosting. A little nudge. A slight adjustment and . . . perfection. Now all she needed was some well-placed sprinkles. Maybe even a few leaves to propel the cupcake past pretty into gorgeous. "What are all these for anyway?"

"My wedding."

J. J. jumped in surprise, squishing the candied leaf in her hand. Her gaze snapped to the left. "Jeepers, Tania. Sneak up on a body, why don't you?"

"Ah, back to the good old days." Brown eyes gleaming with mischief, her sister threw her arm around her shoulders and gave her an affectionate squeeze.

"Better be careful, Sis. You know I'll get even and—"

"Ten times worse, no doubt."

"Exactly. So watch your ass," she said, enjoying the taunt and tease, 'cause . . . yeah. Tania was right. It did feel like old times. "And while you do . . . fill me in." J. J. raised a brow. "Wedding?"

"A double feature."

J. J. frowned, meeting her sister's gaze while she racked her brain. Although, she hadn't met him yet, she knew all about Mac. Tania couldn't stop talking about him. Or rather . . . singing his praises. Every time she mentioned him, her brown eyes sparkled and J. J. smiled. She couldn't help it. She loved her sister. Wanted to see Tania happy and fulfilled. And after a lifetime of listening to her fantasize about Mr. Right? It pleased her beyond anything to see her sister's dream come true as Mac stepped into the role.

She pursed her lips. But back to the original puzzle. A double feature meant . . .

Ah, yes. "Ange and Rikar too?"

"Mac and Ange are best friends, so it only makes sense to do it at the same time."

"Thought you always wanted a lavish ceremony?"

"I don't care about that anymore." Tania gave her another squeeze, then let go to settle on the stool next to her. "All I want is him."

"You love him that much?"

"More."

"I'm so happy for you, Tania. Proud of you too. You found him . . . held out for the right one," she whispered, emotion filling her heart so full the words came out raspy. Tears filled Tania's eyes. Hers followed suit. J. J. breathed through the emotional heave-ho, and fighting to stay even—breaking down in the presence of candy and frosting, after all, seemed counterintuitive—used the only weapon at her disposal. "Here. Have a cupcake."

Wiping beneath her eyes, Tania huffed. "I've had two already. There won't be any left for later if we eat them all now."

"Screw it. We're celebrating." Picking the prettiest one off the plate, J. J. handed it to her sister. "Daimler and I will just make some—"

"Speak for yourself, my lady." Made a little teary-eyed by their exchange, Daimler tried to pull off a stern look. He ended up sniffling instead. "You eat all the wedding feast cupcakes, and you're on your own. I'm not explaining their absence to my boys."

Her sister rolled her eyes. "*Boys.* You do realize you're talking about grown men, warriors who . . ."

Tania's breath caught on the last word, stealing the rest of her sentence.

Perplexed, J. J. stared at her sister, then flinched as a tingle ghosted over the nape her neck. Awareness expanded, morphing into a signal inside her head. Her focus snapped toward the hallway leading toward the front door. Wick. He was close . . . so very close she felt his proximity as sensation prickled. The heated curl clung a moment, then changed course, swirling down her spine in a—

"Oh!" Tania whacked her on the arm with the back of her hand. As J. J. said "ow," her sister hopped off the stool and made a beeline across the kitchen. A second before she disappeared into the corridor, she said over her shoulder, "Come on, baby J. They're home."

No doubt as to who "they" were.

Her first clue? Her sister's excitement and speedy exit. The second indication? The clang of dishes from the dining room as Myst and Angela abandoned table-setting duty and, skirting the end of the massive table, made tracks in her sister's wake. Watching the mass exodus, J. J. slid off her perch but stayed put. No sense jumping the gun. Or making a fool of herself when she didn't know where she stood . . .

Or if Wick wanted her to greet him.

The assumption seemed like a stretch. But then, everything did when it came to him. It was an odd state to be in . . . wanting to get to know him better without having any clue how to go about it.

Balancing on her good leg, J. J. nibbled on the inside of her lip, debating what to do. Go or stay? Be safe or bold? She glanced toward Daimler, hoping for a bailout. An expectant expression on his elfish face, he raised a brow. Well, wasn't that a kick in the pants? As helpful as the Numbai had been over the last few hours, he refused to give her any clues. Instead, he remained silent as stone, no doubt waiting to see which way she would hop.

J. J. glared at him. Flipping elf. He looked as though he was enjoying—

"Ah, Master Wick," Daimler murmured, a knowing twinkle in his eyes. "Welcome home."

A death grip on the edge of the countertop, her attention snapped toward the opposite end of the kitchen and . . . oh my. Lord have mercy. Wick in all his glory, looking better than the cupcakes she'd made, and twice as sweet. His golden gaze raked over her. Her heart went AWOL, dipping low only to rebound into her throat. He skimmed her again, making her feel as though she'd just been strip-searched. Stripped bare within a blink of an eye . . . all without him touching her.

Dear lord. She'd never experienced anything like it. Or him. He made her burn just looking at him, and in that moment, she understood primal attraction. Grasped the magnitude and rawness that pulled her into his orbit. Accepted the need. Reveled in the want. Felt the underlying tug as fate locked her into place.

Completely ridiculous? Nothing but hocus-pocus infused balderdash?

Maybe. Maybe not. All J. J. knew was that she didn't want to fight it. Exploring it sounded way more fun.

Drawing a deep breath, J. J. opened her mouth to greet him and—

"I'll be in my room."

She blinked.

Daimler nodded. "Very good, Master Wick. I'll see to your supper."

And just like that, he was gone, heavy footfalls echoing as he turned and strode into yet another corridor.

J. J.'s brows collided. A moment later, she scowled at the empty spot where he'd stood. "What the heck was that?"

"Go after him, my lady. But before you do, I would ask one thing of you."

"What's that?" Frustration riding shotgun, J. J. limped around the end of the island.

"Be patient with him," Daimler said, giving her pause. "He's had a hard life, one I believe you will understand better than most. Better than any female, in fact, so . . . please, be patient, my lady. He needs you more than he knows."

The entreaty settled her down.

She understood hardship. Had lived with the reality day in and day out . . . and now with the memory of it. She would never forget its effects. Or the chaos it left in the aftermath. So, no problem. She could be gentle—tough, patient—whatever Wick needed. Forbearance, after all, was her friend. But as she hobbled out of the kitchen and into the corridor, doubt came calling. What if he turned her away? Not an improbable outcome considering he'd just taken one look at her and run in the opposite direction.

❀ ❀ ❀

Wick registered her presence long before she approached his bedroom. Standing in front of his easel, his gaze riveted to the door, he wiped his hands on a rag that had seen better days. Stained with old paint, frayed around the edges, the cotton served as his catchall. Something he used while painting during the day. Tossing the scrap of cloth on the table beside him, he plucked his favorite brush from a large mason jar. Wood rattled against the glass rim. The familiar sound did nothing to break his fixation. His senses were too attuned . . . on fire for a female he craved, but knew he didn't deserve.

He should turn her away. Be safe. Act sensibly. Do the right thing and leave her locked on the other side of his door. As far away from him as possible.

Sounded like a plan, but for one huge problem.

He wanted her too much. Needed to know what made her so different from other females. Yearned to touch her again and discover if it was all in his head. Or if Jamison was as incredible as she seemed, able to banish his phobia—stoke his appetite, interest his dragon half by the simple virtue of existing.

Drawing his thumb over boar-hair bristles, Wick frowned at the painting he'd been working on for days. Almost finished, the urban landscape called for a few more details. The final touches, a series of well-placed highlights that would take it from good to great. As he studied the piece, he brushed his hand over his bare chest and waited, heart thumping, half holding his breath, hoping the knock would come. Would she be brave enough? Did she really want to know—about him, about them, about what it meant to cross the threshold and enter his domain?

Wick blew out a long breath. No mercy. That's what it meant. What she would get. What he would give her if she chose to walk toward him instead of away. Unfair? Probably. But he didn't care. Despite his phobia, he wasn't a coward. And with curiosity running rampant, Wick refused to back away. He wanted to explore. Take a closer look at the growing connection between them and identify the variables.

Which . . . yeah . . . put Jamison in the hot seat.

The soft thud of uneven footsteps stopped outside his door.

The muscles bracketing his spine tightened. The moment of truth. Would she? Or wouldn't she?

Knuckles struck wood, the sound hesitant yet somehow certain at the same time. His mouth curved even as he shook his head. And there it was . . . the answer. Bold, beautiful Jamison had just gone all in, playing her hand, dealing him his, sealing her fate. The realization made him nervous. Yet even as his stomach dipped, excitement circled too, making him buzz with sensation. On a precipice. He stood on the edge, the need to jump battling the fear of falling.

The soft knock came again.

"Go easy." Rolling his shoulders, he attacked the tension, forcing himself to relax. But it was hard. The brief glimpse of her in the kitchen had wound him tight. "Don't scare her."

Sound advice. A good strategy going forward too.

Wick heeded both and unleashed his magic. With a sharp mental flick, the dead bolt flipped open. A moment later, the door swung wide and . . . oh fuck. Could she be any more beautiful? Even in too-big sweats and a faded T-shirt, she looked incredible. Fresh-faced without an ounce of makeup to hide her beauty. Strong. Sure. Beyond sexy with her dark hair cascading around her slim shoulders.

Eyes bluer than a cloudless sky met his. His heart rebounded, trying to escape through the center of his chest as she looked him over. Gaze traveling, she showed no mercy, skimming over exposed skin to move to his paint-splattered jeans. She stared at his bare feet a moment before her lips tipped up at the corners.

Wick swallowed past the knot in his throat. Ah, hell. Talk about bad etiquette. He was half-dressed, for fuck's sake. "Shit. Sorry. I'll put a shirt on."

"Don't worry about it. It's a good look for you." As he blinked, wondering what the hell she meant, she asked, "Is it okay if I come in?"

Unable to find his voice, Wick nodded.

Weighed down by the walking cast, she limped over the threshold. He frowned as his gaze slid over her. Favoring her right side, she kept her elbow tucked against her rib cage as though one wrong move would send pain spiraling. He bit down on a growl and, tapping into her bio-energy, read her vital signs. Fucking hell. She was still hurting. Not a lot, but enough for him to want to kick his own ass.

He should've known one go-around with him wouldn't be enough. Not after the injuries she'd sustained. So time to jump back on the energy train. She needed another infusion, and compulsion dictated he feed her again. Provide what her body needed to heal up nice and tight.

"Jamison," he said, hearing the anticipation in his voice. He couldn't help it. The thought of touching her did something odd to him. Instead of reacting with revulsion, the prospect excited the hell out of him. "Come here."

"In a minute."

Wick's brows collided. What the hell did she mean *in a minute?* "You need more healing energy. I can help if—"

"I know," she said, closing the door behind her. The click sounded loud in the silence, cranking him tighter as she made her way past the fireplace and over to the custom bookcases. Jammed full of hardcovers, the floor-to-ceiling built-ins occupied one corner of his room. With a hum of pleasure, she ran her fingertips over a colorful spine. "Tania explained all the Meridian stuff."

"She did?"

"Uh-huh," she murmured, glancing over her shoulder. Her attention bounced from him to the unmade bed.

Shoved up against the wall, the king-size mattress and box spring sat on the floor. No bed frame. No silk sheets or froufrou pillows. Nothing fancy. Just a tangle of sheets twisted up in the middle of Serta's finest. Wick grimaced. Not his finest hour. Half-dressed. Messy bed. Trashed workstation. Maybe he should've tidied up a bit. Made a good impression and dazzled her with neatness, but . . .

Well, it was too late for that.

His slob-like tendencies were out of the bag. So was his habit of tossing damp towels into the corner beside the door. A fact she'd already noticed (goddamn it). Daimler usually took care of that, but with preparations for the mating ceremony in full swing, the Numbai had been too busy to make the rounds. Add that catastrophe to all the canvases stacked against the far wall and . . . yeah. He wouldn't be getting the award for Tidiest Male of the Year anytime soon.

Stepping around his easel, he scooped the duvet off the floor, folded it into quarters, then set it on the end of his bed. As he relinquished the load, Jamison slipped the book she held back into its spot. Her focus narrowed on the canvases leaning against the wall by the window. Nervous tension got the better of him. Not sure what to say, he shoved his hands into the front pockets of his jeans and waited—for inspiration to strike, for her to break the silence first, for the moment she gave him the green light to touch her again.

Pain or not, the decision was hers. Which meant he'd better start praying 'cause . . . shit. It wasn't looking good so far.

"Wow," she said, stopping in front of a stack of paintings. Fingering the white edges of the canvas frames, she ran her hand over the top of the first group, then moved on to the next. At least forty pieces strong, the collection represented the work he'd done over the last eighteen months. "Did you paint all of these?"

"Yeah."

Her gaze skimming the artwork, she smiled, and his heart flip-flopped, somersaulting inside his chest. Did she like what she saw? The artist in him wanted to know . . . to be appreciated for his efforts. The more practical side of him scoffed. He didn't paint for anyone but himself. The pastime helped him relax, giving him an outlet after a hard night of fighting. End of story. No need to court anyone's praise. But as he watched her flip through painting after painting, Wick craved a good word. Anything that would tell him what she thought about his work.

Which was so much bullshit. And the entire reason he never showed anyone his art.

Not even Venom.

Other than Daimler—and now Jamison—no one knew he painted. All right, so all his brothers-in-arms knew about his love for art. They would have to be blind not to notice. The evidence hung the length of the corridor outside his room . . . all over the lair for that matter. But he never talked about it, and none of the other Nightfuries knew the extent of his obsession. Or rather . . . passion.

Given half a chance, Wick preferred to keep it that way.

He'd involved Daimler out of necessity. At first, he'd disliked depending on another. Over time, however, the Numbai had proven to be a true partner, keeping him well stocked with painting supplies, helping him hunt down and purchase precious works of art from all over the world while sneaking every bit of it past the other warriors. All without complaining or sticking his nose where it didn't belong.

Awesome didn't begin to describe the male.

"Holy moly, Wick." Pure, unadulterated awe on her face, she glanced at him over her shoulder. "These are gorgeous. How long have you been painting?"

"A while," he murmured, his gaze on hers. The wonder he spied in her eyes sent him sideways. Pride surfaced, filling him so full he struggled to contain it. Jesus. He got off on her admiration. But more than that, Wick loved the way she looked at him. Interest tinged by a sharp sense of longing rode her expression, making him feel valued. Worthy. Like an upstanding male deserving of her attention. "Almost twenty years."

"You need to hang these. They belong in a gallery."

He shrugged, hiding his pleasure. "I'm not the gallery type."

"No, I don't imagine you are . . ." She paused, and turning toward him, crossed the room on a slow shuffle. "You're too modest for that."

Wick stifled a snort. Totally laughable. He was about as modest as a peacock in full preen. He just preferred to fly below the radar before he showed his true colors, that was all.

Limp more pronounced than before, she skirted the end of the bed. Giving him a wide berth, she walked behind him. His skin tingled as her aura flared, ringing her body, making her glow from the inside out. Wick inhaled deep and exhaled smooth. She stopped at his workstation and, reaching out, fingered his brushes, then turned her attention to the assortment of tubes littering the tabletop. She touched each one, bypassing blue, green, and red to pick up ochre yellow.

Wick shifted his weight from one foot to the other. As his bare feet brushed over the wood floor, he flexed his hands, telling himself to be patient, but . . . Jesus. Less than five feet away. She stood so close, yet still too fucking far away.

His dragon half urged him to move, close the distance and walk up behind her. Instinct warned him to wait. Attuned to her mood, he felt her tension as clearly as his own. She was stalling for a reason. Maybe for time. Maybe for space. Maybe for a bit of both. Whatever the case, Wick refused to rush her. If she needed him to back off and—

"All right," she whispered, the strain in her voice palpable as she turned to face him. Taking a deep breath, she met his gaze head-on. "I'm ready now."

Concern washed through him. "What's wrong?"

"Nothing."

"Don't lie to me." The rough edge of his voice made her flinch. "I want your honesty. Every bit of it, Jamison."

"All right. I guess I owe you that much," she said, looking so unsure he bled for her. "Being alone with you makes me nervous. I know it's stupid. I mean, you've touched me before and everything, but right now I'm . . ."

He raised a brow as she trailed off.

She bit down on her bottom lip. "Extremely coherent. As in, no drugs in my system."

"Are you afraid I'll hurt—"

"No," she said, her denial so quick it soothed his pride. Made Wick believe he could help her while he helped himself. "I know you would never hurt me."

"But?" he asked, prompting her, encouraging her to talk to him.

A furrow between her brows, she looked away, then back again, letting him see her vulnerability. The sight made him ache for her. He knew what it felt like to be insecure and uncertain. To live with unease every damned day. But as he waited for her to continue, patient in the wake of her silence, Wick wanted nothing more than to soothe her. To carry her burden, banish all the angst and replace it with comfort and confidence.

"Look, if you really want the truth, I'll be honest. I came in here with every intention of getting close to you, but one look at you, like that and . . . God, Wick. You're so strong. So much bigger than I am, and . . ." Shaking her head, she blew out a shaky breath. "It's second nature for me to protect myself. My track record sucks. I've never been with a guy who hasn't hurt me, and even trusting that you won't, I'm just . . . I don't know . . . freaking out a little."

"I understand, Jamison." He really did. His hands-off policy predated the Second World War. A helluva long time to live in darkness, without the warmth of another's touch. But here . . . right now . . . in the presence of a female he couldn't resist, Wick saw a chance to change tack and head in a healthier direction. Fear was a terrible thing, and trust more than just about knowing. It was about showing. So instead of backing away, he took his hands from his pockets and stepped toward her. When she didn't shy, he raised his arm and held out his hand, palm up, in invitation. "Come, *vanzäla*. Let me show you how gentle I can be."

The entreaty surprised him. The meaning behind it even more so.

He'd never thought of himself as a gentle male. A killer without conscience? Without a doubt. But as Jamison slipped her much-smaller hand into his, trusting him to keep his word, Wick reevaluated, seeing himself in a new light. Maybe change was possible. Maybe he wasn't destined to be alone. Maybe . . . just maybe . . . he'd finally met his match.

Chapter Twenty

With a gentle tug, Wick drew her into the circle of his arms. J. J. shivered in reaction, but let it happen. Resistance wouldn't help her solve the mystery. Nor give her what she longed to collect . . . answers that would unlock the paradox he presented. Intense warrior vibe. Comforting touch delivered by gentle hands. Delicious dichotomy. Beautiful polarity. And as she waited—breath hitching, heart thumping, uncertainty rising—she wondered what he would do next.

Pick her up. Lay her down. Strip her bare.

All seemed like excellent possibilities. The kind most girls wanted. Problem was . . .

She wasn't *most* girls. Not with her past and prison record. History had taught her caution. Her ex had taught her fear. So the question—the one she really needed to answer . . . and fast—went something like: respond with the desire she already felt or run scared?

Her hand still in his, J. J. exhaled long and slow. Such a big decision. So little time to decide which way to jump. Stay and discover. Or run and hide. The second option was the safest, but the first tugged at her, urging her to be brave. To move forward instead of away. To take what she wanted for a change and seize the moment.

So few opportunities, after all, ever came her way.

Good thing fate had a funny sense of humor, tossing her into circumstance, feeding on her curiosity, making her yearn to know him. Really *know* him every way a woman could a man. And as he closed his arms around her, and she settled into the hard curve of his body, J. J. let it all go. Every bad deed done. Every hurt suffered. Every punishment received. She deserved to know. Had earned the right to explore, and to a little happiness. So here . . . now . . . today, she would find the courage to reach for what she wanted. No fear. No second guessing. Self-preservation be damned.

The thought made her smile.

His eyes reflected her mood, shimmering like golden stars as Wick pressed her closer. Her palms met the wall of his bare chest and . . . oh my. Skin on skin. The zap of physical and emotional connection, two souls reaching out to touch each other. Instant recognition. J. J. perceived the shift, felt her world tilt on its axis, heard his low growl before she relaxed and leaned in, moving toward the inevitable instead of away.

Her cheek brushed the wall of his chest, then touched down over his heart. The steady thump picked her up, making hers catch and tumble until it kept time with his. Unable to resist, she caressed his shoulder. Muscles rippled beneath her fingertips, chasing her chill away.

"Beautiful," she whispered, her head nestled beneath his chin. In an exploratory frame of mind, she played, allowing her hands free rein. Her touch soft, she stroked over his biceps, then changed direction. Brushing over the tops of shoulders, she moved lower to draw gentle circles down his spine. A tremor rumbled through him. She sighed, marveling at the incredible size and strength of him. "You're always so warm."

"Curse of a fire dragon."

No way. Not even close to a *curse*. She liked that his temperature ran hot. "Do you breathe fire?"

"Kind of," he said, his voice hoarse as she continued to caress him. Getting in on the action, Wick flicked at her T-shirt. J. J. sucked in a quick breath as his hand dipped beneath the cotton hem. Fingers spread wide, he palmed the small of her back. She arched. He took advantage of her slight twist and slid his free hand beneath the fall of her hair to cup the nape of her neck. White-hot sensation slithered down her spine. As her breath caught, he dipped his head, brushing his mouth against her temple. "My exhale is candy coated. Three layers of deadly. Magma surrounded by poisonous gas . . . fire on the outside."

"A fireball with attitude." As he chuckled, she rubbed her cheek against his. Day-old whiskers scraped across her skin. Hmm, yeah. She'd made the right decision. He was going to feel so unbelievably good in bed. "Must set the Razorbacks back on their heels."

"That's the idea." Retreating a little, he raised his head and met her gaze. Molten heat made his golden eyes shimmer, sending shockwaves through her. Holding her immobile, he shifted his hips, pressing the bulge behind his button fly against her belly. "Where we going with this, Jamison?"

Ah, and there it was. The demand for truth. Do or die time.

Rubbing her lips together, she dragged her gaze from his and glanced over her shoulder. A messy tangle of rumpled sheets, the bed sat in the center of the room. No more than ten feet away. A ripple of excitement shivered through her. Desire picked up the cue, sending her sideways, urging boldness, making her give him the honesty he demanded earlier.

"We're going over there," she said, a husky shiver in her voice. "I plan to take you to bed."

His grip on her nape tightened. "Is that a fact?"

"It is."

"Probably should warn you, then."

"About what?"

"I'm not good at this shit, *vanzäla*. Never had much practice," he murmured, color spreading across the tops of his cheekbones. "I don't know how to please you in bed."

Tension rode each syllable, infusing his admission with emotion. Shame. Humiliation. Raw honesty. Wick owned every bit of it. And as his words tore at her heart, J. J. felt herself tumble down a slippery slope and straight into love. The fierce kind that came with compassion and a healthy dose of respect. For Wick's courage. For his honor. For the vulnerability he showed her.

Beautiful, uncompromising man.

He might be strong—without equal physically—but Daimler was right. He needed her to show him the way. Back to himself. Into the man he was meant to become. And as he looked away, unable to meet her gaze, she yearned not only to soothe him, but to prove he was more capable than he believed.

Confidence, after all, came to those who practiced.

"Wanna know a secret?" Cupping his jaw, she forced him to look at her.

"Sure."

"Your inexperience makes us even, because I don't know what pleases me either." His brows popped up. J. J. fought the urge to smile. God, he was adorable, unlike anyone she'd ever met. A good man in every way that counted. He wasn't anything like her ex. Quite the opposite, in fact. Adam hadn't cared whether he pleased her or not. Never given her an orgasm, either. But Wick? She could already feel the slow build of sexual attraction. The explosion hovered a breath away, making her blood sing, infusing her with the need to touch while being touched in return. And oh baby, she couldn't wait for him to take control and make it happen. "So how about we make a deal. You do what pleases you, and we'll discover if it pleases me too."

He threw her a dubious look.

Balanced on her good foot, she raised up on her tiptoe. Her mouth brushed his. His breath caught. She pushed her hands into his hair. Hmm, so soft. So thick. Pure heaven. A place she couldn't resist, and as J. J. played in the dark strands, raking her short nails over his scalp, she purred. The sound of pleasure made him vibrate in her embrace. She made it again and brushed her lips against his, kissing his disbelief away. He inhaled hard and fast. Pushing her advantage, J. J. nipped his bottom lip, then delved deep, invading his mouth with a quick stroke of her tongue.

The sharp taste of cinnamon made her moan. Mmm, mmm good. He tasted like spiced candy, a slice of the darkly erotic on a lazy afternoon. Decadence in all its glory. Beyond sinful as he opened his mouth, submitting beneath the onslaught. Bliss danced across her skin as his hands traveled over her bare back, setting her alight with desire. With want and a yearning so deep, she struggled to contain it . . . and take her time. She didn't want to rush him, but—

"Holy fuck, baby." Done following her lead, he growled against her mouth. "You taste so damned good."

Super to know. Better to experience. "Kiss me again."

"I'm gonna kiss you all over." His arms tightened around her as he dipped his head and took the lead, teasing her with the flick of his tongue. She egged him on, asking for more, begging him with each kiss. Giving her everything she demanded, he turned and walked her backward. The bed. Oh God. Fantastic idea. She needed to lay him down . . . or be laid down. J. J. didn't care how it happened, just as long as it happened fast. "Between your thighs too. Right on your curls."

The promise sounded like a threat. A delicious one, but for one thing. She'd never actually, well . . . ah, done that. Or rather, had that done to her.

Her legs bumped the edge of the bed.

Palming her waist, Wick picked her up. She went weight-less for a moment. Cotton sighed as her shoulder blades settled on the sheets. His thigh between hers, he followed her down, caging her with his body, chest rising and falling on harsh exhales. Golden eyes full of promise, he shoved at her shirt. The material brushed over her torso, rising to expose her bra. Racy rather than plain, the frilly lingerie didn't hide much. His nostrils flared as he shifted onto one elbow. Awe winged across his face a second before his fingertips touched down, caressing her nipple through the lace. He lowered his head. She moaned in anticipation. Please, God. She wanted him to—

His mouth touched down. Heat exploded, spreading over her skin.

With a whimper, she twisted, arching beneath him, rising hard, asking for more. He didn't deny her. As he suckled, wetting the lace, increasing the pressure when she begged, he fingered the front of her bra. A quick snap released the clasp. Cool air washed over her breasts. The tip of his tongue flicked over her. She moaned his name. Wick licked her again, then raised his head to look at her. The heat of his gaze touched her skin. J. J. arched, riding a wave of desire, loving the burn as he groaned in reaction.

"Jesus, Jamison. You're so beautiful," he murmured, his tone full of wonder. "I want to see the rest of you."

Fingers spread wide, she stroked his back, hands playing against his skin before pushing beneath the waistband of his jeans. Taut muscle met her exploration and . . . oh yeah. He was incredible, every flipping inch of him. Undulating beneath him, she pressed up and rocked her hips into his. "Take the Levis off first. Then I'll let you strip me."

"Tit for tat?"

"Something like that."

Amusement sparked in his eyes. "Only fair since I get to fuck you."

"*Fuck* me?" The outrage in her tone set him off. He smiled at her, flashing straight white teeth, looking so mischievous it made her want to let him get away with pretending she was a fast lay on a fine afternoon. The devil. Playing along, she tugged a lock of his hair. "You better rephrase that, mister, or I'll rescind my offer."

His expression went from playful to serious in a heartbeat. "Make love to you, then. I get to make love to you . . . touch you everywhere, stroke deep when you're ready, make you come so hard you scream my name." The pad of his thumb traced her mouth, then dipped inside, treating her to the stunning taste of his skin. "A dream come true, *vanzäla.* I thank you for the privilege."

Her breath caught. Oh wow. What an incredible thing to say. "Wick?"

Tugging the T-shirt over her head, he drew the bra over her shoulders and threw it over the side of the bed. "Yeah?"

"Hurry," she whispered. "I don't think I can wait much longer."

"Impatient?"

"Needy. I want you."

He kissed her softly. A second later, his jeans disappeared, leaving him naked in her arms. J. J. moaned in relief. Thank God. Tania had told her all about the disappearing clothes thing all the guys used, and . . . oh, Nelly. Her sister had been right. The trick belonged in the record books, in the oh-thank-you-baby-Jesus section.

Planting his fists on either side of her, Wick pushed upward to land on his knees. As he straddled her leg and palmed her walking cast, J. J. ran the gauntlet, letting her gaze skim over him. She swallowed. Had she said strong earlier? Well, stacked sounded better. Ripped worked too, 'cause . . . holy moly. He was a golden-skinned god, muscle poured over bone, so hard-bodied he took her breath away. Anticipation sizzling in her veins, her mouth parted on a long, drawn-out sigh. The rip of Velcro sounded as Wick undid the straps holding her footwear in place.

J. J. barely noticed. She was too busy staring, wondering if he would . . .

Curiosity made her reach out.

Licking over her bottom lip, she caressed him with her fingertip. His erection bobbed. White cream pearling on the tip, Wick twitched. Hands still cupping her calf, he cursed and closed his eyes. She stroked him again. His hips curled toward her as though asking for more. Growing bolder, she pushed up onto one elbow and wrapped her hand around him.

"My God, Wick." Soft skin poured over hot steel. So hard. So thick. So ready to please her. "How about we put this to work?"

With a snarl, Wick ripped that last strap free. Gentle hands pulled the cast from her foot. Impatient ones flung it over the end of the bed. "Not until I taste you."

The reminder of what he wanted to do to her set her cheeks on fire. As the blush spread, heating her face, J. J. tightened her grip and stroked him from base to tip. "Later. We have lots of—"

"No. Now. "

With another "fuck," he grasped her wrist and pulled her hand free. Hooking the waistband of her sweats, he peeled her out of her pants. The lacy panties went next, leaving her wearing nothing but skin. J. J. froze as he looked her over, skimming her body with predatory intent. Possessiveness too. And in the moment, she felt owned . . . as though he held the deed to every inch of her. With a low growl, he cupped her breasts. His thumb brushed over her nipples, teasing her, exciting her, making her want as his gaze traveled to the dark curls at the junction of her thighs.

Breathing hard, she watched him swallow and . . . oh God. She knew what he was thinking. He was imagining what she tasted like there. She could see it on his face, hear the whisper in his mind, feel the anticipation rushing in his blood. The connection should've scared her. Instead it heightened the intensity, sending bliss unfurling like a whip. As each stroke lashed her, J. J. lost control. She pulsed deep inside, squirmed on the sheets, the mere thought of having him between her thighs making her throb with anticipation.

"Please. Wick, please just—"

"As you wish." Tracing her curves, he stroked over sensitive skin, his focus absolute. The heat of his mouth brushed over her belly, then drifted away. Needing an anchor to ground her, J. J. buried her hands in his hair, begging without words to be taken. Leaving moist tracks on her skin, Wick paused to kiss her mound of top curls. "Invite me in, baby . . . I'm hungry."

So was she, but J. J. obeyed anyway and—

"Oh God. What are you . . . holy shit . . . oh . . . my . . . God!"

J. J. writhed as he settled between her thighs. He showed no mercy, stroking deep with his tongue, licking between her folds, whipping her into a bliss-fueled frenzy. And she begged. Begged for release. Begged for more pleasure. Begged for him. Promised him whatever he wanted in return for the orgasm she could feel coming, but couldn't catch. God, she wanted it. Needed the rush of delight, and for him to keep his word. He'd promised to ride her hard and make her scream. But even as she reminded him, he took his time, extending his enjoyment as he reveled in her taste. As he worshiped at the source, tongued the nub at the top of her sex, driving her mad as he drank deep and made her body weep.

"Mmm baby, you're so wet. So hot. So fucking sweet." Treating her to another round, he sucked harder, arching her spine off the mattress. As she whimpered, he growled, "Come for me, Jamison. Right now. I want to taste it."

His words released her, flinging her into a pleasure palace of his making.

The explosion set her free, and as she flew into the bliss of rapture, Wick lifted his head from between her thighs. His hips replaced his mouth, pushing her legs wider. Whispering her name, he set the thick head of his shaft against her core and . . .

She came again the second he thrust deep.

Shockwaves lit off, drowning her in delight. Buried to the hilt inside her, he shouted, the sound half-roar, half-curse, and withdrew only to come right back. Flex and release. Thrust and retreat. He rocked her with the power of his body, giving her everything, taking it all, doing what he promised, making her scream his name as he pushed her to the brink, throbbed inside her, then followed her over the edge into oblivion.

❀ ❀ ❀

A whole afternoon spent in sexual play.

Wick still couldn't believe it. He'd not only survived, but thrived in the circle of a female's arms. *His* female. Jesus. Talk about amazing. He hadn't shied away from physical contact or felt sick once, and he knew why. Jamison. It all came back to her. She was incredible. A rare treat. A beautiful gift. One he knew he didn't deserve but craved just the same.

Lucky bastard didn't begin to describe him.

Still deep inside her, not wanting to let go, Wick gripped her hips and fell back onto the mattress. Breathing hard from the latest round of lovemaking, she moaned—amping him up, making him so proud his heart expanded—and slumped forward, falling into him, trusting him to catch her. Cupping her face, he kissed her again, licking into her mouth before enfolding her in his embrace. She murmured his name as her breasts touched down on his chest and . . . yum. She felt like heaven, and he couldn't get enough: of the contact, of her inferno-like heat, and the way she trusted him to keep her safe. Skin-to-skin. Heart-to-heart. She made him believe she belonged to him. And as she nestled in, pressed her cheek to his heart, and sighed in contentment, Wick thanked his lucky stars yet again.

Beautiful, beautiful female. Precious beyond words.

"My God," she mumbled, shifting her hips before she went boneless against him. The wiggle pushed him deeper inside her. Wick groaned, loving the raw burn of pleasure. Man, he was sensitive. So ready to go again. Insatiable when it came to her. Unable to get enough of what she did to him. "I had no idea it could be so good."

Neither had he. Live and learn. An excellent way to go.

And he just might, considering Jamison's appetite . . . and his need to appease it. She'd ridden him hard that last time. Liked being on top. Enjoyed watching him while she taunted and teased. Reveled in the rasp of his voice as he begged her for release. Another first. He didn't beg. For anything. It was one of those rules he lived by, but . . . shit. She blew that to hell about an hour in, forcing him to submit while she took the wheel.

And drove him straight over the edge.

For the . . . well, he didn't know what number that had been.

He'd lost count—along with his mind—somewhere after the second round. Now all he wanted to do was hold her and wallow in the afterglow of physical conquest. Hers over him. His over her. Wick didn't care which qualified. It didn't matter. Both worked for him, even though he knew it couldn't last.

The thought weighed on his heart. A heavy burden to carry. Especially since their time together was almost up.

He could feel the stir in the lair. His brothers were awake, up for the night and busy helping Daimler prepare for the mating ceremony. Any minute now someone would come bang on his door . . . and steal Jamison away. Take her from his arms and tell her to get dressed. To do her part. To take her place around the sacred circle. Bare witness as Tania married a member of his pack.

Battling the urge to lock her in his room and keep her all to himself, Wick brushed her dark hair over her shoulder. One hand playing in the thick strands, he stroked the other down her back. She purred, stirring beneath his touch. He hummed. So soft. So sweet. So unabashed in her passion. "Jamison?"

"Hmm?"

"Tell me another secret."

Jamison huffed a second before her lips curved against his chest. Wick smiled in reaction. She liked this game. So did he. They'd been playing it all afternoon. Talking between bouts of lovemaking. Asking personal questions. Revealing secrets long kept. Well, some of them anyway. Although she'd traced over his scar, fingertips lingering on the numbers burned into his forearm in Dragonese, she hadn't asked. Instead, she waited, patient in the swell of his mounting hesitation. He didn't want to tell her about his past. Didn't want to explain what had happened or see the pity in her eyes as he told her about the cage and collar. About the fighting. Or about the killing he'd done to save his own life.

Deceitful much? No question. She deserved to know the truth. Needed the insight in order to understand him . . . the who, what, and why of the male he'd become. Selfishness stayed his hand. He wanted their time together to be without shadow. Untainted by his past. Unblemished by guilt. Pure in every way. So he held back, omitting the one thing he knew he should tell her.

"Let's see. Another secret." Sky-blue eyes met his as she raised her head. Folding her forearms on his chest, she set her chin down on the stack. She pursed her lips. "I stole a guitar off my neighbor's porch when I was eleven."

"Really?"

"Un-huh."

"Did you get caught?"

"Kind of. Lady caught me red-handed." When he raised a brow, she huffed. "Mr. Hufferson's bulldog."

"Mr. Hufferson." Brushing a stray lock of hair from her temple, he grinned at her. "The owner of the guitar in question."

She nodded. "I didn't know it at the time, but the dog always hid in the front flower bed, squishing all the petunias. Funny thing, though, she never told on me."

"If only dogs could talk."

"If only." Her expression dimmed a little. "I felt really bad about it, but—"

"Not enough to return it?"

"No." As she broke eye contact, a frown pushed her brows together. "It was a terrible thing to do, but I wanted a guitar so badly. We didn't have a lot growing up. Most days we didn't have enough to eat, so no way Mom could afford to buy me an instrument, never mind send me to music lessons."

Her voice cracked, and Wick ached for her. Could see her as an eleven-year-old girl, big blue eyes brimming with tears as her Mom said no to the one thing she couldn't do without. Her music.

"All I wanted to do was write my songs," she whispered. "And Mr. Hufferson always left the Bedell beside the rocking chair. I walked by it every day after school, so—"

"The Bedell?" Needing to soothe her, he caressed her back, running his hand over her soft skin, telling her the only way he knew how that he understood.

"The guitar." Drawing a circle over his shoulder with her fingertip, she cleared her throat. "And that stupid dog. Lady might not have given me away, but she started waiting for me every day after school. Would follow me home, give me the evil eye the whole way . . . like she knew I was a thief or something."

"She probably did. Dogs are smart."

"I'll say. I'd lock the gate to keep her out, but she'd head-butt the thing open every time. After a while, I stopped shooing her away and started talking to her instead. Sang to her a lot too, sharing the songs I always have in my head . . . treating her more like a friend than a dog." Tears threatened, making her eyes glisten. Jamison blinked them away and, with a huff, shook her head. "Stupid, right? But I loved her. And therein lies the secret."

"The reason you love dogs so much?" he asked, even though he already knew the answer.

His female was easy to read. An open book most of the time. So trusting that when he asked, she shared, opening up to show her true self. Alluring in some ways, scary in others, 'cause . . . shit. One wrong move, and he'd ruin it.

Destroy her trust. Hurt her without meaning to, simply by being himself.

He was nobody's prize, and as she smiled at him, Wick knew he should thank her for a lovely afternoon and walk away. Cutting ties—doing it quick and with respect—would be best. The kindest thing he could do for her. Despite the enlightening interlude, and the depth of his feelings for her, he wasn't relationship material. Knew without a doubt he would break her heart, along with her spirit, if he promised her tomorrow. She deserved better than him, a male incapable of letting go of a savage past and the rage that went with it. A warrior without conscience and very little honor. She needed a male that would put her first and think of her always. But as she brushed her mouth against his and whispered "Lady the bulldog's to blame," he added selfish bastard to his considerable list of terrible traits and kissed her back.

One more time. Just another hour with her before time and circumstance took her away.

Then he'd do the right thing and let her go for good.

Chapter Twenty-One

With the final "I dos" said, Wick stood on the edge of the sacred circle, beneath the soaring rotunda at the heart of Black Diamond. Colorful wall mosaics, depicting his comrades in dragon form, brushed shoulders with huge white columns. Normally, he loved visiting the ceremonial chamber. Full of color and dimension—architecture and light—the room spoke to the artist in him, soothing him from the moment he mounted the steps and strode beneath one of the four archways leading to its center.

Today, he felt nothing but pain.

Pain for the decision he'd made. Pain for the hurt he would cause Jamison when he told her the truth. Pain for his inability to walk away clean.

And as he watched Jamison exclaim from across the rotunda over the mating mark Tania now wore across the back of her right hand, he choked on self-hatred. He was a first class fool. For so many things. Not the least of which was allowing her to kiss him good-bye. In the fucking hallway. In plain view outside the bedroom her sister shared with Mac. He hadn't meant to let her get that close again. Had planned to deliver her for the ritual dressing of the bride and then walk away, but . . .

Hell. She'd surprised him with that kiss. And with her lithe body pressed against his, her small hands buried in his hair and her tongue deep in his mouth, he'd lost his mind, leaving her with the wrong impression. She expected something from him now. A commitment? Something long term? Forever? Wick didn't know, but he could tell by the way she looked at him. So happy. So excited. So hopeful as she cupped her sister's hand and studied the intricate silver tattoo that signaled a mated couple with yearning in her eyes.

As though she wanted to wear a mating mark of her own.

The thought freaked Wick out. He couldn't do that. Couldn't stand in the center of the sacred circle—as Mac and Rikar had just done with their chosen females—and say the vows that would bind Jamison to him forever. It wouldn't be fair. Despite his greed for her—and the amazing hours spent in her arms—he refused to do that to her. He wasn't up to par. Didn't deserve the privilege of taking her as his mate. Would never be able to give her the kind of life that she wanted. But even as he faced the truth head-on, primal instinct grabbed hold, tempting him to ignore right, embrace wrong, and mate her anyway.

Before he revealed too much of himself, and she came to her senses.

Which made him worse than a fool. It made him an asshole.

Dragging his gaze from her face, Wick turned away. Nothing good would come from trapping her. Or forcing her to stay in his life. He must find the strength to let her go, otherwise—

"I can smell her on you." Quiet, perhaps even a little pensive, the deep voice came from behind him. "Had a fun afternoon, did you?"

"Careful, Ven." Wick glanced over his shoulder. His eyes narrowed on his best friend, he curled his hands into fists. "Show her any disrespect, and it'll be the last thing you do."

"No disrespect intended. I'm just surprised, is all. Happy for you too, but . . ." Expression solemn, Venom met his gaze then shook his head. "Everything's changing. I guess I'm just wondering if you're okay. If *we're* okay going forward."

The unexpected concern—and Venom's insecurities—hit Wick like a body shot. He absorbed the blow, stifling his reaction. Jesus. He should've known Venom would react like this. He knew the male better than anyone. Understood his best friend's desire to protect. Venom needed to be *needed*. It was written in his DNA. Put the major savior complex Venom carried around like luggage together with the history they shared and . . . yeah. It was only natural that his friend react to the shifting landscape—the one in which he cleaved to Jamison instead of Venom.

Sixty years was a long time to look after someone else. To be relied upon. To sacrifice for another without a thought to the toll it took on yourself. Wick understood. He felt the same way about Venom. They were brothers—by choice, if not by blood—but time didn't heal all wounds, and habits had a way of becoming chains.

Maybe it was time he freed Venom of the burden.

Blowing out a breath, Wick opened his mouth to do just that.

Venom cut him off. "Are you going to keep her?"

"No," he said, his gaze seeking and finding Jamison. She laughed at something Angela said. His heart lightened at the sound, then sank again, making dread pool in the pit of his stomach. "I'm going to set her free instead."

Venom frowned. "What the hell is that supposed to—"

"Lads," Forge said, Scottish accent drifting across the rotunda.

Meeting the Scot's gaze, Wick assessed the damage. The shadows in Forge's eyes told the tale. He'd already been cornered by Bastian, information the name of the game. Everyone wanted to know what the male knew—the why behind Rodin's sudden fixation, the reason behind the call to arms. Or rather, the planned assassination. Not that B would tell them. At least, not yet. His commander was good like that, respecting a male's privacy, keeping a lid on secrets until no other option existed but to share the intel with the rest of the pack.

Wick admired B for his tactics. Most days anyway. But as Forge approached, the hem of the navy-blue ceremonial robe brushing over his bare feet, he ached for his comrade. Whatever the sins of his past, the Scot didn't deserve to be singled out by the Archguard. Or carry the guilt of putting the entire Nightfury pack in the limelight, a giant bull's-eye on each one of their backs.

A frown furrowing his brows, Forge adjusted his hold on his son, holding him against his shoulder as he came abreast of him and Venom. Eyes the same deep purple as his sire's locked onto Wick. Giving him a stern look, the baby babbled an incomprehensible string of syllables. Wick's lips twitched. Man, the kid was talkative . . . and kind of funny looking with the dark mohawk sticking up in the center of his head.

Brushing past him, Forge headed for one of the archways. "Meeting in the living room, lads. We got five minutes. After that the wedding feast goes on the table and—"

The kid squawked again, eyeballing Wick from over his father's shoulder.

"Daimler kicks our asses," Wick said, finishing the Scot's sentence as he smiled at the kid. He couldn't help it. G. M. might be pint-size, but he was opinionated. Not to mention cute as hell.

Kissing the top of his son's head, Forge nodded. "Pretty much verbatim."

With a tug, Venom tightened the belt on his robe. "Better get a move on then."

No kidding. Only an idiot crossed Daimler. One who didn't care if he ever ate well again.

Following the Scot's lead, Wick trotted down the steps into the living room. The epitome of casual, the space invited a male to sit down and stay a while. A usual occurrence considering the size of the couch. Kitted out in leather, the custom sectional took up all the real estate in front of the double-sided stone fireplace separating living from dining room. Floor-to-ceiling windows marched along one side, giving moonlight a frame as it peeked from behind the roll of thunderclouds. Throw in the foosball and twin pool tables. Kick up the comfort with fifteen deep-seated armchairs set up theater-style in front of the huge flat screen TV complete with a high-tech video game console. A catchall, the room functioned as a hangout, drawing the Nightfury warriors into the play zone most afternoons.

Heading for his usual spot, Wick strode in behind the couch . . . and the Nightfury resident computer genius. Assplanted on the back of the sectional, combat boots on the seat cushions, computer in his lap, Sloan frowned at the screen. Wick glanced over the male's shoulder, getting a quick snapshot on the flyby. E-mail up and running. Video conference software blinking. A map of Prague on-screen.

"Anything?"

Sloan shook his head. "No word yet."

Fuck. Not good. Where the hell were Gage and Haider hiding? "B know?"

"Yeah," he muttered, sending a furtive glance in Bastian's direction. A scowl on his face, their commander sat down opposite Sloan and set his size fourteens on the glass-topped coffee table. "He ain't happy about it."

"I can see that," Wick said, getting the lay of the land with a quick scan.

All the boys were in attendance. Still dressed in their ceremonial robes. Bare feet sticking out from beneath each hem. Looking like a bunch of thuggish monks. Wick swallowed a snort. *Monks*. Right. The sex-crazed lot he called his brothers had never come close to the distinction. He'd been the only one who qualified for the title. But after a day spent with Jamison, the official report was in. There wasn't a monkish thing about him.

Not anymore.

Thank fuck.

His eyes narrowed, Wick swept the interior again. AWOL. His female was no longer in the room. Ears tuned, he shut out the low rumble of masculine voices to listen for female ones. He picked out a trio of them as he skirted one of the pool tables. The vantage point gave him a clear view into the dining room. Ah, and there she was, standing beside the table, chatting with her sister and Myst, looking incredible in an off-the-shoulder gown. The amber silk complemented her coloring, making her skin glow and her dark hair seem more black than brown. Accepting a lighter from Daimler, she flicked it, no doubt planning to light the candles in front of the place settings.

A single flame sparked to life.

Wick snuffed it out.

As she frowned and shook the lighter, he sent his magic swirling. Fire flared, attacking individual wicks, setting candles aglow. With a soft indrawn breath, Jamison glanced his way. He tipped his chin. Gifting him with a slow, sexy smile, she mouthed "thank you," making him feel ten feet tall.

"Yo, Wick. You with us, laddie?"

The comment brought Wick's head around. Forge raised a brow, the look sending a clear message. One that sounded like "hello, anybody home?" Wick killed the need to cringe. Shit. He really needed to pay better attention. Not the easiest thing to do at the moment. Jamison distracted the hell out of him.

"I'm good," he said, getting back with the program. A couple of strides put him even with the fireplace. Settling into his usual spot, Wick propped his shoulder against the timber-beamed mantelpiece. "Lay it out."

Shifting in his seat, Bastian glanced over his shoulder. "You're up, Ange."

"Like I was saying . . . we've got a lead. I found a couple of interesting references in a financial statement." Decked out in an ice-blue gown, the ex-cop held up a red file folder. A sharp gleam in her hazel eyes, she skimmed over the crowd in the room. "Any of you ever heard of Deuce's?"

"I have. It's a private club downtown. BDSM, I think. Very exclusive. Very expensive." Stepping alongside his best friend, Mac plucked the folder out of Angela's hand. As he flipped it open and scanned the contents, he whistled long and low. "Wasn't Vice looking into this when you worked with that squad, Ange?"

"Yeah," she said. "We knew lots of illegal crap was going down inside. Drugs. Prostitution. Illegal gambling too. Problem was—"

Bastian cursed. "You couldn't prove it."

"Exactly. It was like trying to hit a moving target with a peashooter. Totally impossible to get a line on, never mind make anything stick."

"Stands to reason," Rikar said, lacing his fingers with Angela's. Treating his mate to a heated look, the Nightfury XO pressed his mouth to the back of her hand . . . against the mating mark that matched his own. As Wick watched, his throat went tight. Deep-seated sorrow followed, surprising him even as he accepted it. He would never do that . . . never treat Jamison with such open affection. "If the club is a Dragonkind asset—"

"It'll be surrounded by powerful magic," Bastian murmured, interrupting his best friend. "A smoke screen to keep the humans off the trail. One worthy of Ivar."

Wick hummed, excitement sinking deep. Finally. A viable lead. Something to stick a target on. "Could be his new lair."

"A good source of cash flow too." Big hands gripping the back of the couch, Venom leaned in, making the sectional groan. "We need to check it out. See if there's an underground complex beneath it."

"Then blow it sky-high." Wick cracked his knuckles. Fucking A. A club full of Razorbacks. A contained space with limited exit points. Or rather, escape hatches. God, he couldn't wait to unleash hell and hit the bastards where they lived.

"And so we will." Swinging his feet off the table, B stood. "But not tonight."

A litany of curses rippled through the room.

Green eyes flashed in warning as Bastian shook his head. "Tonight is for celebrating. To relax and get some much needed R & R. Deuce's isn't going anywhere. We'll do some more research, get an action plan together, and hit the club tomorrow night. In the meantime . . . Sloan, you got anything for me?"

With a nod, Sloan hit a few keys. Dark eyes unreadable, he swung the laptop around on his thighs. "DNA's a match, B. Azrad's telling the truth. He is your sire's son . . . your brother by blood."

The pronouncement landed like a bomb, sucking the air out of the room.

No one moved. No one said a word. The entire pack waited, poised on the edge, wondering which way to jump. And where Bastian would land. On the safe side of sanity? Or in Guiltsville for leaving his younger brother to a fate worse than death after the murder of their sire. The fact B had been abused, confined, made to submit to the Archguard's cruel guardianship before he went through his *change* didn't matter. Neither did the fact he'd fled as a fledgling male in order to save his own life. Nor that he hadn't known of Azrad's birth. Not to Bastian. Wick knew it just by looking at him. An honorable male, his commander couldn't stand the thought of abandoning those he considered his family.

No one got left behind. Pure and simple.

It was part of the Nightfury code. A credo Wick lived by, loved, accepted without question. Except in this case, someone had gotten left behind. Azrad. So only one thing left to do. Figure out how to make it right. For Bastian. For the brother his commander didn't know. For the entire Nightfury pack.

"Fuck." Raking both hands through his hair, B hung his head. "What the hell am I supposed to do? He was sent here by Nian. Has ties to the Archguard, for fuck's sake. Despite what he says, I can't trust him."

"No, but you can test him," Wick said, stepping into the breach . . . as much for Bastian as for Azrad. He understood the male. Had shared experience to guide him, and something—instinct, intuition . . . a misguided sense of duty to the warrior who'd suffered the same fate he had—wanted him to give Azrad a chance to prove his loyalty. "Set him up. Tell him about Deuce's. Give him the entire plan . . . the when, where, and how. Down to the last detail."

"Goddamn." A predatory gleam sparked in Venom's eyes. "If we walk into an ambush tomorrow night, we'll know he's in deep with the rogues. If not . . . ?"

Rikar huffed. "We work him as an asset inside the Razorback camp until we're 100 percent certain he's ours, then we'll reel him in. Make him a member of our pack."

"All right." Exhaling hard, Bastian scrubbed his hand over day-old whiskers. The rubdown left red marks on his jaw, broadcasting his unease and upset. "We'll go that way. Set it up, Sloan. Let Azrad and his crew know what we're up to. And the rest of you? Send a good word upstairs . . . pray I'm not forced to kill my own brother before this is through."

Good idea. An excellent item to put on a wish list, Wick decided as he followed his comrades into the dining room.

Killing blood kin, after all, always came at a terrible cost.

❁ ❁ ❁

As dusk folded into night, giving way to the dark skies and the violence of the season's first snowstorm, Nian checked his computer again. Palms pressed to the desktop, frustration turned the screws, twisting his muscles into knots. Hellfire and brimstone. What was taking so goddamn long? Gage and Haider should've contacted him by now. Taking a deep breath, he exhaled smooth, combating the tension, and scrolled through his messages again. He clenched his teeth. No video message. Not a single e-mail. Nothing from the warriors he wanted—no . . . *needed*—to help.

How incredibly disappointing.

Dangerous too. For him as much as the Metallics. Everything hinged on the Nightfury warriors, the ones both here and abroad. He needed the powerful pack's support to secure his position. But if the pair got swept into Rodin's net before he could get them out of the country? Bastian would kill him. But not before the Metallics died inside the Archguard's three-ring circus. And honestly, a double beheading at the closing ceremony of the festival wasn't his idea of a leap in the right direction. The second Rodin spilled Nightfury blood all bets would be off. So would all his best laid plans. The strategic power play would be dead in the water. Without movement. Or enough current to carry him into future greatness.

But worse? Bastian would abandon restraint, murder him, and declare war on the Archguard.

God have mercy on them all if that happened.

Nian didn't hold any illusions. Not after talking to Bastian. The Nightfury commander was a force of nature, a powerful figure able to curry favor, devotion, support, and

. . . yes, even love . . . from the Dragonkind community. The second Bastian sounded the call to arms, thousands of warriors would answer. Starting a war unlike anything their kind had ever seen.

"Come on," he murmured, staring at the blank screen. "Call me."

Silence greeted the entreaty.

With a growl, Nian pushed away from the desk and strode past the wall of windows. Snow swirled beyond the glass outside his study, howling along with the winter wind. He watched it a moment, wondering if staying home had been the best decision tonight. Maybe he should've abandoned his computer and gone downtown to the Emblem Club instead. A favorite spot of the Metallics, the swanky cigar bar drew the pair like a couple of magpies. The warriors had spent most of the festival entrenched in a back corner booth, drinking expensive Scotch, smoking cigars, pleasing whatever female approached them.

A trio of vices. Add the love of a good poker game to the mix, and their sins multiplied.

At the moment, though, he hoped the pair weren't anywhere near the Emblem. He prayed Gage and Haider were smarter than that. The cigar bar was too obvious. Every member of the Archguard knew the males favored the place. Nothing about the Nightfuries had gone unnoticed by the high council. Which made Nian nervous. Rodin hadn't risen to power by being stupid. He might already have the Metallics in custody. Not an impossibility, considering the numerous death squads the bastard commanded.

Which explained the radio silence, didn't it?

With a muttered curse, Nian stopped in front of the sideboard. Snatching a glass tumbler off the gold tray, he grabbed a bottle of bourbon by the neck and splashed himself a finger of the alcohol. As he turned and leaned against the antique, he glared at the computer. He wanted to toss the thing out the nearest window. Just wind up and—

A thump sounded outside his study.

Listening hard, Nian stared at the closed double doors. Nothing but quiet came back. Pushing away from his perch, he crossed the room. The Turkish rug whispered, cushioning his footfalls. With a quick mental flick, he turned the handle and pulled the door wide. The threshold opened into the soft glow of candlelight.

Another bump-thump rattled through the silence.

He frowned. "Lapier?"

When the call went unanswered, Nian stepped into the central corridor, searching for his servant. The noises were no doubt the male's doing. True to his Numbai nature, Lapier never went the night without tidying or polishing something. And yet as Nian scanned the shadows at the end of the hall, a chill snaked over his skin. Something was off. Not by much, but . . .

His night vision sparked. Nian pivoted toward the front foyer. He called out for Lapier again and jogged down a set of five stairs. Huge oak doors that guarded his home loomed in the shadows. As he cleared the last step, he saw Lapier. On the floor beside the round table sitting in the center of the vestibule, the Numbai lay in a limp sprawl: arms flung wide, head turned away from him, tuxedo vest in disarray.

"What the hell?"

Concern for his servant followed his outburst, sending him across the mosaic floor. The second he knelt next to Lapier, Nian realized his mistake. But it was too late. The enemy was already inside the gate. As he spun to protect himself, a whistle sizzled through the air. Pressure lanced the back of his shoulder. Two prongs cut through his shirt to puncture his skin. An electrical charge lit him up, making his muscles seize, paralyzing him with the press of a button.

God help him. A Taser.

Complete electrical overload. The only thing that could render a Dragonkind male powerless. The smart bastards. They'd used his weakness to effect. No mercy or the slightest hesitation, the male hit him with another forty thousand volts. His body spasmed, tunneling his vision, locking the air in his lungs, stealing his ability to move. Unable to breathe, Nian wheezed, falling facedown on the floor as agony threw him over the edge and unconsciousness reached up to claim him.

Chapter Twenty-Two

Hidden inside a cloaking spell, Ivar touched down in the parking lot. Gravel crunched beneath his paws, scraping against his claws. The grating sound drew him tight. Worry took him the rest of the way, plunging him into uncertainty. Dependence on another. Not his strong suit. Relying on anyone when it came to his science seemed, well . . . unnatural.

A kind of cop-out that sat beneath his skin, irritating itch inevitable.

A leader in the field of virology and microbiology, he never allowed another to take the wheel. Or rather the microscope. But as the water treatment plant rose in the man-made clearing, standing alongside ancient trees, rising beneath moonlight, Ivar admitted that after two failures in his lab, Hamersveld's idea held the most promise. The best chance for success, and honestly? After all was said and done, it didn't matter who hatched the plan. The prospect of unleashing one of his babies—supervirus number three—upon the world outpaced his unease, jazzing him like nothing else had in a while.

Granite Falls, Washington. Everytown, USA.

With a population of just over three thousand, it was the perfect target. Rural. Picturesque. Nestled in the shadows of the Cascade Mountain Range, northeast of Seattle . . . not too far, but close enough. But better than that? The municipality was home to couples and families, a young community full of healthy immune systems. A shiver of excitement skittered through him, rattling the spikes along his spine. So much promise. So much fun. So much to do. If he could infect Granite Falls and get his virus to spread, then he could do it the world over.

In any city he wanted.

Humming with anticipation, Ivar bared his fangs. A bona fide test run in the wilds of human society. God. Other than fucking a female while he drained her dry, he couldn't think of anything better.

Coming in on a slow glide, Hamersveld landed beside him. The big male wing flapped. Smooth shark-gray scales clicked together, and tribal ink danced, rippling beneath heavy muscle. Shifting into human form, the Norwegian glanced skyward. *"Fen . . . on the roof. Keep watch. Any sign of trouble, give us a shout."*

The wren shrieked in answer. The terrible sound throbbed in the air, obliterating the quiet, invading his skull, slamming against his temples.

Ivar cringed. "Jesus, he's loud."

"That's nothing," Hamersveld murmured, watching Ivar stomp his feet into his boots. Gravel skittered sideways, pinging off the metal base of a lamppost. "Wait until you hear him in combat. He'll bring a male to ground, completely disorient him with his cry."

"Then gut him?"

"Pretty much."

"Good thing he's on our side, then."

"Believe it." Amusement in his gaze, Hamersveld raised a brow. "Are you ready?"

"Born ready."

As the male laughed, Ivar smiled and, allowing his excitement free rein, strode between two parked cars. His new comrade fell in behind him, following him across the parking lot toward the front entrance. Brand spanking new, the facility was a towering example of technological advancement. Good for him and his plans. Not so great for the humans who called Granite Falls home.

Not that Ivar cared. The whole idea was to wipe them from the face of the earth. Eliminate the unending strife, the environmental reign of terror their race committed day after day . . . year after year. A few dead kids along the way didn't mean anything in the grand scheme of things.

With nothing more than a thought, Ivar swung the front doors wide. The work of seconds, he disabled the security system. As the beep-beep-beeping settled into silence, he scanned the corridor. Not a human in sight. Perfect. Not that it would've mattered. Still cloaked in magic, the inferior race would see neither him nor Hamersveld.

Handy, wasn't it? Invisibility. The calling card of his kind.

After a series of twists and turns through labyrinth-like hallways, past advanced filtration equipment and pipework, Ivar stood where he wanted to be . . . in front of a holding tank. Full of purified water, the contents were good to go. A mere turn of the tap away from being pumped into a human's home. Unleashing his magic, Ivar conjured the hermetically sealed test tube. As smooth metal settled against his palm, Hamersveld stopped beside him, putting them shoulder-to-shoulder.

Black eyes rimmed by light blue met his. The male held out his hand.

Ivar's stomach clenched. Time to pay the piper. With a nod, and a boatload of trust, he handed his baby to his new buddy. "Just like in the lab."

"No deviation. A walk in the park," Hamersveld said, his voice hushed. Full of reverence, the Norwegian's quiet tone put things into perspective. They were about to make history. Change the trajectory of the planet's future for the better. "I'll infuse the water molecules with the viral load, magically fusing the two. Any human who comes into contact with it will be infected. Then we'll—"

"Sit back, record the RO factor, and see how fast the disease spreads." Ivar knew the plan. He'd helped put it together, for Christ's sake. Had spent the better part of twenty-four hours testing the delivery method alongside Hamersveld in his lab. But now that he stood on the precipice, nerves got the better of him. Jesus. He hoped like hell it worked outside a sterile environment. Blowing out a breath, Ivar gave the go-ahead. "Do it."

With a nod, Hamersveld pivoted. Leaving Ivar standing beside the holding tank, he walked to a large pipe running the length of the room. He stopped in front of a raised hatch embedded on top of the water mainline. The warrior unleashed his magic. Prickles exploded across Ivar's skin, raising the hair on his nape as the airlock released with a hiss. Purified water bubbled up through the opening. With a murmur, his new friend controlled it, making it rise like a cobra from a basket. Plunging his hand into the wet swirl, he relinquished the test tube. Hamersveld pulled his hand free of the water. Ivar watched the stainless steel casing float in the waves for a moment, then cracked the cryogenic seal.

The microorganism entered the stream. Hamersveld bared his teeth and, unleashing magic, tweaked the spell. The deadly virus fused with H_2O molecules, becoming one with the water supply.

Wonder picked Ivar up and carried him along. Finally. After all this time . . .

"It's done."

"No going back now," Hamersveld murmured, Norwegian accent thicker than usual. Pride in his eyes, he watched the water retreat into the pipe. Metal hinges whined as the hatch swung closed and the valve spun, sealing the mainline. "We should celebrate."

"Hell, yeah." Elation tightened his chest. He'd done it. Really done it this time. Slapping Hamersveld on the shoulder, Ivar cupped his new best friend's nape. A grin. A hardy jostle. A howl of triumph threatening, he asked, "What do you feel like, Sveld . . . Deuce's?"

Eyes gleaming, Hamersveld gave him a playful shove. "Deuce's will do."

Fantastic. One superbug unleashed and on its way. *And* the promise of multiple females to fuck inside his club. The night couldn't possibly get any better.

Chapter Twenty-Three

Set up on the rooftop across from Deuce's, Venom crouched behind a low wall. Out of sight. Undetectable. His mouth curved. The quiet before the storm. The Razorbacks didn't have a clue he'd descended on their little patch of heaven.

Just the way he liked it. Exactly the way he wanted to keep it too.

At least, for now. Later—after all the recon was in the can—would be soon enough to send a wake-up call . . . in the form of a firestorm.

Rotating on the balls of his feet, he shuffled left, gaze narrowed on the building opposite him. Stone face awash with moonlight, the nothing-special facade looked innocent enough. No awning out front to welcome visitors. No bouncers or doormen either. Just a plain black door emblazoned with a gold plaque. Venom huffed. Smart ploy. Big payoff. A passerby would never guess the private club existed, never mind that it catered to upscale, wealthy people with bizarre tastes.

Or so he'd heard. But after laying eyes on the place? Seeing slid into believing, 'cause . . . oh yeah, there were plenty of Dragonkind inside. He could feel the bastards.

Not hard to do. The magical trace each male left in his wake sent out a clear signal. So did the scent of sex in the air. Hell, he could smell the coital heat from all the way across the street.

A rogue playground in the middle of Seattle.

With a hum of anticipation, Venom pinged his comrades. *"We're good to go. All's quiet on our end so far."*

"Here tae." Hunkered down with Mac a couple miles east of the club, Forge sighed, the sound one of exasperation. *"Shouldae brought a pack of cards tae pass the time. I'm bored tae tears."*

Mac grumbled, seconding the opinion.

Clenching his teeth, Venom swallowed his amusement. No sense laughing at the wonder twins. The pair might take it personally. Which would suck. Particularly since he wouldn't be able to do anything about it. Not while stuck on outlook without any hope of kicking their asses when they mouthed off. Besides, his heart wouldn't be in the squabble. He understood their impatience. Stakeouts weren't his favorite thing either. He preferred to start shit, not sit around waiting for it to happen.

But a plan was a plan. Three fighting units: Rikar and Bastian to the north; the wonder twins to the east; while he, Wick, and Sloan kept eyes on the prize. The setup was a good one, providing three avenues of attack if Azrad screwed them over . . .

And the rogues came out to play.

"Stay sharp, boys," Rikar said, the crackle of frost in his undertone. *"Let it play out."*

"Fifteen more minutes." Heavy footfalls came through mind-speak along with B's voice. As the thud-thud got going, Venom realized his commander was pacing. Unusual

for Bastian. The male was rock solid, as calm as they came under normal circumstances. But with Azrad in the mix, B's edge was sharper than usual. *"If Azrad proves trustworthy and doesn't show, we go in. KO every rogue inside. Burn the fucker to the ground."*

Venom rolled his shoulders, beyond ready for the green light. He adored the seek-and-destroy missions. The covert ops—the thrill of the hunt—jazzed him like nothing else could. Anticipation prickled through him, cranking him tight. He wanted to go right now. Just leap over the roof edge, put feet to asphalt, and cross the street. The work of seconds, and he'd be through the outer door, in prime put-the-screws-to-the-enemy position while Wick set fire to the club. An excellent strategy, but for one thing . . .

He glanced to his right. Yup. No change there. Wick was still distracted as hell.

Crouched a few feet away, Wick stared at his knuckles instead of the target. Not a good sign. Venom frowned as unease spiraled into concern. He'd never seen Wick act like this before, so . . . well, he didn't know exactly. Unfocused. Oblivious to his surroundings. In a world of his own, mind on something other than the mission.

Which scared the hell out of Venom.

Wick might not say much, but he always . . . *always* . . . paid attention. He never missed a thing and saw more than most. So, yeah . . . a not-so-present Wick was cause for concern. No one wanted to go into battle with Wick's focus split. Their most vicious warrior, Venom and the others needed him onboard, raring for fight, not lost in thought. Thinking about what? Venom cursed under his breath. Making the leap from supposition to certainty wasn't difficult. Jamison Jordan. Goddamn it. The female was screwing with his best friend's head . . . all the way from the frigging lair . . . messing with Wick's ability to concentrate.

A serious problem, considering the game plan.

Worry made Venom glance over his shoulder. Perched on a chimney in dragon form, scales clicked as Sloan shook his head. He registered his buddy's tension, and the disquiet that drove it, all the same. The male knew what was up with Wick and didn't like it either.

"Wick," he growled, his tone harsh. His best friend flinched. Shimmering golden eyes snapped in his direction. Thank God. Wick might be acting dumb, but at least he wasn't deaf. *"Pull your head out of your ass. I need you focused . . . in the here and now, not half back at the lair."*

His brows furrowed, Wick nodded, but didn't look convinced. *"I'm fucked, aren't I?"*

"When it comes to the female?" Venom raised a brow, his expression all about "damned right you are." No matter how much he disliked it, he saw no reason to lie. Wick didn't need coddling. He needed to be dropkicked into reality. In the same way he'd been when he realized his friend had bonded with a female. But denying the truth never worked, so forget about sticking his head in the sand. It had happened. It couldn't be undone. Time to accept it. *"Yeah, you're totally screwed."*

Wick dropped another f-bomb.

"Energy-fuse is serious stuff, Wick. I know it scares you. Hell, I don't like it either. Change sucks, and much as I don't want to say it, I'm going to . . ." Eyes aglow, a red wash rolled out in front of him, staining the icy patches on the roof as Venom shuffled sideways. Wick's gaze narrowed on him. He glared back. It was so much bullshit: clinging to the past, being selfish, refusing to share his best friend with anyone. But no

matter how much he wanted things to stay the same, they never did. J. J. was here to stay. Wick couldn't go back, and neither could he. *"Stop being such a pansy. Accept her. Love her. Take her to mate and be happy."*

"Screw happy," Wick growled, cracking his knuckles. *"This is about her, not me. She deserves more . . . someone better. I can't give her what she needs long term."*

"How do you know?" he asked, playing devil's advocate. *"You haven't even tried."*

"Fuck off, Ven."

Ah, and there it was. Wick's favorite comeback, the go-to that heralded the end of a conversation.

Sloan didn't get the memo. Or maybe he just didn't care. *"You know he's right, Wick. Man up and grow a pair. I'd give my left nut to find what you—"*

A burst of magic detonated, sending out shockwaves. As the pulse rippled, the night air warped into a wormhole. Gaze narrowed on the anomaly, Venom tensed, getting ready to move. A dragon materialized over Deuce's, red scales flashing, pink irises aglow, power shimmering around him. And on his tail? Hamersveld, along with a miniature dragon.

Wick snarled. *"Ivar."*

"Wick, don't—" With a quick twist, he reached for Wick. His fingertips brushed leather, but . . . goddamn it. He missed by a mile, catching nothing but cold air. *"Bastian . . . man overboard."*

"Shit." The rattle of scales rippled through mind-speak. *"Hold on. We're airborne. ETA . . . sixty seconds."*

Claws snicked as Mac and Forge took flight from their hidey-hole.

But it was too late.

Ivar was already on the wire, sending out a distress call, rousing the rogues inside the club. As Venom felt them rise and head for the exits, he shifted into dragon form. Hands and feet turning to talons, he zeroed in on Wick and . . . ah, hell. No way would he catch him now. His friend was already out of range. Exploding over the roof edge. Black amber-tipped scales flashing, golden gaze aglow as he painted a target on Ivar's chest. With a muttered curse, Venom bared his fangs and leapt after him. Goddamn it. So much for the element of surprise. Wick had destroyed their advantage with one clean swipe. A dumb-ass move. One that might get his friend killed if Venom didn't move fast.

❀ ❀ ❀

As a squadron of Razorbacks took flight from Deuce's roof, Wick called himself an idiot. Straight up, stone-cold, dead to rights, he'd just earned the Boy Scout's imbecile badge by breaking cover too soon. Shit . . . shit . . . and triple *shit*. Impulse was a bitch, making him move before his brain entered the equation.

Not his usual MO.

Mistakes didn't happen around him. Ever. Then again, there was a first time for everything. Now happened to be a perfect example. Had he used the sense God gave him, he'd still be hunkered down, waiting for Ivar and his posse to land. The trio would've made one hell of a target sitting on Deuce's rooftop. Instead, the rogue leader was in full flight, hauling ass in the opposite direction with his new buddies—the river-rat and company—while enemy soldiers closed ranks around him.

Fucking hell. Had he said idiot earlier? Well, strike that. Asshole made way more sense.

Tucking his wings, he rocketed into a spiral, threading the needle between two rogues. The pair snarled and lashed out. Enemy claws raked his side. Blood welled on his rib cage. Wick embraced the pain, let it expand, knowing he deserved it. For not thinking straight. For making a mistake. For dragging his brothers-in-arms into his fuck up. And as his pack flew in behind him to engage the enemy, Wick wanted to kick his own ass. Or ask Venom to do it for him.

His best friend was bang on. Dumb-ass move was right. Idiocy to the next power. Especially since what drove him had nothing to do with the mission.

Anger. Doubt. Despair. All those fit the bill, explaining the *why* behind the *what,* pushing him to the brink, sending him into the fray without thought to the consequences.

All because he needed a fight.

A ball-busting brawl to help him forget. To blot out the reality of what he must do when he got home. Let Jamison go. Send her away. Free her to live the life she was meant to, not the one he knew she would suffer with him.

The right thing to do. It was the best thing for her. But even as he faced the truth, he hated the outcome. He didn't want to do it. Keeping her sounded better to him. And claiming her . . . in the way of his kind? Shit, that seemed like the best plan of all. A selfish male would do it. Say to hell with the consequences and take what he craved. Too bad egocentric wasn't on his dance card.

And didn't punch his ticket.

Despite his many faults, he refused to trap her. Jamison deserved more than he would ever be able to give her. So no matter how much it pained him, he would force himself to let her go. Push her away. Be honorable for once. Do whatever it took to make her leave Black Diamond and start a new life without him.

But first? He would get his fight.

With a snarl, he sideswiped a Razorback. As the male squawked, Wick flipped up, rotated over and . . . crack! A fast grab. A quicker twist snapped the enemy dragon's neck. Leaving him to ash out in midair, he went after another. Senses sharp, he kept an eye on Ivar's retreat. Not that he could go far. Forge and Mac were on their game, playing the trump card. Wick grinned as he cracked another skull. Score one for the wonder twins. The pair were right where they needed to be: cutting off Ivar's retreat, hemming him in, making him fight instead of turn tail and run.

Speed supersonic, a rogue went wings vertical, rocketing along Wick's right side. Sound warped. Dragon scales rattled. Claws gleaming in the moonlight, the bastard took a shot at him. Wick arched, torqueing into a sidewinding flip. Up. Over. Around and . . . oh yeah. The enemy caught nothing but air, missing him by inches.

He bared his fangs and hissed in satisfaction. Aerial acrobatics . . . his specialty.

One that worked like a charm as he twisted out of the spin. The move put him in prime position behind a trio of Razorbacks. In the strike zone, Wick lashed out. Claws met scales. He dug in. The razor-sharp tips punched through bone. His talon closed around the fucker's beating heart. With a snarl, Wick yanked. Arterial spray splattered across the back of his paw. The smell of blood expanded, then disappeared as the enemy's heart ashed in his palm. His wing-mates roared as their buddy disintegrated in midair, and Wick got ready.

Oh baby. Imminent attack. Not much better than that.

Wings spread wide, he banked hard as the other two rogues attacked. Timing it to perfection, Wick rolled into a somersault. Meathead number one tried to adjust. Too late. He was already in position, poised to strike above the male's spine. Wick didn't hesitate. Coming out of the tuck, he fisted the rogue's horns. The enemy dragon screamed. He twisted, snapping the fucker's neck, and swung around. His eyes narrowed on the last rogue. In full panic mode, the male wing flapped for a second, no doubt trying to decide. Take him on. Or run and hide. Wick banked wide right, hoping for the first, but . . .

No such luck. Wick growled in disgust. Aw, come on. Was the idiot really going to—

"Shit," he muttered as the Razorback turned and fled in the opposite direction.

Increasing his wing speed, Wick chased after him, slicing between two skyscrapers. Glass rattled in steel frames. Refusing to lose the male, Wick banked around the bend, his wing tip inches from a building corner. His sonar pinged, narrowing his senses. Street lights blurred into streaks beneath him. He hummed as he came within range of his target.

Less than fifty feet away. Excellent. Right in the sweet spot.

A bull's-eye locked on the rogue's back, Wick drew a deep breath, filling his lungs to capacity. A fireball gathered at the back of his throat and . . . yum. He loved the taste. Couldn't get enough of his arsenal's cause and effect either.

Deadly. Efficient. Incendiary. The trifecta of nastiness was a gift that kept on giving.

One the Razorbacks underestimated all the time. The enemy never saw it coming. Not that Wick lamented the fact. The chemical complexities of his exhale elevated his game. Had all kind of layers: blue flame on the outside, the ooey-gooey goodness of lava on the inside, a layer of poisonous gas between the two.

Sweet and sour with a hit of hot sauce.

The rogue zigzagged, dodging between buildings. Wick hopscotched a smokestack. Time to head the asshole off at the pass. Magma splashed over his back molars. Whipping into a tight turn, Wick bared his fangs and started the countdown.

Three . . .

Fire licked over his tongue.

Two . . .

Lethal gases combined, rising up his throat.

One . . .

Wick pulled the trigger. The ravenous ball shot from his throat. Heat went cataclysmic. The inferno sucked the oxygen out of the air, hellish tail streaking behind it, hissing through the darkness, obliterating the chill. The Razorback yelled and scrambled, trying to get out of the way . . .

Boom!

The rogue screamed in agony. Wick dodged to avoid the splash-back of lava-infused fireball. Smoke billowed upward. The smell of burning scales and scorched bone putrefied the air, and—

Mission accomplished. One roasted Razorback plummeting out of the sky.

Wick watched him burn a second, then wheeled around, looking for his next target. Huh. None in sight. Which could only mean one thing. He'd flown far afield, chasing the rogue out of the kill zone . . . where his brothers-in-arms still fought. Leaving the rogue to dissolve into a pile of cinders, he stayed low and rocketed over an apartment complex.

The blow back from his wings rushed over the neighborhood. Treetops swayed. Vehicles rocked on their tires. Car alarms started to shriek. A few lights came on. Wick tightened the cloaking spell, strengthening his magic. Invisibility was an absolute must. Scaring the neighbors, after all, was never a good idea.

Neither was showing up on the evening news.

Night vision pinpoint sharp, Wick scanned the sky. Nada. No one in sight. He sent out an exploratory ping. *"Venom."*

"What?"

Wick swallowed a snort. Wow. His friend sounded pissed off . . . and out of breath. Looked like he'd arrived just in time. *"Four down. I'm free and clear."*

"Bully for you." Scales rattled. Venom grunted. *"I still got three on my tail."*

"Should be a walk in the park for you, Ven."

"Screw off, Sloan," Venom growled. *"Get your ass over here and help me."*

Sloan huffed. *"If you want my help, move the hell over. I'm coming in hot."*

"About frigging time."

Following his buddies energy signal, Wick rocketed over a rooftop. A yellow Razorback came at him out of nowhere. Collision inevitable, Wick put the brakes on and ducked. The bastard streaked past, clipping him with a wing tip.

The burn streaked over his shoulder. Holy shit. That had been close, and . . . he blinked, plucking the cause of the male's hysteria out of thin air. Well, all right then. The enemy dragon had good reason to haul ass.

Right on the rogue's tail, Rikar's white scales flashed in the gloom. Frost swirling in his wake, the Nightfury XO glared at him. *"Good of you to join us, hotshot."*

"I was a little busy." His XO *"uh-huhed."* Wick grinned, enjoying the artistic blast as Rikar blew by him.

"Wick," Bastian said, a snarl in his voice. Wick's focus snapped right. Scanning the horizon, he spotted B. Deep in combat, claws gleaming in the moonlight, his commander lashed out. A male screamed as B applied pressure, cracking the enemy's spine in half. *"Help Mac and Forge. Get an angle and take a shot. Down Ivar, but don't incinerate him. We need him alive."*

Good plan. Ivar the Asshole had a nasty agenda. One that included a breeding program and a stable full of unwilling HE females. So yeah. Taking the rogue leader alive made a ton of sense. The problem? Ivar wasn't stupid . . . or alone. He'd armored up and buttoned down, keeping a scaly wall of muscle between him and the wonder twins.

Which meant tactical advantage time. He needed a solid one. An approach the enemy wouldn't see coming.

Eyes narrowed, Wick looked for an avenue. He needed a window just wide enough to slip through while Mac and Forge kept the rogues busy. Not a stretch by any means. The warriors were doing a good job of it already, hammering Ivar's front line of defense. Wick hummed as Forge exhaled. Fire-acid shot between the male's fangs, lighting up the night sky. Hamersveld countered, throwing up a wall of water. The stream of fire hit the barrier with a popping hiss, then flickered and went out like a lightbulb. Mac growled and unleashed his magic. The tidal wave evaporated, throwing mist toward the clouds like confetti.

"Heads up," Wick murmured, keeping a low profile, slithering in like a snake. *"Get ready to bug out."*

Elbowing a rogue, Mac spun around and fed him a mouthful of water spear. As the male went *poof*, he growled, *"Line it up."*

"Say when." Flipping sideways, Forge took out another sentry.

"Give me a second . . ."

Sneaking in from behind, Wick rolled in on a smooth glide. His gaze narrowed on Ivar, painting a target on red scales. Three hundred and fifty yards out. Not close enough yet. Just a little further. Just a little longer. Ten seconds tops before he entered the kill zone. The optimal distance to ensure he singed Ivar's wings. The second his exhale reached Ivar, burning the vulnerable webbing, the bastard wouldn't be able to fly. And once on the ground? He'd hit him hard. Make him hurt. Exact the toll, keeping him just alive enough to answer B's line of inquiry.

Answers. Wick wanted them as much as his commander.

The enemy was hurting those most vulnerable. Females like his own. It didn't matter that he refused to mate her. The claiming was irrelevant. He needed to know when he let her go, Jamison could walk out of Black Diamond into a safer world. One in which Ivar didn't exist, and the code most of Dragonkind lived by held sway.

Preserve life. Protect the weak. Respect a female's right to choose.

Drawing a deep breath, Wick let his magic roll. His exhale gathered, spilling into the back of his throat and—

The wren protecting Hamersveld whipped full circle. Yellow eyes met his, then widened. Baring his small fangs, the miniature dragon shrieked in warning. Thunderous sound erupted like a volcano, blowing sky-high, blasting Wick with debilitating shockwaves. Mind-bending pain hammered his temples. Pressure expanded, warping perception, ripping at his eardrums, making his head whiplash.

His vision dimmed.

The wren screamed again.

Auditory overload battered the inside of his skull. Wick roared in agony. His muscles spasmed. He lost control of the fireball. The blaze shot from his mouth and heat roared, eating through the frigid air. Mac cursed and dodged. Forge shouted as he got caught in the crossfire. But it was too late. The ravenous ball clipped him, hurling the Scot sideways. As his body whiplashed, the inferno slammed into a skyscraper behind him. A sonic boom rippled, spreading like poison over the cityscape. Lava splashed in a deadly arc. Glass and steel exploded. Shrapnel blew outward, ripping through Forge's side.

Dragons—Razorback and Nightfury alike—screamed in pain.

The horror expanded, and Wick gave voice to his anguish, yelling his throat raw as he watched Forge fall from the sky.

Chapter Twenty-Four

Sitting cross-legged in the middle of a gym mat, J. J. flipped through another file. Worn by time, water stains dotted the dog-eared paper. Finished reading the page, she flipped it up, folding it over the top of the folder, and frowned. More gobbledegook. An equal amount of nothing special. Just like the last . . . hmm, let's see. How many was that now? File number ten or eleven? She's lost count a couple of hours ago.

Not that she was complaining. Busy was preferable to twiddling her thumbs.

Especially since Tania had abandoned her to the stacks. Probably a good idea, all things considered. Her sister's mind wasn't in the game. She was too busy dreaming big, drawing a new set of architectural plans. Ones that included an outdoor garden along with a swimming pool for Mac. Thumbing the corner of the page, J. J. smiled. Landscape design. The story of her sister's life.

Well, that and being a worrywart.

An honorable pastime, really. Concern for another, after all, carried weight. Signaled caring . . . deep-seated love too. J. J. huffed. Ironic, wasn't it? Before tonight she never would've qualified as a worrier. But over the last few hours? She'd done little else, so . . .

Bring it on. Pile on the paperwork. Make it last 'til morning.

Until Wick walked back through the door. Safe, sound, and into her arms once more.

Raking her hair behind her ears, J. J. shook her head. Such craziness. Her concern for him amounted to idiocy. He was a warrior: born strong, bred to fight, lethal beyond compare. She knew it. Had seen him in action and accepted the facts. Not that it mattered. Logic had nothing to do with it. Not while worry ruled, making her act like an idiot.

One with a terrible headache. And no sense.

Exhaling a pent-up breath, J. J. turned another page and scanned the typewritten text, seeing it, but not really. She didn't understand it. The draw. The pull. The ridiculous yearning she felt every time she thought of him. Which, God help her, was a lot. She scowled at a dark smudge on the corner of the folder. Two days. A measly forty-eight hours of knowing him. Peanuts. A drop in the bucket on time's sliding scale, and yet the bond she shared with him was irrefutable. Undeniable. So rock solid she couldn't resist its tether. But the truly crazy part? As it tied her down and locked her in, she didn't struggle. She submitted, allowing the magic to flow and the Meridian to have its way. Energy-fuse, love's holy grail. A seductive elixir, the thing every woman searched for, but rarely found.

Hers. For the taking.

Just one problem. Fairy tales happened to other people, not her. Never her. Despite all the hoping and dreaming. Despite what she felt for Wick. Despite everything. It seemed too good to be true, and even though she wanted to believe, J. J. couldn't help herself. She kept waiting for the other shoe to drop.

With an audible sigh, she flipped another page.

"You wanna talk about it?"

Surprise made her flinch. J. J.'s focus snapped to her right. Her gaze traveled across a sea of blue exercise mats. Serious hazel eyes met hers. She blinked and . . . oh, right. She wasn't alone. Angela sat just a few feet away. File boxes stacked like Lego blocks behind her, Angela raised a brow. Unease hit J. J. like a hurricane, blowing the roof off the house where confidence lived. As it escaped into the ether, she nibbled on her fingernail and looked down at the file in her lap.

Alone in a gymnasium with an ex-homicide detective. Oh goody. Every convicted felon's wet dream.

"You know I don't give a shit, right?" The question came out soft, the meaning behind it didn't. Acceptance and more rang in Angela's tone. Strange—more than a little baffling—considering J. J.'s history with SPD. "Wick's not the only one who read your jacket, J. J. I know what happened. Your ex was an abusive jerk."

Disbelief made her huff. Hope made her ask, "So you don't mind that I shot him?"

"I understand the necessity." Propped against a table leg, Angela rubbed her shoulder against the wooden corner. Done chasing the itch, she crossed one foot over the other and shrugged. "And I'm not judging you for it. Besides, you did your stretch."

"Paid my debt to society?"

"Something like that."

"Right," J. J. whispered, not quite believing it. If only it were that simple. If only she could forget. If only the pain would leave her alone, let her breathe, stop twisting the screws. Wishful thinking, she knew. Guilt didn't work that way. It never went away. Like outstanding debt, it stayed until either it was paid off or forgiven. Two things that would never happen for her. "I still have nightmares about it sometimes."

Angela threw her a startled look.

She didn't blame her. Her admission surprised her too. Chewing on her bottom lip, J. J. frowned. What the heck was she doing? Bringing it up. Laying it out. Baring her soul. None of those things fit her usual MO. She never talked about it. Not even with Tania. But for some reason—instinct, the allure of sisterhood, and the need to be understood—J. J. wanted to tell her. Something told her the ex-cop would understand. Angela had seen things, been a part of *that* world . . . the one J. J. had inhabited the past five years.

Which, strange as it seemed, put them on equal footing.

Pressure banded around her chest. J. J. breathed through it. Go hard or go home. There were no in-betweens here. Just straight-up honesty or complete silence. Swallowing, she worked moisture back into her mouth. "Some nights, I wake up in a cold sweat unable to breathe. A scream locked in my throat. The feel of his hands around my neck . . . squeezing."

"I've had a few of those too."

And there it was. The detail intuition had told her was there. Unearthed. Deep in the vault. That place where secrets went to die. A shiver crawled down J. J.'s spine.

"I got caught in the crossfire a couple of months ago." Haunted. No other word described Angela's expression, and as J. J. met her gaze she tried not to flinch. To stay strong in the face of her pain. Her new friend wouldn't accept pity.

Didn't want sympathy either, but . . . God. She recognized that look. Had seen it on her own face while looking in the mirror. "I was raped by a Razorback . . . imprisoned in one of their lairs. Rikar got me out."

"Oh, Ange, I'm so sorry. I didn't know," she said, the admission splitting her wide open. She knew what that felt like: to be cornered, held down, and . . . forced. That it had happened at the hands of her boyfriend didn't make the experience any less horrific. Young. Stupid. Naive. She'd trusted him not to hurt her. Instead, he'd torn her apart, obliterating her confidence along with any sense of self. "How long were you there?"

"Not long. Twelve hours, but then . . ." Angela's voice cracked. As she regrouped, she flexed her hands, making twin fists. "It doesn't take long to destroy a person . . . take their life while leaving them alive . . . does it?"

"No, it doesn't."

Shuffling the papers in her lap, Angela cleared her throat. "You should share how you feel with Wick. He'll help you let go of the pain, along with the past. Rikar does wonders for me."

J. J. nodded, believing every word. Wick was power personified. Intense, yet kind. Lethal in a fight, yet gentle with her. Unassuming yet oh-so-hot in bed, he made her want, need, yearn in ways she never had before. An image of him, golden eyes shimmering as he loved her, flared in her mind's eye. Desire rose on a heated wave. J. J. shifted on the mat and . . . yup. Sex kitten tendencies, here she came. Just thinking about him—how he felt against her, inside her, his skin brushing over hers, his taste in her mouth—and . . .

Good lord. She needed to get a grip. Or hop into a cold shower. Quick. Before she embarrassed herself in front of an ex-cop who missed nothing and—

"Accept it and move on." A twinkle in her eyes, Angela grinned. "Rikar does that to me too. I get hot just thinking about him."

"Must make for an interesting scene when he walks through the door each morning."

"You have no idea."

"Uh, hello," she said, making a funny face. "I think I do."

Angela laughed. J. J. joined in. God, it felt so good to laugh . . . seemed normal to share a moment without studying the angles. Without wondering if what she said would get her killed. Or in hot water with the prison guards. But then, that wasn't her life anymore. She was safe in a place where no one wanted to hurt her. The thought stilled her mind. The realization shifted her perspective, and as it sank deep, so did the idea of freedom.

From everything: the fear, past mistakes, all the pain.

Now she possessed the power to choose a different path and create a new reality. So time to pack up the past and put it away. No good would come from denying the truth. Or fighting what she felt for Wick. He was part of the equation now, and were she honest? Everything she wanted for her future.

The truth tightened her throat, even as it set her free. "Hey, Ange?"

"Yeah?"

"Can I ask you something?"

"Anything."

"Can you read Rikar's mind?" As her new friend blinked in surprise, J. J. hurried to explain. "I mean, how powerful is the connection . . . all the energy-fuse stuff, 'cause I know things about Wick that I shouldn't. Things he hasn't told me about his past. I know it sounds weird, but when I'm with him, it's as though I'm plugged in . . . being fed information. Images. Experiences. How he feels about both."

"Welcome to the club," Angela said. "The connection between mates is a powerful one. I cherry-pick stuff off Rikar's mind all the time. Thoughts. Worries. The stuff he doesn't want me to know because he's trying to protect me. Sometimes, it's just a feeling . . . like a vibration. Other times, I get snippets of residual memory."

Snippets. Right. Made sense. Except she'd gotten a heck of a lot more than that from Wick. A full-on movie seemed like a better description. While lying in his arms, listening to him breathe, watching him sleep, she'd seen things he tried to hide. Borne witness to the cruelty: the cage and collar, the fighting and killing . . . that first day when he'd balked, and that awful man had tied a knife to his hand, then thrust him into the ring. God. The images made her ache from the inside out. For the little boy with the golden eyes, looking so lost and afraid. For the young man as Wick struggled against chains, screaming in agony as the red-hot poker seared his skin.

Leaving the terrible brand behind on his forearm.

Goddamn sons of bitches. The bastards had hurt him so badly.

Tears stung her eyes as sorrow invaded her heart. J. J. willed them away. Crying would only make Angela ask questions. Ones she refused to answer. Wick deserved his privacy. His past was his own to share. Or not. The decision belonged to him and—

"My lady!" The bellow echoed down the corridor.

Sharing a look with Angela, J. J. vaulted to her feet. Something was wrong. She could hear it in Daimler's voice. Heard it in the rapid thump of footfalls outside the gymnasium door. Felt it in every beat as her heart picked up the vibe, hammering the inside of her breastbone.

"My lady, where are you?" Daimler yelled, his tone so panic-filled it raised the fine hair on J. J.'s nape. "Myst!"

"In the clinic, Daimler," she shouted even though she couldn't see the butler yet. Ahead of Angela, J. J. sprinted across the gym. As she reached the door, Daimler sped past, tuxedo tails flapping, arms and legs pumping. Oh no. Oh shit . . . shit, shit, shit. Not good. The elf seemed an unflappable sort, but right now? Calm was history, leaving nothing but alarm in its wake. "She's in the clinic!"

"What's wrong?" Shoving past her, Angela skidded to a stop in the middle of the hall. Breathing hard, her eyes glued to the elf, she watched him run toward the clinic. "Who's injured?"

Dark eyes wide with fear, Daimler glanced over his shoulder without breaking stride. "I don't know, my lady, but it's bad and—"

The wall dead-ending the corridor wavered.

Rooted to the floor, J. J. held her breath. Waiting. Hoping. Praying.

"Please, God," Angela whispered, gaze riveted to the magical entrance. "Not Rikar. Please don't let it be . . ."

A dull roar in her ears, J. J. didn't hear her friend say the last word, but filled in the blank, erasing Rikar's name to insert Wick's. *Please, don't let it be Wick.* As the words bounced around inside her head, J. J. understood true desperation, and how very awful she could be. God, how depraved. How completely bent . . . to wish harm on another so that the man she loved stayed whole. But she couldn't help it. The thought of Wick injured sent her into a tailspin. Did terrible things to her sense of right and wrong. To her sense of fair play. All she wanted in that moment was for it to be anyone but him.

Selfish. Twisted. Beyond terrible, considering she stood beside a woman mated to a Nightfury warrior. One who would die the instant he did.

Her throat closed as ancient stone rippled, undulating in the low light. The portal expanded to form a doorway, allowing her to see into the cavern beyond. A trio came into view. Three dark heads bent, two warriors bookended one, half carrying, half dragging the injured party. Her gaze riveted to the group, J. J. shook her head. Tears stung the corner of her eyes as one of them looked her way. Fierce golden eyes met hers. J. J.'s knees went weak. *Oh, thank God.* Not Wick. It wasn't Wick. He wasn't hurt, but . . .

Jesus be merciful. Forge.

The warrior was in bad shape. Worse than *bad.* He looked dead: unconscious, toes of his boots dragging on the ground, blood covering his torso—as Mac and Wick carried him into the clinic, leaving bloody streaks on the floor in their wake.

❂ ❂ ❂

Head pounding like a motherfucker, Wick lifted his injured comrade onto the examination table. *Injured.* Fuck, what an understatement. Forge was torn wide open, still bleeding like a sieve, so close to death Wick didn't know what to do. Scream in agony for his fallen comrade. Or pick up a scalpel and gut himself for hurting his friend.

Death seemed preferable. To the pain. To the shame. To the guilt.

Fisting his hands in his hair, he stepped back from the table, but refused to look away. From the blood. From the gaping wounds. From the certain knowledge he'd put Forge at death's door. Fucking hell. He'd done this. Was the cause and effect. The one responsible for all the chaos and pain. Had he done his job and stuck to the plan, instead of jumping the gun—going off half-cocked into battle, dragging his pack with him—his comrade wouldn't be laid out on the table. A heartbeat away from losing his life.

His fault. It was all his fault.

"Jesus," he rasped, glancing down at his hands. Smeared with blood, he watched them tremble. His throat clogged as remorse and self-loathing collided. The sound of ripping fabric brought his head back up. An intense expression on her face, Myst cut Forge's blood-soaked shirt away, revealing the extent of the wounds. His eyes stung as he met her gaze. "You have to save him. Please save him, Myst. What can I do? Tell me what to—"

"Get out of the way," she said, her tone so calm it jolted him. In control. In command of her domain. In her element. The realization gave Wick hope. He took a step back. And then another, giving her space, doing what she asked, praying hard as his shoulder blades collided with the back wall. "And get Sloan. I need another set of hands."

Pacing the floor in front of him, Mac spun toward the exit.

The glass doors slid open.

"I'm here." Sloan sprinted into the room, cutting Mac off. "Talk to me."

Her hand rose, then fell as Myst sewed another suture. "Get an IV going."

"On it." Boots thumping, Sloan rounded the end of the table. He slid to a stop next to a rolling table. Grabbing a bag filled with clear liquid, he prepped the kit, and working around Myst, pierced Forge's vein. Tape hissed as Sloan peeled it from the roll. As he secured the IV, he treated Wick to a worried look. "Get Angela and J. J. in here. Myst can't feed him because of her pregnancy, and he needs an infusion of energy. And Mac?"

"Yeah?"

"Go get Tania. We may need her too."

Mac nodded. Wick cringed as his buddy ran for the exit. Shit. Jamison feeding Forge. The idea struck him as dangerous. Particularly since the thought made his dragon half rise with aggression. A bonded male didn't share his female. Ever. But as he watched Myst work, Wick knew no other option existed. Nothing else would work. Forge needed to feed. If he didn't, the warrior would die. Wouldn't survive the hour, never mind last the day. Even with the energy-fuse, he might not make it anyway, but—

The airlock hissed, opening the door into the corridor.

Out of breath, Jamison jogged into the clinic. "Mac said you needed us."

"What can we do?" Angela asked.

"A lot." Eyeballing Jamison, Sloan waved her over. "J. J., you first. Come here. I'll talk you through it."

With a nod, his female headed toward the table. A growl rolled up Wick's throat. Primitive. Possessive. Predatory. The soft snarl curled through the quiet. Like razor-sharp dragon claws, warning gouged at the underbelly of sanity, taking Wick out of his head into another place. A space where instinct ruled and logic didn't live. His gaze on his female, he bared his teeth. Magic thundered through him, rumbling in his veins, making him twitch with the need to possess her.

His hands curled into fists, Wick took a step toward her.

Seeing his expression, Jamison sucked in a quick breath, and halfway across the clinic, stopped short. Her gaze locked on him, she whispered his name. In welcome. With need. With so much heat, Wick lost all sense of himself and his surroundings.

He wanted her. Right now. He needed to dominate. Prove his dominion and show everyone that Jamison belonged to him. She was his.

All *his*. No one else's.

"Jesus H. Christ." Dark eyes shimmering, Sloan fired up mind-speak. *"Venom, get your ass in here. Bring B and Rikar with you. Wick's losing it."*

Staring at him, Jamison licked her bottom lip. Lust spiraled deep, igniting a longing so profound Wick couldn't contain it. Another growl rolled out of him. Venom skidded to a stop in front of the clinic with B and Rikar on his heels. A cacophony of cursing drifted in from the corridor. Unclenching his fists, Wick went after his female. His best friend vaulted over the threshold. In less than a second, Venom grabbed hold. Fighting the lockdown, Wick spun full circle and raised his arm. Bone cracked against bone.

Venom's face snapped to the side. "Goddamn it!"

He cranked his fist back again. Right. Wrong. Neither held sway. Only one thing mattered. Jamison. He needed to reach her. Now. Before anyone touched her.

"Oh my God." Shock flared in his female's eyes. The uncertainty came next, making her raise her hands. She held them palms up, the gesture one of reassurance. "Wick, stop. It's all right. Don't—"

He lunged toward her, dragging Venom with him.

"Fuck," Bastian growled, entering the fray. Electricity crackled, supercharging the air. Hard hands clamped down. Wick roared as he got hauled backward. Away from Jamison. Over the threshold. Out of the clinic into the hallway. Tag-teamed by B and Venom, he struggled, muscles straining, shitkickers sliding on concrete, his dragon half fixated on *her.* He surged forward again. Bastian's grip slipped. "Holy shit. Rikar . . ."

"Got him." Frost spread over his leather jacket as Rikar joined the party. With a roar, Wick twisted. His XO cursed and went hard core, pushing arctic air into his lungs. Oxygen disappeared. He wheezed, using what little remained to yell "no!" as his brothers dragged him from view. "Sloan . . . get it done, then get her into the corridor. We'll keep him locked down until she's finished."

Flipping him belly down, Bastian pinned him to the concrete floor. Still fighting, Wick tried to break his hold. B dropped another f-bomb, and grabbing his arm, cranked it behind his back. Then sat on him while Rikar secured his legs. "I'm sorry. I'm sorry, my brother, but Forge needs it. He *needs* it, Wick."

"No," he rasped, even though he knew the truth. But shit, it wasn't about being reasonable. Or doing the right thing. The territorial bastard inside him had taken over. Now he couldn't control his reaction. Or think straight. "She's mine. *Mine.* I can't . . . don't . . ."

"I know." On his haunches beside him, Venom cupped the back of his head. "But it'll be over soon. Hang tough. Just give it some time."

Some time? To what . . . feed another male? Fuck that. "Let go."

Bastian tightened his grip. "In a minute."

One minute turned into two. And then four. Wick counted off the seconds, each ticktock drove him closer to the edge of insanity. Taut muscles grew tenser, then started to shake. Venom murmured, trying to calm him. It didn't help. He wanted to kill everyone. Rip his brothers limb from limb for getting in his way. For throwing Jamison in the hot seat, and him into emotional meltdown. And as mind fuck expanded, turning his skull into a pressure cooker, Wick groaned in agony. Even after years of battle, all the injuries, he'd never felt pain like this. Wretched. Debilitating. Life-altering anguish. It drilled deep, boring into him until heartache bubbled through the fissure, hollowing him out until all that remained was an empty shell.

His face pressed to cold concrete, Wick moaned her name.

"Here, baby. I'm right here," a soft voice whispered from behind him. Her scent reached him on a heated curl. Wick exhaled hard, needing every little piece of her. "Please, take your hands off him."

"I don't think that's a good idea, J. J.," Rikar said, refusing to let him up.

"He's too wound up. He might—"

"He won't hurt me. I can handle him, Bastian. Please, let go."

B loosened his grip. Baring his teeth, Wick threw off the clampdown. An explosive surge landed him on his feet. His brothers scattered, backing off as he spun to face his female. Serious blue eyes met his. Whispering his name, she reached for him. He didn't hesitate. Desperate for her, he exploded into her arms. Palming her bottom, he picked her up, wrapped her legs around his hips, and dipping his head, invaded her mouth. Unable to resist, he tangled his tongue with hers. With a hum, she buried her small hands in his hair. Heat went cataclysmic as desire blew sky-high. She kissed him harder, opening wide, inviting him in, her nails scraped over his scalp, her hips rocking into his, egging him on.

Shivers exploded down his spine. Oh God. Jesus help him. She tasted so good. So hot. So needy. So sweet. And as he deepened the kiss and carried her down the hall, Wick knew he was done. On the verge, about to ignore right and dive headfirst into wrong. No matter how hard he tried, he couldn't resist her allure. Or stop the awful pull.

Pure madness. Selfishness made manifest.

But Wick didn't care. He needed her. She wanted him. So fuck it. He would take her. Make her slick with need. Ride her long and hard. Let her love him blind in return. The future didn't matter. Tomorrow could wait along with the consequences.

Chapter Twenty-Five

Stripped to the skin, laid out in the middle of the gym, J. J. struggled to catch her breath. An impossibility. Wick refused to let up. Or give her a break. He pinned her to the exercise mat instead, driving her toward pleasure and the pinnacle waiting at its summit. As she gasped, begging for release, he growled her name. Showed her no mercy. Spread her thighs wider. Thrust deep only to retreat and come back, making her moan as he pushed her beyond reality into a world fueled by passion. By devastating delight and—

Oh God. Ecstasy times a million.

He moved like a dream. Felt unbelievable in her arms, and she wanted more. More of his scent on her skin. More of his taste on her tongue. More of the pleasure he fed her.

But only if he let her come. Right now.

"Wick . . ."

"Mmm, baby."

"Now . . . please, now."

"Not yet." Planting one hand beside her ear, he palmed her knee with the other, drew it up, pushed it out, opening her wider. He stroked even deeper. Her breath caught, bliss unfurling fast, the fury of it driving her closer to the edge.

Wick raised his head. Shimmering gold eyes met hers. He snarled at her. She sobbed, so ready to come she clenched hard, the pleasure-pain making her writhe beneath him. "Not until I say."

"No fair."

"No one said it would be fair," he rasped, chest brushing over hers. "No mercy, *vanzäla*."

"Why?"

Dipping his head, he licked over her nipple. "I still smell him on you."

"What . . . oh Jesus," she gasped, losing her mind as he sucked, drawing on the sensitive peak. He nipped the tip, then moved on, lavishing its mate with equal treatment. God help her. He was going to kill her . . . with rapture. Normally not a problem. She wanted to die happy, but as heat spread, setting a blaze beneath her skin, need turned to desperation. "W-who?"

With a growl, he upped the pace, rocking her hard, punishing her with pleasure. A bliss-filled cry left her throat. Beyond pride, she arched, grinding her hips into his. Sensation spiked, then spiraled on a jagged wave. Catastrophic. Desperate. Beautiful. Desire turned incendiary.

His breath hitched.

J. J. pressed her advantage.

"It's mine. *Mine*. . . do you hear?" Fisting her hands in his hair, she pulled his head down and licked into his mouth. He groaned. She took it up a notch and sent her hands searching. Caressing his back, she pressed her palms to the base of his spine. He bucked in her embrace. She sucked on his tongue and . . . yum. He tasted like exotic lands and spiced rum. A deadly combination, one that made her bold.

Breaking the kiss, she bared her teeth. "I want it. Give it to me. Now!"

An order given. A message received, and . . . oooh, baby. Did he deliver, stealing her breath, circling his hips, pressing so deep he rubbed just . . . the right . . . spot. She tittered on the brink a moment, unable to breathe as Wick dipped his head. The heat of his mouth touched her skin an instant before the sharp edge of his teeth scraped her throat. He nipped her pulse point, and ecstasy arced, lashing her with white-hot pleasure. Suspended in glory, J. J. screamed his name. Wick shouted, muscles tensing, body throbbing, coming deep inside her.

As he twitched against her, she wrapped him up and held him close. He sighed and settled warm and heavy against her—hips pressed between her thighs, strong arms around her, his face tucked against her throat. Trusting her completely. Giving J. J. her due. Relaxing into her embrace as he drifted into the heated curl of afterglow.

So amazing. Unbelievable. It was beyond anything.

J. J. hummed in satisfaction. She loved making love to him. But holding him in the aftermath? Having him in her arms, skin-to-skin and heart-to-heart? Pure heaven. And as he murmured her name, she whispered back, her heart so full she could hardly contain it. Beautiful man. Incredible in so many ways, and as repletion drew her into relaxation, she pressed a soft kiss to his shoulder, so very thankful he belonged to her.

Or at least, he would . . . when she got done with him.

❁ ❁ ❁

Too sated to move, Wick lay in the shelter of his female's arms. Still deep inside her, unwilling to leave the warmth of her body, he breathed her in, loving the richness of her scent along with the fact she no longer smelled of another male. Ridiculous, he knew. Unconscious from blood loss, Forge hadn't touched her. No sex involved. Just the touch of her hands, a connection that allowed Jamison to share her life-saving energy. Exactly what his brother-in-arms needed to heal and rebound.

Knowing it, however, didn't make it any easier to bear.

He hadn't been able to stand it. Had needed to wipe all trace of Forge from her skin by replacing it with his own. Stupid. Possessive. Irrational. But there it was . . . his dragon half out in full force, being bitchy even in the face of his comrade's need.

But it was over, and now she lay in his arms. His for the taking. His for the loving. His in the here and now . . . in a very public place. Wick grimaced. Fucking hell. He'd made love to her in the middle of the gym. Under the bright lights, on an exercise mat, in the shadow of a basketball net where anyone might open the door and see them.

Not the smartest move.

Then again, he hadn't been thinking straight at the time. And right now, he couldn't bring himself to care. She felt too good against him, and as he nestled in, Wick took another breath. His mouth curved against the side of her neck. Cinnamon and spiced candy. It never failed. Her natural essence suited her. Called to him. Made him yearn and commit it to memory, imprinting it on his senses and in his heart. He needed to remember everything. Every last detail. How she tasted, the way she smelled, the softness of her skin, and how well she fit in his arms . . . so delicate yet oh-so-perfect.

Small things. Big impact.

Each one must last him a lifetime. Endure years without fading. Tide him over and bridge time, allowing him to remember her with perfect recall. He knew it would come to that . . . to disappointment and the inevitability of good-bye. She would leave. A female of her caliber would never choose a male like him. Wick accepted it with certainty, but instead of making it easy, doing the right thing and pushing her away, he hung on tight. A few more minutes. Maybe an hour if he got lucky. After that, he'd find the strength to let her go. To allow her the life she deserved instead of the one he could give her, and then learn to survive.

Without her.

It wouldn't be easy. He mourned her already. Losing her would hurt like hell. It would be easier to ignore the truth, but Wick refused to lie to himself. There was no going back. No chance of erasing the last few days. He didn't want to anyway. Jamison made it impossible to regret meeting her. Instead, he felt grateful. Such a short amount of time, and yet, her impact on him was undeniable. Irrefutable. Incredible too. He hadn't believed himself capable of loving a female. But fact didn't allow for fiction. He loved her deep, loved her true, craved her in ways he didn't understand yet somehow knew to be right.

A bitch of a thing. Especially while faced with the prospect of leaving her.

Fingers stroking through the soft strands of her hair, Wick pressed his mouth to her pulse point. A gentle kiss against her skin. A tough good-bye said in silence. An excellent reminder of what he must do. Taking a fortifying breath, he raised his head and lost his heart all over again.

Fuck, she was pretty.

Lifting his hand from her hair, he traced her eyebrow with his fingertip. She sighed as he drew a gentle circle on her temple, then drifted down over the curve of her cheek. Eyes closed, relaxed in his arms, she accepted his touch, turning her face into his palm. So trusting. Too vulnerable. Beyond beautiful. Unable to resist, he leaned in and brushed his mouth against hers. She hummed in welcome, allowing him to play, one hand caressing his nape while the other moved over his shoulder. Her touch made him needy. Her taste made him kiss her again, long, slow, and sweet. As he tangled his tongue with hers, Wick called himself a fool. Nothing good would come from putting off the discussion. Best to get it over with, instead of prolonging the unavoidable. But as he drew away, she opened her eyes and met his gaze head-on.

Which . . . shit on a stick . . . made him kiss her again.

How long it went on, Wick didn't know. A minute? Ten? He lost track somewhere after the second kiss. Not surprising. Half the time he couldn't remember his own name around her, but with her hands in his hair and her taste in his mouth? Sad to say, but sensible didn't stand a chance.

Mustering every ounce of willpower he owned, Wick turned his face away. She grumbled in protest. He cleared his throat. "Jamison, we need to talk."

"Don't," she whispered, touching her fingertip to his bottom lip. "Forget about sending me away. I'm not going anywhere."

Wick blinked as surprise blindsided him. He hadn't expected that, but as he met her gaze, he saw the acceptance.

Along with a shitload of determination. He frowned, trying to make sense of her reaction. No way should she be . . .

Jesus. He didn't understand. "It would be better if you left."

"For whom?" Both brows arched, she gave him a no-nonsense look. "You or me?"

"You."

"Not true. I'm exactly where I need to be . . . right here with you."

"*Vanzäla,*" he said, despair creeping into his tone. Shifting against her, he brushed a renegade lock of hair away from her temple and shook his head. "I'm trying to do right by you . . . give you an easy out. A way to—"

"I don't want one. And if you're honest with yourself, neither do you."

"It's not about what I want. It's about what you need."

With a curse, Wick planted his hand on the mat and pushed away from her. He needed some space. A lot of it. No way could he hold the line while touching her. But as he left the cradle of her thighs, she refused to let him go. Giving him a shove, she sat him down, and throwing a leg over, straddled him. Wick twitched. Small hands pressed to his chest, she nestled in, setting her exquisite ass in his lap and . . . Jesus help him. So much for holding out. He couldn't help himself. He palmed her waist, reveling in the softness of her skin, temptation urging him to toss aside hesitation and claim her for his own.

He went the honest route instead. "Jesus, Jamison. I'm not built for this shit. I don't know how to be your mate. I'll fuck it up. I'll hurt you without meaning to and ruin everything."

"Bullshit," she said, her bad language surprising him. Again. Par for the course, he guessed. At least, for the current conversation, 'cause . . . wow. Everything she said seemed to shock the hell out of him today. "I don't accept that. You wanna know why?"

"Tell me," he murmured, unwilling to shut her down.

A bad decision? Probably. But hope was a bastard with an axe to grind—amping him up, making his heart pound, whispering softly until he dared to believe that maybe . . . just *maybe* . . . Jamison might want him as her mate. A long shot? No contest. It was a Hail Mary pass in a losing game, but regardless of the outcome, he wanted to hear what she had to say.

Leaning in, she set her mouth to the corner of his. A quick brush of her lips. A faster retreat. Hardly a kiss at all, but . . . shit. It proved effective, grabbing his attention like nothing else could. "Nothing is perfect, Wick. The best things in life don't come easy. They take commitment and hard work, and you know what else?"

Focus raptor sharp, he stared at her. "What else?"

"Everybody screws up . . . *everybody*." A furrow between her brows, she trailed her fingers over his collarbone and scanned his face. The worry in her eyes almost did him in. He didn't want to hurt her. He wanted to free her, provide her with opportunity instead of hemming her in. But as she chewed on her bottom lip, Wick lost his way. Right. Wrong. He couldn't tell one from the other anymore. "I'm a prime example, the poster girl for doing it all wrong. So I want you to listen to me . . . *hear* me when I tell you . . . I'm not looking for perfect. Easy doesn't interest me, but you do. All I want is to be with you. Just you. No one else."

Struggling to believe, Wick swallowed hard. "You barely know me."

"I know you better than you think." Taking his hand from her waist, she turned his wrist out, revealing the scar on his forearm. He tensed, fisting his hand, trying to pull away, not wanting her to see it. Or ask what it meant. Her grip firmed, holding him still while she traced the brand with her fingertips. "I know where you've been. I've seen your past."

"Impossible." No way. Jesus help him. She couldn't possibly know.

"God's honest truth." Eyes steady on his, her fingertips danced across his puckered skin. Sorrow clogged his throat, making his eyes sting, resurrecting the past while he burned with shame. Cupping his jaw, Jamison shook her head. "Stop it. You have nothing to be ashamed about. What happened to you was done without your consent, neither was it your choice. If I could go back and kill the bastard again for hurting you, I would. Ten times over."

Fuck him. He couldn't breathe. Didn't know how to respond, never mind feel. He never intended to tell her, but somehow, some way, she'd unearthed the truth. "How . . . I don't understand."

"Energy-fuse," she said. "I feel you . . . hear you . . . like a heartbeat. You shared your past without knowing it . . . through the bond we share . . . and guess what? I'm still here. It doesn't scare me and neither do you."

Her admission laid him bare, cracked him open, leaving him without protection. From the hope. From the need. From the certain knowledge that despite his past, she claimed him for her future. And as the floodgates opened, his throat closed, leaving him unable to do anything other than whisper her name.

"Please, Wick. Don't shut me out. Don't send me away. I want you for my own." Tears in her eyes, she pressed her palm to his chest, right over his heart. "You belong to me, and I love you. Nothing else matters."

Undone by her, Wick folded beneath the onslaught. He couldn't resist her. Or deny his need. He'd tried to be honorable. Had made an attempt to do what he believed was right. But Jamison disagreed, and honestly? He wanted her too badly. Was too weak to turn away from all she offered. So he accepted instead. Bowed to fate along with her wishes. "You deserve so much better than me."

"Then earn it," she whispered, holding him close, her cheek against his. "Be with me. Accept me. Love me, Wick. That's all I ask. All I'll ever need."

"I do love you."

"Then it's settled. I stay."

Gratitude hit him like a body shot, punching through to his heart. "You stay. But I want something in return."

"What's that?"

"Marry me, *vanzäla* . . . in the way of my kind." Hands flat against her back, he kissed her collarbone and raised his head. "Stand in the sacred circle with me, say the vows and—"

"Yes." Sky-blue eyes alight with pleasure, she smiled. "Just tell me when."

"Now."

She blinked. "Really? What about the rotunda, the ceremony, all the fancy froufrou stuff?"

"Nothing but bells and whistles."

Her mouth curved. "No need for any of that."

He grinned back, and tightening his hold on her, pushed to his feet and swung her into his arms. She settled like a gift, warm and willing against him as he stepped off the edge of the exercise mat. Chilly floors brushing his bare soles, he walked to the middle of the basketball court. As he put her down at its center, anticipation thrummed through him. Soon. In just minutes, she would belong to him.

No second guessing. No going back. His mate in every way that mattered.

Drawing his hands from her, he took a step back. Magic flared, prickling over his palms as he conjured the first stone. Oval in shape with smooth, round edges, the heavy weight settled in his palm. His gaze on hers, he placed it on the floor, then called forth another. And then another. Until eleven identical multicolored gemstones formed a perfect circle around his female. With a murmur, he opened a channel to the Meridian and evoked the spell, imbuing each of the eleven with the source that fed all living things.

Energy snapped, humming in the air like electricity.

Summoning a length of yellow ribbon, Wick pushed to his feet. "Ready?"

Naked, standing unashamed in bright light, Jamison didn't answer. She held out her hand instead. Releasing a long breath, Wick reached out and slid his palm into hers. She tugged. He accepted her invitation, moving toward fate instead of away as he joined her inside the sacred circle. He stopped in front of her and raised his right hand. Lifting her own, she pressed her palm to his. Within seconds he looped the ribbon up and over, threading the length of satin between their fingers, completing a necessary part of the ceremony, tying them together in a ritual older than time.

Coreene Callahan

"I remember the words from Tania's wedding," she said, reverence in her quiet tone. "I'll go first."

"Jamison?"

"Yes?"

"Never forget that I love you."

Tears welled in her eyes. One fell, tipping over her bottom lashes. He brushed it away, and she smiled. Not a lot, just enough to reassure him as she inhaled soft, exhaled smooth and began the rite that would tie them together for all time. "Fate of my fate. Light of my light. Kindred of spirit without shadow or slight. You are mine. And I am yours. Two hearts intertwined forevermore."

Her vows finished, he began his own, speaking to her in Dragonese, the language of his kind. Gaze steady on hers, his voice rose and fell over rolling *r*'s and long-drawn *s*'s. Her breath hitched. Another tear escaped to flow down her cheek. The gemstones started to glow. White light writhed from their centers, dancing in a decadent swirl around their feet. Awe rushed through his veins, making his heart stall as the binding spell took hold, marrying his life force with his female's, and hers with his.

Pain seared the back of his hand.

The yellow ribbon caught magical flame. Satin turned to cinder as the mating mark burned over his knuckles. Beautiful in design, silver lines drew matching tattoos on their skin. Emotion tightened his throat. Jamison started to cry, and as she laced their fingers, he reeled her in. The warmth of her skin met his. Wick hummed and, holding her close, kissed each tear away. She'd given him a gift beyond measure. His female. His mate. His equal in all things. And as she tucked her head beneath his chin and whispered that

404

she loved him, Wick vowed to protect her always, cherish her forever, and love her until the end of time.

Chapter Twenty-Six

Moving slow and steady, Wick slipped from between the sheets and out of bed. As his feet touched the cold floor, Jamison grumbled, protesting the loss of his body heat. His mouth curved as he watched her curl onto her side in the dark. Night vision pinpoint sharp, he saw everything. Every strand of her hair. Each one of her thick eyelashes. The beautiful lines of the mating mark on the back of her hand, telling him plainer than words she was all his.

He flexed his fist and stared at his knuckles, examining his own tattoo.

A mix of emotions tumbled through him. Pride. Thankfulness. But most of all, an overwhelming sense of contentment. So light. So bright. His heart had never been so full before . . . or so vulnerable. But hell. He couldn't stop the slippery slide into happiness. Didn't want to either. Jamison made him feel good: valued, honorable, and needed too.

All things he'd craved, but never believed possible. Until now.

Still, the switch-up startled him a little, tossing the usual red flags, raising his internal alarm system. Old habits died hard. Wick shoved them aside anyway. Locked down doubt, let the tension go, and accepted that things had changed. He didn't need to be on his guard with her. Jamison would never hurt or betray him. His secrets were safe with her, and so was his heart.

Unable to resist, he pressed his hands into the coverlet on either side of her. As he leaned in and touched his mouth to her temple, she reached out. Her palm slid across his pillow. A frown marring her brow, she murmured his name.

He kissed her softly again. "Sleep, *vanzäla*. I'll be back soon."

The moment she settled, he pushed away from the mattress and, conjuring his clothes, rounded the end of the bed. Worn jeans and a faded T-shirt brushed his skin. He didn't bother with boots. He wouldn't be that long. Would slip right back into the bed next to his female the second he finished his errand.

Which . . . shit . . . wasn't going to be pleasant.

To be expected. Apologizing, no matter the circumstances, sucked.

Bare feet silent against the hospital-grade floor, Wick crossed the recovery room. His choice of beds furthered his goals. Had been purely strategic, for a number of reasons. First, he hadn't been able to wait to make love to Jamison again after the mating ceremony, and—fuck him, but his own bedroom had seemed too far away at the time. And second? Forge. Laid out one room over, the male was passed out, recovering from brutal injury and sleeping like the dead.

Or had been until a few minutes ago.

Dragon senses keen, he heard the voices. Uh-huh. No doubt. The wonder twins were up and at 'em. Not surprising, considering the lateness of the hour. Walking past a round table with a pair of chairs, Wick glanced at the clock above the bank of stainless steel cabinets. Each ticktock sounded loud in the quiet, skinny hands walking around its wide face, speeding time along. 2:43 P.M. Mid-afternoon, prime wake-up time for the Nightfury warriors. So no time like the present. He needed to get a move on and the conversation over before B and the others rolled in to check on Forge.

Unleashing magic, Wick flicked the handle and shoved. The connecting door swung wide. Strides even and sure, he crossed over the threshold and—

"Bloody hell." Propped up in bed, looking like a thundercloud, Forge scowled at his apprentice. A deck of cards between them, amethyst gaze narrowed, he studied his cards as Mac tossed his hand down on the mattress. The Scot cursed under his breath. "You wanker."

"You wanna win?" Seated in a chair next to the bed, Mac reached for the pot. Colorful poker chips rattled as he raked them in. "Beat me fair and square."

"Fucking Irish," Forge grumbled, tossing his own cards. Spades and diamonds slid against the bedspread, triple sixes bumping into a pair of jacks. A sliver of pleasure thrummed through Wick. Straight Up Texas Hold 'Em, his favorite game. "Bone-headed brats, every last one of you."

With a snort, Mac flipped his buddy the bird, then gathered up the deck and started shuffling.

Standing just inside the room, Wick closed the door behind him. The soft click joined the quiet buzz of halogens.

Two pairs of eyes swung his way. Only one, though, concerned him. He met Forge's gaze. "How are you feeling?"

"Like I want tae beat the shite out of Mac."

Their resident water dragon rolled his eyes.

Wick's lips twitched. "Better then."

"Aye."

The male's low tone drew Wick further into the room. He stopped at the end of bed and, planting his forearms on the lip of the footboard, leaned in. He frowned at the individual stitches dotting the top of the handmade quilt, then cleared his throat. Jesus. How to start? What to say? Where to begin? He didn't know. Remorse never entered his equation, but as he looked up and saw the thick bandage crisscrossing Forge's chest, regret hit him hard. God, he'd almost killed one of his brothers.

The thought made him sick to his stomach.

"I'm sorry," he said, staring at his hands, his throat so tight the words came hard. "I didn't mean to hurt you."

"I know." Shifting against a pile of pillows, Forge sat up a little straighter. "Friendly fire, lad. It happens."

"Not to me."

"Tae every male, if he lives long enough."

He shook his head. Despite Forge's willingness to forgive, Wick couldn't let it go. A mistake had been made. He must pay for his part in it. "I owe you restitution. A blood debt of—"

"Bullshite. You owe me nothing," Forge growled. "'Tis the other way around. You shared your female. Saved my life by letting J. J. feed me."

Let her? What a big, fat lie. "I wasn't exactly willing."

"Neither was I." Expression serious, Mac split the deck with one hand. A pro move. Not surprising. The newest

member of the Nightfury pack excelled at the poker table.
Was a regular card shark, even by Wick's lofty standards.
"Venom and the others held me down too when Tania took
her turn. And Rikar?"

Wick raised a brow, waiting for the punch line.

"The corridor turned into a winter wonderland. Total
Frostville the second Ange entered the fray. We couldn't
hold him back, so Bastian hammered him. Knocked him
out cold." Mac huffed, cards moving rapid-fire, a silent shuffle in his hands. "You should see the shiner he's sporting.
Ange is still babying him."

"Seems tae be going around," Forge said, gesturing to
the back of Wick's hand. "You've gotten some of the same."

"More than just some." He flexed his fingers, making
the mating mark move across his knuckles. Pride settled
deep. A swirl of happiness followed. "Didn't think I had the
balls to claim her, did you?"

"Courage isn't your problem, Wick." Picking up a poker
chip, Forge flicked it at him. He caught it in midair and,
running his thumb over the ridged edge, turned the piece
over in his hand. Mischief in his eyes, the Scot smirked.
"People skills, on the other hand?"

"Fuck off, Forge," he said, unleashing his favorite phrase.

As intended, the comeback made both males laugh. And
just like that, the tension eased, and it was over. Apology
accepted. Back to normal. Forgiveness sent and accepted.
Fantastic. But as relief took away the burden, another worry
popped up to replace it. A big one that had nothing to do
with the warriors already safe inside the lair.

Skirting the end of the bed, Wick unloaded on the mattress. His back against the footboard, he stretched his legs
out on top of the quilt and crossed his feet at the ankles.

Gaze ping-ponging between his comrades, he asked, "Any word from Gage and Haider?"

Mac shook his head. "Nothing. B's worried."

Wick was too. The Metallics never went this long without checking in. The fact they'd gone radio silent wasn't a good sign. "What about Nian?"

"Sloan's sending him messages, but so far he hasn't answered."

"Shite."

"No kidding." Sliding into a slouch, Mac leaned back in his chair. Plastic creaked as he lifted his legs and set his shitkickers down beside Wick's bare feet. "We got another option, though."

"Azrad," Wick murmured, picking up his buddy's line of thought.

Forge hummed. "A good bet, considering his connection tae Nian. The male might know something."

Fingers crossed. Information was step one. Action would come next. "Is Bastian setting up another meeting?"

"Yeah. Not sure when it'll go down," Mac said. "He wants Forge on his feet first."

Wick nodded. Made sense. "All hands on deck."

"Bloody well better be." A sour look on his puss, Forge glared a warning. "You leave me at home, I'll kick your arses from here tae Saint Paddy's Day."

"Could be worse." Flashing pearly whites, Mac grinned, half devil, all eager. "At least, there'll be lots of beer to drink."

"Green ale," Wick said, joining in on the fun.

"Total wankers . . . the pair of you."

Mac laughed.

Wick shook his head, even as appreciation for his fellow warriors sank deep. Despite their newness to the pack, Mac and Forge fit like marrow inside bone. They belonged. Were family in every way that counted. Which meant he should be able to ask them anything. He frowned. Right? After a moment spent thinking it over, the answer came to him. No question. Both males were solid, safe, smart as hell too, so . . . yeah. Asking for their advice seemed like the thing to do.

But for one small problem.

He'd never asked anyone for help before. Wasn't sure how to go about it either. Should he jump right in? Was there a protocol he needed to follow? A code of etiquette of some kind? Shit, he didn't know, so . . .

Fuck it. He might as well wade in. "Hey, Forge?"

"Aye, lad?"

"I hear you're good with a hammer."

An understatement. A huge one. Particularly since Wick had seen his work. A master carpenter, Forge owned serious tools and a shitload of skill. Ones he put to good use every afternoon, carving out a spot for his collection of fine wines and aged whiskies. The passion fueled his project, keeping the male happy as he built a wine cellar in one corner of the underground lair. Barely begun, the space reeked of style and sophistication, with exotic woods taken from foreign lands, and a sense of tradition brought over from the old country.

From a Highland heritage and a history that endured.

Rapt interest in his eyes, Forge perked up. "What are you building?"

"A gift for Jamison."

Chasing an itch, Mac rubbed his shoulder against the seat back. "Lay it out."

Simple as that, the conversation began. Amazing, really. Something as basic as a question could give birth to camaraderie. The kind he'd only ever experienced with Venom. But as Wick shared his idea, his brothers accepted him without question: helping him shape his vision, hashing out the details, and making a list of materials. Extraordinary. Wicked fun too, and as he listened to Forge and Mac argue about the best wood screws to use, his excitement lit off like a rocket. Watch out world. He was headed into the great unknown, about to attempt something he never had before with his friends' help. The fine art of pleasing a female. And oh baby, he couldn't wait to get started. Couldn't wait to see Jamison's face when he unveiled his gift and surprised the hell out of her.

❁ ❁ ❁

Perched on a stool at the kitchen island, J. J. rapped the end of her pencil against the notepad and frowned at the cake in front of her. The eraser bounced against paper, punishing a curlicue treble clef and the adjoining lines containing a flurry of music notes. Two birds with one stone. Musical composition while baking . . . a happy accident. One she'd discovered with Daimler's help. A pastime she would be enjoying, but for one simple thing.

Her design wasn't working.

Oh, not the song. The melody was taking shape just right, the up-tempo chorus flowing into each verse like a river into the sea. On cue. Perfect rhythm keeping time. No problems on the musical front at all. It was the dragon cake she worried about. The legs were too fat, the neck too skinny, and the head? Gosh darn it all. The thing looked more like a triangle than the smooth, sculpted contours she wanted. Chewing on her lip, she added another string of notes to the music staff, then dropped the pencil to pick up the baker's knife. She drummed its tip against the marble countertop. The rat-ta-ta-tat barely registered. She was too busy figuring out where she'd gone wrong.

Not in the actual baking. The white cake looked okay. So no, it couldn't be that. Tilting her head one way and then the other, she pursed her lips, hoping a different angle would help, but . . .

No such luck. The head still looked awful.

She scowled at it. Dumb thing. Who knew baking a fancy cake could be so difficult? Not her. Not after decorating the cupcakes had gone so well. Nudging the base, she pushed the notepad aside and turned her crappy-looking dragon full circle, studying it from each side, then glanced at the knife in her hand. Maybe if she scalped it a little more. Trimmed down the body. Reinforced the neck. Added the horns, scales, and spikes with colorful marzipan. J. J. grimaced. Maybe she should just start over. Much as she hated to admit it, that seemed like the best option.

"Frick'n frack," her sister grumbled. Seated across from her, Tania chewed on the end of her own pencil. A sketch pad bobbing in her other hand, she cursed under her breath. "It still doesn't look right."

"Join the club."

Startled from her own creative dilemma, Tania's head came up. "What?"

J. J. poked the dragon head with the tip of her knife. "Well, just look at it. Catastrophe central. It looks like something out of a bad horror flick."

Tania snorted in laughter. "The neck's too skinny."

"Thanks for the news flash," she muttered, tossing her sister a perturbed look. Tania grinned. J. J. rolled her eyes. Ah, snap . . . she might as well admit it. She'd bitten off more than she could chew. And with Daimler out of the lair—off on some secret mission for Wick—she didn't have a chance in hell of heading the baking disaster off at the pass. "What's your problem?"

"The waterfall."

J. J. raised a brow.

With a sigh, her sister flipped the sketch pad in her direction. J. J. blinked. Wow. Get a load of that. The three dimensional drawing practically leapt off the page, depicting a moonlit lagoon surrounded by lush forest and smooth stone. Staring at the picture, Tania shook her head. "I want the water to flow down the rock face and into the pool, but . . . I don't know . . . the perspective's off or something. I can't figure out why it's not working."

"You got me." Eyes narrowed, J. J. studied the design. "I don't know the first thing about—"

A warm tingle swept over the nape of her neck.

She drew in a soft breath as the soft sensation buzzed down her spine. Well, well, well, it was about time. Wick was headed her way, and after pulling a disappearing act all afternoon? She was ready to see him. Ready to ask him again too: poke, prod, beg, borrow, and plead for a clue. He was up to something. She felt it in her bones. Saw it in the knowing gleam in his eyes. Smelled it on him too. But the cherry on top . . . the proof in her pudding? He'd been AWOL from lunch until dinner for the last three days.

Along with the other Nightfury warriors.

Suspicious much? Uh-huh. Beyond mysterious, a puzzle worth solving.

Anticipation running hot, J. J. slid off the stool. As her bare feet touched warm tile, she glanced at her sister. "See yah."

"Rah, rah, sis-boom-bah," Tania said, mischief in her eyes. "Go get him, tiger."

Laughing, J. J. rounded the end of the island. All her senses locked on Wick, she turned into the corridor and . . . oh man. There he was, halfway down the hallway, looking good enough to eat as his long legs carried him forward. Getting a move on, she walked toward him, heart pounding, body humming, her desire for him rising like a heat wave. Golden eyes shimmering, a slow grin spread across his face. Her stomach flip-flopped. A buzz of happiness followed. God, she loved it when he looked at her that way: with a hunger born of passion and need, and so much love it took her breath away.

"Hey," she said, getting up close and personal as she stepped into him. Hard muscle rippled as he wrapped his arms around her. Hmm, he always smelled so darn good, like wood smoke and male spice. Breathing him in, she pressed a kiss to his T-shirt-clad chest and, tipping her chin, offered him her mouth. He didn't hesitate. Dipping his head, he brushed his lips against hers. She smiled against his mouth, running her hands down his back, loving the feel of him, then got back on track. Curiosity demanded an answer, and she wanted to know. "So, you gonna tell me now?"

He shook his head. "How about I show you instead?"

Oh, yes, please. Especially if the *showing* included getting horizontal with him in bed. "Where we going?"

Wick didn't answer. He grabbed her hand instead and, lacing their fingers together, led her down the corridor. Away from her sister and the kitchen. Past the bedroom J. J. now shared with him. The thump of his boots sounding loud in the quiet, she followed without question. Where to . . . where to? The question heightened her anticipation until she couldn't stand it.

She wanted to know. Right now.

All part of his plan, she knew.

Sneak that he was, Wick had played her to perfection, letting her know something was up without giving the game away. He'd even shut her down in the mental sphere, refusing to allow her to read him via the bond they shared. Which, naturally, sent her need to know into orbit. Grinning like an idiot, she wrapped both of her hands around his and hopped like an excited five year old. She couldn't help it. Whatever he had planned must be big. Huger than huge, 'cause . . .

He stopped in front of a set of double doors. Eyes alight with anticipation, he met her gaze. "Ready?"

So eager her voice vanished, she squeezed his hand and nodded.

"Close your eyes."

Taking a deep breath, J. J. obeyed. He shifted beside her. The doorknob clicked, the soft snick echoing inside her head. With a gentle tug, Wick drew her forward, guiding her over the threshold, walking her deep into the room. It felt large, open concept, high ceilinged, more like a living area than a bedroom. The smell of fresh paint hung in the air too, along with a hint of sawdust. But the floor felt smooth, like hardwood and . . . oh, wait. Soft fringe touched her bare toes. She'd just stepped onto an area rug, a big one judging by the distance she traveled before Wick stopped walking.

Untangling their fingers, he released her hand.

J. J. squirmed, curling her toes into plush carpet. "Now?"

"Yes," he murmured, his mouth brushing the side of her throat. A shiver erupted, raising goose bumps on her skin as he nipped the shell of her ear. "Now. Open your eyes, Jamison."

She did and . . .

Holy God. J. J. blinked. A baby grand piano. A freaking *baby grand piano* sat across the room. Glossy black paint shining. Ivory-white keys glowing. Padded bench seat calling her name. And beside it, standing proud in a guitar stand, a brand new Bedell . . . honey-colored wood gleaming in the low light. Disbelief warred with overwhelming emotion. Without mercy, it punched through to grab her heart, squeezing so hard she struggled to breathe. Her hands started to shake. Tears pooled in her eyes, blurring her vision, making her throat close, kicking shock up a notch.

She opened her mouth, then closed it again. It was too much. Way too much. The most beautiful thing she'd ever seen. Beyond anything she could've imagined for herself.

"Oh, Wick," she whispered, so overwhelmed she didn't know what to do. Sit down and cry like a baby. Or hug Wick so hard she'd crack his ribs. "Oh my God. You . . . I . . . it's . . ."

"How'd I do?"

"I can't . . . I don't even know how to . . ." A rasp in her voice, J. J. struggled to answer. She shook her head, knowing she needed to give Wick his due, but . . . God. His gift stunned her into stupidity. A music room. Beautiful, crazy man. He'd built her a music room. A place for her to compose. A spot designed for play. A space all her own. Gratitude collided with appreciation, looping around her heart, combining with her love for him. A sob lodged in her throat, J. J. dragged her gaze away from the Bedell and turned toward him. He stood a few feet away, golden eyes intent, watching, waiting . . . no doubt wondering if she liked his gift. "It's phenomenal. Beyond gorgeous. I love it. You're just . . . crazy incredible."

Pleasure sparked in his eyes a second before his mouth curved.

More tears fell, and unable to stay away a second longer, J. J. reached for him. Bridging the distance, he moved in tight and hugged her close, making her feel precious. Amazing . . . in every sense of the word. No one had ever made her feel important—cherished, needed, worthy of this kind of attention. No one except Wick, and as she pressed her cheek to his chest and listened to his heartbeat, she understood, for the first time, what true love meant.

"Thank you," she said, her tears soaking through his T-shirt. "The words will never be enough, but . . . thank you, Wick. Thank you so very much."

With a hum, he kissed the top of her head. "I have another gift."

"Oh jeez," she said with a sniffle. "Are you trying to kill me?"

He laughed, flashing straight white teeth, and pivoted with her in his arms. Slow dancing with her, he twirled her in lazy circles across the room and into a seating area. One she hadn't noticed until now. Totally understandable. She'd been too busy staring at the piano and her new guitar to notice anything else, but as Wick sat her on the couch, her power of observation came back on line. A present—a big one with a floppy red bow—sat on the coffee table. Wick slid onto the sofa next to her, his hard-bodied, long-limbed frame depressing the seat cushions.

Over the initial shock of the baby grand, curiosity got the better of her. Her gaze cut to his. She raised a brow.

Arms flung along the back of the sofa, Wick settled in to watch her. He tipped his chin. "Open it."

"You're spoiling me."

"A mate's prerogative."

Pleasure shivered through her. *Mate.* Oh, how she liked the sound of that, and as she broke eye contact and slid to the edge of her seat, she wanted to forget about the gift. Postpone it until later and make love to him instead. Glancing over her shoulder, she treated him to a saucy look. Heat sparked in his gaze. She licked over her bottom lip. Wick shook his head and pointed to the present.

"Okay, okay." Grabbing the gift, J.J. dragged the tall box across the tabletop. "Better get ready, though, 'cause afterward, you're gonna pay for making me wait."

"Deal."

Undoing the bow, J. J. flipped the top off and, peering over the edge, peeked inside. She froze. Good lord. It couldn't be. No way would he—

Her present moved.

J.J.'s mouth fell open. Shock expanded. All thought vanished. Complete and utter adoration replaced it.

"Oh my goodness, Wick . . . you didn't," she whispered, disbelieving even as she reached inside and lifted her gift from the box. White with gray markings, the puppy stared at her, dark-brown eyes solemn, black button nose inches from her own. Speechless, J. J. stared back. Good heavens, a dog . . . and not just any breed either, but a perfect, pudgy-nosed baby bulldog. "You just didn't."

"Seems I did." Focus absolute, he took in every nuance of her expression. "Do you like her?"

"Do I . . . holy moly, no. *Like* doesn't even come close. I *love* her." Another round of tears rolled over her lashes. A music room and a puppy. All on the same day. Totally surreal. So completely unexpected, J. J. couldn't wrap her brain around it. But as she hugged her new dog and looked at Wick, the truth finally hit home. This was her life now. *He* was her life. She belonged to the most incredible, generous, gorgeous man in the world, and he to her. "Have I told you how much I love you today?"

"Words, *vanzäla*," he said, a growl in his voice. The dark tone hinted of amatory afternoons and untold naughtiness. Desire spiraled on an incendiary swirl, making her toes curl. "Show me instead."

With a "hell, yeah," J. J. rose to the challenge and set the puppy down beside the couch. Nose to the floor, the little darling went exploring, and she didn't hesitate. She slipped into Wick's embrace, buried her hands in his hair, and kissed him deep, knowing she would never get enough of him. So lucky. Despite her mistakes. Despite a rocky past and rough start. Despite all the guilt and heartache. Fate smiled down on her, granting her the one thing she hadn't known she couldn't do without . . .

The best kind of forever with the man in her arms.

Acknowledgements

I've discovered along the way that every book I write is different. Each story comes together in its own time, at its own pace, the ideas, themes, and characters melding to form a transformative kind of story magic. This book, however, touched me in ways I have difficulty explaining. Maybe because I fell in love with Wick, the hero of *Fury of Desire*, the instant I met him. There is just something about a bad boy, isn't there? Particularly one with a shady past, an uncertain future, and a bad attitude. But for all his stubbornness, he made me a better writer, challenging me in ways no story ever has . . . and for that, I thank him.

Many thanks to my literary agent, Christine Whitthohn. You rock, baby!

A huge thanks to Eleni Caminis and Melody Guy. Thank you for all your hard work, dedication, and support. It means the world to me. And to the entire Amazon Publishing team whose talents, enthusiasm, and commitment never cease to amaze me. I so enjoy working with all of you!

To my friends and family, I love you all. Thank you for putting up with me and my distraction when I'm deep in Storyland.

Last but never least, to Kallie Lane, fellow writer, critique partner, and friend: You make me better. You always have. Thank you!

I raise a glass to each and every one of you!

About the Author

✿ ✿ ✿

Image © Julie Daniluk

As the only girl on all-guys hockey teams from age six through her college years, Coreene Callahan knows a thing or two about tough guys and loves to write about them. Call it kismet. Call it payback after years of locker room talk and ice rink antics. But whatever you call it, the action better be heart stopping, the magic electric, and the story wicked-good fun.

After graduating with honors in psychology and working as an interior designer, she finally succumbed to her overactive imagination and returned to her first love: writing. And when she's not writing, she is dreaming of magical worlds full of dragon-shifters, elite assassins, and romance that's too hot to handle. Callahan currently lives in Canada with her family and writing buddy, a fun-loving golden retriever.